MISS PRIM AND THE DUKE OF WYLDE

A CYNSTER NEXT GENERATION NOVEL

BOOK THIRTEEN

STEPHANIE LAURENS

ABOUT MISS PRIM AND THE DUKE OF WYLDE

#1 New York Times *bestselling author Stephanie Laurens explores what happens when Fate tosses two people who had no intention of marrying each other into the hothouse of a noble betrothal under the avid eyes of the ton.*

A gentleman seeking a suitable wife is forced by Fate and unhelpful circumstance to become engaged to a lady who had no idea that in selflessly assisting him she was auditioning for that part.

In the leadup to her tenth Season, Meg Cynster—known to the ton's eligible bachelors as Miss Prim—takes to the country to ponder the question: If not marriage, then what? She has yet to find an answer when she comes upon a supremely elegant curricle, drawn by a pair of high-spirited horses presided over by an unconscious gentleman. Others present know where he's staying, but can't manage the horses. With no real choice, Meg accepts the responsibility and drives the gentleman home. Unfortunately, he's too inebriated to just leave, so she rouses him enough to help him inside.

But then others arrive, and Meg learns the gentleman is none other than Drago Helmsford, the notorious Duke of Wylde—and in order to protect her reputation, she and Drago are forced to declare that they are engaged.

Although a shocking surprise for everyone, by all measures, the match is highly desirable. Meg and Drago have no option but to allow the engagement to stand until the end of the Season, when they can quietly call it off. Consequently, they have to keep the fact that their engagement is a sham an absolute secret from everyone, including all members of their families.

Through the ensuing whirl of the Season, with all eyes focused avidly on them, they duly pretend to be an affianced couple—roles that, to their surprise, come to them remarkably easily. With every member of their families and all the powerful in society being unrelentingly encouraging, both Meg and Drago, with eyes wide open, start to consider the possibility that marrying the other might just be the answer they'd each been seeking when they'd first met.

Then accidents start happening and quickly escalate to attacks, and it becomes clear that someone is intent on preventing Meg from marrying Drago. Why is unclear, but with the threat hanging over them, the Cynsters and Helmsfords rally around to ensure Meg makes it to the altar. But even after the wedding, when Drago and Meg retreat to his estate, the attacks continue until, with their hearts and future on the line, Drago and Meg risk all in a gamble to expose the faceless villain and bring the ever-present danger to an end.

A classic historical romance laced with intrigue set in the ton's ballrooms and drawing rooms and in the green depths of the English countryside. A Cynster Next Generation novel. A full-length historical romance of 113,000 words.

OTHER TITLES BY STEPHANIE LAURENS

The Tempting of Thomas Carrick

A Match for Marcus Cynster

The Lady By His Side

An Irresistible Alliance

The Greatest Challenge of Them All

A Conquest Impossible to Resist

The Inevitable Fall of Christopher Cynster

The Games Lovers Play

The Secrets of Lord Grayson Child

Foes, Friends and Lovers

The Time for Love

Miss Flibbertigibbet and The Barbarian

Miss Prim and the Duke of Wylde

A Family of His Own (March, 2024)

Lady Osbaldestone's Christmas Chronicles

Lady Osbaldestone's Christmas Goose

Lady Osbaldestone and the Missing Christmas Carols

Lady Osbaldestone's Plum Puddings

Lady Osbaldestone's Christmas Intrigue

The Meaning of Love

The Casebook of Barnaby Adair Novels

Where the Heart Leads

The Peculiar Case of Lord Finsbury's Diamonds

The Masterful Mr. Montague

The Curious Case of Lady Latimer's Shoes

Loving Rose: The Redemption of Malcolm Sinclair

The Confounding Case of the Carisbrook Emeralds

The Murder at Mandeville Hall

Bastion Club Novels

Captain Jack's Woman (Prequel)

The Lady Chosen

A Gentleman's Honor

A Lady of His Own
A Fine Passion
To Distraction
Beyond Seduction
The Edge of Desire
Mastered by Love

Black Cobra Quartet
The Untamed Bride
The Elusive Bride
The Brazen Bride
The Reckless Bride

The Adventurers Quartet
The Lady's Command
A Buccaneer at Heart
The Daredevil Snared
Lord of the Privateers

The Cavanaughs
The Designs of Lord Randolph Cavanaugh
The Pursuits of Lord Kit Cavanaugh
The Beguilement of Lady Eustacia Cavanaugh
The Obsessions of Lord Godfrey Cavanaugh

Other Novels
The Lady Risks All
The Legend of Nimway Hall – 1750: Jacqueline

Medieval (As M.S.Laurens)
Desire's Prize

Novellas
Melting Ice – from the anthologies *Rough Around the Edges* and *Scandalous Brides*
Rose in Bloom – from the anthology *Scottish Brides*
Scandalous Lord Dere – from the anthology *Secrets of a Perfect Night*

Lost and Found – from the anthology *Hero, Come Back*

The Fall of Rogue Gerrard – from the anthology *It Happened One Night*

The Seduction of Sebastian Trantor – from the anthology *It Happened One Season*

Short Stories

The Wedding Planner – from the anthology *Royal Weddings*

A Return Engagement – from the anthology *Royal Bridesmaids*

UK-Style Regency Romances

Tangled Reins

Four in Hand

Impetuous Innocent

Fair Juno

The Reasons for Marriage

A Lady of Expectations An Unwilling Conquest

A Comfortable Wife

MISS PRIM AND THE DUKE OF WYLDE

MISS PRIM AND THE DUKE OF WYLDE
Copyright © 2023 by Savdek Management Proprietary Limited
ISBN: 978-1-925559-58-3

Cover design by Savdek Management Pty. Ltd.
Cover couple photography by Period Images © 2023

First print publication: August, 2023

Savdek Management Proprietary Limited, Melbourne, Australia.
www.stephanielaurens.com
Email: admin@stephanielaurens.com

The names Stephanie Laurens and the Cynsters, and the SL Logo, are registered trademarks of Savdek Management Proprietary Ltd.

❀ Created with Vellum

CHAPTER 1

MARCH 28, 1855. BENENDEN, KENT.

"*I* never thought that it would come to this."

On hearing that pronouncement, Drago Helmsford, Duke of Wylde, looked up to find his close friend, Lord Harry Ferndale, heir to the Marquis of Tavistock, gazing at him through bleary eyes filled with drunken commiseration.

Drago arched a brow. "This what? That I would stand on the cusp of offering for a lady?" He snorted softly. "Given the terms of my father's will, there was never any option other than to solicit the hand of some likely damsel."

The two of them were seated at a table in the corner of the taproom of Benenden village's Bull Inn, along with George, Viscount Bisley, and Thomas Hayden. The four had been firm friends from their first day at Eton and had remained inseparable through their years at Oxford and the subsequent nearly fifteen years that they'd spent inhabiting the social circles favored by the wealthy bachelors of the ton.

"At least," George said, his words only slightly slurred, "this Alison Melwin doesn't sound the sort to be overly demanding. To want to trim your sails, so to speak." George squinted at Drago. "She's a local, you say?"

Drago took another swig of the inn's strong ale before replying, "A neighbor. Her family owns a property along the Court's southern boundary, and of particular note"—he wagged a finger at the other three—"she's the daughter of my aunt Edith's childhood friend and longtime bosom-bow."

Thomas frowned as if trying to concentrate. "The aunt you asked for help in finding a suitable bride?"

Drago nodded. "The same." He paused, his tankard poised before his lips, then admitted, "All in all, I have to concede that in every respect, Alison is an excellent candidate for the position of my quiet, conventional, and most importantly, amenable duchess." So saying, he drained the tankard, then lowered it to the table.

He glanced at his friends. They'd all been drinking steadily since they'd arrived at the inn several hours ago. In response to his summons, the others had driven down from London to join him in farewelling his bachelor days, and after assuaging their hunger with large servings of the inn's game pie, they'd settled in to drown his sorrows.

In actual fact, he wasn't all that sorrowful. Offering for Alison's hand was simply one of those unavoidable steps he had to take as part and parcel of being the Duke of Wylde.

"I still can't believe that your father even thought of using his will to blackmail you into marriage." George looked far more mournful than Drago.

He lightly shrugged. "Of all men, the pater knew what he was dealing with—would be dealing with even from the grave."

Harry nodded soberly. "He was a canny one, your pater."

"Still," George persisted, "leaving you to inherit the entailed properties while, after a certain date, withholding the family funds required to keep them going seems a trifle heavy-handed." He suddenly looked worried. "I hope my old man doesn't get wind of this and think to do the same."

Remembering his father with genuine affection, Drago replied, "Papa saw it as his duty to ensure the succession, and he knew that, just as he had, I would avoid the Marriage Mart for as long as I possibly could. At least he gave me until my thirty-fifth birthday to do the deed."

"Your thirty-fifth birthday that comes around this August." As well-flown as the rest of them, Thomas clarified that point.

Harry frowned. "August is months away. You could play the field for the whole upcoming Season—"

"And risk Aunt Edith or—God forbid—m'mother deciding to let slip my rapidly approaching need of a bride?" Drago shook his head. "Thank you, but no. Can you imagine the matchmakers' reaction? I wouldn't be safe setting foot outside Wylde House."

"Lord, no!" George looked suitably horrified, while Harry looked chastened.

Thomas had been staring into his empty tankard. He glanced at the others, then pointed at their likewise empty mugs. "'Nother round?"

Harry blinked myopically, then hauled out his fob watch and squinted at the face. "Sad to say, old man, but I think we'd better get on the road."

Drago pushed his tankard away. "Given I can't offer you beds at the Court—or at least, given Edith's in residence, beds you'd want to avail yourselves of—you probably had better head off."

Even Drago wasn't staying at his nearby estate, the dukedom's principal seat of Wylde Court. He'd driven down from London intending to spend the evening carousing with his friends, then remain overnight at the Court and offer for Alison's hand on the morrow, only to discover that his aunt, who had arranged tomorrow's meeting with Alison and her parents and was presumably intent on ensuring Drago performed as she hoped, had already arrived.

On driving into the Court's stable yard, he'd been informed of her presence and had left a message redirecting his friends and headed for the small cottage in Benenden that he'd acquired years before as a local bolt hole.

Harry had driven the other two from London in his curricle. On arriving at the Court, they'd received Drago's message and continued as directed to the Bull Inn, but as the cottage was too small to accommodate them as well as Drago and his valet and groom, all three had decided to head back to the capital that night.

Drago pushed away from the table and rose. The others followed suit, and after signaling to Morrow, the publican, to put all charges on his slate, Drago led the way out.

The evening air was crisp and clear, the temperature low enough to have their breaths fogging.

While the inn's ostlers rushed to put Harry's team of bays into the shafts, the four friends settled their hats on their heads and hunted in their coat pockets for gloves and pulled them on.

The ostlers led the horses and curricle out.

Drago thanked Harry, George, and Thomas for their support "at this pivotal time in my life."

Harry blinked as if only just realizing the momentous threshold upon which Drago stood poised. "Sadly, after tomorrow, you won't be the same man."

Startled, Drago laughed, but even to his ears, the sound seemed hollow. "No, indeed. By noon tomorrow, I'll be an affianced man."

Glumly, George shook his head. "It'll be the end of an era."

Drago smiled slightly. "I'm only the first of us to fall."

Accepting the reins, Harry shuddered. "Just as long as you don't start a domino effect."

"Lord preserve us!" Somewhat unsteadily, George thrust out his hand to Drago. "Good luck, old man. May it all go smoothly."

"I'm sure all will be boringly predictable." Drago shook George's hand, then Harry's and Thomas's.

Awkwardly and with telltale care, the three climbed into the curricle and shuffled and sorted themselves out.

Drago shoved his gloved hands into his pockets and stepped back.

Gripping the reins, Harry glanced at him. "Sure you don't want to clamber up? We could take the lane past your bolt hole's front door."

Drago smiled and shook his head. "You'll be faster going the other way, and the cottage is only a hundred or so yards up the lane. The walk will help clear my head."

George frowned. "Were I in your shoes, I'm not sure I'd want my head all that clear."

Drago laughed and raised his hand in farewell.

The others whooped and waved, and Harry shook the reins and drove off, turning left through the village on their way back to London.

Drago listened to the rattle of the wheels fade, then with his hands once more in his greatcoat pockets, he paced across the intersection directly opposite the inn and set off to find his bed.

Of the four of them, he'd always had the hardest head, and despite the quantity of ale he'd consumed, his abilities were only mildly affected. Observing him now, no one was likely to realize he was, in fact, quite drunk; he'd long ago learned to master his expression and not grin like a besotted fool.

Several years ago, he'd bought the cottage he'd commandeered for the night so that a local woman recently widowed due to a tragic accident on one of the estate's farms could have a roof over her head. Conveniently, the cottage stood on the edge of a farm the woman's son-in-law and daughter owned, which meant that on the rare occasions Drago had need of a bolt hole, the widow could easily decamp to spend a few days with her family.

Drago had insisted the widow was doing him a service in keeping the cottage neat and the small garden cared for and had flatly refused to accept any rent. Although initially, the widow and her family had been uncomfortable with the implied charity, given their financial position compared to Drago's, it really would have been silly to insist on paying the dukedom, and as Drago had used his bolt hole several times over the years—whenever he wished to avoid his mother and relatives at Wylde Court—all parties had come to accept the arrangement.

He walked at a slow and steady pace. With the night still and silent about him, inevitably his thoughts slid to his unavoidable life-changing appointment the next morning. Confronted with having to find a bride by August, in January, he'd bitten the bullet and asked his paternal aunt Edith for help. He hadn't asked his mother for the simple reason that she knew him far too well. Additionally, Edith—being a Helmsford by birth— had a finely honed understanding of what the wider family would expect in Drago's duchess.

Almost certainly, Edith had been waiting for him to ask and had immediately directed his eye toward Alison Melwin. Lady Melwin, Alison's mother, remained one of Edith's closest friends, yet beyond that, Drago accepted that Alison possessed most of the attributes the family and society would deem desirable in his bride.

He'd met Alison only once, a month ago at a local party hosted by the Melwins specifically for that purpose. Although he and Alison had been born mere miles apart and each had always been aware of the other's existence, as she was twenty-four to his thirty-four, while growing up, they had rarely crossed paths. And given the circles he inhabited in town, they had never crossed paths there, either.

But Alison had, indeed, seemed everything that Edith had labeled her —quiet, willing, and sensible. Not a silly young girl expecting him to hang on her every word and constantly dance attendance on her. Being a local, Alison would know how to manage the household at Wylde Court, and as the Melwins were an old family and entrenched in the ton, presumably she would know or readily learn how to manage the reins of the London house, too.

Most importantly, when he'd managed a few words with her alone, she'd given him to understand that she was entirely willing to embark on a marriage of convenience with him.

He'd been relieved that she hadn't been looking for love. Indeed, she'd been as clear-eyed as he in acknowledging that she wasn't in love with him any more than he was with her.

On that basis, he believed they could rub along well enough.

His decade-long career prowling through the ton had predominantly been spent in those circles eligible young ladies did not frequent. Regard-less, he had never encountered or so much as glimpsed any of that species who even remotely stirred his heart much less evoked any of the reac-tions that, from observing his parents' marriage, he knew stemmed from love. Consequently, in light of his father's demand, a sound, agreeable marriage of convenience was the best he could hope for.

As he paced along, he told himself that was the logical conclusion and he should be grateful that he'd found a suitable lady like Alison so easily.

Yet the prospect of tomorrow and the step he intended to take had settled like a lead weight on his chest.

Should he have made a greater effort, girded his loins, and stepped into the bright lights of the ton's ballrooms and drawing rooms and actively searched for a lady capable of engaging his emotions? Yet he had no reason to believe that such a female existed, and he had only so much time. Offering for Alison was the sensible way forward.

Dragging his mind from such unhelpful retreading of the arguments, he raised his head, looked along the lane, drew in a deep breath, and walked on.

* * *

"RISE AND SHINE, YOUR GRACE."

His face half buried in a pillow, Drago groaned and, raising his arm to shade his eyes, rolled onto his back. After a second or two's effort, he managed to crack open his lids.

Maurice, Drago's valet, had opened the curtains, and daylight seared Drago's senses.

Wincing, he closed his eyes and mumbled, "What time is it?"

"Nine, Your Grace." Maurice cheerily added, "You told me to wake you so you'd have plenty of time to get spruced up for your outing to claim your bride."

Don't remind me. "So I did." Drago gathered his willpower. "Right, then." Lowering his arm, he threw back the covers. "Let's get to it."

Maurice was busy laying out his clothes. Despite the name Maurice, which Drago strongly suspected was assumed, the valet—in his late thirties, short, stocky, and round of face—was a product of London's East End, a fact that occasionally showed in his speech but concerned Drago not at all. Maurice had an eagle eye when it came to clothes and appearance, a talent Drago had learned to respect. If Maurice decided that one of Drago's most severe suits, teamed with a waistcoat in silver brocade and an ivory-white silk stock, was the correct raiment in which to present himself before his prospective bride, Drago wasn't about to argue.

Determinedly not thinking about what he would shortly be doing, he washed, then, swathed in a silk dressing gown, allowed Maurice to shave him. Maurice had taken one look at Drago's heavy-lidded eyes and firmly taken the razor from his hand.

Once Drago was stubble-free and patting his cheeks dry, Maurice wiped the razor and carefully stowed it. "How hungry are you?"

Drago paused to consider, then replied, "I could eat a horse."

His mouth felt as dry as the bottom of an Egyptian tomb, and his stomach was a hollow pit.

Making for the door, Maurice cast an assessing glance his way. "Hair of the dog?"

Drago grimaced. "Possibly. Let's see how I feel once I get downstairs."

As other than Maurice and Tisdale, his groom, he'd brought no staff to the cottage, it fell to Maurice to cook breakfast.

Although lean, Drago was tall; by anyone's assessment, he was a large man. He also had a healthy appetite, and the dinner the previous evening, while acceptable as an inn's dinner offering, hadn't been all that much for someone used to multiple courses and large portions.

And drinking copious amounts of ale always left him ravenously hungry.

He dressed in the clothes Maurice had laid out, then secured the silk stock with his diamond pin. He brushed his dark hair, grateful as always to his London barber, who had the knack of making sure Drago's dark locks always fell as they ought, even after he'd raked his fingers through the heavy mane.

After deciding he was as "spruced up" as he was likely to get, he headed for the door. The stairway was narrow; almost bouncing from one shoulder to the other, he descended with care, eventually reaching the ground floor and the small hall before the front door. He turned to the open doorway on the right and walked into the parlor, which also served as a dining room.

The windows looking onto the front garden were open, and a light, flirtatious breeze wafted in.

Drago drew in a careful breath, then walked to where a single straight-backed chair had been set at one end of the small table.

He sat and surveyed the dishes. "Eggs, bacon, sausages, and lots of toast. You're invaluable, Maurice."

"Thank you, Your Grace." Maurice breezed in from the kitchen, bearing a dish of butter. "Do endeavor to remember that." He placed the butter beside the toast and critically surveyed Drago.

Reaching for a slice of toast, Drago arched a brow. "Do I pass muster?"

After studying Drago's hair, Maurice nodded. "You'll do. Now, do you want coffee or something stronger?"

The pressure in Drago's head spiked every time he allowed his gaze to drift toward the brightness outside. "Given I have to drive to Melwin Place, you'd better make it half and half."

Maurice glanced at the window, then turned toward the kitchen. "A wise choice."

Minutes later, he returned with a large mug filled with coffee and whisky.

Drago had made good inroads into the eggs and sausages, and the toast was almost gone. He accepted the mug, sipped, then took a long swallow. Setting the mug down, he nodded. "That should do the trick."

"Tisdale and I were wondering whether we're going to remove to the Court later today, after you do the deed. If not, we'll need to go to the market in Rolvenden and get more food." Maurice nodded at the nearly empty platters. "There's nothing much left."

Drago frowned. "Us repairing to the Court depends on whether Aunt Edith is still there and whether I want to avoid her." He grimaced. "She probably will be, and I probably will. Her preening over my impending leg shackling will be insufferable."

"So we need food."

Drago nodded. "Get more than we need. We can leave the rest for Mrs. Kennedy in thanks for her hospitality."

Maurice muttered something about Drago owning the damn cottage, but dutifully loaded his arms with the now-empty platters and headed for the kitchen.

Drago called after him, "Do you need more funds?"

"Still have what you gave us before we headed down here. That's more than enough."

Drago glanced at the small clock on the mantelpiece and raised his voice. "Tell Tisdale to put the grays to and leave them tied in the yard. I won't be much longer."

"Right you are. We'll hire a gig from the inn."

Replete, Drago drank his heavily laced coffee and, finally, shifted his gaze to the window. The sunshine outside still threatened to give him a headache, but having a full stomach definitely helped.

He sighed, drained the mug, then trudged back up the stairs. The mirror in the bedroom was small, but a duke about to propose really ought to look his best.

* * *

Margaret Cynster—Meg to all who knew her—strolled through her cousin Christopher's fields, the woods lining the Walkhurst Road her destination.

She'd come to Kent, to Christopher's home, Walkhurst Manor, to spend the weeks before the Season commenced by helping Christopher and his wife, Ellen, cope with the demands of their three-year-old daughter, Julia, and their one-year-old son, George, after the birth of Marcus, the newest addition to their family.

For the past two weeks, while Ellen tended Baby Marcus, Aunty Meg had proved the perfect distraction for the rambunctious toddlers.

Meg and Ellen were much the same age, and although their interests were wildly disparate—Ellen being very much a country dweller while Meg delighted in spending most of her year in London amid the circles of the haut ton—after Ellen and Christopher had married, Meg and Ellen had quickly become close friends.

And in this instance, in the weeks leading up to what would be Meg's tenth—*tenth!*—Season, she'd welcomed the chance to spend time in the country away from her immediate family and friends. She needed to think about where her life was heading. After ten years of trawling through the ton searching for the right gentleman, she'd grown disillusioned, disaffected, and even—*gasp!*—bored.

Bored, she'd discovered, was not a state that suited her.

Yet despite having spent the past two weeks weighing up this notion and that, she was no nearer to making any decision on what she should do next—on what to do with her life if her ideal gentleman never appeared.

She was no longer sure such a gentleman existed, and if he didn't, she needed to develop a goal beyond becoming said gentleman's wife. To date, her entire ambition had been fixed on attaining that state, but without her ideal gentleman deigning to appear, she saw no prospect of achieving it.

She was not a naturally restful person. She needed something to do, some active role to fill. That was an aspect of her character the past ten years had made plain.

Sadly, she'd yet to define any suitable role she might make her own.

Be that as it may, that morning, with the sun beaming down, warming the air and dispelling the last memories of winter, she had ventured out on a specific quest. She often sallied forth for a ramble once the first rush of the morning was past, and Mrs. Hambledon, the manor's cook, had asked if Meg could gather some dandelions, wild garlic, and nettles.

Meg had agreed, and Mrs. Hambledon had assured her, "You'll find plenty of good clumps of wild garlic and nettles in the woodland bordering the road, and you'll pass any number of dandelions in the fields along the way."

So it had proved. As Meg passed into the cool shade of the trees, the trug swinging from her hand was half filled with dandelions, roots as well as leaves as requested.

A gentle breeze caressed her warm cheeks. As usual, her straw hat had slipped back on her head and now hung over her nape, secured by the ribbons looped about her throat.

She wended her way between the trees, following the twisting paths made by wildlife. As Mrs. Hambledon had predicted, Meg found several clumps of wild garlic and had soon harvested a goodly pile of leaves, then she moved on in search of nettles. Possibly due to the lack of sunlight deeper in the woods, there didn't seem to be any nettles growing beneath the trees. She vaguely recalled spotting nettles in the roadside verge the last time she'd ridden to the village and made directly for the road, but between her and the verge, brambles had grown into clumps higher than her head, forcing her to detour around the prickly masses.

Rounding a massive bramble bush, she glimpsed the road through the trees ahead.

Men were darting about in the lane.

Surprised, she stopped and took in the sight of two woodsmen leaping about in the middle of the roadway as they attempted to catch the halters of a pair of magnificent grays harnessed to what was unquestionably the most elegant curricle Meg had ever seen.

She was a Cynster; she'd seen elegant curricles aplenty. Excellent horses, too, and the pair of grays also ranked highly.

Yet there was no one sitting in the curricle. No driver, no groom. No one at all.

And at any moment, one of those lovely horses was going to rear and injure itself or lash out at the woodsmen.

She recognized the men. Carter and Miller worked for Sir Humphrey Martingale on the Bigfield House estate, which lay on the other side of the road from Walkhurst Manor. Sir Humphrey was Ellen's uncle, and her brother, Robbie, managed the estate.

Without further thought, Meg ran for the road. After leaping across the ditch some yards behind the woodsmen so as not to startle the already frightened horses, she set her basket down on the verge, then walked toward the curricle.

Carter and Miller—every bit as panicked as the horses—glanced over their shoulders and saw her.

"Miss Cynster! You want to stay away, miss. These horses—"

"I'm used to handling horses." She spoke calmly, evenly, and continued walking forward.

As she neared the grays, both of whom were rolling their eyes, she started crooning. She might refer to horses as "smelly beasts," but she knew more than she'd ever wanted to know about how to handle them. How to soothe and calm them.

She kept her gaze locked on the animals, catching their eyes, capturing and holding their attentions, impressing on them that she was calm and untroubled, so they could be, too.

Gradually, the horses quieted, and first one, then the other, allowed her to catch their halter and draw their head down enough to grasp the reins.

With both sets of long reins in her grasp, she stroked and patted the long noses. "There, now. How did such a pair of beauties as you get loose?" Her gaze traveled along the reins—to the figure slumped lifeless across the curricle's seat. "Oh." She managed—just—to keep the shock from her voice. The last thing she wanted was to set the horses panicking again, but she felt her eyes grow huge as she stared at the dark-haired gentleman. Not a muscle, not a finger, not an eyelash twitched.

"Is he dead, do you think?" one of the woodsmen whispered.

"I don't know," Meg heard herself whisper back.

The man—judging by the quality of his clothes, let alone his horses, he was beyond doubt a gentleman and a wealthy one at that—lay motionless, his chin sunk on his chest, his arms lax at his sides. Only his long, black-trouser-clad legs, bent with his knees wedged against the front board, were holding him in place on the leather seat.

The shoulders slumped against the seat's back were broad, encased in a dun-colored greatcoat worn over a coat that just a glance told her hailed from Savile Row. The waistcoat, too, was top of the trees, richly embroidered without being glaring. And in the folds of silk below the man's chin, a diamond blazed in a stray beam of sunlight.

Drinking in the vision, Meg felt strangely shocked. His face was lean with the long planes, patrician nose, and chiseled cheekbones of an aristocrat. His jaw was squarish without being aggressive, his lips, in repose, finely drawn. His brow was wide, with locks of black hair falling rakishly over the expanse, shadowing eyes well set beneath the angled slashes of black eyebrows.

His lashes were impossibly long and thick, forming black crescents on his cheeks.

Even inanimate, his was a face so outrageously handsome the sight of it literally stole her breath.

A novel reaction for her, along with the errant yet compelling thought that surely a man as beautiful as this shouldn't simply die.

She frowned, then to herself as much as to the stunned woodsmen, murmured, "He looks too young and healthy to have died of an apoplexy."

Or indeed, any other natural cause, and there was no sign of violence anywhere.

Despite his utter stillness and a pallor she suspected was natural, there was enough color in his complexion to suggest he wasn't dead.

Still frowning, she blew out a breath. "Let's see."

Reorganizing the reins as she went, she walked along the side of the curricle, then boldly mounted the steps.

The well-sprung carriage dipped with her weight, yet the man didn't stir.

Grimly determined, she rearranged the reins, grasping them in one hand, then telling herself he couldn't be—wouldn't be—dead, she steeled herself, reached out, and searched for a pulse in the man's throat, just beneath his chin.

His skin was warm to her touch, and his throat felt strong. It was also long; seeking a pulse point, she was forced to dip her fingers beneath the silk of his stock.

She slid her fingertips down the long tendon and, at last, felt the solid throb of a heartbeat.

Yes! There.

The man's lashes fluttered, then rose.

Dark-chocolate-brown eyes met hers.

Startled, she pulled back her hand and was about to straighten, but discovered she couldn't seem to move.

She blinked, caught—trapped—in that mesmerizing dark-chocolate gaze.

Drago stared at the vision leaning over him.

A vision, indeed.

Curls of spun gold haloed a face of feminine perfection, of smooth cheeks and a flawless peaches-and-cream complexion. Not a classically oval face but one with a wide brow, delicately arched brown eyebrows, large—huge—summer-sky-blue eyes, and a tapered chin that held just a hint of determination.

Delighted, with his gaze, he traced her features, the pert straight nose and long eyelashes. He registered the perfect symmetry of her beauty even as her lips caught and held his attention.

Lush lips shaded the palest rose, they were the evocative shape one associated with a cherub.

Or perhaps an angel.

Have I drunk myself to death?

No. He hadn't had that much. He was drunk but not that drunk.

Which meant he was awake, and this was real, and she was, too.

He returned his gaze to her sky-blue eyes and allowed his lips to curve into a seductively charming smile, one all but guaranteed to work on even the starchiest of ladies.

Still holding her captive with his gaze, he raised a hand and gently— very gently so as not to startle her—ran the backs of his crooked fingers down one satiny cheek. "I really would like to get to know you better."

The slight slur edging the words, uttered in a deep, dark voice that rendered them nothing less than an outright invitation to sin, jolted Meg free of the sensual web the devil had so effortlessly cast. The stunningly effective web he'd snared her in just by looking at her with those gorgeous, fathomless, *dangerous* eyes.

Abruptly, she wrenched her gaze from his and straightened, registering the combined scents of coffee and whisky. "Good God!" She would have stepped back, but the curricle was only so wide. "You're *sozzled*! And it's not even noon!"

The horses shifted, and she turned to calm them. They settled, and she swung back to their owner to find him frowning faintly as if not quite understanding her reaction.

"Yes, well." Making an obvious effort, he attempted to lever himself upright. "There's a reason for that, I'll have you know."

Clinging to temper as her best defense, she gave vent to a disgusted sound. "So you did this to yourself." She waved at the horses. "You set out driving a fabulous pair of high-steppers while thoroughly inebriated and put them as well as yourself at risk!"

Her tone had risen enough to make him wince.

Good. He deserves the sharp edge of my tongue.

She planted her hands on her hips and glared at him.

Still appearing vague and puzzled, he looked up at her, then shifted his gaze past her.

Then his lids lowered, and every vestige of returning tension drained from his long frame, and he slumped onto the seat again, this time with his head lolling against one shoulder.

Meg stared, then frowned. She reached out, gripped his shoulder, and shook him—or tried to. He was far heavier and more solid than she'd thought. She jabbed his shoulder instead. "Wake up!"

Not so much as a flicker of an eyelash.

Frowning more direfully, she debated slapping him—not lightly.

"Miss? I think he's passed out again."

She glanced at Carter, who'd come up to stand beside her and the carriage.

He pointed to the man's hand where it lay relaxed, palm upward, on the edge of the seat. "See how slack his hand and fingers are?"

Meg stared at the hand. Long-fingered, narrow-palmed, the hand of a musician, it lay apparently lifeless on the leather seat.

Miller came up on the curricle's other side. "Aye." He nodded sagely. "Out of it, he is. Sure as eggs are eggs."

Meg suspected they were right. Frustrated, she blew out a breath, then glanced at Miller and Carter. "Do you know who he is?"

"Oh, aye!" Carter nodded. "It's his lordship. Heard he was back in the old Vere cottage, which is where he sometimes stays." Carter stepped away from the curricle and pointed down the lane in the direction from which the curricle had come. "The cottage is just along there a ways, on the corner of the last lane on the right, before you get to the village road."

Meg drew the image of a two-story cottage from her memory. "Isn't that where Mrs. Kennedy lives?"

Miller nodded. "That's the one. His lordship here owns the place, but she keeps it for him, so to speak."

"I see." If Mrs. Kennedy kept for the man, then despite current appearances, he couldn't be all bad. Sadly, the cottage was too far away to ask the woodsmen to walk the horses and carriage—and comatose driver—home, and regardless, she wasn't comfortable leaving the high-bred horses in their care. She sighed. "I'll have to drive him back to the cottage."

Neither Carter nor Miller argued.

She remembered her basket, turned and located it on the verge where she'd dropped it, and pointed to it. "Could one of you take my basket to Mrs. Hambledon at the manor and tell her that once I've delivered the gentleman to the cottage, I'll walk back?"

"Pleased to, miss." Carter saluted her and loped back to the basket.

Miller looked uncertainly at her, then at the slumped body taking up the bulk of the seat. "Can you manage, miss?"

"Perhaps if you shove him back a little more?"

She watched as Miller came around the curricle and did his best to rearrange the large body and long limbs, ultimately clearing a section of seat sufficient for her to sit.

She turned and wiggled into position. "Thank you." Expertly, she looped the reins about her hands.

Miller looked unconvinced. "Are you sure you'll be able to handle 'em, miss?"

"Quite sure." Meg smiled reassuringly at Miller. "I am, after all,

Demon Cynster's daughter. Although I'm not that fond of horses, I can definitely manage them."

Her confidence rang in her tone. Miller heard and nodded respectfully. "Right, then." He stepped back.

"I'll have to go up to the Bigfield House drive to turn them." Meg dipped her head Miller's way. "Thank you and Carter for your help."

"Thank *you*, miss," Miller called as she flicked the reins and set the horses trotting. "We'd never have managed if you hadn't come along."

Meg smiled to herself. Helping others always made her happy. Satisfied and fulfilled.

She glanced at the figure lying boneless beside her. "I suppose I'll be helping you, too." Facing forward, she grinned. "My halo will be shining."

The horses recognized a firm and knowledgeable hand on their reins and responded accordingly. Under her guidance, the pair stepped smartly along to where the road widened at the mouth of the Bigfield House drive. She slowed the horses and executed a neat, smooth, uneventful turn.

Feeling pleased with herself, she straightened curricle and horses and set the lovely grays trotting rapidly back down the road.

CHAPTER 2

*M*eg would never have admitted it to anyone, but she thoroughly enjoyed driving the magnificent grays south to the cottage. The curricle lived up to expectations, too, bowling along with amazing smoothness. Reluctantly resisting the temptation to prolong the drive, she turned down the narrower lane that bordered the small plot on which the two-storied Vere cottage stood.

It was a cheery country cottage with gingham curtains in the windows. The small front garden was a mass of daffodils and jonquils, their bright, bobbing heads softening the lines of the local gray stone, as did the white-painted wood of the windows and doors.

As Meg had expected, just past the cottage, an open gate gave access to a small stable yard. The yard filled the space between the rear of the cottage and a surprisingly large barn big enough to accommodate both horses and carriage.

She slowed the horses and turned them through the gate, and they obediently clopped into the yard and halted.

She looked at the barn. The door was shut. There didn't seem to be any groom or stableman about. Certainly, no one came running, alerted by the sound of wheels and hoofbeats on the gravel.

Meg transferred her gaze to the cottage. No Mrs. Kennedy opened the rear door and came rushing to assist with her drunken employer. There was a stillness about the place that assured Meg that there truly was no one at home.

"Damn!" She looked at her still-comatose passenger. "Now what?"

Could she just leave him snoring on the seat?

She glanced at the horses. If she tied them up…

No. They would grow restless, and then who knew what they might do? They could easily injure themselves, let alone someone else.

She returned to studying their owner's long, relaxed limbs and wide-shouldered frame. There was no possibility that she could even shift him; he would have to move under his own steam.

How to revive him? She couldn't sit there all day, just waiting for him to rouse.

She ought to have asked Carter and Miller if they knew which lord he was. She'd dismissed the point as inconsequential at the time—she hadn't needed to know who he was to deliver him to the cottage—but now… It would be nice to have a name to bark at him.

Instead, she used the point of one elbow to nudge him sharply. "Wake up!"

He sucked in a breath, then softly snorted. Two seconds later, his absurdly long lashes fluttered, then squinting warily, he eased up his lids.

Raising his head, he squinted at her, then his gaze went past her. Slowly, he looked around, then struggled upright. "You brought me back."

"Carter and Miller—the woodsmen who found your horses wandering along the road without a compos mentis driver—told me you were staying here." She glanced at the cottage, wondering if the men had got that right.

"I am."

"There doesn't seem to be anyone here."

"My valet and groom went to Rolvenden, to the market."

He sat fully upright and, frowning, scrubbed the fingers of one hand through his hair, disarranging the black locks thoroughly, yet when he lowered his hand, his hair appeared merely fashionably windblown.

She swallowed a humph and, in increasing dismay, stared at the cottage. "So there's really no one here?"

"'Fraid not. And my head's still spinning. If you'll excuse me, I should go inside and lie down." Before she could stop him, he swung his long legs out of the curricle and stepped onto the gravel. He stood tall, settled his coat over his shoulders, then promptly collapsed, falling back against the curricle's side and slowly sliding down to end in a heap on the ground.

Startled, the horses shifted. Immediately, Meg gave them her attention and spent the next minute calming them again.

Exasperated, she sighed and listened, but no sound of retching reached her ears. That was better than the alternative.

Seeing no other option, she pulled on the brake, climbed down on the other side of the carriage from where its owner now lay, and playing out the reins, discovered they were long enough to tie to the hitching post outside the barn door.

That done and the horses secured, she walked around the carriage and halted, looking down at the rumpled figure now sprawled against the curricle's wheel. His dark head was once again down, his chin sunk almost to his chest. "Are you still awake?" she demanded.

"Sadly, yes." He raised a hand to his temple. "There's no need to shout."

She pressed her lips tightly together to suppress an unholy grin, then bracingly said, "Come on. You have to get up. Although I'm sorely tempted, I'm too well brought up to leave you lying there."

A moment passed, then he raised his head and angled a dark glance up at her. "I promise you I would get up if I could. Unfortunately, for reasons of their own, my limbs aren't cooperating."

"The reason is probably all the whisky you've drunk."

"I only had one half mug this morning. It was all the ale last night that's to blame."

She shook her head. Several of her male cousins turned talkative when drunk. Stupidly so. Just like this lordling, whoever he might be.

Seeing nothing for it, she heaved a theatrical sigh. "All right." She stepped around and positioned herself in front of him. Facing him with her feet planted at what she judged to be the appropriate distance from him, she held out her hands and wriggled her fingers. "Give me your hands. Obviously, you're a great deal heavier than I, but with the carriage behind you, we might just manage to get you on your feet."

He focused on her hands, then sighed, too, as if her direction was a massive imposition. But obediently, albeit slowly, he sorted out his arms and legs, got his feet planted before him, then reached up and grasped her hands.

His grip was firm and cool, not tight, yet she sensed reined strength behind it.

"Right, then. On the count of three." She braced herself. "One. Two. Three!"

She hauled with all her might, and he pushed up, using her for balance as he straightened his long legs and got his weight over his feet.

At the last moment, he swayed, and she feared he would go down again, but he staggered back and caught the curricle's side and managed to steady himself.

Then he smiled, nearly blinding her with charm. "There!"

Blinking, she saw that he was looking absurdly pleased. Smothering a snort, she freed her hands from his and stepped back.

Carefully balancing against the curricle, he straightened to his full height, which proved to be significantly taller than she'd thought. She was used to tall men; her brothers and most of her cousins were over six foot tall, yet this lordling would, she thought, be even taller than they.

"That's better." He risked taking his hand from the curricle's side to tug his exquisitely cut black coat straight, then he fixed his gaze on the cottage's rear door. "Now, to get inside."

He took one step, and his leg buckled. She rushed to catch him, and he lurched into her, and she staggered as well.

For an instant, they teetered, and she prayed they weren't both going to end on the gravel. In desperation, she wrapped her arms as far around him as she could reach. "Don't go down!"

"I'm trying not to." His arm descended across her shoulders, and his hand wrapped about her upper arm.

For several fraught seconds, they shuffled and shifted, but then steadied, and she breathed again.

For a moment, they both rested, simply breathing and taking stock. She had her arms wrapped halfway around his lower chest, hands splayed to hold him, and one heavy arm lay over her shoulders. They seemed to have achieved stability of a sort.

"My apologies. My limbs are definitely not behaving as they ought."

He was entirely serious and sincere.

She angled a glance at his face. "Have you ever been this drunk before?"

He appeared to trawl through his memories, then hedged, "Not that I recall."

She swallowed an entirely inappropriate laugh. "All right. Just concentrate on putting one foot in front of the other."

He did as ordered, and they advanced step by shuffling step toward the cottage's rear door. When they stood on the low stoop, he braced one hand against the doorframe, allowing her to release him and open the door, which was helpfully unlocked, as most doors in the country were.

She clamped her arms about him again, and his arm settled across her shoulders. With her on his left still bracing his weight, they angled through the doorway and moved into the small kitchen.

She glanced around and saw a deal table and counters lining the walls, but nowhere to sit.

"That way." He pointed to a narrow corridor leading toward the front of the house.

Given the width of his shoulders, negotiating the corridor without letting him go was a trial. When she attempted to ease her hold, he staggered and almost fell, and she quickly clutched him again.

Finally, they reached the small front hall.

The front door lay ahead, with open doors giving access to rooms on either side, while immediately on their left, the stairs rose steeply.

"This way." He urged her on.

As they neared the doorways, she peered through. To the right, she glimpsed a dining table, while on the left, she saw a sitting room. Relieved, she headed that way.

As they drew level with the newel post, she glanced at his face.

He'd noticed her looking toward the sitting room and shook his head. "Only armchairs. I need to lie flat."

She opened her lips to waspishly inform him that he would have to make do, but he gripped the newel post and, using it as a fulcrum, swung around to face the stairs, of necessity taking her with him.

Before she could react, they were stumbling up the steep flight.

It was a tight fit, and he was leaning forward, his weight and the arm across her shoulders compelling her to climb with him. "Bed's upstairs."

From his tone, deep and reassuring and somehow inviting, she wasn't at all sure that he didn't expect her to join him in it.

She would have halted where they were—midway up the steep flight —but momentum and the weight of his arm across her shoulders propelled her inexorably on.

But when they stepped onto the landing at the top of the steep flight, once more on level footing, she dug in her heels. "This," she stated in a tone that was the definition of resolute, "is as far as I can take you."

He looked down at her as if momentarily confused, then he blinked, and his lips—his most distracting feature—lifted in an almost-innocent smile. "Ah, yes. Propriety and all that."

His dark gaze swept her face as if he was committing her features to memory, then he grinned a boyishly charming, tempting grin. "I must thank you for your rescue. You've been the opposite of a damsel in distress."

Then his gaze locked with hers, and once again, she fell into the snare of those mesmerizing eyes.

"Such a lovely angel." The words were a croon imbued with impossible-to-resist seductive charm.

She felt his palm and fingers brush her cheek, then slide lower to frame her jaw.

Then he was lowering his head, his lips slowly approaching hers.

She should jerk back and avoid the kiss.

She knew she should, and he gave her plenty of time to do so, yet...

Overwhelming curiosity of a type and tenor she'd never before experienced held her immobile.

Her lips throbbed with heated anticipation the like of which she'd never felt before.

She waited, breath bated, held—wanting and yearning—in the invisible net of his charm.

With their lips a bare whisker apart, he paused, then on a grateful sigh, as if understanding that permission had been granted, he closed the distance and kissed her.

Of course, she'd been kissed before—many times by multiple gentlemen—yet never had she been kissed like this.

He didn't devour or seek to dominate or seize. Instead, his lips tempted, the exchange a medley of subtle challenge and blatant encouragement perfectly crafted to ensure she couldn't resist—that she wouldn't even think of resisting.

She fell into the caress as warmth spread through her, ignited purely by the simple contact between his lips and hers.

Seconds later, unable to hold back much less retreat, she raised her hands and framed his lean cheeks, and then she was kissing him.

Deliberately. Determinedly.

A low growl—a deep purr in his throat—only encouraged her further.

When the tip of his tongue traced her lower lip, she boldly opened her mouth and, with a giddy abandon that was so unlike her, welcomed him in.

He wasn't slow to take advantage. Within a minute, the exchange—entirely mutual—had teased desire to life and was steadily stoking their passions into a roaring blaze.

His hands had long ago lowered, and his arms had locked about her. She gloried in the hardness of the long frame against which she was held. Eager and sure, riding the crest of a passion she had never even guessed she possessed, she moved into him, exulting in his immediate response, in the ravenous, rapacious desire she sensed lurking behind his expertise.

The front door was thrust open.

"Drago! Where are you? If you think—" The forceful words cut off, followed by a much weaker, "Oh, my heavens!"

"Good gracious!" rang out in a second voice.

"What...? Oh, good Lord!" came from a third, much more censorious female.

"Oh." And there was a fourth present as well.

Meg was trapped in the rapture of the kiss, and the exclamations reached her as if through a fog. Her wits in abeyance, her senses only gradually refocusing, she was slow—very slow—to react.

Not so the man in whose arms she stood.

The effect on her partner in the illicit engagement had been immediate, instantaneous. At the first sound of the door opening, every single muscle in that long, large body had tensed to rocklike hardness, and he'd broken the kiss and looked down on the interlopers.

Meg saw his features before he wiped all expression from his face. He'd come very close to snarling at whoever had interrupted...

She followed his gaze down, into the front hall. To the bevy of four ladies, shocked into silence, clustered in the open doorway.

But then the name the first lady had used finally penetrated Meg's brain, and with her eyes flying wide, she snapped her gaze back to the gentleman's face.

To that too-handsome-for-anyone's-good face.

Her brain seized.

Feeling as if someone had upended a bucket of icy water over his head, Drago took in his aunt Edith's shocked and furious face and, beside her, the stunned look on Mrs. Compton's face; Edith's companion looked ready to swoon.

The pair had halted just inside the door. Beyond them on the stoop stood Lady Melwin and Alison Melwin. Predictably, hatchet-faced Lady Melwin was glaring, her eyes shooting daggers at him, while Alison stood staring upward, mouth agape and...apparently not that shocked.

He and his angel were standing at the top of the stairs, illuminated by a shaft of light lancing through the window above the cottage door. They were perfectly lit, perfectly recognizable.

Seeing astonishment being rapidly replaced by outrage in his aunt's and Lady Melwin's faces, after one swift glance at his angel's stunned expression, he did the only thing he could.

He lowered his arms from around her, but captured her hand and squeezed it briefly in warning as he turned to face the threat. He smiled as if delighted to behold the cluster of ladies about the door. "Aunt. Mrs. Compton. Lady Melwin and Miss Melwin. You're the very first to learn our happy news."

He felt the fingers locked in his twitch, but his angel didn't pull away. Instead, beside him, she shifted to face the newcomers, too.

His aunt blinked. After a fraught second, somewhat weakly, she inquired, "Happy news?" Her gaze drifted to his angel, and her eyes widened.

"Indeed." Raising the hand he held to his lips, he brushed a kiss to knuckles only he could see were nearly white and, smiling down at the assembled ladies, with his customary arrogant assurance stated, "This lovely lady"—*What the devil is her name? I should have asked*—"has just done me the honor of agreeing to become my wife."

His aunt's eyes couldn't get any wider. Her startled gaze had fixed on the lady by his side. "Miss Cynster. Is this true?"

Cynster? It was his turn to smother a flinch of pure shock. *What the devil have I got myself into?*

His fingers had spasmed about the lady's, and she turned her head and regarded him, then with a smile that, to his surprise, matched his, she met his eyes, then she looked down the stairs and trained that utterly assured smile on his aunt. "Indeed, Lady Catterdale. I daresay our announcement is a surprise."

To his continuing astonishment, she—Miss Cynster—started down the stairs, and still clasping her hand, perforce he descended behind her.

With her other hand, she gestured his way. "His Grace and I have only recently become acquainted, but, well…" She aimed her smile, along with an indulgent look, at him. "Here we are."

He didn't trust that look one iota.

"I…see." Edith's tone stated very clearly that she didn't see at all.

Halting on the lowest step and thus retaining the high ground, the diabolical Miss Cynster calmly continued, "Drago and I had no idea you might call. Had we known, we would have welcomed you in more appropriate fashion."

He dutifully looked as innocently sincere as he could and merely blinked when Lady Melwin snorted, "Indeed!"

"But…" Mrs. Compton frowned uncertainly. "Wasn't His Grace supposed to call at Melwin Place at eleven o'clock to…?" She broke off in a fluster and flapped her hands ineffectually. "Well, clearly, that won't be happening now."

"Obviously not!" Lady Melwin's eyes spat sparks. "It seems His Grace has made other arrangements." Abruptly, she stepped back. "Come, Alison! Clearly, we are not required here!"

With that, Lady Melwin swung on her heel and stalked down the path to the cottage's front gate. Looking past her, Drago saw the Melwin barouche standing in the road behind the gig his aunt used when in the country.

To his surprise, instead of immediately following her incensed mama, Alison smiled brilliantly at him and Miss Cynster and darted forward to grasp and squeeze Miss Cynster's hand.

"Thank you," Alison whispered. "Thank you so much!" Her gaze flicked to him. "I hope we'll meet again soon." Then she whirled and rushed after her mother.

Utterly confused, Drago stared after her.

"Well!"

His aunt's exclamation drew his gaze. Her gaze, he noted, was flicking between him and Miss Cynster. He could almost see the wheels whirling in her brain as she calculated the benefits of him marrying a Cynster rather than Alison, who despite being the daughter of a dear friend was, relatively speaking, a nonentity within the wider ton.

To his relief and also his delight, Miss Cynster withstood his aunt's scrutiny with as little reaction as he.

"I believe..." his aunt began, then ventured, "Margaret, isn't it?"

Miss Cynster nodded. "Meg."

His aunt's gaze turned limpidly innocent. "Have you known my nephew for long?"

Calmly, Miss Cynster replied, "I've known Denton for many years. However, I only recently became acquainted with His Grace. I often visit my cousin and his wife at Walkhurst Manor, and this year, I decided to spend the weeks leading up to the Season in Kent."

Drago very nearly applauded that piece of masterly misdirection. He would wager that everything she'd said was true.

Of course, knowing that he often paid lightning visits to Wylde Court, which lay only a few miles from Walkhurst Manor, his aunt leapt to precisely the conclusion that wily Meg Cynster had intended. "I see." His aunt met his gaze. "So you recently became attached. Really, Drago, you might have thought to mention it. I could have smoothed matters over with Agatha had I known."

He conjured up a suitably contrite expression and shot a glance at his new partner in deception. "I apologize, Aunt, but in truth, I wasn't at all certain until...well"—he waved up the stairs—"just now."

His aunt primmed her lips, but it was clear she wasn't the least displeased with how her attempts to get him suitably wed had played out. "Very well. We'll say no more about it. But now I must rush after Agatha and smooth her ruffled feathers, pour oil on troubled waters, and all that. Miss Cynster, you will excuse us."

"Of course, Lady Catterdale."

"Come, Millie." His aunt collected her companion, who had been a silent observer of the entire scene, with a sweeping glance. "We need to be off."

"Yes, of course." Mrs. Compton beamed at Drago and Miss Cynster. "So thrilling to be the first to know!"

With that, she whirled and fell in behind his aunt as she marched determinedly back to her gig.

Drago remained in the open doorway, and Miss Cynster—Meg—remained fixed beside him until his aunt and her companion had climbed into the gig and rattled off down the road.

Only then did Drago reach for the doorknob and carefully close the door. Then he turned to face his unexpected fiancée, only to find her frowning.

She met his eyes. "For what did Alison Melwin thank me?"

He arched his brows. "An excellent question." He waved her into the sitting room and, when she consented to enter, followed her in. "I'm not sure I know the answer." Replaying Alison's words, he frowned. "I was assured Alison had no prospective suitors."

"Suitors?" Meg halted before the window in the small room, then swung to face him. Sudden suspicion filled her blue eyes. "Just what was that all about? Surely you weren't expecting such a visit." Her eyes narrowed. Holding his gaze, she crossed her arms and demanded, "Tell me all and tell me now."

He was a duke; no one issued demands to him. All but instinctively, he arched an arrogant brow that should, by all rights, have firmly depressed her pretensions.

He wasn't entirely surprised when that didn't work.

Her chin firmed, and her eyes narrowed to sapphire shards. "You got me into this. The least you can do is explain exactly what 'this' is."

He wagged a finger at her. "You were an equal partner in that kiss."

"And what has that to say to anything? You're Drago Helmsford. It's common knowledge that you can kiss life into a statue!"

"Really?" He looked suitably impressed.

Her eyes flashed. "Don't let it go to your head!"

"Permit me to observe that you're not a bad kisser yourself." While she continued to stand, he couldn't sit. He halted facing her, two paces away.

Close enough to discern that she wasn't entirely sure how to take his compliment.

"Yes, well." She flicked the fingers of one hand dismissively. "The fact that you managed to draw me in is the only thing preventing me ringing a peal over your head."

He couldn't resist. "Good Lord! Your peal is louder than this?"

"Much!" She glared at him, then pointedly stated, "I'm waiting."

Meaning he hadn't succeeded in distracting her from her initial question.

He sighed. "All right." He paused, selecting his truths as she had earlier. "The situation is this. I want to get married. I'm nearly thirty-five, and it's time." As a scion of a noble house, she would understand his not marrying previously and his wishing to marry now. "However, I saw no reason to subject myself to the brouhaha of openly searching for a bride during the upcoming Season." He caught her gaze. "You can imagine what that would have been like."

She blinked, then nodded. "You looking for a bride would create an outright frenzy. It would be matchmakers at twenty paces."

He laughed and, grinning, inclined his head. "Indeed. All in all, it didn't bear thinking about. So instead, I asked my aunt, Lady Catterdale, if she could make any suggestions."

She frowned. "Why not your mother?"

Because she knows me all too well and wouldn't have approved of or assisted in me embarking on a marriage of convenience. "Because I felt that Mama making any moves on that front would be too obvious, and I hoped that working through my aunt would be more...discreet. Regardless, I suspect Aunt Edith had been waiting for me to ask, because she immediately suggested I consider Alison Melwin."

"Why?"

"Firstly, because Edith understood I was seeking a marriage of convenience, and Alison is an entirely acceptable, quiet, presentable, and amenable candidate for the position of my duchess."

"Quiet and amenable being your most desired qualities."

She was almost as cynical as he. "Just so. More importantly from my aunt's point of view, Alison is the only daughter of Agatha Melwin, who is my aunt's closest childhood friend and longtime bosom-bow. Additionally, Melwin Place, although a much smaller estate, shares a border with Wylde Court."

Frowning slightly, she digested that, then arched a brow at him. "So what brought on this morning's visitation?"

He grimaced. "I'd made an appointment to call at Melwin Place at eleven this morning. Although I'd made no mention of it, my intention was to use the opportunity to offer for Alison's hand."

She regarded him levelly. "But instead, you got drunk, fell asleep in your curricle, allowed me to rescue you, and ended by thinking to thank me by kissing me, thus landing us in this predicament."

He considered each point, then nodded. "Yes."

She continued to study him, then remarked, "At least we seem to have made Alison happy. Who told you she had no other suitors? Her mother?"

"My aunt. Who would have had it from Alison's mother, so yes." He frowned. "Obviously, Lady Melwin is not a source to be trusted on that point."

"Apparently not." Meg shifted her gaze to the window, to the peaceful scene outside.

The situation was beyond outrageous, yet in all honesty, she couldn't see what either of them could have done differently. Step by step, the interplay of people and actions had led them inexorably to this point, and instead of feeling pointlessly incensed, she felt...curiously engaged. Immersed and drawn in, more or less willingly. Indeed, the scenario felt more like an adventure. A challenge to see if they—she and the notorious Drago Helmsford—could together extricate themselves from the mire into which some mischievous Fate had gleefully tossed them.

After a moment's further consideration, she muttered, "I suppose this teaches me not to come to the aid of inebriated gentlemen." She glanced at Drago. "Even if I did so mostly for your horses' sakes."

Her coconspirator looked genuinely contrite. "I do most sincerely apologize. As you no doubt realize, I was not myself—or at least not operating with my usual incisive wit and well-informed acumen."

His dry tone had her lips twitching.

"I truly had no idea my morning would end like this." He shook his head in apparently sincere befuddlement. "It was supposed to be quite different."

"Well," she replied, "you are still betrothed, only not to the lady you expected."

He dipped his head in agreement, then met her gaze. "So what now?"

That didn't require much thought. "Given we're now unofficially engaged, I believe our next question should be, How are we going to manage this situation?"

From the seriousness of his expression, she judged his wits and his acumen, despite previously being in abeyance, were now fully active.

Eyes narrowing as if assessing some vision, he said, "It's your reputation we need to protect. Given mine, everyone will be perfectly willing to believe the story we've concocted thus far, and anything the world thinks subsequently won't affect me in the least." His dark gaze returned to her face. "But in all we do henceforth, we need to ensure no opprobrium of any sort clings to you."

She had no wish to argue with that, so simply nodded.

"Ergo," he continued, "that means we'll have to maintain the façade— the charade, if you like—of being engaged for some months." He arched a brow at her. "Possibly to the end of the Season?"

She weighed the prospects. "If we don't want to set tongues wagging, then June at least."

"Very well. Let's say June." His features easing, he nodded. "We hold our line until then, doing whatever we need to do to keep our façade intact, and then in early June, you can call off the engagement on the grounds that we've agreed that we won't suit."

Openly curious, she studied him. "You're willing to be jilted?"

He shrugged lightly. "It won't worry me, and everyone will think that you're remarkably clear-headed."

She could see that he was entirely sincere; regardless of the social cost, it wouldn't worry him in the least if it meant protecting her. She was well acquainted with the innate attributes of those born to the nobility; most of the males instinctively protected females of their class, and patently, he was no different.

In this case, his entrenched instincts would work in her favor.

"All right. With that goal in mind, we need to plan our next steps." She thought of the obvious ones. "We're going to have to have our story straight and stick to it."

"Indeed. Speaking of which... Margaret. Meg." He caught her gaze. "I can't recall if I ever knew, but which branch of the family do you belong to? I know you're not one of Devil Cynster's brood."

"No, they're my cousins. Well, second or third cousins to be accurate. My father is Demon Cynster."

"Ah." He nodded. "Devil's cousin. So that's why you could manage my horses. I was wondering about that. That means you're Nicholas and Toby's sister."

"Younger sister. I'm the youngest. Pru is the oldest. She's now the Countess of Glengarah."

He wrinkled his nose. "Given your family and mine, we'll need to tread carefully." He looked at her, faintly puzzled. "Why haven't we met before? No—of course." He waved the point aside. "Stupid question."

"Indeed. You and I might both inhabit the more rarefied echelons of the haut ton, but socially speaking, we've never moved in the same circles. That's something almost everyone will know." She considered him. "In fact, I had heard that the major hostesses had despaired of luring you to their ballrooms and drawing rooms."

He thrust his hands into his pockets and huffed. "Had I ever appeared at such events, I would have caused heart attacks. And of course, you've never been allowed to attend the sort of parties I frequent." He paused, then added, "We're going to have to be convincing in our story of meeting down here."

Puzzled, she asked, "Apropos of that, why are you staying in a cottage and not at Wylde Court?"

"I drove down from London yesterday only to learn that Edith was already in residence at the Court, so I rattled on down here." He met her eyes. "I set up the cottage years ago as my local bolt hole, for use whenever I want to avoid family at the Court."

"Given your aunt knew to look for you here, your bolt hole is clearly no secret." If Carter and Miller had told her that their "lordship" was staying at the Court, she would have guessed who he was and taken him there, where staff would have been plentiful and none of the subsequent difficulties would have arisen.

I wouldn't have experienced that kiss, either.

She bundled the thought aside as being neither here nor there. He'd started to pace, clearly thinking, and she refocused on him. "Do you visit the area often enough to make a story of us meeting down here believable?"

"I'm down here every few weeks. I was last at the Court…a little over a week ago."

"I was here then, at Walkhurst Manor."

Still pacing, he nodded. "So by chance, we met then." He arched a brow at her. "Why are you in Kent?"

She explained about Christopher and Ellen's new baby. "I've been close to Ellen ever since they wed, and I was free, so offered my services."

He frowned and glanced at the small clock on the mantelpiece. "Won't they be missing you?"

"I sent word with the woodsmen, so they won't be panicking yet."

"All right." He paused, then said, "It occurs to me that we might want to bolster our story of meetings somewhat. As I recall, Christopher married about four years ago?"

When he looked at her inquiringly, she nodded. "That's right."

"And you've often visited Walkhurst over those years?"

"Yes."

"In that case, we could have met previously—say at the market in Sissinghurst."

"Or in Benenden village. Or at church."

"Not church. We want this to be believable, remember?"

"Well, we could add the shops at Rolvenden, then."

"All right. So our revised story is that we've met occasionally, purely in passing and entirely innocently, over the past four or so years at Sissinghurst, Benenden, and Rolvenden. We should be vague as to how long we've been aware of each other. But this time, over the past two weeks, we met...how?"

"Driving is possible. I often drive alone around here. Or walking in the woods."

"We met while you were driving the gig and I was riding," he insisted, "and then we went walking in the woods and found ourselves discussing our potential futures and given our..." He paused, then looked at her. "What's the word I'm looking for?"

She opened her eyes wide. "Inclinations?"

"That will do. Given our inclinations, we broached the subject of marriage, and"—he halted and spread his arms wide—"here we are." He met her eyes. "Will that suffice, do you think?"

She reviewed the tale and nodded. "I can't see why not." She, too, glanced at the clock. It was nearly one o'clock. "We'll need to break our news to Christopher and Ellen immediately, before they hear it from anyone else. The family will consider Christopher as in loco parentis, even though he's only a few years older than me." She studied Drago. "Are you and he acquainted?"

"Acquainted, yes. Close, no. He was a year ahead of me at Eton and Oxford, and of course, I've seen a bit of him over the years in town, and we occasionally cross paths down here. The Wylde estate lies north of the road to East End and Biddenden, so we're not immediate neighbors."

He frowned at nothing for a moment, then met her eyes. "I think we should speak with Alison first."

She held his gaze. "You certainly owe her an explanation, if not an apology."

He nodded. "I would also like to learn why she seemed so relieved and happy about not receiving an offer from me."

Meg studied his perfectly serious expression, then lips reluctantly lifting, said, "I should take issue with how conceited that sounded, but... you're right. Virtually every young lady I know would leap at the chance to be your duchess."

"I know." He shook his head. "That's been the bane of my existence to date, and as there's no denying it, that begs the question of why Alison wasn't at the very least put out by our unexpected declaration."

"Where is Melwin Place? I've heard the name, but never visited. Is it far?"

"Your uncle Vane and aunt Patience would know the Melwins, but I doubt the younger generation—Christopher and the rest—would have mixed with Alison, who truth be told has always struck me as something of a mouse, and even less with her older brother, Hubert, who is the definition of a pompous stuffed shirt. But to answer your question, Melwin Place is off the road to Biddenden, some way northeast of and farther away than Walkhurst Manor."

Meg frowned. "Given the time..." She glanced at Drago. "Is there any food in the kitchen?"

"No. That's why my men went to Rolvenden." He met her gaze. "Let's go to the Bull. We can have a bite in the dining room there, then drive over and see Alison before circling back to the manor and informing Christopher and his wife of your change in status."

She huffed, but after a second's consideration, nodded. "And once we speak with Alison, we can decide for how long my change in status should stand."

CHAPTER 3

"*G*ive me your hand, and I'll help you over."

Meg looked up at Drago, who was balancing on the uppermost stone of a fallen section of the wall around Melwin Place. He was holding out his hand to her and attempting to look encouraging.

After seeing to his horses, then walking down to the Bull, where they'd enjoyed a quick and unexpectedly tasty lunch, they'd returned to the cottage, and with her help, Drago had put the horses to, and they'd driven around the lanes to Melwin Place.

But rather than bowl up the drive, Drago had turned his horses down a narrow track beside the small estate's perimeter wall. The horses were now safely tied to some trees.

When she'd asked why they were leaving the curricle there, Drago had replied, "Trust me, at this particular point in time, neither you nor I want to encounter Agatha Melwin."

As she suspected he was right, she'd followed him to this spot where, some time ago, a tree had fallen and the wall had crumbled and been left unrepaired.

With his long legs, Drago had hopped up easily enough, but she was rather shorter. Luckily, she was dressed for rambling, and her skirts of blue cambric would withstand a fair amount of rough treatment.

Resigned, she scanned the wall and noted several gaps that she could use for her feet, then she walked forward, set the toe of her half boot in one crevice, and gave him her hand.

He grasped her fingers, and she fought to smother the frisson of awareness that shot through her, then nearly swallowed her tongue when he pulled her up as if she weighed nothing at all.

Fighting for balance, she teetered beside him on the top of the wall.

He promptly gripped her waist with both hands and steadied her. "All right?"

No! Him being so near, let alone having his hands so firm about her middle, sent her senses rioting. "Yes," she lied. She forced her eyes to the park ahead of them. "Where to now?"

"Down, first." He released her and stepped off the wall, dropping easily to his feet, then turned to her. "Come on."

Without any by-your-leave, he reached up, gripped her about the waist again, and swung her down with senses-stealing ease.

The instant he released her, she hauled in a much-needed breath.

He'd already turned to survey the house, just visible through the trees. "Alison mentioned that she spends a lot of time in the summerhouse by the lake." He glanced at Meg. "Let's see if she's there."

She followed him through the trees of the park, keeping within their shadow. They came to the lake. As it was out of sight of the house, they took to the gravel path like civilized visitors.

The summerhouse was a small white-painted wooden structure, and sure enough, as they neared, they saw Alison, who must have heard their footsteps, peering out of the open doorway.

Alison's face lit. "Oh! I'm so glad you've called."

"She certainly doesn't appear cast down," Meg murmured.

They started up the steps.

"Alison," Drago began, "I wanted to apologize—"

"Oh, no apologies are necessary, Your Grace! None at all!" Alison beamed at them both. "I'm so very happy for you, and I can't thank you enough, Miss Cynster, for, well…" Coloring, Alison let her words trail away and glanced at Drago.

Bemused, Meg filled in, "For taking the Duke of Wylde off your hands?"

"Yes!" Alison beamed anew. "Please." She caught their hands and drew them into the small room. "Do come in. I want you to meet"—she released them, whirled, and gestured to a tall, lanky gentleman who was standing in the shadows—"Joshua Bragg, my sweetheart."

Meg cut a glance at Drago and saw him looking at Bragg.

Then Drago shifted his gaze to Alison. "Your mother led me to believe that you were unattached."

"Yes, well," Alison said, "that was so at the time." She smiled at Joshua as he came to stand by her side. "You see, Joshua and I…well, I suppose you might say we're childhood sweethearts. We've known each other since we were small, and we've always felt...well, a connection. But then we grew older, and Joshua went away to grammar school and then to his legal studies and...well, I thought that was the end of things between us."

"It wasn't." Joshua claimed Alison's hand and smiled at her, and the appropriate description was that he had his heart in his eyes. "But as I'm sure His Grace will understand, I had no prospects—nothing to offer you and no right to imagine I could claim your hand."

When the pair seemed lost in each other's eyes, Meg prompted, "But now?"

Joshua straightened and met her gaze. "I heard from my parents—they live nearby—that there was talk Alison might soon accept an offer." Joshua glanced at Drago. "I didn't know from whom, but as I've never forgotten Alison and my circumstances have recently changed—I've been offered a full partnership in my firm—then I felt I had to come down and chance my hand." He shared a glance with Alison and squeezed the hand he held. "And my darling girl has just accepted my suit."

Smiling, he looked at Drago and Meg. "As I understand the pair of you had already reached an agreement, thus releasing Alison from any implied arrangement, that left her free to accept my proposal and bestow her hand on me."

Meg glanced at Drago to see how he was taking being thrown over for a solicitor, but he was all smiles.

Apparently perfectly genuine smiles.

"I'm very glad you've found each other again, and I"—Drago glanced Meg's way, one eyebrow faintly arching, then he returned his gaze to Joshua and Alison and amended—"we wish you nothing but happiness."

"Thank you." Joshua shared with Alison another glance brimming with joy. "I can't thank you enough for giving me the chance to make Alison happy."

Meg thought to ask, "Do you envisage any difficulty in convincing the Melwins to accept the outcome—both Drago's retreat and Joshua's offer?"

"Oh no," Alison earnestly assured them. "Although naturally, Mama will be disappointed that I won't be a duchess, she's always had a soft spot for Joshua, so I'm sure she'll come around."

"And Alison and I together will be more than a match for her papa and Hubert," Joshua added. "If necessary, we're willing to wait and wear them down until they consent to our engagement."

"Indeed. We're in no huge hurry," Alison said.

The pair were all but bubbling with optimism.

Drago glanced at Meg, then looked at Alison. "We should leave you to break your news to your parents. Once again, you have our warmest felicitations."

"And you have ours," Alison leapt to say.

Meg smiled, and they made their farewells. Leaving the happy pair discussing their declaration to Alison's family, Meg and Drago walked back around the lake and across the park.

She couldn't resist observing, "Alison seemed overjoyed at the prospect of being Mrs. Bragg rather than the Duchess of Wylde."

"Indeed. If I'd ever had an inflated ego, it would surely be sadly punctured by now."

She eyed him curiously. "For a duke who had been on his way to offer for a lady's hand just hours ago, you don't seem all that cast down."

He shrugged. "I was never set on marrying Alison, only on achieving the married state."

Meg wondered why—or at least, why now—but before she could frame a question, Drago went on, "Given Bragg's suit and his and Alison's obvious happiness, I feel compelled to maintain our charade at least until they've secured their chance for a happy marriage." He glanced at her. "If we break off our engagement before their betrothal is well established and their eventual wedding an accepted fact, I wouldn't put it past Hubert—I did mention he was a pompous snob—to do his damnedest to block Joshua's suit and pressure Alison to try to win me back."

"Hmm. If Hubert is half as bad as you've painted him, that seems a distinct possibility." She met Drago's dark gaze. "In the circumstances, I agree we should do all we can to give them time to cement their relationship. It seems the least we can do."

He nodded and faced forward. "June, then. Let's stick with that."

They reached the damaged wall, and she steeled herself and allowed him to lift her up and help her down again.

Once back in the curricle, Drago set course for Walkhurst Manor. "So, regarding our fictitious engagement, how, exactly, are we going to present it to the ton, and following on from that, what do we tell Christopher and his wife? What's her name again?"

"Ellen."

"Ellen. Do we tell them the truth or...?"

They debated their options and the likely ramifications of each possible pathway; some were clearly more fraught with danger than others.

"We can't afford anyone guessing the truth," he stated, "meaning that at no point can we allow our behavior to suggest our charade isn't real."

"Indeed." After a moment, she heaved a huge sigh. When he glanced at her, she met his eyes. "I can't see any way for us to get from here to early June without courting catastrophe other than by behaving consistently and constantly as if our engagement is real."

Somewhat grimly, he nodded. "I agree. Given the Season is about to start and given who we are, we're going to have to spend from now until June parading through the ton as an affianced couple, and there is no chance that any lack of conviction on either of our parts will go unremarked."

"They'll be watching us like hawks."

"Every moment of every day." Full realization of what they were going to have to do was sinking in.

He turned his horses down the Walkhurst Road. After a moment, he asked, "You don't have any other suitor in the offing, do you?"

"No." She cast him a sharp glance. "You?"

He knew what she was asking. "I was anticipating being engaged, remember? Therefore, I presently have no active liaisons."

She nodded and faced forward. "Returning to the question of what we should tell whom, it seems to me that the fewer people who know the truth, the better. If I tell Christopher and Ellen the truth, they won't behave toward either of us as they should, and worse, I can't guarantee they won't tell the rest of the family, and once the wider family knows, someone is sure to slip up and forget to act appropriately." She glanced at him. "Once family know the truth, it will be difficult to keep it from spilling out."

"I don't disagree." He caught her gaze. "But will you be comfortable deceiving your family?"

She didn't shrug off the question but instead thought long and hard before replying, "I truly can't see any other option—not given all that's at stake." Once again, her blue eyes met his. "Can you?"

"For myself, I can't see any way around spinning our families our concocted tale. The truth would place a far more onerous weight on their shoulders, and in reality, no one—family included—will be harmed by our charade." He pulled a wry face. "Other than you and I, Alison and, through her, Joshua are the only ones directly impacted, and in their case, the effect is very much for the better and welcomed."

Meg thought about that, then nodded decisively. "Yes. You're right. Our charade will certainly raise hopes and expectations in others, but no actual harm will be done when we call things off."

He smiled, straightened, and flicked the reins to set his grays trotting more rapidly down the road. "Perhaps we should consider our charade as us entertaining the entire ton."

She laughed and conceded the point with a dip of her head. "Sadly, I think we can be sure that the entire ton will be avidly interested."

After a moment, she said, "As we have to speak with Christopher and Ellen first, and neither of them are fools, let's see if our fabricated tale will withstand their scrutiny. They are, after all, the ones most aware of the time I've spent in this area."

Drago murmured ready agreement.

Content enough with their plan, at least to that point, he mentally canvassed whether there was any angle they hadn't covered. He couldn't think of anything more he could viably do to better protect Meg Cynster. Any adverse impact that accrued to him, he probably deserved, but she had stepped in and rescued him, his favorite horses, and his rather expensive curricle, and something within him was adamantly opposed to her being ruined—indeed, harmed in any way—because of that spontaneous act of kindness. One that, albeit unintentionally, had also freed Alison Melwin to claim her own, much happier destiny.

Clearly, in all that followed, protecting Meg Cynster had to be his overriding goal, and Drago had no argument with that.

He was also curious as to how this charade of theirs would play out. Somewhat to his surprise, he was actively looking forward to the challenge of being her fiancé, pretense or not. Such eagerness stood in sharp contrast to his lack of enthusiasm over being engaged to Alison. Considering that, he could only conclude that being engaged to Meg, who as a Cynster was on equal footing with him socially and who had already displayed an independent mind and will, would be a significantly greater challenge, and being the sort of gentleman he was, meeting challenges was what life was all about.

Conquering challenges was the essence of living, at least to him.

When Meg pointed ahead, he slowed his horses and turned them onto the gravel drive leading to Walkhurst Manor.

He drew up in the forecourt before the manor steps, and a stable lad came running to take charge of the horses.

Drago tossed the lad the reins, swung down, and rounded the carriage to hand Meg down, but she hadn't waited and had already clambered to the ground.

"Thank you, Jeb." She smiled at the lad. "We'll be at least an hour, possibly more."

The lad saluted her. "I'll take good care of these beauties, miss." He dipped his head to Drago. "Your Grace."

As Drago accompanied her up the steps, she muttered, "Even the stable boy recognized you, but I didn't."

"He's a local. You're not."

The butler had already opened the door and, having seen Drago, stood straight and tall.

"Good afternoon, Pendleby." Calmly, Meg crossed the porch. With one hand, she indicated Drago. "This is His Grace, the Duke of Wylde."

Pendleby bowed low. "Your Grace. Welcome to Walkhurst Manor."

Entering the front hall, Meg continued, "We were hoping to speak with my cousin and Mrs. Cynster. Are they at home?"

Pendleby assured them that his master and mistress were, indeed, in the house, and at Meg's suggestion, she led Drago to the library, apparently Christopher Cynster's domain, while the butler hurried to summon the lady of the house.

To say that Christopher Cynster was astonished to see Drago arrive with Meg would have been a massive understatement. Christopher was also instantly suspicious, although he hid it well, and Drago, for his part, did his level best to project an air of relaxed bonhomie appropriate to a male of their ilk in throes of delight over having secured his desired bride.

That endeavor and maintaining that façade through greeting and being greeted by Christopher's wife proved surprisingly easy.

Once they were all seated in the comfortable armchairs, Drago largely left it to Meg to break their news, putting in his tuppence-worth only on points that required further clarification or on which she needed support. His judgment that she would be far better than he at reading her relatives' reactions proved sound; on several occasions, she fleshed out their tale, adding a new but logical detail that patently answered a question only just forming on Christopher's or Ellen's lips.

All in all, Drago was impressed by how convincingly Meg spun their tale, making it ridiculously easy for him to be equally convincing in playing his prescribed part.

He'd always possessed a marked facility for reading people, especially those of his own class. Ellen, he judged, readily accepted the picture they painted, and her expressions of happiness for Meg and Drago were entirely sincere.

Christopher, on the other hand, while outwardly accepting, tended to watch Drago rather than Meg, and that with an assessing eye. Drago had to wonder if Christopher—who had once been very much of Drago's ilk —scented something of the truth, yet when Meg concluded her explanation, establishing that she and Drago were informally betrothed and hoped to make their new status formal in the upcoming weeks, once their wider families had been informed and suitable arrangements made, Drago could have sworn he saw amusement lurking in Christopher's eyes.

"This is all so exciting!" Ellen positively beamed. "I'm so pleased for you both."

Christopher added his felicitations with every appearance of sincerity.

And the first hurdle in gaining Meg's family's support was successfully cleared.

"It's heading toward six o'clock." Ellen, still beaming, looked hopefully at Drago. "Do say you'll stay to dine. It's just us, and we don't stand on ceremony."

Meg, no doubt remembering that he was hiding out at the cottage with only his valet and groom, arched a questioning, faintly challenging brow his way.

Interpreting that as encouragement, he smiled at Ellen and half bowed. "I would be delighted, Mrs. Cynster. Especially as, quite soon, we'll be family of sorts."

"Indeed, we will be, and apropos of that, you must call me Ellen."

Christopher, still smiling in a knowing way Drago wasn't sure he liked, also nodded. "Christopher for me. We leave the nicknames to our elders."

Drago laughed and nodded. "I had noticed that." He met Ellen's eyes. "Everyone calls me Drago."

And just like that, they all relaxed and, when they were summoned to the dining table, went in to dinner exactly as if they were, indeed, family.

Once they'd started on the first course, Christopher glanced at Drago and asked, "I assume you drove over?"

Drago nodded. "At the moment, my grays are in your stable."

Predictably, a discussion of carriage and riding horses ensued, followed by an even more detailed exchange regarding local farm production, in which Drago and Christopher, and Ellen, too, had a vested interest.

Meg listened to the conversation with unexpected focus. The topics didn't excite her, but the engagement gave her the opportunity to observe Drago in this milieu. It was plainly one into which he effortlessly fitted.

She was quietly amazed at how easily their revelations had gone, at how little effort on her or, it seemed, his part had been required for them to pass themselves off as an engaged couple.

Drago's charm was, she realized, an innate part of him. He was entirely relaxed and not trying at all, yet he'd won over both Ellen and Christopher without exerting himself or striving to project any false image.

This—the nobleman sitting opposite her—was who Drago, Duke of Wylde, was. No fabricated façade, no added gloss. He was being himself, and that alone was enough to draw people to him.

She was pondering that insight when they rose from the dining table. They paused in the front hall, and after tendering his thanks to Ellen and Christopher, Drago took his leave.

Meg accompanied him onto the porch and went with him down the steps to where Christopher's groom held Drago's horses.

She halted on the last step while Drago accepted the reins and thanked Pullman, who saluted and returned to the stable.

Darkness had fallen, but the lamps on the porch threw steady light into the forecourt.

Drago turned to Meg. "I need to return to London tomorrow morning to inform my mother and brother of our news. As agreed, I'll spin them our tale. However, I will also need to speak with the three friends who were down here at the Bull with me yesterday evening."

Lips twisting, he shook his head. "Hard to believe it was only yesterday evening." He met Meg's eyes. "The thing is, the three of them know I was planning to offer for Alison this morning. They know that Edith had arranged an appointment at Melwin Place for eleven o'clock. They also know I've never mentioned even meeting you before, and I very likely would have if we'd formed any degree of attachment."

She held his dark gaze. "You think they need to be told the truth."

He grimaced and nodded. "I can't see any way around it. They'll know this sudden, out-of-the-blue engagement of ours is a sham, and not telling them the truth might lead them to speculate and imagine a cause far less innocent."

She pulled a face. "I see." After a second, she asked, "What are their names?"

"George Bisley—Viscount Bisley—Lord Harry Ferndale, and Thomas Hayden." He studied her face. "I doubt you'd know any of them any more than you were acquainted with me."

She nodded. "You're right. I don't think I've met them." She searched his face for an instant, then conceded, "As they already know so much, I accept they'll have to be told the truth, but I assume you'll swear them to secrecy."

"Absolute, unwavering secrecy. I've known them since Eton and have no qualms on that score."

"Very well. Is there anyone else who needs to know the truth?"

He thought, then shook his head. "Not that I can think of." He arched a brow at her. "Anyone on your side?"

Meg had to review their tale again to be sure, but... "I don't think so. We've been vague about the dates on which we supposedly previously met, and those occasions were all down here, so my friends in town would have known nothing about them, and I wouldn't necessarily have mentioned such...fleeting distractions."

His quick grin suggested he was amused at being classed as a fleeting distraction.

She raised her chin. "I'll go up to town later tomorrow and break the happy news to my parents. Their house is in Half Moon Street."

His expression sobering, Drago nodded. "Tomorrow's Friday, and by the time I see everyone, it'll be too late for a formal call." He met her eyes. "Shall we say eleven o'clock on Saturday? I'll call at Half Moon Street, meet your parents, and formally apply for permission to pay my addresses to you."

She made a dismissive sound. "My parents won't care about any formal application. All they'll want to know is if I want to marry you."

His smile utterly distracted her. "In that case—"

Before she had any inkling of his intention, he caught her to him, bent his head, and kissed her.

Thoroughly.

Wickedly, sinfully, evocatively.

She was immediately plunged back into the kiss they'd shared on the cottage stairs, only this time, the reaction—her to him and him to her—was even more immediate.

Even more intense.

For uncounted moments, nothing else mattered—nothing else existed in her mind—other than the sensations and desires so potently stirred by the ravenous and ardent melding of their lips.

Transparently reluctant, he raised his head and brought the hungry exchange to an end.

Briefly, from under his black lashes, his dark eyes met hers, then with a wry twist to his lips, he set her back on her feet.

The instant she was steady, he stepped back and grinned devilishly at her. "Just in case you need a memory to bolster your persuasiveness."

With that, he saluted her, leapt into the curricle, flicked the reins, and set his grays trotting smartly down the drive.

Her lips throbbing, Meg stood on the step and watched until the shadows cast by the trees lining the drive hid him from sight.

What the devil have I got myself into?

She really didn't know.

After a moment, she turned and started up the steps. "At least this Season, I won't be bored."

* * *

Drago walked into Wylde House, his mansion on Park Lane, and paused to allow his butler to remove the greatcoat from his shoulders. "Is my mother in, Prentiss?"

"She is, Your Grace. I believe you'll find her in her sitting room."

Drago eyed the stairs; his mother's sitting room was on the first floor.

He'd told Maurice and Tisdale of his engagement to Meg Cynster. Luckily, neither had known for whose hand he'd intended to offer the previous morning, so they hadn't needed to be regaled with the truth. However, both would even now be making their way to the servants' hall, where Mrs. Prentiss, the housekeeper, reigned supreme...

"I have news, Prentiss, that you are free to share with the household. Although the alliance has yet to be formally announced, I have offered for Miss Margaret Cynster's hand, and she's accepted."

"Your Grace!" Prentiss's face lit. "That's wonderful news! On behalf of the entire staff, permit me to offer our felicitations."

"Thank you." Noting how thrilled Prentiss transparently was—indeed, almost rapturous with delight—Drago, amused, observed, "I take it the alliance meets with your approval?"

Prentiss colored. "I would never presume—"

"No, no." Drago waved the protestation aside. "I'm genuinely curious as to how you view the connection."

"Ah. Well, as to that, Your Grace, it's deeply pleasing and, indeed, gratifying to know that the House of Helmsford will be allying with the House of Cynster. The Cynsters are every bit as old a family as the Helmsfords. Such an alliance will be viewed as eminently fitting."

Drago smiled. "Eminently fitting" meant his mother would be pleased by the match. "Excellent." With a nod of dismissal, he strode for the stairs.

On reaching his mother's sitting room, he tapped on the door and walked in.

With the beading of the widow's cap she'd taken to wearing after the death of Drago's father glinting against her fair hair, Constance, Duchess of Wylde, a tall, still-slender, and commanding figure despite her years, was sitting in one of the pair of armchairs by the fire. She looked up from the letter she'd been reading, saw him, and smiled. "Drago." She held out a graceful hand.

"Mama."

She waited while, returning her smile, he approached her chair, grasped her hand, and bent to kiss the cheek she proffered. As he straightened, she regarded him shrewdly. "Well, what news? How was Wylde Court?"

Drago spared a smile for Mrs. Weekes, his mother's companion, who was ensconced in the window seat, embroidering, then sat in the armchair on the other side of the fireplace. "I take it Aunt Edith hasn't sent word."

He knew his aunt had kept her scheme to have him marry Alison Melwin a complete secret, knowing, as he had, that his mother wouldn't have approved. On his way back to town, he'd called into the stable yard at the Court and had confirmed that Edith was still there, but he'd forgotten to ask if she'd sent a messenger to London; he wouldn't have put it past her to steal his thunder.

His mother blinked her eyes wide. "What word?"

He smiled. "I realize this might come as a surprise, but I've offered for Margaret—Meg—Cynster's hand, and she's accepted."

His mother regarded him levelly for several seconds before, plainly seeking confirmation, she repeated, "Meg Cynster."

Drago nodded. "Demon and Felicity Cynster's youngest daughter."

"I know who Meg Cynster is. I'm just surprised you do."

He knew well enough to keep his pleased, relaxed, entirely open smile in place. "We'd crossed paths several times in recent years, down in Kent. She often visits the Cynsters at Walkhurst Manor—Vane and Patience's son Christopher and his wife. She—Meg—was down there when I visited the Court last week, and…" He continued spinning their prepared tale, being careful to avoid unnecessary details.

As always, he wasn't entirely sure his mother swallowed his story; throughout his childhood and beyond, she'd had the knack of seeing through his prevarications and obfuscations. He was always very aware that she knew and understood him, in some respects better than he knew himself; after all, as people constantly told him, he was very like his father in virtually every way.

But by the time he came to the end of his explanation, his mother looked genuinely pleased.

"Well, my dear, while I would never have imagined you would decide on a Cynster, I must commend your choice." Constance looked across the room at Mrs. Weekes. "Trudy, what say you to Meg Cynster becoming Drago's duchess?"

Mrs. Weekes, who had known Drago from childhood, studied him in her usual straightforward, assessing fashion, then she smiled and nodded. "I can see such a union working quite splendidly."

"Indeed." Returning her gaze to Drago, Constance added, "Meg is one who will keep you on your toes."

Seeing the gleam in his mother's eye, Drago deduced that was intended as a challenge to him and steadfastly quashed the urge to ask why.

"Have you spoken to Meg's parents yet?" Constance asked.

"Meg is due in town later today. I've made arrangements to call at Half Moon Street tomorrow morning to meet her parents and formally apply for her hand."

Constance nodded approvingly. "Please tell Felicity—and yes, of course, she and I are acquainted—that I will call on her on Sunday afternoon so that we may discuss further arrangements. *And*"—Constance fixed Drago with a look that warned him that acquiescence with what she was about to decree wasn't optional—"I will arrange for your uncles and aunts, on both sides, I think, to call tomorrow afternoon so that you may break the news of your upcoming nuptials to them all at once, in person and, if at all possible, with Meg by your side."

From the window seat, Mrs. Weekes nodded enthusiastically. "That would, indeed, be most appropriate."

Drago looked from one lady to the other and knew better than to argue. He inclined his head to his mother. "I will leave those arrangements in your hands."

He rose and took his leave of the pair and, with well-disguised alacrity, got himself out of danger.

He paused in the corridor outside the sitting room, then strode back to the stairs. Once on the ground floor, he headed for the library, always the domain of the current duke. There, he tugged the bellpull, and when Prentiss appeared, organized the dispatch of three footmen to carry simple verbal summonses to George, Harry, and Thomas.

He was confident all would respond immediately, even Thomas. Although it was only just after four o'clock, the chambers of Crawthorne and Quartermaine in Lincoln's Inn kept civilized hours, at least in terms of summonses from the Duke of Wylde. As for George and Harry, both would almost certainly be at home, getting ready to go out on the town.

While he waited for his friends to arrive, Drago nursed a glass of whisky and considered what he needed to say and what else he needed to do. Eventually, he rounded the library desk, sat, set aside the glass, drew out a sheet of paper, and jotted a list of those he needed to apprise of his impending change in circumstances. His and Meg's engagement might be a sham, but he needed to behave in every way as if it were real.

Not long after—when he was staring at the list and wondering whom he'd missed—he heard voices in the front hall. He quit the desk, and when Prentiss showed George and Harry in, Drago was standing in front of the fireplace, once more sipping from his glass.

As with a bow, Prentiss withdrew, Drago held up the glass. "Drink?"

"Yes, please!" George and Harry chorused.

"It's getting nippy out there." While Drago went to the tantalus, George came forward to hold his hands to the blaze in the hearth.

"Well, it is still March," Harry pointed out. "And this is England, not the south of France."

Drago carried their glasses to them, having also refilled his own.

George and Harry eagerly accepted the crystal tumblers, then George arched an expectant brow at Drago. "Are we here to drink to your engagement?"

Drago inclined his head. "We are, but there's been further develop-ments. Let's wait for Thomas. He should be here soon."

"Actually," Harry said, lowering his glass after taking an appreciative sip, "I'm rather surprised you're back in town already. I would have thought the Melwins and your aunt would have pressed you to stay in Kent, at least for a few days."

Sounds of an arrival reached them, saving Drago from having to respond. A moment later, Thomas joined them, plainly eagerly expectant, and once Drago had poured a drink for him as well, the four sat in their usual places in the well-padded armchairs arranged before the fire.

It was Thomas who raised his glass to Drago and said, "To your health, Your Grace, and that of your soon-to-be duchess."

"Hear, hear!" George and Harry responded.

Lips twisting, Drago inclined his head, then replied, "There has, however, been a pertinent change."

"Change?" George blinked. "What sort of change?"

"The lady in question." Drago swept the three with an amused glance. "I've called you here to inform you that, contrary to your and my expec-tations, I offered for the hand of Meg Cynster, and she accepted."

To say the three were flummoxed, confounded, indeed stupefied, would have been understating their reactions. They stared at him in complete silence, mouths acock, for at least a minute before Harry managed to hoarsely repeat, "Meg Cynster?"

Drago nodded. "Indeed."

"But"—bewildered, George held out his hands in appeal—"how on earth did she get involved?"

Drago sighed. "It's rather a long story. Suffice it to say that when I woke—or rather was woken—that morning, my head wasn't as clear as it might have been."

"You mixed up the ladies?" Harry shook his head. "Never known you to be that foxed before."

"No. I didn't mix them up." Drago proceeded to explain what had happened, all the way to being discovered on the landing, kissing Meg Cynster witless.

Aghast, George whispered, "By your aunt, her companion, Alison Melwin, and her mother? Good Lord!"

"Indeed. That being so, there was really only one thing I could do," Drago explained. "I stated that Miss Cynster had just done me the honor of agreeing to be my duchess. And she, of course, had to go along with it."

"So"—Thomas sounded almost devastated with shock—"you're going to marry Meg Cynster. Just like that."

"No, of course not." Drago cradled his glass between his hands. "We hardly know each other."

Although kissing her already ranks as one of my most-highly-desired pleasures.

"Ah." George calmed. "This engagement is merely for show—to preserve Miss Cynster's reputation."

"And to preserve me," Drago said. "Admittedly, I hadn't realized she was a Cynster when I made my declaration, but can you imagine the reaction from the Cynster clan if I hadn't moved to protect her?"

"Lord, yes." Harry had blanched. "I wouldn't have wanted to be in your shoes had you tried to somehow avoid a declaration, Duke of Wylde or not."

Thomas looked relieved. "So this engagement is actually a sham."

Drago inclined his head. "A fiction to preserve Miss Cynster's reputation."

"But what about you having to be married by mid-August?" Thomas asked.

"My plan to find a suitable lady with whom to enter into a marriage of convenience still stands, but due to this development, has had to be postponed."

Thomas frowned, but it was Harry who asked, "How long will you need to allow the engagement with Miss Cynster to stand?"

"Meg has proved to be a blessedly straightforward and sensible lady.

We've discussed our predicament, and allowing for the issues arising due to both our families' status in the ton, we've accepted that we'll have to allow the engagement to stand—and more, to do everything within our power to make it appear entirely genuine—until early June. Then she'll call it off on the grounds we've decided we don't suit, and I'll be free to offer for my amenable bride."

"Early June," Thomas said. "That's cutting it fine."

Drago feigned hurt. "Do you doubt me, Thomas?" Drago grinned. "Never fear. Two months is more than long enough for me to get suitably leg-shackled."

Thomas grinned and dipped his head. "I suppose that's true."

"But that's for later. For now"—Drago raised his glass—"I invite you to wish me well and swear on all you hold holy that you will keep all you know under your hats."

"I'll drink to that," Thomas said, raising his glass to Drago.

"Lord, yes." George, too, drank deeply. "Can you imagine such a piece of gossip getting out?"

"Well, it won't via me," Harry said and drank.

Drago paused, then more quietly said, "All three of you know that I would trust you with my life. And as it happens, other than myself and Meg, you three are the only ones who know the truth of our faux engagement."

He let the words hang in the quiet of the library and sipped and watched as the implication slowly sank in.

He was relieved when George, expression hardening, nodded, as did Harry.

"So if it ever becomes known, it would have come from one of us," Harry said. "But it won't."

"No, indeed," George agreed.

"I believe," Thomas said, "that this is the sort of secret that, collectively, we will take to our graves."

The others chorused, "Hear, hear!" and all raised their glasses and drank.

* * *

AFTER SEEING HIS FRIENDS OUT, Drago inquired of a footman if his brother had come in. On being informed that Mr. Denton had returned to the house and was in his apartments, Drago sent a message up asking Denton to join him in the library.

When his brother arrived, curious as to why he'd been summoned,

Drago told him his news, sticking to much the same tale with which he'd regaled their mother.

Although Denton knew that Drago needed to marry by Drago's birthday in mid-August and that Drago intended to comply with the terms of their father's will, Denton hadn't known of Drago's appeal to their aunt Edith nor of Edith's scheme for Alison Melwin to become the next Duchess of Wylde.

Consequently, Denton had no reason to doubt that Drago's engagement to Meg Cynster was real. However...

"Meg Cynster." Denton repeated the name, shook his head in bemusement, and looked at Drago, sitting in the armchair opposite. "I would never have thought you'd offer for Meg."

Drago hid a frown. "She mentioned she'd met you several times."

"Well, we're much the same age, so when we were younger, during the summer, we were all encouraged to spend time together at various parties—you know how it goes."

Drago nodded. Before he could inquire as to what about Meg Cynster was causing Denton's amused surprise, Denton asked, "Are you going to inform Uncle Warley?"

Drago showed his surprise. "I hadn't thought to do so specifically. Mama is inviting all the relatives to gather tomorrow for our grand announcement. I assume Warley will come and learn the news there."

Denton shrugged. "I suppose that will do." When he saw Drago looking puzzled, Denton explained, "Warley's the secondary heir after me, and we are speaking of a dukedom, after all."

Drago smiled. "Trust me, Warley won't care—or rather, he'll be only too delighted to know I'm finally getting around to doing the deed."

Denton allowed that to slide and, unbidden, returned to the subject Drago wanted to know more about. "I really thought you would pick a quiet lady, one more cipher-like. Instead, you've chosen Meg Cynster." Again, Denton smiled in a way that suggested he was expecting all sorts of entertainment to stem from that fact. "Meg is such a...well, *different* sort of lady. Not only that, but she's known in certain quarters—meaning the bachelor circles—as Miss Prim."

"Miss Prim?" Startled, Drago bit back a too-revealing comment about her ability to kiss. "She's not prim."

"Not in the usual sense, no." Denton was still smiling. "She earned the moniker because of her managing disposition and bossy nature. The 'Miss Prim' came about because she would never, ever, allow any gentleman to cross any line of which she didn't approve. And I do mean never, ever. In horse terms, she's impossible to turn."

Unless she wants to.

"I see." Drago rather thought that his mother, too, knew of Miss Prim. After a moment of revisiting his recent memories, he admitted, "I agree she's a fairly forthright and forceful character—certainly no cipher—but that said, I believe I'll be able to handle her well enough."

Denton cast him an incredulous look, then snorted disbelievingly.

CHAPTER 4

*T*he following morning, at two minutes to eleven o'clock, Meg was dallying in the gallery above the front hall of her parents' house in Half Moon Street, keeping watch on the front door.

She and her maid, Rosie, hadn't arrived in Half Moon Street until the evening of the previous day, and as her parents had been out attending social events, she hadn't had a chance to break the news of her pending engagement until the family had gathered about the breakfast table earlier that morning.

She'd stuck faithfully to the tale she and Drago had concocted.

Given her parents had never heard her mention his name nor had any inkling that she was even acquainted with the notorious Duke of Wylde, they'd initially stared at her in stunned surprise. But then the significance of what she was saying had started to sink in; although neither had ever pressured her to marry, Meg knew they'd started to worry that she never would. As the reality of her news registered, their expressions had reanimated until they'd beamed delightedly and congratulated her, although her father had quickly retreated to sternly insisting that he'd be wanting to assess Drago's worth before he gave his consent to the match.

Both Meg and her mother had simply looked at Demon—the entire ton knew the worth of the dukedom of Wylde—then her mother had gone back to exclaiming and wanting to know details, many of which Meg would have preferred not to have to invent.

Fabrications were always so much harder to remember.

She was saved from having to strain her brain by her brother Toby, the only other member of the family present. He'd initially stared at her as well, although in his case, she'd got the impression he was thinking rapidly—possibly too rapidly for her and Drago's comfort; if anyone was going to see straight through their charade, it would be Toby. But then he had grinned, wished her well, and told Demon that Drago was considered to be "exactly as he appears."

Understanding that to mean that Toby knew of no circumstance that detracted from Drago's apparent eligibility, her father had grunted. "Just as long as he meets *my* expectations in every way."

Meg had jumped in to make her and Drago's request for an audience with her parents at eleven o'clock to discuss the prospective engagement. That petition had been met with approval and, on her father's part, a glimmer of respect.

In the gallery, Meg paced back and forth, her gaze on the door. She'd seen her parents go into the drawing room a few minutes before.

The clocks throughout the house chimed and bonged, marking the eleventh hour.

Deeper in the house, the front doorbell pealed.

Halting at the head of the stairs, Meg watched as the butler, Fletcher, crossed the front hall and opened the door.

Drago's voice reached her as, in the languid drawl he no doubt employed when trading on his standing, he stated his title and informed Fletcher, "I believe Miss Cynster, Mr. Cynster, and Mrs. Cynster are expecting me."

"Indeed, Your Grace." Suitably impressed, Fletcher bowed low and waved Drago inside.

Quickly and silently, Meg went down the stairs and stepped onto the tiles as Drago handed his hat and cane to Fletcher.

Then Drago smoothly swung her way, his features softening as his gaze landed on her.

His heavy lids rose, his eyes fractionally widening. His gaze had locked on her, and for a split second, she sensed that, for him, the world had stopped.

Drago blinked and covered the momentary lapse with a charming smile. He stepped toward Meg, holding out his hands to take hers. "Good morning, my dear. I trust your journey back to town was uneventful?"

She gave him her hands, and he grasped them. Aware of the butler looking on, he raised first one, then the other, to his lips, pressing kisses to her knuckles while attentively searching her face.

The look she sent him was a subtle question; she'd detected the hitch in his concentration. That she'd noticed was itself a surprise; he was normally a past master at concealing his reactions.

But the sight of her had been arresting. Literally. They'd spent most of Thursday together, and he'd grown used to her in what he now realized was her in-the-country mode. Then, she'd been wearing a neat but unremarkable blue cambric gown and half boots suitable for rambling about the fields. Her straw hat had been pushed back most of the time, revealing a face wreathed by untidy, loose golden curls.

Today, she was all young lady of the haut ton, and the change was rather startling.

Fashioned in the very latest style, her morning gown was of expensive figured twill in a greeny shade of bronze that emphasized the creaminess of her complexion and the soft blue of her eyes, while her golden curls had been tamed into a striking arrangement of plaits and sweeping loops that made his fingers itch with an unexpected urge to disarrange them.

For just a second, he'd been fixated by visceral awareness.

He couldn't remember how long it had been since he'd experienced such a moment.

Perhaps never.

Now, however, her parents were waiting, and he and she had a charade to perform.

He smiled reassuringly, released her hands, and offered his arm. "I take it your parents are available. Shall we?"

She took his arm with a look that stated that she was willing to allow the moment to pass. "I believe our way is already well paved, but Papa will still want to grill you."

"Understandable," he murmured as they approached the open doorway leading to the drawing room. "Luckily, given my previous intentions, I already had everything prepared and rehearsed." He briefly met her gaze. "I'll just be making my case to a different papa."

Her lips quirked, and she walked beside him into the room.

A short lady with graying golden curls rose from the sofa to greet him. Her expression was all interest and eager curiosity.

His charming smile in place, Drago took the small hand she offered him and bowed over it. "Mrs. Cynster. It's a pleasure to meet you."

"Your Grace." She dipped into a slight curtsy, but Drago drew her up and, eyes dancing, shook his head.

"Drago, please. As I'm here to plead to be allowed to join your family, formalities are surely unnecessary."

Felicity Cynster beamed at him, her expression open and encouraging. She gestured to the tall gentleman who broke from his commanding stance before the fireplace to prowl to his wife's side. "In that case, Drago, allow me to make you known to my husband, Meg's father."

Drago braced himself as, still smiling with charming ease, he shifted his gaze to Demon Cynster's face and met the man's steady hard blue gaze.

Demon Cynster was a legend in the Thoroughbred horse racing world, and although he had to be in his early sixties now, Drago had no difficulty seeing what it was about the man that had made him one of the select group at one time known as the Bar Cynster. Rakehells, one and all, until they had married and become pillars of the haut ton.

Drago inclined his head. "Mr. Cynster."

His gaze shrewd and penetrating, Demon had been studying him. Now the older man thrust out his hand. "Drago." They shook hands, then Demon said, "I understand you wish to marry Meg."

"Indeed." Drago glanced at Meg as she came to stand beside him. He took her hand and faced her parents. "I hope to convince you to grant me that honor."

That, he realized, had been just the right thing to say; some of the starch went out of Demon Cynster's stance, and with a soft snort, he waved Drago to a chair. "At least you realize that despite your rank, marrying Meg will still be an honor." Demon sank into the armchair opposite. "Come. Sit. And let's discuss your suit."

Somewhat to Drago's surprise, Meg and her mother remained, overtly interested parties if not participants in the exchange that followed.

It was an exchange that rolled from point to point in a smooth, not to say polished fashion. The encounter proceeded more easily than Drago had imagined it might; it soon became obvious that Demon had been this way before, and Drago recalled that Meg had mentioned that her older sister, Prudence, was now the Countess of Glengarah, which no doubt explained Demon's familiarity with the process, which in turn paved the way for Drago's responses.

Forty painless minutes later, his application for Meg's hand had been approved. It was only then, as relief—somewhat unexpected given this was all a charade—flowed through him, that Drago caught a glimmer of...yes, it was definitely expectant amusement in Demon's blue eyes.

The sight reminded Drago of the gleam he'd detected in Christopher Cynster's eyes.

What is it that I don't know?

He had no time to pursue the thought, as arrivals in the front hall brought him and Demon to their feet as a fashionable lady and gentleman swept into the room.

"Pru, my dear—and Deaglan, too!" Mrs. Cynster smiled in delight. "We were wondering when you would get here."

"Mama." The tallish lady bent to kiss Felicity Cynster's cheek. "For once, the winds were favorable." Straightening, the lady looked from Demon to Drago to Meg. Then she returned her gaze to Drago. "Papa. Meg. And I don't believe…" Pru's blue eyes narrowed.

"Drago Helmsford." He used the name she would most likely have known him by. "And yes, we've met, although it was at least a decade ago."

Pru's eyes had widened. "You're Wylde now! Of course." Then she frowned and looked at the rest of her family.

"You're just in time to hear Meg and Drago's news, my dear." Felicity looked decidedly smug.

Demon stated, "Drago has asked for Meg's hand, and we've given them our blessing."

Pru's eyes had widened even more. She glanced at Drago, then looked at Meg. "Him?"

Meg slid her arm into Drago's and tipped up her chin. "Indeed."

Pru's smile was beyond delighted. "Well done, you!" She switched her gaze to Drago and offered her hand. "Welcome to the family, Drago."

Drago took the hand and bowed over it. "Countess."

Retrieving her hand, her smile still lighting her face, Pru glanced around the company. "What a turn-up this is going to be. The Season just got so much more interesting!"

The tall gentleman, almost as tall as Drago, who had until then held his peace, nudged his wife aside and offered Drago his hand. "Wylde."

Drago grasped the man's hand. "Glengarah."

Pru settled on the sofa beside her mother. "Do you two know each other?"

"Same clubs," Glengarah offered and claimed an armchair beside Pru as the others resumed their seats.

"I take it you've just arrived in town?" Drago ventured. He wanted to keep the focus on the newcomers.

"Only a few hours ago, via the boat train." Glengarah glanced affectionately at Pru, who was already whispering with her mother. "And despite my wife's sudden interest in the Season, what in reality lured us here is the upcoming sale at Tattersalls."

From there, the conversation plunged headlong into a discussion of horseflesh, a subject on which, even in that company, Drago could hold his own. After Meg mentioned his grays and he explained how he'd come by them, Pru declared that she wanted to see them. "Especially if your stable is now going to fall within the family fold."

The talk continued in purely equine vein.

Drago noticed that Meg, beside him, remained quiet, listening with what appeared to be a resigned air.

Under the cover of a discussion of the potential of horses in the upcoming sale, Drago turned to her and murmured, "Horses don't appear to be a favorite topic of yours."

Meg smiled wryly and, leaning closer, admitted, "They're not. They are, however, the rest of the family's life, so I've learned to bear with interludes such as this."

Drago met her gaze, but then Deaglan claimed his attention, and he returned to the conversation.

Despite Meg's customary boredom with the topic, she was listening and observing more attentively than usual. Initially, she'd held herself in readiness to intervene at the first hint that Drago needed help, but that hint had never come. Indeed, his relaxed assurance in this milieu plainly ran bone-deep. It wasn't assumed, but a genuine part of him—a result of his upbringing in the same way that her confidence in this sphere was an outcome of hers.

Within ten minutes of Pru and Deaglan's arrival, Meg had accepted that she wouldn't need to metaphorically hold Drago's hand or worry that he would put a foot wrong. In truth, even in chatting with her mother and father, he was incredibly poised and quick-witted, too.

Then the talk swung to the formal announcement of their engagement.

Drago nodded to her mother. "My mother wished me to convey her compliments and that, if convenient, she will call on you tomorrow afternoon to discuss what she termed 'further arrangements.'"

"Excellent!" Meg's mother replied. "Do assure the duchess that I will be at home."

Drago undertook to do so. "Also"—he glanced at Meg—"Mama hoped you would be free to meet with her and others of the family this afternoon. At three o'clock, if that suits?"

Meg had to assure him that she would be available, to which he replied that he would call and escort her to Park Lane.

"One more thing." Drago looked at her parents. "The notice in the *Gazette*. Would you prefer to send a note directly? Alternatively, the editor is a personal friend and will ensure placement in the edition we stipulate."

They agreed that her parents would craft an announcement and send it to Wylde House, and subsequently Drago would add his own note and send both to his friend.

"I strongly advise that the notice should run in Monday's edition,"

Meg's mother said. "This is not the sort of news that will remain secret for long."

"No, indeed," Pru concurred. "But it might pay to set the scene a trifle." Her blue eyes twinkled as she looked at Meg and Drago. "You don't want to be held responsible for any seizures induced by shock." She looked at her mother and arched a brow. "Perhaps via a drive in the park tomorrow afternoon?"

Her mother nodded in decided fashion. "An excellent notion." She patted Pru's hand. "You're right, my dear." She fixed Meg and Drago with a direct look. "Foreshadowing the surprise would be wise."

Drago didn't miss a beat but looked at Meg in smiling acquiescence. "In that case, I'll call around at...shall we say three o'clock on Sunday?"

She nodded. She couldn't help but feel that their fictional engagement had taken on a life of its own.

Drago cast a smiling glance around the company. "And on that note, I should take my leave." He rose, adding, "Mama will be waiting to hear of our decisions."

Meg and the others rose, and with great cordiality, Drago shook hands all around. Then Meg waved him to the front hall and fell into step beside him.

As they walked into the hall, and at a nod from Drago, Fletcher went to fetch his hat and cane, she murmured, "That went well, I think."

Drago cocked a black brow at her; his eyes were laughing. "Better than you'd hoped?"

Her own lips lifting, she tipped her head in agreement.

They were still within sight of her family. Obviously aware of that, Drago remained studiously correct, kissing only her hand in farewell.

He glanced up and caught her gaze and held it as he straightened and, sotto voce, murmured, "It appears we've successfully launched our charade."

"Indeed." Still smiling, she inclined her head. "For better or ill, it's underway."

That diabolical black eyebrow arched even higher. "Let's endeavor to avoid any ills." Then he smiled insouciantly, and his charm rolled over her in a seductive wave. He raised a finger and tapped her on the nose. "Until this afternoon. Au revoir."

With that, he turned, and Fletcher leapt to open the door. Settling his hat on his dark locks, Drago strode through, went quickly down the steps, and vanished from her sight.

Meg stood staring at the doorway as Fletcher shut the door.

There was little doubt that having Drago Helmsford as her supposed fiancé would do her reputation no harm.

But what's going to happen when I call it off?

She wasn't so sure about that.

* * *

ON DRAGO'S ARM, Meg walked into the grand front hall of Wylde House and wondered if, in entering her parents' home, Drago had experienced a similar sensation, as if he were an ancient Christian about to face the lions.

The exceedingly correct butler, middle-aged and garbed in conventional black, bowed low. "Miss Cynster. Welcome to Wylde House."

She smiled. "Thank you." Despite the man's formality, his gaze was warm, and she sensed he was observing her with eager curiosity.

Drago helped her out of her coat and handed it to the butler. "Thank you, Prentiss. I take it the duchess is in her sitting room?"

"Yes, Your Grace."

Drago wound his arm with Meg's and led her toward the massive staircase. "Mama wanted to speak with you first, without the distraction of the rest of the horde who will be arriving shortly. No doubt Mama's companion will be with her. Mrs. Weekes is a longtime widow, a distant cousin of Mama's. She's been a part of the household since I was in short coats."

Appreciating the information, Meg nodded. As they ascended the staircase, her gaze was drawn to the glorious paintings—landscapes in deep, rich tones in heavy, ornate gilt frames—hanging on walls covered in exquisite buttercream silk with a subtle pattern that complemented the dark tones of the walnut paneling. The floor of the front hall was tiled in the classic black-and-white pattern, while the chandelier that depended from a circular skylight high above fractured light from myriad crystals.

The fleur-de-lis-patterned carpet of the gallery into which she stepped was thick and soft, and the light falling through the multipaned windows, framed by long curtains of plush topaz velvet, was golden and warm. Beyond the glass, the canopies of the trees in the garden were ruffling in the slight breeze.

All in all, the ambiance of the house was one of quiet, refined, long-established luxury.

Drago steered her along a corridor leading from the gallery, then paused to open a door. He caught her gaze, arched a brow, and murmured, "Ready?"

Fleetingly, she raised both brows, then walked through the doorway. Head high, with outward calm, she glided toward the fireplace, where two older ladies sat in armchairs, one nearer the fire than the other, with both chairs facing a sofa set perpendicular to the hearth.

Both ladies looked her way and smiled encouragingly.

Meg told herself that their engagement being a charade should make this meeting easier; whatever transpired was unlikely to have much impact on her future life, whatever that might be.

Of course, after weathering nine Seasons, she recognized the Duchess of Wylde. That hawk-faced lady occupied the chair nearer the fire and was regarding Meg through hazel eyes whose expression suggested that their owner was intrigued, curious, and at least at that moment, inclined to be kind.

Meg halted a yard from the chairs and curtsied to the appropriate depth. "Your Grace. I'm delighted to have the opportunity to speak with you again."

The duchess's lips twitched. "In peace before we join the hordes?"

When, straightening, Meg blinked, the duchess laughed and waved at her companion. "Allow me to present Mrs. Trudy Weekes, who keeps me company."

Meg and Mrs. Weekes exchanged nods and murmured greetings.

Then the duchess waved to the sofa. "Sit, my dear, and tell me how you came to know my rakehell son and how he prevailed upon a sensible young lady of your ilk to consent to be his duchess."

"Mama." Drago rolled his eyes and followed Meg to the sofa. As he elegantly sat beside her, he complained, "As you more than anyone are keen to see me wed, there's no sense in queering my pitch."

"Nonsense, my dear." His mother fixed her gaze on Meg. "I'm merely interested, and as all the rest of the family will ask the same questions, it might be wise to practice your answers on listeners who are less inclined to be critical."

She has a point. Before Drago could protest, Meg said, "Over the years, we had occasionally crossed paths during the times I spent in Kent, staying with my cousin and his wife at Walkhurst Manor."

"Ah yes. Christopher and Ellen, is it not?"

Meg nodded and continued with their agreed story, with Drago adding fictional flourishes here and there. While the duchess and even more Mrs. Weekes appeared to accept their tale, Meg wasn't entirely convinced that the duchess didn't harbor some suspicion that all was not quite as they said.

Nevertheless, Meg grew increasingly relaxed in the older ladies' company as the talk segued to expectations of the Season and of how the ton would react to their engagement; the pair were similar to females in her family, and she was so accustomed to their sometimes-dry way of looking at life that she had no difficulty responding suitably.

Indeed, the half-hour audience sped past, then the butler came in and announced, "Your Graces, the rest of the family are gathered in the drawing room. Lord Warley asked if you intended to join them soon."

"Of course he did." The duchess glanced at Meg. "You'll grow used to Warley." She looked back at the butler. "Thank you, Prentiss. We'll come now."

The duchess rose, bringing Meg, Drago, and Mrs. Weekes to their feet. The duchess regarded Meg shrewdly. "Drago, you had better stick to Meg's side, if nothing else than to ensure that she knows to whom she is talking. Trudy and I will lead the way."

Mrs. Weekes laid aside her embroidery and joined the duchess as she glided for the door.

Drago offered Meg his arm. "Warley is my uncle, my father's only brother. He's a bachelor and lives in London and is apt to be a bit abrupt, at least with ladies."

"I see." Meg took Drago's arm, and they fell in behind the duchess, who led the way out of her sitting room, into the gallery, and on to a pair of double doors that presently stood open.

Beyond the doorway, about twenty or so people were gathered, ranging in age from early twenties to the duchess's generation. There were none older, Meg noticed with some relief. In her experience, the older people got, the more inclined they were to speak bluntly, and given that their engagement was a sham, blunt questions could prove tricky.

As Drago, following his mother and with a finely-honed sense of the dramatic, paused on the threshold of the huge, elegant room just long enough for every eye in it to fix on Meg, she became aware of a host of butterflies that, entirely unexpectedly, had taken up residence in her stomach.

Then Drago set his hand over hers on his sleeve and looked down at her in expectant delight. To her surprise, her own smile bloomed, and apparently satisfied, he looked out at the room and declared, "Allow me to present Miss Margaret Cynster, soon to be my duchess."

Scanning the faces, the intrigued and pleased and curious expressions, she kept her smile—appropriately confident yet not overly so—in place as Drago led her forward.

She soon discovered that her momentary trepidation had been misplaced. With Drago making the introductions, she was more than up to the task of interacting with and, indeed, satisfying the understandable curiosity of his assembled relatives. She and Drago moved from group to group, being showered with the predictable exclamations and responding to the subtle inquisitions. In that respect, his mother had been correct as to which questions would most exercise the minds of those there, and their now-practiced answers tripped glibly from Meg's tongue.

The company was served with tea and cakes, which gave everyone something to do with their hands. Once supplied, she and Drago continued circulating among those gathered to meet her.

With Drago adroitly directing the conversations and the duchess occasionally interjecting, the traditional ordeal passed without incident, and indeed, was relatively pleasant and not without its moments of interest.

She renewed her acquaintance with Drago's younger brother, Denton, who was in many ways a milder version of Drago—a fraction shorter, a fraction slighter, and nowhere near as potent a presence.

Drago's uncle Warley was an immediately recognizable character, an ageing bachelor who didn't want anything to interfere with his settled life. He was curious about Meg, but that she was a daughter of Demon Cynster was, in Warley's view, clearly the most important attribute she possessed.

When she laughed at a mild joke he offered, Warley's dark eyes—much like Drago's but rather faded—twinkled.

Drago's aunt Edith had patently decided to be pleased by his defection to Meg in lieu of Alison. Edith was welcoming, but Meg sensed a determination in her attitude, as if Edith was on watch to ensure Drago didn't, somehow, backslide.

Edith might be a problem when we decide to call things off.

Meg tucked the thought away as she surrendered her empty cup to a footman, then at Drago's direction, she turned to find herself facing two couples. Both ladies bore a strong resemblance to the duchess and were several years older than Meg, while the gentlemen were Drago's age or a touch older.

"Allow me to present my sisters and their husbands," Drago drawled. "Claudette, Mrs. Pemberthy, and Melanie, Mrs. Forsythe. And of course, Pemberthy and Forsythe."

Everyone shook hands. "We're absolutely delighted to meet you, Miss Cynster," Claudette said.

"Please, just Meg," Meg replied.

"Well, she's Claud and the older one, and I'm Mel," Melanie said, "so you and I are going to have to listen carefully at family events when everyone is shouting names." She grinned at Meg. "You cannot imagine how much we've looked forward to this day." She transferred her gaze to Drago. "Now our dear older brother will have someone else to fuss over."

Drago arched a superior brow. "I haven't fussed over you since the day I put your hand in Forsythe's. From that moment, you became his responsibility."

Forsythe huffed. "And never a dull moment since, let me tell you." But his gaze as he looked at his wife was fond.

"You see?" Claudette said. "Trust me, Drago will be forever hovering."

Melanie uttered a dramatic sigh. "It runs in the family, sadly. I know of no one who's discovered a way to break Helmsford men of the habit."

Meg laughed. "They sound awfully like Cynster men."

"Oh, that's right," Melanie said. "You come from a similar family, so you already know what you're in for."

Meg glanced at Drago. "I fear I do."

With no more than a lift of one slanted eyebrow, he turned to chat with his brothers-in-law, who apparently wanted a moment of his time.

Claudette and Melanie were very ready to draw Meg into their own circle of three.

"They're chatting about politics," Melanie explained. "Both our husbands hold seats in the Commons."

"Often, their discussions are quite boring," Claudette said, "but we'll learn what it's all about on the way home. Sometimes, Parliament's business is worth knowing."

"Especially if," Melanie said, "as sometimes occurs, we can...adjust their thinking."

"Indeed." Claudette cast a swift glance at Drago and their husbands, who appeared momentarily absorbed. Lowering her voice, Claudette said, "One thing—just a word to the wise. Drago appears so easygoing and, indeed, malleable, but there's not one person here, or in fact anywhere, who has ever succeeded in controlling him."

Melanie nodded. "If he thinks your suggestion will suit him, he'll go along like a lamb, but if he wants to go in some other direction, nothing on earth will sway him."

"Which," Claudette concluded, "is why we're so pleased he's chosen *you* as his bride."

Melanie explained, "We've been dreading who he might choose, you see, because once he'd decided, there would be no arguing, and while we're entirely happy that he's marrying, we would greatly prefer that he does so without creating any social waves."

Claudette rested her hand lightly on Meg's sleeve. "As you'll understand, anything that affects the dukedom is always of interest to the ton and also to the political classes."

Meg blinked. "I hadn't thought of that, but yes, I do understand." She was aware that some of her relatives, the Duke and Duchess of St. Ives, were of necessity quite involved in political affairs.

"Of course," Melanie assured her, "once you and Drago are wed, Claud and I will be around to help you navigate the political shoals."

Claudette grinned and nodded. "It'll be quite a family effort." Her expression stated she was looking forward to the challenge.

A minute later, Drago appeared by Meg's side, and he and she moved on to another group of relatives.

While chatting with the ladies, Meg overheard enough of the men's conversations to realize that Drago was very much on top of the varied enterprises and estates that made up the dukedom. She knew something of what was involved; her cousin Sebastian, heir to the dukedom of St. Ives, was already shouldering much of that burden for his father.

She also heard enough to comprehend that Drago had been successfully managing his estates since his father's death some nine years ago. Despite his reputation for hedonistic indulgence, he hadn't ducked the responsibility. She was also impressed by how sensitively he dealt with several of the gentlemen's comments, hints, and carefully worded appeals.

When they moved on again, it was to join a group of Drago's younger cousins, most younger than Meg, and she had cause to appreciate how deftly Drago steered the conversation, without effort keeping his more boisterous male cousins from crossing any social line.

As she and Drago moved on, she murmured sotto voce, "Timothy and Jarrad should thank you for keeping them from embarrassing themselves."

"Yes, they should." Drago met her eyes, his own alive with laughter. "Trust me, I'll remember that at an appropriate time."

She chuckled, and they joined the group of older ladies gathered about his mother and Edith.

The duchess looked up and fixed Drago and Meg with a look. "We've just been discussing your plan to place an announcement in Monday morning's *Gazette*. While that is, indubitably, the correct thing to do, you would, we all feel, be well served by appearing in the park tomorrow."

"A half-hour drive along the Avenue would do it," Edith added.

Meg nodded. "My mama and my sister Glengarah said the same." She glanced at Drago. "We've agreed to make an appearance tomorrow afternoon."

"Excellent!" The duchess smiled upon them both.

Meg glimpsed the face of the pillared ormolu clock on the mantelpiece; she'd been at the house for over two hours. "On that note"—she glanced at Drago—"I really should take my leave."

He looked past her at the clock and arched a brow in surprise. He met her eyes. "The time has, indeed, flown."

Meg made her farewells to the duchess and Edith and the others in that group, and as Drago escorted her to the door, she smiled and nodded to those they passed.

As they started down the stairs, Drago murmured, "That went much more smoothly than I thought it would." She felt his gaze touch her face. "I know that meeting even that much of the family can be off-putting, yet you didn't seem the least overwhelmed, presumably because you hail from a similar background."

She laughed. "I assure you that, numbers-wise, the Helmsfords have nothing on the Cynsters. But I must admit that being able to recognize the types of characters that invariably crop up in any such family helped." She glanced at him and saw his brows rise.

"It's certainly true that we have our quota of odd characters, Warley being one." Smiling, too, Drago met her gaze. "He was quite taken with you, you know. That's something of an achievement."

She chuckled, and they stepped off the stairs and walked to where Prentiss waited, her coat already in his hands. "I've sent for your carriage, Miss Cynster."

"Thank you." Meg allowed Drago to help her into her coat.

Through the narrow window flanking the door, Prentiss confirmed that her carriage was just pulling up and, with a flourish, opened the large door and held it wide.

Meg smiled at the butler as, with her hand on Drago's arm, she walked past.

Drago escorted her down the steps. "I think," he said as they descended, "that we pulled off our charade without a hitch."

"I hope so."

They paused beside the carriage, and as the footman opened the door, Drago caught Meg's hand and smoothly raised her fingers to his lips. His dark eyes caught hers as he kissed the sensitive skin, and she discovered she couldn't breathe.

Every sense came to full attention and quivered with expectation, poised...

Still holding her gaze, he smiled and straightened, then helped her up the steps and into the carriage.

She swung around and rather abruptly sat, and he stepped back. "I'll call at Half Moon Street tomorrow, just before three."

Feeling slightly giddy, she managed a nod.

Drago saluted her, then nodded to the footman, who closed the door.

Her coachman started the horses walking, and Meg blinked and finally drew in a much-needed breath.

Wylde House fell behind, and as the coach turned onto Park Lane, her mind started to clear, and the ability to think returned.

Sufficient for her to realize what she'd been expecting, what she'd been giddily yearning for...

She'd hoped for another kiss.

CHAPTER 5

*D*rago duly appeared in Half Moon Street the following afternoon, handed Meg into his curricle, and drove to the park. It was a pleasantly mild day, with a weak sun playing peek-a-boo with cottony clouds. Garbed in a warm carriage gown in a bronzy-burgundy hue, Meg sat back and admired the skill with which Drago managed his currently fractious grays and held her peace until the curricle was rolling smoothly under the first trees along the avenue.

"I have to say that, thus far, our charade has been embraced by all remarkably readily." She glanced at Drago. "Did you think it would be this…well, straightforward?"

He frowned slightly. "I honestly didn't think beyond the need for us to put on a good show, but just between us, the alacrity with which news of our betrothal is being greeted by one and all is making me a trifle uncomfortable. Even the staff are going around beaming, specifically beaming at me."

"I know just what you mean." She shifted on the seat. "I spent hours last night and again today wondering and weighing up if we're doing the right thing in, well, deceiving everyone."

When she glanced at him, his usually affable expression was faintly grim.

"I've been doing the same thing," he admitted, "but I keep coming back to the fact that if the truth—that without the protection of an imminent engagement, you and I were alone in that cottage and were found kissing on the landing—became known, you would be ruined. And if we allow others to know—our families and those we would normally trust—they simply won't be able to keep up the pretense. One slip is all it will take. We both know that's true." His tone firmed. "So while in general, deceiving our families as well as the entire ton might not be the right thing to do, in the circumstances, it is the only choice we have—the only viable, sensible, and honorable way forward."

She grimaced lightly. "I keep reminding myself that if the scandal gets out, it won't be only you and me affected."

"No, indeed." He paused, then quietly said, "I don't really approve of the justification of it being for people's own good for them to be kept in the dark, but in this case…" He shook his head. "I really can't see any way around it."

She glanced ahead, then nodded at the rows of carriages drawn up to either side of the avenue. "We've been noticed."

Drago sighed and slowed his horses to an appropriately sedate pace, one just fast enough to make it plain that no matter who tried to attract their attention, he had no intention of stopping. "Here we go."

With his expression transforming to that of a gentleman only too ready to indulge his companion, he drove between the carriages pulled up on the verges, pausing only to maneuver past vehicles going the other way.

Meg kept an airy, innocent smile on her face as if she was just a young lady out enjoying a pleasant drive on a Sunday afternoon. And she was perfectly certain that it wasn't the sight of her fetching new gown and matching hat that was responsible for the gasps and second looks and almost comical expressions that dawned on so many faces. Young and old, matrons and grandes dames, the ladies chatting avidly in their carriages turned, in many cases open-mouthed, to stare at them—or more accurately at Drago—as with his attention, smiling and affable, occasionally shifting to her face but otherwise remaining on his horses, he tooled the carriage along.

Given the grays were still acting up, he had a reasonable excuse for remaining apparently oblivious to the multitude of stunned faces.

For her part, Meg met every nod and careful—in some cases startled —inclination of head with a breezy smile and an appropriate acknowledgment.

When they finally emerged at the other end of the social gauntlet and left the last carriages behind, Drago flicked the reins and sent the grays trotting on, then turned onto the northern arm of the circuit. Once they were bowling westward, he glanced at her. "We don't have to go through that twice, do we?"

She tipped her head, considering, then wryly replied, "Given how much attention we garnered, I believe our mothers will accept that we've done enough to seed the ground for the notice in the *Gazette* tomorrow morning." She glanced at him. "I take it the announcement went in?"

He nodded. "Melkinhoff assured me that it will, indeed, appear in tomorrow's edition. In fact, I got the impression that he was salivating at the prospect."

She huffed.

He slowed the horses as they went around the curve that would take them south again. "I rather suspect the irony of Miss Prim capturing the notorious Duke of Wylde will be the cause of much comment over the teacups this afternoon and tomorrow."

She laughed and admitted, "I hadn't thought of that."

His gaze touched her face. "How did you—who don't appear to be prim at all—come by that label?"

"Oh, I can become very prim when the occasion calls for it."

"And when's that?" When she glanced at him, lips curved, he added, "So that I'll know which occasions to avoid."

She thought for a moment, but could see no reason she shouldn't explain. "I've had nine Seasons, and given I'm a Cynster, I always have gentlemen looking my way. And the longer I've declined to choose one of them, it seems the accepted wisdom is that I must be feeling increasingly desperate. From experience, I've discovered that the most effective way to discourage those gentlemen who are convinced I must want to entertain an offer from them is to retreat to being decidedly and severely proper—cool, prudish, missish, and...well, prim."

He blinked. "And that stops them?"

"Usually, they can't find a way around the social hurdles I strew in their path. By insisting on the absolute nth degree of social correctness, I can usually make them reconsider their fixation on me."

"Hmm." With his eyes narrowed in thought, he murmured, "So you make it too hard to reach the real you."

She considered, then nodded. "I suppose that's true." A movement on the lawn ahead caught her eye. "Oh, look!" She pointed. "Isn't that Alison and Joshua, heading toward the bridge?"

Drago glanced that way, then slowed his horses. "It is. In the interests of spending more time under the eye of the ton, shall we stroll?"

"Yes, let's."

There were any number of stable lads from the surrounding great houses who loitered along the avenues in the park, hoping to earn a shilling for holding a gentleman's horse. Drago spotted one he recognized and crooked his finger. The boy came running as Drago halted the horses.

Beaming and pleased to be chosen, the lad saluted. "I'll take good care of 'em, Your Grace."

Drago smiled and tossed him the reins, then descended to the gravel and rounded the carriage to hand Meg down.

She accepted the arm he subsequently offered. As they started to stroll down the gentle slope to the Serpentine, she murmured, "He knew you."

"He knew my horses." Drago grinned. "He knows the grays belong to some duke. He wouldn't know my name, and to him and his cronies, my name's far less of a feather in his cap than being trusted with those horses."

Meg chuckled and shook her head. "Given my family, I should have guessed that."

There were quite a few others taking the air in the fashionable precinct. Thankfully, most were of their age or younger, engaged couples strolling, others in larger groups of gentlemen and ladies, and several bevies of younger ladies with maids or footmen trailing.

None of Drago's acquaintances were likely to be strolling in the park of a Sunday afternoon, but he wasn't surprised when some groups, rather less wary of his notoriety and more willing to be openly curious than their elders, approached and paused to exchange greetings with Meg and, therefore, him.

He was curious to see how such interactions would play out—how difficult they might prove—but it rapidly became apparent that Meg was more than up to the challenge. She handled the introductions and managed the resulting short conversations with a practiced ease that, for all his experience, he lacked.

He listened and—rather humbly—learned from one he quickly recognized as a master. She hadn't wasted her nine Seasons. More, judging by some of her comments and artful questions, she was sharply observant, noticing when others were happy or troubled, and she had at the tips of her mental fingers the family connections of those they met.

They finally caught up with Alison and Joshua, who were strolling arm in arm with Alison's maid trailing a few paces behind.

"Your Grace! Miss Cynster!" Alison's face lit. "How lovely to meet you here." She looked brightly between them. "You must be so excited to be able to announce your engagement just as the Season begins."

Meg smiled. "Indeed." She shifted her gaze to Joshua. "And what of the pair of you?"

Joshua placed his hand over Alison's where it rested on his sleeve.

"We've spoken with Lord and Lady Melwin and made our wishes known. Both have indicated a willingness to accept my suit, so…" Joshua blew out a breath and grinned as if he couldn't quite believe his luck. "We hope to announce our engagement very soon."

"That's wonderful!" Meg beamed at the pair.

Also smiling, Drago added his congratulations.

Glowing, Alison confided, "Mama and Papa wanted to break the news to my brother Hubert in person first, before we make any formal announcement."

"And Hubert had already returned to London." Joshua lightly grimaced and shared with Alison a look brimming with hopeful happiness. "But with any luck, another day or two, and we'll be able to make our betrothal official."

Sincerely happy for the pair, Drago caught Joshua's eyes. "You said you'd recently been made a partner in a legal practice."

Joshua nodded. "Huntley and Cowper. We specialize in estate matters —property, agistments, that sort of thing."

"Based in town?" Drago asked.

"Yes, in Grey's Inn. That said, there's talk of opening an office in Kent, most likely in Tunbridge Wells. There's a lot of estates down that way, and quite a few of our current clients live within reach of the town." Joshua glanced at Alison. "If our plans for the Tunbridge Wells office go ahead, it's likely I'll be placed in charge. Given that my parents live in Tenterden and Alison will feel happier being within reach of her parents at Melwin Place, that would be a helpful development all around."

Drago nodded. "That would be a good result. Do you enjoy the work?"

As Joshua enthusiastically replied and the talk veered to discussion of acres, fields, and fences, Alison rolled her eyes and said to Meg, "I love that color on you. I haven't seen much of the fashions this year, but with an engagement in the offing, I'm hoping to spend more time in Bruton Street, discovering the latest modistes."

"There's several I can recommend." Meg would have preferred to listen to Drago and Joshua's discussion—Drago's questions more than Joshua's answers. She had to wonder what was in Drago's mind. But she dutifully responded to Alison's eager questions; although Alison had visited town before, she hadn't spent even a tithe of the time Meg had in the capital.

Eventually, Alison ran out of questions, and the gentlemen wound up their exchange.

"Oh, my goodness!" Alison peered at a small watch pinned to her lapel. "Look at the time!" She glanced at Joshua. "We need to head back."

He nodded and, reclaiming her hand, wound her arm in his. He smiled at Drago and Meg. "Miss Cynster. Your Grace."

His expression relaxed, Drago smiled. "Until next we meet." He dipped his head to Alison. "Miss Melwin."

They parted, and Meg and Drago walked toward his curricle, where the stable lad was watching over the horses and carriage as if defending a castle.

The sun was setting, and there were fewer others lingering on the lawns.

Pacing beside Drago, Meg glanced at his face. "Why were you so interested in Joshua and his firm's capabilities?"

Drago lightly shrugged. "I've been thinking of engaging another set of eyes to keep track of the various Wylde estates' contracts." Briefly, he met her gaze. "I wouldn't mind having someone more local—someone I could trust who was aware of the various local issues that can impact the Wylde Court farms—to assist there and, subsequently, perhaps with the other estates farther afield."

Meg stared at him for several seconds, but he didn't add anything to that. His expression gave nothing away, either; she'd already realized that, as was the case with many men of his ilk, he allowed only what he wanted to show to manifest in his expression.

She faced forward. As they neared the carriageway and the elegant curricle, she found she was softly smiling.

Fondly smiling.

Drago Helmsford might have been born to great wealth and noble station, but he thought of others and wasn't above helping them when the chance offered.

She observed just that attitude at play as he dealt with the stable lad who had held his horses, leaving the youth not just richer by several shillings but also with his confidence buoyed.

Drago handed her up, and as she settled on the seat, she remembered what she'd learned of him over the hours spent with his family.

As he set his horses pacing again, she glanced at his chiseled profile and felt she stood on solid ground in concluding that, at base, deep down where a person's true character dwelled, Drago Helmsford, Duke of Wylde, was a genuinely, fundamentally kind man.

* * *

THAT EVENING, feeling unaccountably restless, Drago set out for St. James Street and the soothing ambiance of his favorite club, Arthur's.

Once through the unassuming portal, he made his way to the lounge. After claiming a comfortable armchair in a nook tucked along one side of the imposing fireplace and chimney, he ordered a large whisky.

A minute later, he was taking his first soothing sip and wondering what he should do with his evening—and trying to keep his mind from fixating on Meg Cynster—when a shadow fell over him.

He looked up and saw a well-dressed gentleman perhaps a few years older than he.

The man smiled. "Alverton. I married Therese Cynster."

"Ah." Drago waved to the chair opposite. His mind raced. "So, a compatriot of sorts."

Alverton's lips curved. "One might say that." He sat. He was holding a glass of his own; he raised it and, studying Drago over the rim, sipped. Lowering the glass, in a mild tone, he asked, "Have you known Meg for long?"

"Not *known*." Realizing how that sounded coming from an acknowledged rake, Drago quickly amended, "We've crossed paths in the country over a matter of years and more recently grew better acquainted."

"I see. You're what? Thirty-five?"

"Almost."

"And you've decided it's time you got yourself a bride and saw to your nursery?"

Drago wasn't sure there wasn't some sort of unexploded ordnance behind those innocent-sounding words. "As I recall, you followed much the same path."

For an unnerving moment, Alverton looked at him assessingly—as if trying to see into his mind—then the damned man smiled. "Again, you might say that." Still smiling in that unnerving fashion—as if he knew something Drago didn't—Alverton raised his glass and toasted him. "To your marriage." Coolly, his eyes hardening, he added, "One thing. Don't ever cause Meg a moment's anguish, or life as you know it will cease."

Drago blinked in surprise. When he refocused, he saw Alverton on his feet. "Really? A threat?"

"Most definitely not. That was a promise." With a tip of his dark head, Alverton moved on.

Drago stared after him, then raised his glass and sipped. "Really?"

He wished very much that he'd had the sense to ask Meg for a list of her Cynster cousins—titles, marriages, and all.

That wish grew only more fervent when Viscount Breckenridge stopped by to have a word. Luckily, Glengarah—Prudence's husband,

whom Drago had already met and whose assessment he'd already passed
—strolled up before Breckenridge got to the threat stage.

Bemused, Drago sat quietly in his corner and was treated to a procession of Cynster or Cynster-connected males. Even the future head of the
family, Sebastian, Marquess of St. Earith, appeared to—with the specter
of a sword somewhere in the background—wish Drago every happiness
with his soon-to-be wife.

And of course, to warn him, obliquely but definitely, against any
temptation to cause Meg a moment's pain.

Two more whiskies and several Cynsters later, and Winchelsea—who
had exuding menace down to a fine art—was very nearly the last straw.

The very last was Toby, Meg's brother, who, as quiet as a phantom,
appeared by Drago's side as he descended the steps of Arthur's and, his
hands sunk in his greatcoat pockets, turned his feet for home.

Toby fell in beside him.

Drago shot the younger man a sharp and distinctly sour look. "I
suppose you're here to tell me that if I harm so much as a hair on Meg's
head, you'll see me rent limb from limb."

Taken aback, Toby looked at him, then replied, "I wasn't actually
going to go that far."

"But you were going to issue some sort of veiled threat."

"Well, yes. It's customary, isn't it? Expected." Toby waved a hand.
"Especially with you being...well, you."

At the "you being you," Drago's usually inexhaustible well of patience
ran dry. He halted abruptly and, when Toby did the same, pinned him
with his gaze. "Let me make one point crystal clear. When it comes to
protecting Meg from any and all harm, she has and will forever have no
more focused, committed, and devoted champion than me."

In the quiet street, the words rang with determination, and Drago felt
them resonate deep inside him.

Toby, for his part, didn't move, although in the light from a nearby
streetlamp, Drago saw his eyes widen.

Narrowing his own, Drago crisply stated, "I would take it kindly were
you to spread those words to the rest of your clan. They don't and won't
need to watch Meg protectively—they should instead feel sympathy for
anyone who moves against her."

With that, Drago spun on his heel and stalked off.

He listened, but heard no footsteps following. He walked up the street
and crossed over Piccadilly.

By then, the cool of the night had penetrated his fevered brain and
dampened his irritation.

In his head, he heard his words again. He knew how such a declaration would be interpreted by men like the Cynsters, which was exactly what he'd intended.

That, however, wasn't the revelation he was now facing.

In assembling and uttering those emphatic words, he hadn't even stopped to think. No. Because those words were, indeed, exactly how he felt about Meg.

And although that feeling was in some ways familiar—he had sisters and a younger brother and other dependents, after all—when the subject was Meg, the feeling was infinitely stronger. Much more intense.

Indeed, after they'd shared that kiss in the cottage, it had been that nascent feeling surging to life that had prompted him to declare that they were engaged.

He couldn't have said anything else. Not because of any social repercussions but because, in that moment, that was what he'd wanted.

He'd needed to protect her. To secure and take care of her...

He was who he was—Drago Helmsford, the hedonistic Duke of Wylde —and he was rarely unclear about what he wanted in his life.

And that meant...

Frowning, he walked steadily into Mayfair while some part of his brain started to plot how to get what he wanted.

How he could lay claim to everything he now truly wanted of life.

CHAPTER 6

The following evening brought with it the first true ball of the Season.

Standing beside Meg and her mother in the receiving line on the stairs of Devonshire House, Drago murmured, "It hadn't actually occurred to me before, but the timing of our announcement has been rather..."

"Fortuitous?" Meg offered.

"I was thinking more along the lines of being like an incendiary tossed onto a pile of kindling." Careful not to focus on anyone in particular, he scanned the surrounding throng, many of whom were avidly watching him and Meg. "It seems we've given the ton its first sensation of the Season."

The look Meg sent him was curious. "You didn't see that coming?"

He shrugged one shoulder. "To date, the Season hasn't featured as all that important in my life, so no. I didn't."

He'd dutifully called at Half Moon Street to take Meg and her mother up in his town carriage for the short drive to Devonshire House. His first sight of Meg as she'd descended the stairs toward him, superbly gowned for the evening in silk in a muted shade of teal, had temporarily deprived him of the ability to think. He'd been inexpressibly grateful that he'd adhered to correct procedure for a newly affianced gentleman and hadn't arranged to meet them in the ballroom.

As it was, only her mother and father had been there to witness the struck-dumb expression he hadn't been quick enough to wipe from his face. He'd sensed that the older Cynsters had been quietly amused. Meg, of course, had noticed, too, but in her case, a fine blush had risen in her cheeks, which had been some compensation for his own discomfiture.

The receiving line advanced, and they stepped into the foyer before the ballroom's huge double doors, which had been set wide. Through the open doorway, the hum of conversation rolled out in a smothering wave, and the light blazing from multiple chandeliers was almost dazzling.

As they moved forward, the interest of those ahead became more obvious as people turned and glanced back at him and Meg.

"I take it," he murmured, "that we will, indeed, be the cynosure of all attention."

"I expect so." She didn't seem overly alarmed. Her gaze on the group welcoming guests just inside the ballroom's doors, she tipped her head closer and whispered, "The lady beside Her Grace is Lady Otterley, Her Grace's bosom-bow and the biggest gossip in the ton."

"Wonderful."

Meg cast him another of her amused glances. "It is, actually. Because she's receiving, she won't be able to interrogate us. We'll be able to move on quite quickly."

"Ah. I see."

They reached the head of the line, and it was instantly apparent that everyone in sight had scoured their morning's copy of the *Gazette*. The duchess knew Drago well enough, and she was plainly on excellent terms with Meg's mother and Meg herself.

"An excellent outcome," the duchess declared, her haughty features signaling complete approval as she surveyed Drago and Meg. "We are very glad to be able to congratulate you both"—she focused her slightly protuberant eyes on Drago—"and it's a particular pleasure to welcome you into our circles, Your Grace."

Drago half bowed and murmured what he hoped were appropriate responses.

Meg's mother had moved on and greeted Lady Otterley and, by dint of asking after her ladyship's granddaughter, had succeeded in diverting her ladyship's attention.

Meg seized a pause in her ladyship's doting reply to curtsy and murmur a greeting before moving quickly past her mother to curtsy to His Grace, the Duke of Devonshire—the last in the line and unquestionably the safest—and Drago followed her lead.

A minute later, after exchanging a few entirely innocuous words with His Grace, Drago and Meg were free to walk into the milling crowd.

They were joined by Meg's mother, who tapped Drago's arm with her fan and directed his attention to one side of the room. "You need to come with me, but after you weather the next round of greetings, you will have to circulate"—she glanced up at him, and he caught the twinkle in her eye —"or else you'll be mobbed."

"Delightful," he murmured under his breath, but duly escorted Meg and her plainly experienced mother to a grouping of chaises set along one wall to accommodate the older matrons of the ton.

The group they approached held several who, although he wasn't well acquainted with any of them, even Drago recognized as grandes dames. On guard, even more so after Meg's fingers tightened warningly on his arm, he kept his most charming smile in place and bowed over beringed hands and bore with the inevitable inquisitions with outward good humor and as much grace as he could muster.

Meg, he discovered, was an old hand at this. Aside from all else, she was apparently related to several of the most formidable old ladies and treated by virtually all as a favored protégée.

What was even more notable were the comments directed his way, which largely echoed those of their hostess.

"We are," the haughty Duchess of St. Ives announced, "delighted to see you finally taking your rightful place in this sphere."

Gracefully, Drago inclined his head and, somewhat to his surprise, found the truth on his tongue. "I have to admit I hadn't previously appreciated the...significance of such events."

The energy in the room was palpable, and while female heads predominated, there was a large contingent of gentlemen present, all engaged in avid conversations. He hadn't previously considered balls as venues at which important connections might be made and information exchanged, but he was rapidly revising that opinion.

The duchess's dark eyes sparkled, and her lips curved. "You'll learn." She tipped her head at Meg, currently engaged in a discussion with another of the group. "And you've chosen a most excellent guide."

Another older lady arrived, and Drago and Meg stepped back. After seeing Meg's mother ensconced with the other older ladies, as instructed, he and Meg moved into the crowd.

A crowd Drago now viewed through new eyes.

Meg had taken the arm he'd offered. He noticed her glancing at his face.

When he raised a brow at her, she arched hers back. "What is it?"

He glanced around, saw several others converging, and remembering her mother's warning, started strolling through the crowd as if they had their sights set on someone in particular. "Until this evening, I hadn't realized that becoming your fiancé would function as a ticket of sorts, permitting me entrée to this arena."

When he glanced at Meg, she looked confused.

"Until now, I've avoided the ballrooms." He glanced swiftly around, confirming his earlier assessment that this ball at least was an event at which meaningful matters might be discussed and useful connections made. "And while that was definitely by my choice, if I'd simply changed my mind and appeared here tonight without you by my side, I would have been viewed with a certain suspicion."

She tipped her head. "Yes, I agree. You would have been looked at askance because no one would have felt they understood why you were here."

"Precisely." He paused, then added the rest. "But as the Duke of Wylde, I have responsibilities to the dukedom, to the family—even to the realm in terms of my seat in the Lords." Steering her past a group who were plainly debating intercepting them, he dipped his head and met her eyes. "But to fulfill those responsibilities to the best of my ability, I should be—I need to be—here. Don't I?" He glanced at those around them. "Attending events such as this?"

When he looked back at her, her expression was serious, and she nodded. "Yes." She met his eyes. "You probably do." She, too, glanced around. "I know Alverton, Winchelsea, St. Earith, and even Glengarah will be here, meeting with others and sharing opinions on this and that." She brought her gaze back to his face. "Sometimes, they stay for only an hour. At other events, they stay the whole time." She frowned. "But you would have been invited to every event ever since you came on the town."

"Indeed. All the major hostesses invariably send invitations to me and every other gentleman of birth and standing, but of course, once past our callow youth, most of us never attend events such as this." He raised a brow at her. "Can you imagine what would have happened had I attended this gathering while still unattached?"

She nearly choked on a laugh. "Regardless of any suspicions, a frenzy would have ensued."

"Exactly." Had he not sent that announcement to the *Gazette* and had she not been on his arm, he still wouldn't have been able to step foot into Her Grace's ballroom, even though, as the grandes dames had been at such pains to point out, this was a function at which he rightfully belonged.

They'd reached the other side of the ballroom and turned to survey the chattering horde.

"Meg. There you are."

He and Meg turned to greet the Countess of Alverton and her husband.

Meg smiled, grasped hands, and touched cheeks with Therese. "I hoped I'd catch up with you here." She nodded to Devlin. "Devlin." After introducing Drago, she returned her gaze to Therese. "How are the children?"

Therese happily filled her in on the latest exploits of her growing brood, leaving Devlin to chat with Drago.

From there, by artful if impromptu design, she and Drago progressed from one family encounter to another via various cousins including Louisa, Marchioness of Winchelsea, Antonia, Marchioness of St. Earith, as well as Meg's sister, Pru, all with husbands in tow.

After parting from Pru and Deaglan, Drago murmured, "Was this organized?"

Meg grinned. "No. But they understand that you might be feeling a trifle out of your depth and are trying to help by easing your way."

He smiled. "I have to admit I'm obliged to them. We've kept the hordes at bay for over an hour."

But there was no escaping forever, and they were soon engaged in conversations that had them accepting congratulations, approbations, outright encouragements, and not a few commendations on their good sense in getting engaged to each other, before the conversations inevitably devolved into overly inquisitive probing into how and when and where they had met. Meg was an old hand at sliding around such queries, and Drago proved even more charmingly adept at giving answers that were both true yet entirely misleading.

Indeed, listening to him as he successfully deflected old Lady Harrington, Meg found herself in awe of his skill.

She was delighted when Drago's sisters and their husbands stepped in to ease the pressure, and Claudette made a point of steering them to where several of Drago's more distant connections were pleased to make Meg's acquaintance and chat for a short time with Drago, who, it seemed, they rarely saw.

Once again, comments genuinely supportive of their match came thick and fast.

Soon after, the dance floor cleared, and the musicians set bow to string, and with considerable relief, Drago solicited Meg's hand for the first waltz.

Our first waltz as an affianced couple.

As with Meg in his arms, he stepped out, Drago inwardly frowned as he remembered that this was, in fact, all a sham.

He refocused on her, on the supple feel of her in his arms as he steered them around the floor. They whirled, and she looked up and, smiling, met his gaze, and the rest of the room fell away.

She was featherlight in his arms, effortlessly matching him step for step, the skirts of her gown swirling as they precessed down the room. Then her smile deepened, and she murmured, "I had wondered if you enjoyed dancing."

It was patently obvious she did.

"I enjoy all forms of dancing." He clamped his lips shut and hauled his mind from the track it had taken. No need to think about that particular age-old dance and even less of enjoying it with her.

Why not?

He shoved the thought aside and whirled them through a turn, and as they started up the room again, observed, "I just realized. As we both enjoy waltzing and we're engaged, there's nothing against us indulging in however many dances we wish."

She studied his face. "So we can avoid more questions about the how and where and when?"

Among other reasons.

He nodded. "There's only so many times one can repeat oneself and still sound believable."

With a smile, she tipped her head in concession. "There is that."

Meg just hoped that she could hide her intensifying awareness of him. She'd thought the leaping of her pulse, the skittering of her senses whenever he drew close, would have worn off by now, but no. If anything, the sensations had only grown more intense, more distracting.

The pressure of his hand splayed across her back and the grip of his fingers on hers left her lungs cramped and her breath shallow.

She concentrated on appearing unaffected throughout the succeeding dances. Somewhat contrarily, she breathed a silent sigh of relief when the musicians finally paused for a break, and she and Drago were once more forced to engage with those seeking to congratulate them. With the first rush of exclamations and congratulations waning, inquiries as to their engagement ball grew more frequent. While she felt confident in fending off such questions, and thankfully Drago was, too, the process definitely wore on their nerves until she was almost wishing for the musicians to return.

Luckily, when they did, it was for a set of only three dances, one of which was a country dance. Drago insisted on retaining her hand for all three, and as supper mercifully followed the third dance and Drago managed to secure them a small table for two, her hyperaware senses gained a short respite.

When they returned to the ballroom, it seemed the worst was over. They strolled in more relaxed fashion along the side of the room that boasted long windows opening to a paved terrace. It was a blustery night, and no one had ventured outside. Nevertheless, Drago eyed the terrace speculatively, then glanced around the room. "I don't suppose," he murmured, "that we could steal away?"

Meg huffed repressively. "With your reputation? Regardless of our engagement, no. That would cause all sorts of whispers, which, after all, is precisely what we're striving to avoid."

He heaved a resigned sigh, making her grin.

Then she spotted a trio of well-dressed gentlemen gathered in a knot by the wall. They appeared to be trying to surreptitiously attract their— or at least Drago's—attention, but as he idly scanned the room, they weren't in his line of sight.

She pinched his arm. When he looked down at her, she nodded toward the three. "Do you know them?"

He looked, then smiled widely and replied, "George, Viscount Bisley, Lord Harry Ferndale, and Thomas Hayden."

"Your three friends?"

"Yes. And I'm amazed to see them here." He set course for the three.

"So they know…" She left the question hanging.

"Yes. But don't worry. They won't say a word."

She had to accept his assurance on that point.

They joined the trio, and Drago introduced them.

In turn, Meg offered her hand, over which all three very correctly bowed.

"Delighted to make your acquaintance, Miss Cynster." George, Viscount Bisley, was a bluff-looking sort but, like Drago, very nicely turned out, with his expertly trimmed golden-brown curls gleaming.

"As am I." Lord Harry Ferndale possessed shining brown hair and hazel eyes that signaled very clearly that he was curious about her, but not in a pushy way.

Thomas Hayden, also brown haired and almost as tall as Drago, had pleasant, even features and a winning smile. "We"—he cast a swift glance around the room—"felt we should come in case you needed rescuing."

For would-be rescuers, all three appeared distinctly nervous, of which Drago was plainly aware.

"Are you sure that was wise?" His eyes were dancing. "You three are almost as eligible as me and, until now, have proved equally elusive."

"Don't tempt Fate," George warned.

"I have to admit"—Harry cast a wary eye over the still-considerable crowd—"I had no idea how well attended this event would be—I've seen my mother and two aunts, for pity's sake—nor that so much attention would be focused on you two." He smiled apologetically at Meg. "I hadn't truly appreciated what a prime event Drago and you getting engaged would be."

"Indeed." Thomas looked a trifle wide-eyed as he took in the gazes that had drifted their way. Lowering his voice, he went on, "I have to wonder how on earth you're going to…well, unravel this."

Drago was jolted by an instinctive impulse to brush the notion aside. Subduing it, he coolly replied, "Don't worry. Meg and I know what we're doing."

His head raised, Thomas was scanning the crowd. "Is Alison here?"

"I spotted her earlier," Drago said. "She's most likely still here, somewhere in the scrum."

Thomas returned his gaze to Drago's face. "That could prove awkward."

Drago allowed his lips to curve. "No, it won't." He glanced at Meg and allowed his smile to deepen. "My getting engaged to Meg allowed Alison to accept another—a gentleman who will assuredly suit her much better than I."

Meg grinned in agreement, but the other three looked stunned.

"Really?" George looked around as if trying to spot Alison.

At that moment, three ladies approached, and Meg slipped her hand from Drago's arm and stepped away to engage them, leaving him free to converse with his friends in reasonable privacy.

He appreciated the opportunity. "Yes, really." He lowered his voice to a whisper to add, "So even though Meg and I plan to part at the end of the Season, I won't be marrying Alison. With luck, by the time June comes around, Alison will have wed her beau, so regardless of what transpires, I won't be looking in that direction again."

Harry frowned. "But that will leave you only a month, two at most, to find an alternative bride."

Drago smiled with rakish assurance. "Oh, ye of little faith. Trust me, a month will be more than long enough. How can you doubt me?"

At that moment, Meg returned to his side. Well aware that she didn't know the true reason for him wishing to marry, Drago asked, "Any difficulty?"

"No." Meg waved dismissively. "Just the usual curiosity as to when our engagement ball will be."

"And when will it be?" Thomas asked.

Drago waved languidly. "We haven't yet decided."

"I say. Meant to mention"—George looked eager—"I saw a smashing hunter at Tattersalls this morning." He beamed at Meg. "Miss Cynster might be interested in taking a look."

Ignoring Drago's questioning glance, Meg smiled and let the comment slide past, but Harry leapt in with a description of his latest equine acquisitions, waxing lyrical about their lines and gait. Thomas threw in a comment or two, but it was George and Harry who continued to feed the conversation.

The pair were making such an effort to please and entertain her that she had to shake her head and put them straight. "Gentlemen, I regret to inform you that I'm the one Cynster who doesn't like horses."

All three stared in varying degrees of stupefied surprise.

Finally, George managed, "Don't like horses?" He glanced at Drago. "But Drago said you'd managed his pair when...you were in the country."

Smiling, Meg explained, "I'm Demon Cynster's daughter, so of course I can manage horses. I just don't particularly like them as animals." In an attempt to redirect their thoughts, she offered, "I much prefer dogs."

That earned her a curious look from Drago. "You do?"

She nodded. "Sadly, I've had to leave my dogs at home in Newmarket, and from what I've heard, they seem to have transferred their allegiance to Adriana, my brother Nicholas's wife."

"Well," Harry said, "you should get Drago to give you one of his wolfhound pups."

"Wolfhounds?" Meg turned wide eyes on Drago. "Scottish or Irish?"

"Russian. One of my great-uncles was the ambassador in St. Petersburg years ago, and on retiring and leaving the country, he was gifted with a breeding pair. Of course, no one had thought to ask if he liked dogs, and he didn't—they made him sneeze uncontrollably. So I took them, and ever since, I've raised them and their offspring at Wylde Court."

"Don't they mind if you stay away for months?" Meg asked.

Drago shook his head. "They have their keepers, but as soon as I appear, they immediately take to following me. They're loyal to the bone."

"I would love to meet them. Aren't they large?"

He held his hand at waist height.

George nodded while Harry shuddered. "Trust me, you don't want to meet any of them while stumbling around the corridors of Wylde Court in the dark. Almost gave me a heart attack, once."

The others all laughed.

But George, Harry, and Thomas abruptly sobered as their hostess—backed by two other matrons with a total of three younger ladies hovering just behind—swept up to their group.

"Bisley, as I live and breathe." The duchess smiled in predatory fashion. "Your mother would never forgive me if I didn't introduce you to Sophie here." The duchess reached back and drew one of the blushing young ladies forward. "She comes from your neck of the woods—the Micklehams from Denbigh."

Meg could tell the information meant nothing to George, but he knew there was no escape. He managed a weak smile, murmured a greeting, and bowed to Miss Mickleham. As he straightened and she rose from her curtsy, the musicians started up again.

"Ah!" The duchess's smile deepened. "Just in time. Off you go, my dears."

Drago promptly grasped Meg's hand and nodded to the duchess. "If you'll excuse us, ma'am."

The duchess flicked her fingers at them. "Yes, yes—you may go." She turned her gaze on Harry. "Now, Ferndale—"

As Drago urged her toward the floor, Meg met his eyes and struggled not to laugh.

Smiling, he halted and swung her around, then she was in his arms, and they were once again whirling.

Repeated exposure to the swooping, soaring sensations evoked by waltzing with Drago Helmsford hadn't muted their impact in the least. Meg still felt as if she were floating, swirling through a haze of delight.

She'd waltzed with so many gentlemen over the past years, yet it had never occurred to her that a waltz—a simple waltz—could be this absorbing. This captivating and engrossing. The sheer power Drago brought to the moment was disguised by the ineffable and never-failing grace that imbued his every movement. Quite shocking strength was so superbly harnessed that every swoop and twirl was smooth and effortless.

The hardness of his thigh pressing between hers as they went through the sharp turns at the ends of the crowded floor left her giddy.

Pleasurably so.

The dance came to an end, and she honestly wasn't sure if she was glad or not. One part of her was hugely relieved, another part disappointed.

Drago glanced over the heads, then steered her away from where he'd been looking.

When she peered at him questioningly, he murmured, "Best, I think, to leave George, Harry, and Thomas to fend for themselves. I doubt our hostess would be pleased if we gave them a chance to escape her coils."

Meg grinned. "No, indeed."

"So." Drago glanced around again, then as they continued to move through the crowd, met her eyes and murmured, "How do you think our charade is holding up?"

It took effort to hide the shock of cold reality that washed over and through her.

She'd forgotten—utterly and completely—that this was, indeed, a charade.

To give herself a second to gather her wits, she glanced around assessingly, then tipped her head closer and whispered back, "Surprisingly well."

Possibly because I—and perhaps even you—forgot about our engagement not being real.

She glanced at him, but reading his expression while in public was wasted effort. Whatever showed in his features did so only when he intended it to be seen.

Redirecting her gaze to those about them, she swallowed the unhappiness that had surged inside her and felt it settle in a cold hard knot in her stomach.

"Are you all right?"

She looked up to find Drago with concern in his eyes. She found a smile and tipped her head toward where her mother and the grandes dames sat. "People are starting to leave. We can, too."

He looked toward the sofas by the wall. "All right."

As he steered her toward her mother, Meg wondered if the note of disappointment she thought she'd heard in those two small words was real or merely a figment of her fancy.

* * *

DRAGO CALLED at Half Moon Street a little before noon the following day and took Meg up in his curricle for a turn around the park. In light of their reception at the Devonshire House event, both of their mothers had strongly recommended the outing.

As he guided his grays through the park gates, he grumbled, "I'm not at all sure I see the point. They had at us all yesterday evening. Why do we have to give them another opportunity?"

"Because," Meg said, "given our families' standings, we're obliged to ensure that none of the grandes dames missed out. Sadly, not all were present last night."

He felt like whining, but quashed the urge.

Ahead, the twin rows of carriages lining the avenue loomed. He studied the battlefield. "Can we walk, do you think?"

She looked at the carriages. "You mean along the verge beside the carriages?"

"Yes. While managing this pair, I can't really concentrate on conversations, and I don't like the idea of constantly halting if the ladies hail us, as I assume we should."

"We should, indeed, and I see your point." She waved ahead. "Pull up at the end of the row, and we can stroll from there."

He did as directed. After leaving the grays in the hands of his favored stable lad, who had seen him draw up and had come running to tender his services, Drago offered Meg his arm, and they set off, strolling along the line of fashionable barouches, all with their hoods down the better to allow the occupants to observe all those driving, riding, or walking by.

Unsurprisingly, their appearance on the lawn beside the carriages caused a stir.

"Miss Cynster! Your Grace!"

Meg wasn't surprised to hear them hailed the instant they drew level with the first carriage. Smiling confidently, she nodded to Lady Melrose, an old but still-influential hostess who had not been present at Devonshire House. With Drago beside her, Meg diverted to the side of the old lady's equally elderly barouche.

"Good morning, Lady Melrose." Meg bobbed a curtsy.

Beside her, Drago inclined his head. "Ma'am."

"A good morning, indeed. Glad to see you both about. Read about your news yesterday morning." Her ladyship didn't beat about the bush. "Quite a shock, albeit a pleasant one." She regarded them shrewdly. "I daresay this is one of those connections not even your great-aunt foresaw, miss." Switching her gaze to Drago, she continued, "As for you, Your Grace, I have to admit I was a member of the camp that would never have credited you with such good sense. Seems your mother had it right. She always maintained that despite your hedonistic ways, when the time came, you would choose wisely." She drew back to include them both in her approving smile. "As you've amply demonstrated. I wish you both well."

With a nod of dismissal, she released them.

Her smile in place, Meg bobbed again, and Drago nodded, and they stepped away.

A few paces on, Drago bent his head to Meg's. "Is that all it takes—just listening?"

"If we're lucky."

The succeeding carriages belonged to ladies they'd met the previous evening, where a smiling nod and called greeting sufficed. When Drago glanced at Meg—clearly waiting to take her lead—she explained, "They won't expect us to stop and chat unless we have something we especially wish to tell them."

"Which we don't." He faced forward. "That's a relief." After a moment, he asked, "So how many of these carriages do we need to stop and chat at?"

She cast a knowledgeable eye over those she could see. "A fifth, possibly fewer. The reason our mothers suggested an appearance before luncheon is that the grandes dames we need to placate will most likely be here, but the majority of the matrons with daughters in tow—whom we don't need to specifically court—won't appear until later."

"Ah. I see." After a moment, Drago murmured, "Who is your great-aunt, and why would she have foreseen our connection?"

"Great-aunt Helena, the Dowager Duchess of St. Ives, is widely regarded as eerily prescient. Of course, in this case, she could have had no idea that we might become engaged."

"Is she here, in town? Am I likely to run into her at some event?"

"At present, she's still in Cambridgeshire, at Somersham Place, but she'll most likely come to town at some point."

Drago made a mental note to be especially wary of the Dowager Duchess. The notion of a lady who might, somehow, see into his mind made him uneasy.

They continued strolling, pausing to chat wherever they were hailed. By his estimation, that was rather more frequently than every fifth carriage, but not often enough to prevent them moving down the line in reasonable fashion.

Among all the congratulations and exclamations, one comment was repeated so often that not even he could ignore it or its implications.

"Such a wise choice, Your Grace."

"Really, it's hard to imagine how you might have chosen better."

"An excellent choice that will stand you in good stead in the future."

The same message came again and again, in slightly different words but with the one clear meaning, one not even he would deny.

Meg Cynster was an excellent choice for the position of his duchess.

Conversely, Alison Melwin—sweet, gentle, mild of manner, and generally faint of heart—could never have managed.

By the time they reached the end of the line, crossed the avenue, and started back along the other side, still being hailed, still doing the pretty by countless older ladies and grandes dames, he'd seen that truth in action, had it drummed repeatedly into his brain.

Courtesy of his self-limited interactions with the ton over the past decade and more, in now moving through the hallowed halls, he recognized enough gentlemen to get by, and he knew some of the ladies, but not enough to successfully navigate the shoals of ton expectations.

And as the Duke of Wylde, more than anything else he needed to be able to succeed in that.

Although he'd made no request of her, Meg seemed intuitively to have grasped his difficulty; in acknowledging every hail, she invariably used the lady's name and title. And where the lady's title was obscure or not particularly informative, Meg followed up with a question that gave him a clue as to how the lady fitted into the wider web of the ton.

The ton lived and breathed through connections, and Meg had everyone's at her fingertips.

Previously, immersed in his hedonistic and largely private life, he hadn't really thought about what his married life would be like, how it would differ from the life he'd led as a bachelor. How marriage would change the way he interacted with his world.

He was thinking of that now.

With the specter of his father's will hanging like Damocles's sword over his head, he had to face facts, namely, that he didn't just need a wife. He needed the *right* wife.

A wife who could perform in the manner in which Meg currently was.

With the end of the second row of carriages in sight, he found himself viewing her through newly opened eyes.

Feeling far more entertained than she'd expected, Meg cast a teasingly amused look at Drago. "Almost there."

He'd been studying her face, but now he looked ahead and grunted.

She laughed. "You sound just like my brothers and cousins."

"All sane and sensible men."

"Never mind." Buoyed by unquenchable good humor, she patted his arm. "The ordeal is nearly over. Only Lady Conningham and then Lady Palmerston and we're done."

She steered Drago toward Lady Conningham's carriage. As they drew near, she advised, "Don't show any awareness of how loudly she speaks. She's rather deaf—you just have to talk at the same level, but pretend all is normal."

As they approached her carriage, Lady Conningham waved her cane by way of summons.

Meg sensed Drago's instinctive resistance but, smiling, towed him to the carriage's side. "Lady Conningham! You are looking well!"

"Thank you, my dear!" her ladyship boomed. She nodded to Drago. "Your Grace. I understand you've managed to convince this young lady that her place is by your side." Her ladyship snorted. "About time someone did! And that applies to both of you!"

Meg countered, "We're happy our proposed union meets with your approval, ma'am."

"P'shaw!" Smiling herself, Lady Conningham waved them away. "I can see Emily over there just waiting to pounce, so you'd better get on, or she'll frown at me over afternoon tea."

Meg bobbed, and Drago—who looked as entertained as she but trying to hide it—bowed elegantly, eliciting another loud snort from her ladyship.

As Lady Conningham had noted, seated in splendid state two carriages along, Lady Palmerston's gaze was, indeed, trained on them.

Short, sweet-faced, with slightly protuberant soft-blue eyes, Emily Temple, Viscountess Palmerston, appeared the epitome of everyone's favorite aunt, yet she was one of the original patronesses of Almack's, had buried one husband in Lord Cowper, and had subsequently married her great love, Palmerston. She was widely appreciated as having sound sense, delicate sensibilities, great beauty as well as charm, all linked with shrewdness and devoted loyalty to her husband's cause, political and personal.

For decades, her salons had been renowned the length and breadth of the country and, indeed, far beyond its borders.

As Meg and Drago neared, her ladyship beckoned imperiously.

With smiles, they presented themselves.

Her expression one of gracious approval, her ladyship looked from one to the other. "Meg Cynster and Drago Helmsford. I must admit I am quietly amazed. The pair of you have managed to turn the ton on its collective ear, but in the opposite of the usual way. I have not heard of anyone, grande dame or otherwise, who had even dreamed of matching the two of you, but now you've presented us with the fait accompli, the alliance seems so very obvious and so obviously perfect in every way." She beamed at them both. "I predict great things will come of this. Indeed, your marriage will be the making of you both."

Meg hid a wary blink behind an appropriate mask of glowing happiness. "Thank you, ma'am."

"Indeed." Also smiling genially, Drago bowed.

"Yes, well, now I've made that pronouncement, I will, of course, expect you to live up to it." Lady Palmerston held up a warning finger. "And before you slope off, apropos of living up to expectations, I am holding a soirée—one of my usual gatherings—next Monday evening. You will both receive invitations shortly, and I will expect to see you there."

Meg slanted a look at Drago, even as she said, "Of course, ma'am. We'll definitely attend." Regardless of any other invitation, one could not refuse a summons from the current Prime Minister's wife.

"Excellent." Lady Palmerston nodded. "Now you've declared your intention to wed, there's no reason not to embark upon establishing yourselves within the necessary circles."

With that, she released them, and they moved on, past the last carriages.

"Done." Drago looked ahead to where his curricle waited in the care of the stable lad.

"Indeed." Despite their morning's foray having gone without a hitch, Meg felt strangely discombobulated. Not unhappy, no. In fact...

Drago took her hand, and her senses, as usual, leapt and skittered—a sensation she was, at last, learning to ignore. He helped her up to the seat, and she sat and, while he paid the stable lad and exchanged a few words, she stared at the carriages lined up along the avenue—the scene of their recent triumph.

That was it. For the hour and more it had taken them to complete the circuit, she'd been absorbed, engaged, and actively focused, using her knowledge and her social skills to further the fiction of their engagement. And during those minutes—all those minutes—the restless inner yearning she'd grown so accustomed to over recent years had simply not been there.

She'd felt satisfied. Fulfilled.

She still did.

Mulling that, when Drago climbed up to sit beside her, she agreed that they could return to Half Moon Street, where luncheon awaited them along with their mothers, keen to hear how their morning had played out.

CHAPTER 7

The following day saw Drago and Meg strolling the lawns of Lady Derby's riverside pavilion in Chelsea. The thick grass was dotted with round white-painted wrought-iron tables and matching sets of chairs, and at the lower end of the gently sloping expanse, beyond a line of trees, the waters of the Thames rippled and gleamed.

The sun was beaming strongly, which was just as well as her ladyship had somewhat recklessly declared her event would be a picnic.

Drago cast a decidedly jaundiced eye over the many matrons with daughters in tow and the more youthful gentlemen hauled along as escorts. "If her ladyship wasn't a connection, I trust we wouldn't be here."

Fetchingly gowned in a plum-colored dress trimmed with ivory lace, Meg dipped her head his way. "Probably not." She glanced at the other guests and confirmed, "I suspect we've been touted as the main attraction. Otherwise, there's little benefit to be gleaned for us—few new connections we might be thought to need to forge."

"In that case, let's keep walking." When they'd attended the theater the previous evening, he'd discovered that, just as at the ball, as long as they were on the move, people tended not to intercept them. In his opinion, such behavior was more driven by said people wanting to see with whom they were intending to engage rather than any hesitation over boldly accosting them.

Yet even here, in rather less exalted circles, there were those with whom Meg informed him they needed to engage.

He wasn't entirely surprised that she included his aunt Edith in that number, especially as she was seated alongside two of his older connections.

One of those was Lady Rampling. After exchanging kind words with Meg, her ladyship fixed him with a knowing look. "You are to be commended, Wylde, for exercising the sense you were, as a Helmsford, undoubtedly born with. To have snapped up a Cynster—one of the last available of your generation, too—shows a fine sense of what is due to your position."

Drago couldn't think of how he was supposed to respond to that, so he merely arched a laconic brow.

Yet as he and Meg circulated, twined with the often-effusive felicitations ran a steady stream of approbation, mostly directed at him—that he'd been so clever to offer for Meg—but occasionally at her, too. Old Lady Connaught even went so far as to ask—more or less seriously— whether Meg's spurning of all other suitors over the past nine years had been because she'd always had her eye on becoming the Duchess of Wylde.

He had to hand it to his supposed betrothed; she laughed and blithely agreed, which everyone listening correctly interpreted as her being too kind to coldly deny the ageing lady's ridiculous notion.

The event was well advanced—the picnic served and consumed and the guests relaxing in a postprandial daze—when he spotted George and Harry sidling along in the shadow of a tall hedge.

Meg also noticed. "Good Lord!" she whispered. "Have they been here the whole time or just sneaked in?"

"I have no idea." He'd been so engrossed in watching Meg handle the other guests, he hadn't looked for anyone else.

Meg glanced at him. "No Thomas?"

Drago shook his head. "Thomas's father was rather impecunious, and Thomas has to make his own way, so he's a partner in a law firm in Lincoln's Inn. At this hour, he'll be in chambers."

"Ah. I see." Meg studied his face, then smiled. "There are several of my close acquaintances over there"—she pointed to a bevy of ladies of similar age to herself seated on a low stone wall—"who I would like to catch up with and who don't need to have their tongues tied by your rakish presence."

He grinned devilishly. "In that case, I'll talk to George and Harry for a while."

She laughed and flapped a hand at him, then headed for her friends.

Drago watched her go, then sauntered over to join Harry and George. "I didn't expect to see you two here."

"Lady Derby knows we're friends of yours, so she sent invitations, and we thought we should come, in support as it were," Harry explained. "But I say, it feels awfully dangerous being here."

"Especially after the Devonshire ball." George looked a touch grim. "The duchess insisted on introducing me to three young ladies, and"—he nodded in the direction Meg had gone—"two of them are over there."

Drago fought to straighten his lips. "Well, you're all the way over here, so safe enough for the moment."

"Hmm." George didn't look entirely convinced, but he exchanged a meaningful look with Harry, who shrugged.

"Actually"—George turned to Drago—"as Harry said, we're here in support, and in that vein, we thought we ought to mention...well, what we've observed."

"As you might imagine," Harry took up the explanation, "we've been watching you and Meg, and we've noticed something that you, being more caught up in the moment, might not have."

"Oh? What's that?" Drago didn't need to feign interest.

"Well," George said, "when meeting with others, you work together very well."

"It's almost like passing a baton back and forth," Harry said. "One of you takes the lead, then hands the conversation on to the other." Harry nodded across the lawn. "You were doing it before, even with your aunt."

"The thing is," George said, "as your friends, we feel...well, obliged to point out that Alison Melwin, lovely girl though she doubtless is, wouldn't, simply wouldn't have been able to..."

"Stand by your side like that." Harry nodded in definite fashion. "Given the circles we three will be expected to join once we wed, then whoever you marry, it has to be someone like Meg."

"Don't forget that while, thus far, you've only had purely social events to contend with," George went on, "you even more than we—at least not until we inherit the titles—will need to cope with the political sphere as well."

"Heaven help you!" Harry muttered. "There's always so much going on—spoken, unspoken, just simply understood, let alone subtly implied— that to manage in that arena, you will assuredly need some lady like Meg."

Some lady like Meg.

That understanding had been coalescing in Drago's brain over the past few days.

Along with the corollary.

Why not Meg?

Secure in the knowledge that his expression would reveal nothing of his thoughts, he slowly nodded. "You're right." Unbidden, his gaze shifted to the lady in the plum-colored dress who was sitting on the stone wall across the lawn. "In whatever comes, I will, absolutely and indubitably, bear that in mind."

Unaware of Drago's distant scrutiny, Meg had been drawn into a discussion of several charities currently in favor among the haut ton.

"You're so lucky to be marrying a gentleman as well-heeled and also well-connected as Wylde," Miss Stanhope earnestly told Meg. "You'll be able to donate to any of the major foundations and, if you're so inclined, take positions on their boards."

Miss Cartwright nodded. "Mama is on the board of the local work-house, but she says that without the weight of money and a noble title behind one, it's difficult to push the administrators into improving conditions, even though the need is obvious to all."

Miss Fitzgibbon was one to get stars in her eyes. "Just think of how much good you might be able to do!"

Meg smiled. "I have cousins-in-law who are deeply involved in the affairs of the Foundling House. I might find it easier to make a start there."

"Oh, that's one of the most *worthy* charities," Miss Fitzgibbon assured her, which pronouncement was confirmed by many nodding heads.

Meg was rather relieved when the talk swung to whom Miss Fitzgibbon currently had hopes for, and the other young ladies' attention shifted to the pretty blonde who had yet to settle on any gentleman as the one for her.

But I haven't, either. Not really.

Despite acknowledging that, Meg surrendered to the impulse to imagine how and with which charity she might become involved were she to marry well enough. In terms of her search for some purpose in life, such a prospect held definite appeal.

It wasn't something she'd considered before, given it wasn't a path open to her unless, as Miss Cartwright had noted, she was to marry a gentleman with both title and money.

As the Duchess of Wylde...

Several moments later, she blinked, refocused, and saw Drago on his way across the lawn to join her.

Of George and Harry, there was no sign.

She checked the tiny watch pinned to her lapel, then rose and, after excusing herself to her friends, walked to meet her supposed betrothed halfway.

He halted and arched a brow at her. "Can we leave?" His tone was almost plaintive.

She laughed and wound her arm in his. "Yes, we can. According to the clock, we've given Lady Derby her due and can consider ourselves free to find her, tender our thanks, and be on our way."

"Thank God!"

* * *

THE NEXT AFTERNOON SAW MEG, surrounded by a crowd of ladies, in her grandmother's drawing room in Dover Street. Some of those present were relatives, others connections; only a select few were neither, as a larger gathering would have overflowed the room. The extended Cynster family—grandes dames, older matrons, younger matrons, and the few young ladies not yet wed—were present, at least all those currently in London. As the Season had only just commenced, some, such as the Devon contingent, Lucifer and Phyllida's tribe, had yet to arrive.

As the guest of honor, teacup in hand, Meg dutifully moved from group to group, appeasing the curious without revealing more than was wise and accepting congratulations on both her and Drago's behalf.

The older ladies occupied the sofas and armchairs, while the younger generation, cups of tea in hand, remained standing. All were avidly chatting, and a conversational hum blanketed the room. As most were members of the wider Cynster clan, sharing family news predominated, yet several older family members and also Louisa and Therese commented on the challenge Meg had chosen to undertake.

With her cup, Therese gestured to the assembled ladies. "I—well, all of us, really—are thrilled on the one hand, but also relieved that you've elected to accept Drago's proposal. Quite aside from the fact that he is clearly going to need the help of a lady of your talents, and it's reassuring that he has, apparently, recognized that, the position of his duchess is precisely the right role for you."

Louisa nodded in definite fashion. "I completely agree. Filling the position of the Duchess of Wylde is exactly the right challenge for you. The challenge you obviously need in life and, indeed, deserve."

Given it was widely accepted that Louisa had inherited her grandmother the Dowager Duchess's renowned perspicacity, that pronouncement wasn't one Meg could easily dismiss.

Parting from her more-established cousins, she embarked on a turn around the room, seizing the moments to consider Therese and Louisa's point.

She couldn't deny that, over the past days, during all the events they'd attended, Drago had, indeed, relied heavily on her to smooth his path. He'd accepted her direction and suggestions without question. Indeed, he and she had worked surprisingly well together. So well, in fact, that she—and he, too—had slid comfortably into their mutually supportive roles, roles that, in truth, fitted them both very well.

The only problem was…

Through the crowd, she glimpsed Drago's aunt Edith and his mother—who naturally had been invited—and also Lady Melwin. Meg's mother had earlier murmured that the Melwin ladies had been invited at Edith's suggestion as, for reasons Meg's mother and grandmother didn't entirely grasp, the Helmsfords wished to signal their approval and backing for a match between Alison and a certain young solicitor, a Mr. Joshua Bragg. Meg had been quick to lend her voice in support of the match as well.

Scanning the assembled ladies, she located Alison, chatting with two others, and made her way to her side.

Alison looked up and smiled in welcome.

Meg smiled back. She was acquainted with the other two ladies and slid easily into the ongoing conversation.

A few minutes later, the other ladies moved on, and Meg turned to Alison. "How is your engagement to Joshua progressing?"

Alison's face clouded. "It isn't." She rushed to clarify, "Progressing, that is. Joshua and I are still determined to wed, but Hubert has decided to be difficult."

Meg glanced around, then drew Alison aside, into one of the window alcoves. "Tell me. Perhaps we—Drago and I—can help."

Alison sighed. "I wish that were so, but at present, none of us know what it is that Hubert is objecting to. This only came up yesterday evening, when Hubert arrived at a family dinner intended to introduce Joshua to the wider family. Papa had already informed Hubert of Joshua's offer and hadn't received any hint that Hubert would oppose it, but Hubert arrived just before the rest and insisted, with much huffing and puffing, that it wouldn't be socially wise to announce our betrothal publicly, not at this time, given you and Drago have only just announced your engagement."

Frowning, Alison shook her head. "It's almost as if Hubert thinks the clock will somehow turn back and Drago might glance my way instead." She looked at Meg. "It's quite nonsensical."

Meg's pulse leapt. *Could Hubert know…?*

Trying to make sense of the situation, she asked, "Is Hubert's approval essential?" She studied Alison's face. "I thought your father and mother had agreed to Joshua's suit."

"They did, but these days, both tend to bend to accommodate Hubert's views on most subjects. Although Mama has always had a soft spot for Joshua and we're fairly confident of her support, Papa has taken the line that as Hubert will eventually inherit and become the head of the family, then his approval is needed as well."

Alison heaved a sigh. "Don't worry. Joshua and I are resolute. Ultimately, we'll win through. We've decided to view Hubert's opposition as nothing more than a temporary resistance, one Hubert will think better of soon enough."

Her mind racing and her emotions in unexpected upheaval, Meg managed a reassuring smile. "I'm sure you're right."

At that moment, Lady Melwin summoned Alison with a beckoning hand, and she and Meg parted.

Meg drifted around the outskirts of the still-considerable crowd, sipping and putting into practice her and Drago's proven tactic that as long as one kept moving, others were less inclined to confront one.

Twice during this single event, she'd been reminded that her engagement to Drago was a sham. That when they dissolved their engagement in June, she would no longer fill the position that had already come to fit her like a glove.

The challenge that everyone agreed she was perfectly qualified to meet would no longer be hers.

Nor would the satisfaction of meeting it any longer buoy her.

The purpose she'd unexpectedly found in Kent would be no more.

What am I going to do then?

What other purpose could she find? She wouldn't even be in a position to meaningfully support the charity of her choice.

She told herself that her comprehension of all the above accounted for the sudden lurch in her spirits, the sensation of plunging low at the prospect of their sham engagement ending.

"Meg."

She looked up as a delicate hand closed about her wrist, and she found herself facing Drago's mother. A swift glance around showed that ladies had started to take their leave.

The duchess released her and waved down the room. "Come. Stroll with me a moment. I need to leave soon and would like to assure you of my support with regard to you becoming Drago's duchess."

Meg obediently started walking slowly beside the duchess, more or less against the tide heading for the drawing room door.

"Indeed," the duchess continued, "I wanted to underscore how much I approve of my son's choice."

Meg's wariness increased exponentially when the duchess met her eyes and added, "However he came to make it."

Trapped in the duchess's hazel gaze, Meg understood one thing. *She knows.*

As if confirming that, the duchess inclined her head and went on, "I know my son very well, my dear, and in light of that, I am absolutely, unequivocally certain that you are the very best bride for him."

Despite her unease, Meg couldn't not ask, "Why?"

"Primarily because of a number of attributes that are peculiar to you. First, of course, is your station. By birth, you are Drago's peer, and that gives you a better than average understanding of him as well as entitling you to a degree of consideration from him that comes to him instinctively. You will stand by his side in a manner and with an assurance few young ladies could match. On top of that, there's the undeniable fact that you have caught his eye and also his mind, his cerebral attention. That's no mean feat, and I know of no other who has come even close to fixing his attention in that more meaningful way. Others might be physically alluring, but are unable to capture his interest on any other plane. And that neatly brings me to my last point." Again, the duchess met Meg's eyes. "You already stand up to him, entirely fearlessly, and he pays due attention to your opinions. He respects you and your insights. I cannot tell you how much that will mean in the years to come, only that it is a critical element in being the wife of a Duke of Wylde."

The duchess's lips curved, and she looked ahead. "They did not come by that title accidentally. It may have been bestowed in ancient times, but the family breeds true."

"I see." Meg tried to tamp down the welling desire—almost a hunger—to further explore all the duchess had alluded to.

"And as a parting point, I wanted to tell you that despite his reputation —which I assure you has been well earned—given all I've seen of how Drago reacts to you, once you are wed, he will be entirely and unwaveringly faithful to you, just as his father was to me. In that aspect as well, the Helmsford men breed true."

Meg saw the fondness for both father and son that was, in that moment, visible in the duchess's beautiful face and felt humbled and just a touch envious.

And even more downhearted that she would not have the chance to experience and explore the intriguing prospects the duchess had described.

"So, my dear"—the duchess halted, caught Meg's hand, and leaned in to touch cheeks—"I'll bid you farewell for the afternoon." She straightened, released Meg, and glanced around the slowly emptying room. "It's been very pleasant catching up with your family. They are all as thrilled as the Helmsfords at the prospect of this alliance."

Yet more pressure.

Any chance that the duchess hadn't seen the truth vanished as she met Meg's eyes again. "You really wouldn't want to disappoint so many. If there is any question of breaking things off, do bear that in mind."

With a serene smile, the duchess inclined her head.

Meg dipped into an appropriate curtsy, then straightened, and eyes narrowing, watched the duchess glide away. She now knew from whom Drago got his powerfully persuasive charm.

* * *

In the wake of her grandmother's afternoon tea, throughout the subsequent evening, Meg hadn't been able to speak privately with Drago, not at any point during the dinner and soirée they'd attended.

Both events had only underscored all that Therese, Louisa, and Drago's mother had articulated, all points Meg herself had consciously or unconsciously noted. Being the lady by Drago's side, steering them both through the shoals of society and life, was a role for which she was uniquely qualified and in which she could excel, and doing so was intensely satisfying. On top of that, the interest in them as a couple, especially at the Lansdowne House soirée that had been attended by many of the political set, had been gratifying in one sense, but also unnerving, given their engagement was a sham.

Given that they currently intended to disappoint an increasingly large number of the most powerful in the haut ton.

That prospect had weighed on her, and she'd spent the night tossing and turning, thinking of and rehearsing and editing all she intended to discuss with Drago during the outing she'd arranged for the morning.

She was feeling distinctly on edge when he called at eleven o'clock. Aware of Fletcher holding the door, she ensured she greeted Drago with appropriate delight. A faintly concerned expression lurked in his eyes as, greeting her with his customary grace, he took her hand and led her to his curricle. She held her tongue as he helped her up, accepted the reins, and climbed up beside her.

The instant he'd set his horses trotting, he glanced at her. "What is it?"

As she'd suggested they make for Regent's Park rather than Hyde

Park, he'd brought along his tiger. She didn't want to broach the subject dominating her mind while within anyone else's hearing; that was why she'd opted for Regent's Park. She prevaricated. "What did you think of our reception last night?"

"At Lansdowne House?" He looked ahead and expertly guided his horses around the corner. Once he had the pair trotting smartly again, he replied, "In all honesty, it was a trifle overwhelming. I hadn't expected our engagement, the fact that we're now engaged, to be such a..."

"Major event?"

"Exactly." After a moment, he went on, "I hadn't realized that our engagement would elevate us to such prominence. That it would garner such intense interest."

"Or such approval and encouragement?"

"Indeed." He paused to guide his horses across Oxford Street, then turned the pair north. Soon, they could see dead ahead the green expanse of the Regent's Park lawns bordered by leafy trees. Drago tipped his head toward the sight. "It's as if our engagement has caused us to walk into a landscape I, at least, hadn't foreseen."

Meg nodded. "I hadn't, either. I hadn't even imagined that it might be so."

They reached the park, and Drago drew up in the Outer Circle, near the York Gate. He handed her down and, leaving his tiger in charge of the horses, offered his arm. She steeled herself and took it, and they entered the park.

Regent's Park was always less crowded than the more fashionable Hyde Park, and at that hour, the majority of those walking the graveled paths were nursemaids pushing perambulators or maids and footmen watching over young children set loose to run and play on the lawns.

A few older children were flying kites, and others were sailing toy boats on the lake, but there were plenty of open spaces in which Meg and Drago could stroll—in public yet with their privacy assured.

The instant she was certain that they were out of all others' hearing, Meg drew breath and, looking ahead as they continued strolling, launched into her prepared speech. "The degree of the ton's approbation has been eye-opening. The comments made to me, the allusions to what others see as our joint destinies, the assumptions of the impact our marriage will have in circles I've never dreamed of entering, the views on the desirability of the alliance between our houses—all of that has forced me to see..." She paused, then, her gaze fixed in the distance, went on, "That us becoming engaged is a much bigger, broader, and more powerful proposition than I had supposed."

She glanced at Drago and found him looking down, gazing at the grass as they walked on. She continued, "The encouragement has been blatant and, I suspect, will only grow more so once we conclude the formalities with our engagement ball."

He looked up and met her gaze, and she forced herself to calmly say, "I wanted to ask whether the ton's response has altered your view of our charade, of the wisdom of it, in any way."

He held her gaze for several seconds—searchingly, as if he was trying to see into her mind—then, still pacing beside her, replied, "We've both had many more aspects of our prospective union made abundantly clear to us over recent days." He hesitated, then looked ahead and went on, "Perhaps we would be wise to listen to, ponder, and weigh such opinions and consider whether in light of what we've learned, we wish to revise our plan."

Her lungs seized. "Revise in what way?"

He didn't immediately answer, and they steadily paced on. Then he offered, "We originally saw our engagement as a fabrication—a charade designed to protect your reputation, to deflect a specific scandal."

"True. But now?"

"As I see it, now we stand in a significantly different place. More, on a significantly different field, one on which neither of us imagined we would find ourselves."

She nodded, and they kept walking. Eventually, she prompted, "So?"

Drago had wanted to revisit their arrangement but hadn't known how to introduce the subject. Now, he could barely believe his luck, yet perhaps, given how instinctively they moved together, whether on the dance floor or in a drawing room, he shouldn't be surprised that she had reached the same conclusion—had seen the same potential as he.

"I think," he said, his tone carefully neutral, "that we should continue as planned, but with one fundamental adjustment." He glanced at her, but she was looking down, and he couldn't see her expression. He went on, "Specifically that we should eschew pretense and, instead of viewing our engagement as a sham, explore the possibilities as if it were real. Then in June, we can make our final decision—whether to proceed to a wedding, as all the ton will expect, or call things off as we'd originally planned."

She nodded and looked up, meeting his eyes. "Yes. That sounds like a workable way forward."

His heart, unruly organ that it was most astonishingly proving to be, at least around her, leapt. "Good." He managed to mute the ridiculous smile that wanted to bloom across his face into an approving and pleased expression.

They'd been strolling along a vaguely circular path. She glanced ahead. "June should give us plenty of time to thoroughly explore the possibilities—to gain some idea of how a marriage between us would work and what the benefits would be."

He was more than happy to agree with that. "There have been so many aspects brought to my attention that I hadn't previously realized existed, I honestly feel there's a lot for me to learn and absorb."

"I feel the same." Meg glanced up, met his dark eyes, and smiled. "I'm so glad we've spoken of this and decided on our new tack."

His smile was warm. "I am, too."

She remembered the other issue she'd wanted to raise with him. "On the subject of our engagement being real, I spoke with Alison yesterday, at my grandmother's at-home, and she told me that Hubert is standing in the way of her and Joshua announcing their engagement. Hubert's stance left Alison feeling that he harbored hopes of you and I changing our minds and you possibly making an offer for her." She studied Drago's face. "Could Hubert know that our engagement is—or at least was—a charade?"

Drago frowned. After a moment of thought, he shook his head. "I can't see how Hubert would know." He met her eyes. "Other than you and me, only George, Harry, and Thomas know the truth of our engagement. Well, the truth as it was. But more to the point, I never actually said that I intended to offer for Alison's hand."

She frowned, too. "You didn't give your aunt any indication?"

"No. All she knew was that I intended to call at Melwin Place that morning—and even then, she was the one who made the appointment. I was on my way to take advantage of the opportunity and make an offer for Alison's hand when…"

"When whisky intervened?"

His lips twitched, and he met her eyes. "Just so. But as I didn't speak to any of the Melwins or to Aunt Edith of my intention, then beyond *guessing* that at that time I was considering offering for Alison, Hubert can have no more reason than the next man to suspect that our engagement was a sham."

"What about the next woman?"

Alerted by her tone, Drago looked at her. "What woman?"

"Your mother. She also spoke with me at Grandmother's event, and while she—your mother—didn't exactly say so, I was left with the distinct impression that she knew or at least had guessed."

He grimaced. "I fear she knows me all too well. Guessed rather than actually knows is probably correct." He regarded her curiously. "What was the gist of her comments?"

Meg arched her brows lightly. "She listed all the advantages that will accrue once we marry, and her parting words were that it wouldn't do to disappoint the entire ton, capped with a recommendation that if there was any question of us breaking things off, we really should bear that in mind."

He huffed. "That sounds like Mama. She doesn't interfere until she pulls the rug out from under you." Meg felt Drago's gaze touch her face. "Is Mama's interference what prompted you to suggest we rethink our direction?"

She met his eyes and shook her head. "No. Hers was merely the clearest and most succinct statement of everything I was already grappling with." She paused, then added, "If anything, her summation helped me sort things out in my mind."

He tipped his head as if accepting that.

They'd reached the farthest edge of the large lawn. Wordlessly, they circled and started back.

Unheralded, Drago sighed. He looked ahead. "I have a confession to make."

She blinked at him. "Only one?"

He laughed, then conceded the point with a tip of his head. "As pertains to this, only one." He met her gaze, and his expression sobered. "There's a specific reason I was suddenly set on finding a bride."

Puzzled, she studied his face. "Something more than advancing age?"

"Actually, advancing age does have something to do with it." Having taken the plunge, he laid out the terms of his father's will.

Unsurprisingly, Meg listened intently, then equally unsurprisingly, frowned. "So if, after all, we decide we don't suit and dissolve our engagement in early June, you'll have to very quickly look about you for another suitable candidate."

His lips tightened, but he had to admit, "Yes. But you don't need to worry about that—not if it comes to us deciding to break things off after all." He suddenly had a horrible thought and hurried to say, "Promise me that you won't allow my need of a suitable bride to sway you when it comes time to make our final decision." He met her gaze and, with all the authority he could muster, stated, "When you make up your mind to marry me, I don't want you putting my impending need of a bride on the scales."

Meg studied his face, his eyes. She was starting to be able to tell when he was wearing no mask, and he wasn't at that moment. He was entirely sincere in issuing that last, distinctly ducal command—definitely an honorable one when all was said and done.

When he continued to wait as if for her agreement, she inclined her head. "Very well," she conceded and looked ahead.

They continued strolling toward the gate.

A minute later, she asked, "Could Hubert know about your father's will?" She met Drago's eyes. "Could knowledge of the situation you would face were we not to marry be behind his resistance to Joshua's suit?"

"I was pondering that, but I can't see how he might know. As you can imagine, I've kept that fact a closely guarded secret."

She thought, then huffed. "If that stipulation had become widely known, you would have been fighting off the matchmakers from the moment the will was read."

"Exactly. When I asked Aunt Edith for her help, I swore her to silence on that point, and she's not one to break her word. So I can't imagine how Hubert would have learned of it, nor can I guess why he's interfering in Alison and Joshua's lives."

Meg—and she suspected Drago, too—was still pondering that mystery as they reached the York Gate and passed through. On the pavement, they turned right and were strolling toward where Drago's carriage waited, with his tiger straightening from his slouch against the park rails, when a sudden pained yelp had her and Drago whirling around.

A half-grown, golden-pelted puppy shot out into the street.

Directly into the path of a phaeton-and-four being driven smartly along the paved road.

"No!" Without thought, Meg dashed after the pup. "Look out!"

Drago's heart leapt into his mouth. For an instant, time slowed, and he saw with absolute clarity what was about to occur.

He raced after Meg.

He reached her just as she crouched and scooped the now-cowering pup into her arms. He wrapped his arms around her, puppy and all, and knowing that the driver would haul hard on the reins and instinctively swing the high-stepping chestnuts the other way, he lifted Meg and pivoted sharply so that she was closer to the pavement and protected by his body as the off-side horse's shoulder rammed into his back. He was jolted forward, but he'd braced against the blow and didn't go flying.

Pandemonium ensued. The near-side leader attempted to rear, and the curricle's driver cursed as he frantically tried to manage his panicking horses.

Men ran from all around to help.

Drago's heart was still pounding. He took another step toward the pavement, out of the immediate melee, then ducked his head and looked into Meg's white face. "Are you all right?"

Sky-blue eyes huge, apparently mute with shock, she nodded.

The horses were still restless, shifting and stamping, but more or less under control. A crowd had gathered and were staring and exclaiming, but the danger was past.

"Good God, Wylde! Is that you?"

Drago looked over his shoulder to see Carmichael-Craik sitting on the phaeton's elevated box seat and staring down at him, utterly incredulous. "Daniel," Drago replied. "My apologies. That was...entirely unexpected."

Carmichael-Craik goggled at him.

Imperturbably, Drago rolled on, "I have to confess that, all in all, I'm rather glad it was you behind the reins." He tipped his head toward the four powerful horses. "Not many men would have been strong enough to hold them."

"Yes, well..." Carmichael-Craik, who was well aware of the quality of horses Drago drove, plainly didn't know whether to preen or give in to his justifiable anger.

Before anger bubbled up again, Drago adjusted his arms about Meg and turned so that, with one arm at her waist, steadying her, they were facing the phaeton side by side. "I don't believe you've yet met my fiancée —my duchess-to-be, Miss Cynster."

The name had Carmichael-Craik blinking.

Confirming that while Meg might not like horses, she knew she'd committed something of a sin, she raised a contrite face to Carmichael-Craik. "I'm so very sorry, sir. I would never normally have chanced injuring your superb team, but..." She glanced down at the soft, squirming bundle of golden puppy who was doing his best to bury his muzzle beneath her arm, then looked up at Carmichael-Craik. "I simply couldn't let him be trampled under your horses' hooves. That would have been...dreadful."

Carmichael-Craik stared at her, then cleared his throat. "Indeed, Miss Cynster. Absolutely ghastly." His strangled tone left Drago in no doubt that Carmichael-Craik was envisaging what would have happened had his horses trampled Miss Cynster, fiancée of the Duke of Wylde.

Carmichael-Craik swallowed and shifted his gaze to Drago. "Let's say no more about it."

Drago smiled and shifted to hold up his hand, and Carmichael-Craik bent to take it.

"Thank you, Daniel," Drago said. "Your understanding is appreciated. No doubt we'll see you around town."

With that, Drago urged Meg onto the pavement, and Carmichael-Craik saluted them with his whip, then shook his reins and set his team slowly walking along.

Drago would have felt more sympathy for the man, but inside, he was still reeling. He stuffed his roiling emotions deep and focused on Meg.

She was trying to coax the puppy to pull his nose out from beneath her arm.

Drago noted the small body was still shivering. "He probably won't lift his head and look around until he feels safe again."

Meg raised her head and scanned the pavement. "Can you see his owner?"

Drago searched to both right and left, then shook his head. "There doesn't seem to be anyone interested in claiming him." He looked at the pup, then bent and sniffed. Straightening, he confirmed, "He smells like a gutter. I doubt he's anyone's pampered pet."

"Or if he is, he's well and truly lost."

"Hmm. So what do you want to do with him?" He already knew the answer.

Sure enough, she instantly replied, "Take him home, of course." She looked at Drago. "I didn't save him from certain death to throw him back on the streets."

He suppressed a wry smile. "Of course not." He tightened his arm about her and turned her toward his curricle. "Come on, then. I'd better take you both home."

He helped her, still cradling the puppy, into his curricle. The dog consented to settle in her lap, but burrowed his muzzle under her gloved hand.

Drago reassured his tiger, Milton, that he'd done the right thing in remaining with the grays rather than rushing to help with Carmichael-Craik's horses. After reclaiming the reins and waiting for Milton to swing up behind, Drago shook the ribbons and started back to Half Moon Street.

Halfway there, Meg looked up from the puppy, a frown in her eyes. "I've just realized. Mama's old retriever is at home, and she doesn't like other dogs." Sadly, she looked down at the golden bundle. "I'm fairly certain she won't appreciate a puppy, either, and she has been known to be vicious."

Drago sighed and looked down at the pup. "I suppose I can take him.

I've left my dogs at the Court, and as we're fixed in town until June, he'll have time to grow a trifle before meeting them."

"Thank you!" She looked up, and seeing her face aglow with happiness was worth every complaint he knew would be coming his way. A dog was one thing, a half-grown pup quite another.

Then she frowned. "Your staff…"

"Are very well trained when it comes to dogs." They were also very well paid, which helped.

"Excellent." She poked the pup with a finger. "I hope you know how to behave."

So did Drago.

When they reached Half Moon Street, the only way they could part the pup from Meg was to have Milton tuck it inside his coat. After walking Meg to the door and seeing her inside, Drago returned to the curricle, took up the reins, and with Milton sitting beside him, finally turned his horses' heads for home.

Drago noticed that the puppy's nose was poking out of the enveloping jacket, dark eyes trained on him. Dogs always knew who the dog lovers were.

Returning his gaze to his horses, rather than dwell on the horrific moment outside the park gate and the revelation—the epiphany—the incident had visited on him, he let his mind retread the discussions of the afternoon, drawing unexpected and considerable comfort from the revised agreement he and Meg had reached. He found it reassuring that she had been as willing as he to recast their engagement; nevertheless, he couldn't be certain that their new direction would, in fact, culminate in them facing an altar. He hadn't wooed her or made any of the courting gestures ladies were said to expect.

What if she decided that, after all, marrying him was not to her taste?

He'd set out for Melwin Place to cold-bloodedly offer for Alison Melwin and wound up with Meg Cynster in his arms.

Even now, he wasn't sure if that was a stroke of luck or a disaster poised to slay him.

CHAPTER 8

*T*hat evening, as Drago climbed the stairs of Entwhistle House with Meg on his arm and her mother on Meg's other side, he was still fighting to suppress the lingering reactions that had assailed him in that heart-stopping moment outside Regent's Park.

He understood from where the intensity of his reaction sprang. His inner self had decided that, as his meant-to-be duchess, Meg was already his. His to hold, ergo, his to protect.

Like it or not, convenient or not, that was not an outcome he could alter or ignore.

And if his recollections of how his father had invariably reacted on the few occasions Drago could recall of his mother being in even the most remote danger or subject to the most distant potential threat were correct, then it seemed he was well on his way to being just like his father in that respect as well.

He knew his parents' relationship had been one of deep, unwavering, mutual love. Not affection—nothing so tame. They had each been the light of the other's life, and now his father was gone, his mother held a kernel of emptiness in her heart that Drago accepted nothing could fill.

If that was his fate...

Meg pinched his arm to draw his attention as they stepped forward to greet their hostess. Predictably, Lady Entwhistle was delighted to welcome them and seized the moment to commend them on their sound sense in getting engaged to each other.

The niceties dealt with, they deposited Meg's mother with the other older matrons, pausing to withstand the usual observations and comments from the grandes dames, then with Meg's hand on his arm, he and she moved into the crowd.

Among the first to claim their attention were his sisters, with his brothers-in-law in tow. The six of them formed a comfortable group, with his sisters answering Meg's questions about Wylde Court while his brothers-in-law grasped the chance to sound him out regarding his likely attitude to several upcoming bills.

Just how relaxed Drago and Meg were with the other two couples—how patently as one with them they were—again underscored that their union was, indeed, not just desirable but meant to be.

When the group eventually broke up, each couple going their separate ways, he and Meg did as expected and circulated through the milling throng, then the musicians started playing, and they gratefully escaped onto the dance floor.

Meg enjoyed three waltzes with Drago, interspersed with chatting with others, all of whom were increasingly curious as to when their engagement ball would be held. When the musicians retired, to distract herself from the far-too-pleasurable spiking of her senses—apparently inevitable when whirling in Drago's arms—Meg set herself to determinedly explore the social power that would accrue to her if she became the Duchess of Wylde.

Immediate access to and inclusion in the more powerful circles of young matrons was one obvious advantage.

"We have an active group of politically connected younger matrons who meet every week while Parliament is sitting," her cousin Therese informed her. "Tory or Whig or Liberal—unlike our husbands, we don't shut our ears to the other side's notions. We discuss everything freely. It's really a most useful way to debate and, ultimately, to have our opinions heard. Once you're wed and we all return for the Autumn Session, you'll have to come along."

Melanie had mentioned other groups who came together to pursue various issues from charities to agitating for safer traffic through London's crowded streets.

In short, the possibilities seemed endless.

A noble title and real wealth remained a passport to influence over a broad spectrum of human endeavor.

As they moved away from two young matrons who had urged her—after her wedding—to join their efforts to raise awareness of stray cats and dogs in the capital, Drago murmured, "Speaking of stray dogs, one in particular, have you given any thought as to what name you wish to bestow on your rescue?"

Meg halted and swung to face him. "I meant to ask—how is he?"

Drago arched his brows. "As I haven't been informed otherwise, I assume he's well. Most likely eating his head off in the kitchen." He smiled. "Cook always complains when I bring the dogs to town, but she's always disappointed when I leave them in the country." His expression sobered. "However, I have been informed—by Prentiss, no less—that every beast requires a name." His laughing eyes betrayed the severity of his expression. "So what is the mongrel's name to be?"

"Ridley," she promptly replied. At Drago's inquiring look, she added, "He was such a wriggly little thing, but Wriggly sounds far too nursery like."

He smiled charmingly, and her heart warmed and softened. "Ridley it is, then. No doubt, Prentiss and Maurice will approve."

They turned to go on and, in the crowd, came upon Drago's uncle.

"Warley." Drago looked surprised. "A ton ballroom is hardly your usual haunt."

Warley bent over the hand Meg held out to him, then straightened and fixed Drago with a wary eye. "Take it from me, my boy. The past always catches up to one. I made the mistake of getting to know Hermione Entwhistle far too well in my feckless youth, and look where it's landed me!" He cast a glance at the guests around them and shuddered. "Not my sort of thing at all, but Hermione isn't one I care to cross."

"Uncle!" Drago fought to keep his lips straight. "You shock me."

Warley waved. "Nonsense. You'll learn the way of it soon enough." He half bowed to Meg. "But you must excuse me. If I stand still too long, the vultures descend." He glanced at Drago. "It's almost as if, because you've bitten the bullet, they think *I* will suddenly be overcome with a desire to trip into parson's mousetrap, too!"

Shaking his head in disbelief, Warley lumbered on through the crowd.

Drago met Meg's eyes, and they both burst out laughing.

After they sobered and started ambling again, Drago, curious enough to watch Warley over the sea of heads, murmured, "Much as we might laugh, I can see several widows tracking Warley."

"Ah." Meg nodded sagely. "I suspect that's why Hermione Entwhistle pulled whatever string she has to have Warley attend. There are several widows in her set who have recently come out of mourning."

Drago grinned. "My money's on Warley to evade them all. He has, after all, been doing that successfully for decades."

Soon after, they met Denton, who was also looking a trifle hunted. In response to Drago's questioning look, Denton assured Drago and Meg, too, "I've just dropped in to keep Mama happy. I'm only staying for half an hour."

"I see." Laughing, Meg engaged Denton in a discussion of how he currently spent his days.

Drago watched with both approval and appreciation; if Meg were to become his duchess, she would need to get to know Denton better, and her questioning was of the ilk that his brother didn't truly notice that he was, albeit subtly, being interrogated.

By the time they parted from Denton, Drago suspected that Meg now knew more than his mother did about Denton's current life. His brother had been more relaxed with Meg, presumably through having moved in similar circles in their youth.

For her part, Meg was relieved that both Warley and Denton seemed entirely untroubled by the prospect of her becoming Drago's duchess. Indeed, Denton had been encouraging, more so than she'd hoped.

They continued to stroll and chat. At one point, when she was engaged by several unmarried ladies of her own age and Drago had turned to speak with a gentleman acquaintance, from the corner of her eye, she saw Warley sidle up to Drago and mention something, rather surreptitiously. From Drago's expression, she couldn't guess what manner of comment Warley had made, but after Drago gave a small nod, his uncle vanished into the crowd, and Drago turned to rejoin her.

She farewelled the ladies, and together, she and Drago moved on.

They'd gone barely a yard through the dense crowd when George Bisley and Harry Ferndale stepped into their path, with Thomas Hayden hovering behind.

"What a crush!" Harry exclaimed.

"At least it gives us some cover." George grasped Meg's proffered hand and bowed over it.

When it came their turn, Harry and Thomas did the same.

"We guessed you'd be here," George said. "Thought you might like some support."

Meg smiled, and Drago, in apparent seriousness, thanked them sincerely.

"Yes, well." Like George, Harry kept glancing nervously around. "You are the first of us to fall, so to speak. Seemed like the right thing to do."

"Even if," Thomas added, "it makes us as nervous as skittish horses."

Meg laughed. "Perhaps if we talk earnestly, you'll remain unmolested."

"We can try," George said. "Who knows? That might work, at least for a little while."

Entirely willing, Meg asked how they had all met and by dint of successive questions teased a recounting of their earlier lives from them. Her questions jogged their memories, and soon the four were exchanging reminiscences—which didn't always match—of incidents at Eton and Oxford and, even more entertaining, of when they had been on shared holidays at Wylde Court or at the estate of Harry's uncle, the Marquess of Tavistock, or at George's home in Leicestershire.

Meg noted that they didn't mention sharing holidays at Thomas's home, but recalling Drago's comment about Thomas's father's impecunious bent, she thought better of asking if they ever had.

Indeed, while in response to her questions, George and Harry opened their budgets without reservation, she met with far less success in inducing Thomas to share much of his thoughts.

Then the musicians started up again, and George, Harry, and Thomas took fright at the prospect of Meg and Drago taking to the floor and leaving the three of them exposed. All three stated their intention of leaving and made their farewells, then quickly tacked away through the crowd.

Smiling, Meg allowed Drago to lead her to the clearing floor and draw her into his arms. As they started whirling in practiced fashion, smiling at the now-familiar sensation of floating on air, Meg realized that both George and Harry had, indeed, been openly encouraging regarding her and Drago marrying, while Thomas...hadn't been. He hadn't been discouraging, either, or not openly so, but his expression, like Drago's, was difficult to read. She'd got the impression that Thomas had been standing back, watching, as if waiting to see how she and Drago got along.

Given Thomas's background—or his background as she assumed it might be—perhaps he was understandably more cautious over encouraging their match.

Of course, as far as the three knew...

She refocused on Drago, who, smiling slightly, was staring into her face. "Have you told Harry, George, and Thomas that we've changed our tack?"

Drago met her eyes and shook his head. "Not yet, but you've already won over George and Harry. They've all but told me that I should marry you. Thomas, admittedly, is rather more reserved, but that's just Thomas."

"Ah. I see." Meg smiled more widely. "So even your friends can see the benefits of us turning what began as a necessary charade into our reality."

Drago smiled, too, stepped out, and swept her into a vigorous turn. "Apparently so. Even they. Along with the rest of the ton."

* * *

THE FOLLOWING days and nights passed in a blur of must-attend parties, balls, dinners, and soirées.

On Monday evening, Drago dined quietly with Meg's family at Half Moon Street, a relaxing meal in preparation for the next event on their schedule.

At nine o'clock, the Alverton carriage drew up outside the door, and Drago and Meg joined Therese and Devlin for the short journey to Cambridge House for Lady Palmerston's soirée. As her ladyship had promised, Drago and Meg had received invitations, and Therese and Alverton had likewise been summoned. "And no one refuses Emily," Therese declared. "Aside from all else, she is really such a dear that no one ever wants to dim her happiness."

Although to date his acquaintance with her ladyship was slight, Drago could appreciate the truth of that statement.

"Really," Therese said as they rocked down the well-lit street, "given his past, Palmerston is an incredibly lucky man to have won such an admirable and devoted lady to his side. Politically and socially, she's his best asset."

"And he knows it," Alverton drawled.

"What do you mean about his past?" Meg hadn't really kept up with politics, assuming she would never have to know anything beyond the general facts. Given she and Drago were about to walk into what amounted to the dragon's lair, she needed to make shift to update her knowledge.

Through the dimness within the carriage, Therese blinked at her. "Well, in his earlier years, Palmerston was nothing less than a gazetted rake, and long ago, when Emily was Lady Cowper, she and Palmerston had an affair. On Palmerston's side, one of innumerable liaisons, but even then, most who knew them acknowledged that there was a special link between them, and there was no doubt that she held a palm for him, and he, one for her. When Cowper died, they married and have become the very epitome of a devoted married couple."

Resisting the urge to glance at Drago, Meg arched her brows. "So Palmerston is a flesh-and-blood example of a reformed rake."

"Indeed. That's not to say he doesn't still possess an appreciative eye, but these days, he simply isn't inclined to do more than approve. Of course, no one denies that in marrying him, Emily came into her own. She's found her true place as his wife, a role in which she can and does use her innate talents to the full."

Devlin hummed in agreement. "They've created a formidable partnership. Palmerston brings the greater and wider knowledge and a razor-sharp intellect to their relationship, and in balancing that, Emily has a surfeit of all the softer qualities."

Therese nodded. "You know her well enough to be aware of those, and I assure you they are not merely skin deep. She's a rock of common sense and native shrewdness, colored by delicate sensibilities, and of course, her beauty has always stood her in good stead."

While Meg nodded in understanding, Drago drank in the information. Courtesy of avoiding what might be termed the central establishment of the ton over the past decade, he was having to learn on his feet. As the carriage rocked around the corner into Piccadilly, he looked at Alverton. "Is there any particular topic that's likely to be the focus of attention tonight?"

"Other than the Crimea?"

Drago huffed. "Even I've heard about the war, but I imagine there are particular perspectives and views that might be discussed."

Alverton nodded, and during the few minutes while the carriage turned in to the forecourt of Cambridge House and inched its way to the front steps, he outlined the current thrust of the government, concluding with, "Palmerston is bringing his considerable weight to bear in an attempt to get the execution of the war, as he terms it, 'back on track.' By that, he means focused on the critical aspect of protecting British trade and, more generally, our trading routes."

"You have to remember"—Therese was peering out of the window at those alighting ahead of them—"that Pam was Foreign Secretary for years and then Home Secretary under Aberdeen. His understanding of the importance of our exports to the Ottomans is second to none, and he's vocal about the necessity of preventing the Empire falling into Russian hands."

The carriage halted, bringing Drago and Meg's impromptu lesson on the current state of politics to an end. Drago and Alverton alighted and gave their ladies their hands, then walked beside them up the steps and into the well-lit foyer.

The foyer and the salons opening from it were a hive of activity. A cacophony of voices and a miasma of perfumes and pomades, rising in the warmth generated within the crowded rooms, engulfed them. Looking over the heads, all Drago could see were groups of gentlemen, most groups including a smaller number of ladies, talking earnestly. Wine flowed freely, ferried about by liveried footmen, but everyone's attention was focused on whichever discussion had currently claimed them. Despite the clamor, there was no idle chatter going on.

He spotted Lady Palmerston holding court at the foot of the stairs and, with a nod, directed Alverton and Therese that way. With Meg's arm twined with Drago's, he and she followed.

After greeting Therese and Alverton, Lady Palmerston waved the couple to the salon on the left of the foyer. "Lansdowne most especially wished to speak with you both."

As Therese and Alverton dutifully headed off, her ladyship turned her smile on Drago and Meg. "Your Grace. Miss Cynster! I'm delighted you could join us."

Drago bowed over her ladyship's hand, and Meg dipped in a regulation curtsy.

As they straightened, her ladyship beamed benevolently upon them. "I truly am thrilled to see you here, my dears. In welcoming young couples such as yourselves to our circle, I always feel as if I'm doing my part to guide the country into the future, to ensure there will be safe hands on the reins, so to speak."

Along with Drago, Meg murmured an appropriate response and suppressed the urge to glance at him. It seemed likely that yet more expectations were about to be heaped on their heads.

Sure enough, her ladyship literally took them under her wing. She delegated her place at the foot of the stairs to her arch-bosom-bow, Lady Elliot, and drew Drago and Meg into the crowd.

They spent the next hour being steered from group to group, being introduced to others, learning of those who mattered most and those who might do so in the future, and also being exposed to various concerns and arguments currently before Parliament, especially those bills passing through the Lords.

"We could do with your vote," Earl Granville, the government leader in the House of Lords, informed Drago. "We have the numbers at present, but more always helps to make our point, don't you know."

Throughout, Lady Palmerston—"Emily" as she insisted they call her—proved a font of knowledge. Soon, she and Meg were trading familial connections and links and insights into attitudes espoused by various older families. Some of those whom Drago and Meg met, they already knew—like the Earl of Meredith and Drake and Louisa—but others were known to them only by name and reputation.

At one point, Emily looked at Meg with approval. "My dear, you know more than I do about your generation. Louisa is amazing, of course, but while your circles will certainly overlap, I suspect you will have knowledge in areas neither Louisa nor I nor any of our other peers have." She patted Meg's wrist with a certain satisfaction. "You'll be a valuable addition to our cause."

There was no question in Drago's or—he felt sure—Meg's mind over what that cause was. Firstly, that of her husband, Palmerston, secondly that of his Whig government, and thirdly, the country, although the order in any given circumstances would doubtless vary.

Finally, Emily consigned them to their own devices and left to swoop down on some other couple she wished to encourage.

Drago seized the moment to pause by the side of the room and look out over the gathering.

Halting beside him, Meg blew out a breath. "I feel as if my brain is about to explode! So many facts crammed into it in such a short time." She met Drago's eyes, but there was a smile in hers and a satisfied glow in her expression.

"It's certainly been an education. Some I knew, most I didn't." He studied what he could read in her face, then glanced at the still-dense crowd. "Certainly, I had no idea that this"—he gestured to the people before them, the groups all earnestly discussing important aspects of government—"was waiting for us."

Well, for him, at least.

She nodded. "It's been eye-opening."

He had to ask. "Off-putting?"

She met his gaze and transparently considered the point, then smiled, shook her head, and glanced back at the crowd. "Actually, I find it…fascinating. Enthralling and even exhilarating. I now understand Drake and Louisa's and Therese and Alverton's frequent distraction, not to say absorption, with political circles. It's a never-quite-spelt-out responsibility of nobility. Some might choose not to contribute, but the responsibility remains nonetheless."

"Indeed," Drago murmured. "Most of those here were born to the purple at some level, whether peers themselves—like me—or from secondary branches of noble families, like you. Historically and to this time, we collectively are those most accustomed to wielding power. And as Emily said, we are the ones being actively groomed to manage the reins into the future."

She met his eyes, her expression serious. "It's a challenge, isn't it? One that comes with the title and position, but the chance to make a difference…" She tipped her head. "That's attractive, alluring. Or at least I find it so." She studied his expression. "You?"

He held her gaze and softly smiled. "I wouldn't have imagined so, but yes." He nodded. "I do." His gaze went to the crowd. "As my mother would tell you, I've always been most surely motivated by a challenge, and this is certainly one that has the power to engage me."

"Right, then." She retook his arm and faced the shifting throng in the salon. "In this—in entering this arena and making it ours—we're agreed. That being so, I suggest we make the most of this opportunity." She flicked him a challenging glance. "One is new to a circle only once, so let's not waste our chance to presume and make mistakes."

He laughed and willingly went with her, once more into the fray.

* * *

THEIR ENGAGEMENT BALL—ORGANIZED by their mothers—was only two nights away. Consequently, when, in the middle of the afternoon following the Cambridge House event, Drago called at Meg's home to be informed that she was visiting her modiste in Bruton Street, he accepted the news with equanimity, hailed a hackney, and instructed the driver to take him to the fashionable precinct.

He had the jarvey drop him off at the corner of Bond and Bruton Streets. After sliding his hands into his greatcoat pockets, he ambled down the pavement lined with the discreet windows of modistes and milliners catering to the haut ton.

He wasn't a stranger to the area and, having asked Meg's parents' butler for the name of the modiste she favored, he strolled confidently toward that establishment. He was two shops away when the door opened, setting a bell tinkling, and Meg stepped out, closely followed by a maid of similar age.

"Meg!"

At his hail, she turned, and the smile that lit her face had him smiling besottedly in reply.

As he neared, she arched her brows and gave him her hand. "What are you doing here?"

He raised her hand to his lips and, holding her gaze, dropped an entirely chaste kiss on her knuckles. Then he tucked her hand into his arm and turned her to stroll Mayfair-ward. "I came looking for you." He quickly cast about for a reason and remembered his prepared excuse. "I wondered if you had any further insights to share on our adventures last night. I called at Half Moon Street, and the butler told me you were here." He caught her gaze and raised his brows. "Your gown for the engagement ball?"

She smiled and nodded. "A final fitting."

After glancing back and confirming that her maid was dutifully following two paces behind, Meg faced forward and chuckled. Tipping her head toward his shoulder, she confided, "You have no idea how much excitement arranging every facet of our engagement ball has given my mother and yours. These days, every time I come home, it seems that there's some new idea they've decided on."

"Just as long as they've organized the musicians and instructed them to play plenty of waltzes."

"I've been assured that's the case, although I should also mention that our propensity to spend as much time as possible on the dance floor has been noted and not with unlimited approval."

"Ah, well." He was walking protectively by the curb as they passed a row of shops. "Just as long—" Movement beside Meg caught his eye. His heart seized. "Watch out!"

He shoved her back toward her maid, causing the burly man, who had turned from a window with a knife glinting in his hand, to pull up, cheated of his prey.

Drago shot a fist at the man's face, but the villain was already moving away, and the blow only grazed his head as he turned and fled along the street.

Drago teetered, literally torn between racing after the man and ensuring Meg remained safe. He couldn't do both.

The man ducked into an alley just ahead.

Drago exhaled, drew in a deeper breath, and turned toward Meg, just in time to catch her as she flung herself at him.

"Are you all right?" She patted his arms and chest. "He didn't stab you?"

He caught her hands. "No." He frowned faintly. "It was you he was going to attack."

She frowned more definitely back. "Why do you think that? I thought he was about to push past me and have at you."

Puzzled, he shook his head. "Why would anyone want to attack me?"

Patently exasperated, she widened her eyes at him. "Why would anyone want to stab me?"

They stared at each other for several heartbeats, then he offered, "There don't appear to be obvious answers to either of those questions."

"No." Meg blew out a breath, glanced around, then linked her arm with Drago's, and together, they walked on. Her heart was still uncomfortably lodged at the base of her throat, and her pulse had yet to return to normal.

She kept telling herself that everything was as fine as it had been five minutes before. Drago was unharmed, and she was, too.

Luckily, it was midafternoon, and although the street wasn't deserted, that time of day was not one favored by the ladies of the haut ton for visits to their modistes. Other than a few curious looks, the incident hadn't attracted much notice.

They strolled on, and after some thought, she offered, "Perhaps he was after my reticule." She glanced down at the beaded purse dangling from her wrist by its braided cords. "It was on the side closest to him. He might have intended to slice the cord with his knife."

Drago grunted, but after a moment, conceded, "I suppose that's possible."

His tone stated he didn't think it likely.

She wasn't sure she did, either, but at the same time, she couldn't imagine what else might have been the motive behind the incident.

The weather was fine, and they could easily have strolled home in the mild sunshine, but on reaching Berkeley Square, she wasn't surprised when Drago hailed a hackney. He handed her into the cab, then helped Rosie climb up to share the jarvey's bench seat.

After giving the jarvey their direction, Drago joined Meg in the cab. As the carriage started rolling, he reached for her hand, closed his around it, and gently squeezed. Looking ahead, he said, "I really don't like you being in danger."

An understatement. Memories of the road outside Regent's Park scrolled through his mind while the associated emotions roiled in his gut, all too vividly reconjured.

Meg turned her hand in his and lightly squeezed in return. "Trust me, I don't like being in dangerous situations, either. Especially ones unforeseen and unforeseeable."

He felt her gaze on his face and understood the point she was making.

Accidents. Both incidents had simply been that. Happenings beyond their control.

He tipped his head in acknowledgment. "Indeed."

Inwardly, he comforted himself with the knowledge that their engagement ball—the occasion on which their intention to marry would be formally acknowledged by their world—was only two nights away.

After that, he could be very much more protective without anyone thinking it odd.

CHAPTER 9

To Drago's surprise, the formal dinner that preceded his and Meg's engagement ball, both events hosted by the Duke and Duchess of St. Ives in their Grosvenor Square mansion, wasn't the ordeal he'd anticipated. Primarily because Meg remained by his side throughout, and she was quick to step in whenever he found himself out of his depth in dealing with her Cynster relatives and connections.

He'd thought the Helmsford family large—and by ton standards, it was—but the Cynster clan, as they accurately labeled themselves, was something else again.

But combining the two families, as was achieved about the massively long dining table, was a feat that generated nothing but goodwill and honest enjoyment. Without exception, everyone on both sides was delighted with the proposed alliance and was happy to say so and, more importantly, to show it.

From the first moment—when Drago and his brother, accompanied by Warley, had escorted his mother into the black-and-white-tiled foyer to greet the duke and duchess—all had rolled smoothly along.

Meg reveled in the moments, more than anything else because within the august surrounds of St. Ives House, she didn't need to constantly worry about some knife-wielding man leaping out of the shadows at Drago. There, surrounded by family and loyal staff, she could relax.

Over the past days, she'd relived those fraught moments in Bond Street again and again and was increasingly certain the man's target must have been Drago. She couldn't imagine why anyone would try to harm her, and surely if the man had intended her harm, he wouldn't have come at her while Drago was walking beside her.

No, that she was the man's intended victim made no sense at all. Ergo, he'd been after Drago.

After tonight—after this event that marked their prospective relationship being recognized and accepted by their world—she intended to use her bolstered position to probe further as to who might wish Drago ill.

A cuckolded husband? One had to imagine that might be a possibility.

But she didn't as yet feel she had sufficient standing to badger Drago for information—not yet. And tonight, she didn't have to worry for his safety, so she could relax and enjoy the moment, and she devoted herself to doing just that.

Regardless of whether she eventually married Drago or not—she quashed a sharp pang at the mere thought of "not"—this would be her one and only engagement ball, and she intended to enjoy it to the full.

Appropriate toasts were drunk and wishes for their happiness resonated throughout the long room.

The food was delicious, and the wine flowed freely. The back-and-forth conversation about the table was rapid-fire, consistently good-natured, and often hilarious. Her familial peers were in excellent form, and the comments, observations, retorts, and ripostes came thick and fast.

Laughter was the prevailing sound, with excited chatter a hum overlaying the background *clink* of cutlery on fine porcelain and the occasional *ting* of crystal glasses being tapped.

Eventually, however, after the final course had been consumed, his mother and hers rose and came to drag—accompany—Meg and Drago upstairs to the ballroom, to stand at the head of the reception line for the guests who had started arriving for the ball.

Meg exchanged a quick, feeling look with Drago, but with nothing more than a faintly challenging lift to his dark brows, he rose and pulled out her chair, and together—to the raucous cheers of her cousins and his —they meekly followed their parents from the room.

For the next hour, she stood beside Drago as they welcomed the better part of the haut ton to their event and accepted the congratulations, all surprisingly genuine, heaped upon them.

Finally, their mothers—smiling with approval—released them, just as the musicians struck up for the first waltz.

Drago's mother leaned close and whispered, "Your reward for behaving in such exemplary fashion. Trust me when I say that we"—with her gaze, she included Meg's mother, who was smiling delightedly—"appreciate it."

Laughing, Drago bowed to her and to Meg's mother, then took Meg's hand and, with his gaze capturing hers, gracefully led her to the floor, passing through a parting sea of guests to reach the clearing space.

There, he turned, and Meg went into his arms.

She'd previously thought waltzing with Drago akin to floating on air; tonight, he waltzed her onto a different plane, one on which only he and she existed.

They whirled, and she gazed into his eyes, unable to look away as the magic of the moment descended and wrapped about them, cocooning them in a net of heightened awareness and blatant, pulse-throbbing, sensual longing.

The sensation of his hand splayed across her back, the contact burning through the layers of fine silk, the physical power as he swirled them, step by masterful step, revolution by revolution, down the floor, all effortlessly snared and fixed her senses.

The guests watching were a blur of faces, a distant murmur of sound. Someone started clapping, then the applause spread throughout the room, the percussive beats almost as fast as her heartbeat.

She was enthralled—fascinated anew—by this man who, she was fast learning, had untold facets, all of which she longed to explore. She did not understand where that compulsion came from, from what it sprang; she only knew it was there, and at moments like this, when she was truly a physical captive in his arms, that need rose and thrummed very close to her surface, leaving her skin prickling with lascivious hunger and unsated desire.

Could he tell that he made her feel like that?

Trapped in his dark gaze, she didn't doubt it; from all she'd heard of him over the years—whispers shared among the cohort of unmarried young ladies—the man was a master seducer.

She would have been stunned to learn that, at that very moment, the master seducer was questioning, dazedly, who was seducing whom.

The feel of Meg—*his* Meg—in his arms was a potent invitation to sin.

He knew well enough that he had to resist the tug of that primal urge, yet her eyes—so wide, so very blue—inexorably drew him in. Into imagining a moment when it would be just the two of them, alone and free to explore...

All that he now so desperately wanted to uncover, catalog, and know.

To know and make his in the most primitive fashion, albeit cloaked in his usual charming veneer, disguised by his customary sophisticated expertise.

He knew who he was beneath the elegant outer coating, and it was that man who so powerfully lusted after her, the lady who was almost his.

Who would soon be his. He told himself that as he hauled hard on the reins of his always reckless libido. He would not risk any harm to her, would not permit even a whiff of scandal to touch her.

My perfect duchess.

By the time the musicians played the last chords, and he and she slowed, halted, and he bowed and she curtsied, he was entirely in control, with both halves of him—the reckless and the caring—intent on the same aim. At some point, others had joined them on the dance floor, giving them an easy way of finding their path back to the much-less-exciting reality of their engagement ball.

With Meg on his arm, he smiled charmingly and moved into the crowd, conversing with his usual ease while his libido, unsatisfied and disgruntled with it, slowly retreated deep inside him.

It took Meg two conversational exchanges before she felt that she'd finally caught her breath and realigned her wits and senses with reality.

If he can do that with just a waltz, what will it be like...

She forced her mind away from such giddying speculation.

By Drago's side, she moved through their well-wishers, more or less as he directed. He could see over the heads, while to her, the crowd formed colorful walls on all sides, and she trusted him to find those they really should spend a little time with.

While in the receiving line, they'd greeted most of the guests, including Lord and Lady Melwin and Alison, accompanied by Joshua, with a disapproving Hubert trailing behind. Drago found Alison and Joshua in the crowd, and Meg and Drago spent a few minutes chatting, but with so many others all around, it wasn't the moment to inquire whether Hubert was still being difficult.

As Meg moved on with Drago, she leaned close and whispered, "At least Lord Melwin seemed comfortable with Joshua squiring Alison tonight, so presumably Hubert will eventually come around."

"Presumably," Drago agreed.

In between waltzes, in which they invariably indulged—given their surroundings and the impact those moments had on her senses and her wits, Meg wasn't sure such unfailing pandering to their desires was necessarily a good thing—among the shifting crowd, they joined groups of family and friends and spent a little time with each, cementing connections and deepening family ties.

Supper came and went in pleasant fashion; they spent it at a table with Pru and Deaglan, Claudette and Pemberthy, and Melanie and Forsythe.

Later in the evening, they came upon George Bisley, Harry Ferndale, and Thomas Hayden. All three looked rather nervous, almost furtively looking over their shoulders, but as they chatted with Drago and Meg and no matrons with young ladies in tow appeared to accost them, they relaxed and grew expansive.

"Have to say"—Harry glanced all around—"that everyone in both your families seems thrilled with the prospect of the connection." He slanted a faintly questioning look at Drago.

That look reminded Meg that these three had known of her and Drago's initial plan. She'd forgotten to confirm whether Drago had as yet informed the trio of their revised direction.

Drago's response to Harry's unvoiced question—a serenely assured "Indeed, they are"—gave her no clue either way.

Whether George knew of their altered intention or not, he seemed entirely supportive of their current tack. "Excellent outcome, seems to me. Everyone's happy, which is always a relief with big families. Even your aunt Edith seems content."

Reserved as usual, Thomas had been studying Meg and Drago. "Still… there are other considerations, I expect."

Meg wasn't sure what Thomas meant by that, but Drago merely smiled and, seeming to wave the comment aside, raised the prospect of shooting parties at Wylde Court in the autumn.

Music intervened, along with partners for all three unattached gentlemen, confident young ladies who approached them and all but demanded their attendance in the waltz about to start.

Swallowing laughter, hand in hand, Drago and Meg slipped away and onto the dance floor.

Remembering her earlier question, before the revolutions of the dance and the associated distractions could claim her wits, looking into Drago's face, she asked, "Have you told George, Harry, and Thomas of our revised plan?"

Drago blinked. He clearly thought back—it had been nearly a week since their walk in Regent's Park—then refocused on her. "Actually, no. The opportunity hasn't presented itself."

Given he'd been spending so much time with her combined with the subjects gentlemen of their ilk usually discussed, she wasn't all that surprised.

Drago smiled and whirled her around the end of the floor. When they straightened, still smiling, he observed, "Regardless, it's fairly clear they approve of the notion."

"George and Harry, yes, but what about Thomas? I find him hard to read."

"He's always reserved and…let's say cautious." Drago grinned. "It won't surprise you to learn that of the four of us, he's perennially the most careful."

"The least reckless. I can well believe that."

On that note—as Drago whirled her up the center of the room in a succession of rapid turns that drew envious gasps from some of the younger ladies looking on—she let slide the matter of what he chose to tell his friends.

The crowd was thinning when they came upon a group that included her sister and several married cousins and their spouses.

Meg found herself chatting to the spouses, who were genuinely interested in how she'd found her first foray into political circles.

Meanwhile, Drago was surrounded by her sister and female cousins. Meg should have been on guard, but when she overheard Pru, Therese, and Louisa telling Drago about the old adage that Cynsters only married for love, it was too late to step in and change the subject. Instead, she had to continue pretending to listen to Devlin's and Drake's wise words about how best to deal with some of the other political hostesses who would doubtless soon summon her and Drago to their events—"Where Emily Temple leads, the others will be quick to follow" —while Pru and Louisa teased Drago about the need for him to live up to the Cynster ideal were he to be successful in ushering Meg to the altar.

Damn them!

She understood why the trio had enlightened Drago. All three were shrewdly observant, especially when it came to people and relationships, and also highly protective of her, and presumably they'd sensed enough to move to ensure that Drago knew what was expected of him in becoming her husband. So yes, she appreciated their motive, but they'd just made her way forward much more complicated.

Drago, of course, responded with his usual unrufflable charm, without, in fact, commenting at all on what the trio had said.

Meg inwardly sighed and, masking any sign that she'd heard a word, turned to join Drago in engaging with Pru, Therese, and Louisa. There was no sense in trying to dismiss or contradict what they'd said, much less create a fuss over it, not in public. Meg smiled and chatted and, within a few minutes, succeeded in drawing Drago away.

The instant they were free of others, Drago dipped his head and looked into her face. "What is it?"

She studied his dark eyes; he appeared merely curious. She set her chin. "I think we should talk about our situation. I believe there's an issue we need to address."

His brows faintly rose, but he didn't argue as she drew him through the crowd. As they neared the far end of the room, the musicians help-fully started playing another waltz. Meg glanced swiftly around, but the guests had shifted their attention to the dance floor, quite possibly expecting to see her and Drago whirling around it.

Gripping his hand, she pressed a panel on the wall, and a hidden servant's door sprang open. She stepped through, and Drago followed and closed the door behind him. Sconces, alight, were spaced along the narrow corridor's wall. Meg drew Drago with her as she followed the corridor away from the ballroom, then she paused, opened another hidden door, and stepped out into one of the house's hallways.

She waited while Drago resecured the door—given the size and age of his Park Lane mansion, he was no doubt accustomed to such things—then she turned deeper into the house. "This way."

She led him to a small parlor that, prior to her marriage, Louisa had used. Meg was relieved to find it much as she remembered it. She went straight to the lamp on the sideboard and, once Drago had shut the door, turned the flame high, bathing the small room in a gentle golden glow.

Drago had halted inside the door. He studied her, then slowly walked closer. "What issue do we need to address?"

She stared into his face—that ridiculously handsome, often rather arrogant, but almost always impossible-to-accurately-read face. She couldn't think of anywhere else to start other than by admitting, "I heard Pru and the others telling you about what the males in the family refer to as 'the Cynster curse.'" Hurriedly, she clarified, "Marrying for love." She tipped up her chin. "I want you to know that I don't want any such consideration to..." She paused, groping for suitable words.

Drago studied her face and softly supplied, "Put me off?"

Her eyes flashed. "Yes! Exactly!" Her expression eased into one of reluctant acknowledgment. "I appreciate that, at least for Cynsters, the old adage is the most reliable guarantee of a happy marriage, but I've never heard it said that love has to come first. Initially." She met his gaze. "That it has to be there from the start."

Do you love me? The question all but filled Drago's mind. Carefully, he asked, "In light of this apparent Cynster requirement, can I ask what, at this moment, you feel for me?"

She blinked at him.

He watched as her gaze grew distant, and she plainly looked inward.

After several seconds, she refocused, and he sensed she was, again, grappling for words.

This time, he didn't help her out; he wanted to hear what she truly thought. He held his breath and waited.

Eventually, looking faintly disgruntled, she said, "I know I feel something for you, something unique—a connection, one that makes me anxious if you're in danger, one that draws me to you in various ways. I'm interested in you and what you think in a way I've never before been with any other gentleman. I'm engaged, enthralled, fascinated, and drawn to you, but I don't know what label to put on that." She tipped her head. "Is that love?" Her frown deepened. "I've never been in love before, so I have no yardstick against which to judge."

While that wasn't exactly the answer he'd hoped for, it was one that held out hope.

She'd been studying his face, searching his expression. Before he could distract her, she drew breath and stated, "So that's where I stand. What about you? How do you feel about me?"

When he didn't immediately reply, she added, "More to the point, if we go forward and marry, do you think—is it possible—that you might, at some point, come to love me?"

I'm already so deeply in love with you, there's no going back.

The words rang clearly in his head, but there was no way they could make it past his lips. Like all men of his ilk, admitting to love still ranked at the very top of the list of vulnerabilities no sane male ever owned to. It was simply not done.

However, looking into her face, into the soft sky-blue of her eyes, and reading all she allowed him to see, he accepted her question had to be answered. Somehow.

He, too, had never been in love before, but he knew damned well how it felt. How it affected him…

He caught and held her gaze. "You've described how you feel about me." He nodded slowly as realization burst upon him. "And that's exactly how I feel about you. You being in danger is a powerful and instant prod, galvanizing me into action. Into needing to protect you. That's not simply behaving as a gentleman"—*far from it*—"but a reaction that's driven by an imperative buried deep inside me. It's not something I can easily control." Best to own to that now, given the opportunity had presented itself. "And as for the rest, I, too, feel consumed by the need to know every little thing about you. About how you think about everything and anything."

Awareness—full understanding—of what he was saying glowed in her eyes. Impulse prompted, and he raised a hand and gently cradled her cheek. "As for being drawn to you..."

Slowly, drawing out the moment and the anticipation, he lowered his head, then swooped the last inch and pressed his lips to hers.

Hunger roared, and for the first time, he allowed it to seep into the exchange, and was gratified by the soft sound she made in her throat and the immediate response of her lips against his.

She parted the luscious curves and brazenly invited him in, and the taste of her captured him, utterly, indescribably, and he swept deep and gloried in the astounding sensation.

Gently, so as not to startle her, he drew her closer. Urged her nearer, and eagerly, she came.

She pressed into him, her breasts impinging, firm and warm, against the hard planes of his chest, her hips sinking against his long thighs, cradling his already rampant erection.

He sensed she noticed, but wasn't at all disturbed. Far from it. She seemed to purr low in her throat, then she pressed even closer.

Instinctively, his arms locked about her, and he angled his head and deepened the kiss.

Their tongues tangled and dueled, and sensation and longing and need and want wound together in a compelling incitement demanding oh so much more. Hungrily and greedily demanding satisfaction.

He was so consumed by the moment that his hand was gliding up toward her breast when a mental jab from his own self-interest jarred him and jolted his mind back into the ascendancy.

Into comprehending the reality of what he and she had, between them, wrought.

A situation that—as she'd plainly realized—needed to be carefully navigated.

Even more so now that love had been dealt into their equation.

Not that she seemed in any hurry to step back from the rapidly-approaching-conflagration kiss.

Seizing the reins he hadn't even noticed he'd let slither from his grasp, calling on the extensive expertise of his rakehell years, he eased—gently, carefully—back from the exchange.

When transparently reluctantly he raised his head, she stared up at him. "What's wrong?"

Gently, he grasped her shoulders and forced himself to step back, to create a gap of at least six inches between her alluring curves and his tense frame. He continued to gaze into her face; this time, it was he who was lost for words. He released her shoulders and lowered his hands. "I…" She'd had the courage to speak of love to him. So… Briefly, he closed his eyes. "This is going to sound so conceited, but"—he opened his eyes and looked into hers—"I know, and you know, too, that I could easily take this further. A lot further. Indeed, to the point where there would no longer be any question of whether we would marry or not."

Faint color rose in her cheeks, but mercifully, she didn't argue.

He felt his features set in grim lines and forced himself to go on. "While on the one hand, that would undoubtedly be extremely pleasant for us both, such an occurrence would only compound our problems regarding the issue we were discussing earlier." Love. When she simply stared, faintly uncomprehendingly, at him, he felt compelled to spell it out. "Yes, I want you to marry me, but I want you to choose me out of love and commitment, not because of lust." He paused, then added, "Cynsters aren't the only family who know the value of love."

She tipped her head, studying his face. "Your parents?"

"A love match that lasted until my father's death. And even then…"

"I see."

He wondered how much she truly saw, but being alone with her in such tempting surroundings was fraying his already much-tried reins; they needed to get back to the ball. He cleared his throat. "So to summarize. At this point, we're in agreement—we go forward and see what comes. You want—or at least would prefer to have—love as the foundation of our marriage, and I want or at least would prefer the same thing. Given that, I think it's reasonable to suppose that our married life will be all that we wish it to be. However, to allay all doubts as to our feelings, we'll give ourselves until June before making our final decision." He arched his brows at her. "Is that an accurate statement of where we stand?"

She nodded. "Yes. That's our situation and our agreed direction."

"Good." He felt as if they'd negotiated a major battlefield and emerged alive and unscathed. He reached for her hand. "I have no idea how long we've been absent from the ball, but I'm fairly certain we should get back."

"Indeed." Meg led the way, this time sticking to the hallways and principal corridors of the house. While her lips still throbbed and her skin prickled with unsated need, she was content with what their short interlude had revealed and, even more, with what it had achieved—a far clearer understanding of each other on both their parts.

She felt a great deal more reassured and confident as to where they were heading and what their shared future might hold.

They emerged from a minor corridor into the rear of the ballroom's foyer to find several couples departing, and in the general melee, she and Drago were able to tender their farewells as if they'd stepped out of the ballroom for that purpose.

Once those guests had left, they reentered the ballroom only to be met by more of those intent on departing. Good manners kept them by the open door, thanking guests for attending and sharing their big night.

"Good." Meg's mother materialized beside them and absentmindedly patted Drago's arm. "Your mother and I wondered where you had got to, but apparently, you've been ahead of us." With a nod of approval, she moved back along the lines of departing guests, joining Drago's mother as co-hostess in thanking everyone for their company.

Meg shared a look with Drago, then returned to shaking hands and exchanging farewells.

Apparently, several of her cousins and his had noticed their absence from the ballroom, but while there were several arch looks, knowing smiles, raised brows, and cheeky grins, no one made any reference to them disappearing.

Not, that was, until Thomas Hayden strolled up with George Bisley and Harry Ferndale. With a wide grin at Meg, Thomas jogged Drago's elbow. "Up to your usual tricks, I see."

Drago's expression, until then the epitome of charming geniality, instantly hardened to chiseled granite, and the look he turned on Thomas would have frozen the marrow in anyone's bones.

Meg all but goggled at the transformation; Drago looked positively dangerous.

George and Harry saw the change and both leapt in to seize Drago's and Meg's hands and effusively shake them and compliment them on the evening.

"Although I did have two close shaves," George reported.

"Consider yourself lucky," Harry retorted. "I had to worm my way out of three!"

Meg readily encouraged their nonsense and was relieved to sense the tension in the large body beside hers slowly ease.

"My apologies," she heard Thomas murmur. "That comment was clearly misjudged."

From the corner of her eye, Meg saw Drago curtly nod. "Indeed." Then he held out his hand to Thomas, who shook it, then Thomas made his bow to Meg, uttering all the right phrases, before joining Harry and George. With waves, the trio departed, making for the stairs.

Meg watched them go, then was recalled to her duty by the next group of departing guests.

As she stood beside Drago and farewelled the last stragglers, she pondered his reaction to Thomas's admittedly ill-advised remark. She'd always been told that, when it came to men like Drago, discerning their true feelings was more a matter of paying attention not to their words but to their actions.

Or as the case might be, their reactions.

CHAPTER 10

The following morning, Meg took a piece of their engagement cake, neatly wrapped and tied with ribbon, and went to call on her old governess, Miss Stirling, who lived in a small flat in a genteel building in Manchester Street.

Drago drove her to Manchester Square in his curricle, with his tiger up behind them. He'd arrived at Half Moon Street at ten o'clock and offered to take Meg for a drive in the park, but on learning of her projected visit, he'd immediately offered to drive her there instead.

Bemused, she'd inquired whether he thought to accompany her to meet with Miss Stirling. He'd hesitated, then suggested that perhaps he could meet her old governess when he came to collect her at the end of her visit. "There's a coffeehouse on Manchester Square. I'll spend a quiet hour there, then come and fetch you."

She'd agreed to the arrangement, yet even as she directed him to the correct building on Manchester Street, she had to wonder if this degree of togetherness was what she should expect going forward, given they were now incontrovertibly engaged and—by their own decision—quite possibly heading to the altar.

As she'd anticipated, after drawing his horses to a halt, Drago tossed the reins to Milton, descended and handed her down, then escorted her up the steps, into the building, and up the two flights of stairs to the correct door.

In responding to Meg's knock, when little Miss Stirling opened her door, the ex-governess's eyes flew wide.

Meg fought not to grin too devilishly. "Darling Stirs, allow me to present my fiancé, the Duke of Wylde."

"Oh—oh!" Miss Stirling gasped. "Your Grace!"

Drago's charming side came to the fore. He somehow managed to capture Miss Stirling's mittened hand and bowed. "It's an honor to meet one who has played such a major role in the life of my soon-to-be duchess."

Unsurprisingly, Miss Stirling turned pink and was rendered incoherent.

Meg quickly took charge, explaining that Drago understood that she wished to speak with Miss Stirling privately and that he would return in an hour and hoped to spend a few minutes with them then.

Miss Stirling gabbled agreement, and taking his cue, Drago bowed again, exchanged an understanding smile with Meg, and left.

Meg and Miss Stirling watched him go down the stairs. Even that, he did gracefully.

"Good Lord, Meg—a real duke?" In wonderment, Miss Stirling stared at her erstwhile charge. "Your dear parents must be over the moon!"

"They are, indeed." Smiling, Meg urged the little governess back into her neat parlor and shut the door. Meg usually called every few months; Stirs had been her constant companion from the age of six until she'd left the schoolroom at seventeen, and she was deeply fond of the kind and caring woman.

Once Stirs was settled in her favorite armchair by the fireplace, Meg presented her with the wrapped cake. "A very small token for your help in making me the lady I am today."

Stirs demurred, but happily accepted, unwrapped, and admired the large slice of cake with its royal icing. Once she reached the end of her exclamations, she set the slice aside for later and asked if Meg would take tea.

Meg declined and mentioned that Drago had gone to a coffeehouse to fill in time.

Reassured, Stirs settled and demanded to be told the entire story of how Meg had snared her handsome duke.

Their fictional tale tripped easily from her tongue; the notion of taking Stirs into her confidence didn't even make it as far as a conscious question. The little woman would be shocked and confused and would insist on telling Meg's parents, with whom she maintained a correspondence.

Besides, by Meg and Drago's joint decision, fiction was now fact.

Stirs was an incurable romantic and waxed lyrical about how she imagined Meg and Drago's relationship would evolve. "You must make sure it's a proper partnership, my dear." Stirs blinked somewhat myopically toward the door. "Especially as he seems rather…well-set-up, if you take my meaning."

Meg assured her that Drago was, indeed, a very handsome and charming man and told her of their recent attendance at the Cambridge House soirée.

"Oh, that's quite excellent!" Stirs beamed. "Taking an interest in running the country will keep him occupied. It's essential, I've always thought, for gentlemen to have some real occupation to give them purpose."

Stirs then asked for a description of their engagement ball, and Meg dutifully supplied it, omitting only the half hour or so that she and Drago had spent alone. On impulse, knowing that Stirs was an acute observer of people and often a font of sound common sense, especially in the romantic sphere, Meg asked, "Stirs, what would you say are the signs that a lady is in love with a gentleman?"

Her erstwhile governess's eyes flew wide. "Why, that's simple, my dear. If the lady cares more for the gentleman than for herself, then she can be assured that love is what she feels for him." Stirs's eyes twinkled at Meg. "Nothing else will really achieve that, you know."

"I see." Having broached that subject, Meg could see no reason not to address the other side of the coin. "And is there any way that a lady can tell whether a gentleman is truly in love with her?"

"That, I admit, requires a degree of observation," Stirs replied. "A gentleman's protestations must always be treated with some degree of caution, but reading their minds really isn't all that hard. One simply needs to pay close attention to their reactions in certain situations. It might be a situation in which the lady could conceivably be in some danger—even something simple such as being led astray by some other gentleman, that sort of thing. Pay attention to how he reacts, and you'll have your answer."

"I see." Drago had already rescued her once, admittedly from the consequences of her own actions rather than defending her against another. But in Bond Street, he had very effectively protected her from the thug with the knife. Slowly, Meg started to smile.

"Yes, well! However matters develop between you and your excessively handsome duke, I must say I am truly heartened at the news that you will become a duchess. It's just the right challenge for you, and trust me, my dear, when I say that having a challenge that captures your interest and motivates you will be essential for your future happiness."

Meg had felt that the challenge of being Drago's duchess would suit her; it was reassuring to have Stirs's opinion mirror her own.

A knock on the door heralded Drago. Meg waved Stirs to remain in her chair, but when Meg ushered Drago in, the small woman was, of course, on her feet, ready to welcome her august visitor.

A smile curving her lips, Meg waited until Drago had charmed Stirs into sitting again, then Meg resumed her seat while Drago pulled up a straight-backed chair.

She sat back and observed and was amazed by how easily Drago teased Stirs into losing her understandable awe of him and relaxing enough to laugh at a joke he ventured. He mentioned Ridley, but after a glance at Meg, avoided even alluding to her brush with imminent death. Stirs was delighted at the story of the golden-pelted puppy and enthralled by his antics, at least those Drago described. Meg wasn't sure all the tales were true, but they served to put a wide smile on Stirs's face and a sparkle in her eye.

By the time Meg and Drago rose and made their farewells, Stirs was beaming and happy, and Meg was pleased with the outcome of their morning.

They left the building, and she took Drago's arm, and he turned her toward the square. "I left Milton walking the horses. He'll meet us at the corner."

She nodded and, still smiling, strolled beside him along the pavement. It was a quiet street with only the occasional carriage rattling along the cobbles.

They were halfway to the square when two large men dressed in frieze stepped out of an alley just ahead and halted on the pavement, facing Meg and Drago.

The man on the right was shorter, squat and solid, while the other was bald and as tall as Drago but half again his weight. Both were heavily muscled and carried long, wicked-looking knives.

Meg halted.

Before she could draw breath to scream, Drago swept her behind him and stepped in front of her. She heard a sibilant hiss and, wide-eyed, saw him draw a long blade from his cane.

Swordstick, her brain informed her.

In the time it took the thought to form, Drago had lunged, skewering the stocky man through the arm so that he howled and dropped his knife.

The taller man gave vent to an angry bellow, raised his knife high, and brought it down in a stabbing blow, but already disengaged from his first victim, Drago deflected the knife with the swordstick's sheath and slashed at the man's chest.

Mouth agape, the man stared down at his front, where blood was already staining his none-too-clean shirt.

Drago lashed out with the ebony sheath and knocked the knife from the stunned man's hand, then whirled and kicked the stocky man, who had been reaching for his knife, in the stomach. The man staggered back, then shot his mate a terrified look and kept going, stumbling away into the alley.

For a second, the tall man stared at Drago, then clapping an arm across his wounded chest, rushed after his friend.

On his toes, Drago swayed, driven by the urge to race after the men. To catch them and wring from them the name of who had sent them.

The pair certainly weren't locals.

He gritted his teeth and pushed down on the rage that threatened to override all thought. He wanted to chase the blackguards, but he couldn't leave Meg alone and undefended.

That this was the second time that someone had threatened her with a knife hadn't escaped him. Nor had the fact that on both occasions, there was no per se reason that he should have been with her, there at that precise time.

No reason at all to suppose that, when she was attacked, he would be by her side.

Sword and cane still in hand, he turned to Meg. She'd paled, but her gaze, concerned, was raking him.

He looked past her, then glanced around. Although there were others on the street, strolling along, none had been close enough to notice what had occurred; their incurious attitudes confirmed that.

His breathing slowing, the battle-ready tension that had claimed him ebbing, he returned his gaze to Meg's face. "Are you all right?"

Her wide eyes leapt to his. "Me? I'm not the one who engaged with two knife-wielding thugs! Nor am I the one holding a bloody sword."

He glanced down at the rapier, then huffed and drew a handkerchief from his pocket and wiped the thin blade. "At least this thing finally came in handy. It was my father's."

She stepped closer and placed a hand on his arm. Looking into his face, she asked, "What was that all about?" She glanced toward the alley. "Who sent those men to attack you?"

He raised his head and stared at her. "Attack me?"

She met his gaze, concern clouding her blue eyes. "Why would anyone come after me? It has to be you they were after."

He reran the incident in his mind. He didn't think she was right, but...

Jaw setting, he returned the rapier to its sheath and clicked the blade home, then reached for her arm. "Regardless, I suggest we get off the street. I doubt they'll return, but there's no need to take unnecessary risks."

Unsurprisingly given she was convinced that he was the thugs' target, she was entirely willing to stride quickly beside him to the end of the street and into the square, where Milton was waiting with the grays and the curricle.

Drago helped Meg to the seat, then took the reins and joined her. The instant he felt Milton's weight swing up behind, Drago started the horses trotting.

Meg finally managed to haul in a breath past the constriction that had locked about her chest in the instant that she'd realized the thugs' intention. The moment she'd seen their knives.

What had Stirs said?

If the lady cares more for the gentleman than for herself, then she can be assured that love is what she feels for him.

Given the emotions roiling inside her, Meg was confident she could, with absolute assurance, conclude that she was in love with Drago. For a moment there, she'd been poised to fling herself into the fray to protect him. Only the experience of having been close to so many brotherly and cousinly fights—wrestling and fisticuffs, not all of which had been benevolent at the time—had held her back. She'd known beyond question that Drago wouldn't have thanked her for getting in his way and distracting him.

She made a mental note to ask Louisa about the small revolver Louisa routinely carried in her reticule. As a soon-to-be duchess, Meg rather thought she should carry one, too.

The reassurance of feeling Drago—hale, whole, and as far as she had ascertained, without a scratch—sitting close beside her brought her turbulent feelings down a notch.

But only a notch.

As they rattled along, the flaring concern triggered by the attack solidified into determination.

She now knew, on a wholly conscious and even visceral level, that she wanted to be the Duchess of Wylde. It was, therefore, right and proper that she work to protect her husband-to-be.

As they rattled smartly back into Mayfair, that determination grew.

She focused ahead. "Where are we going?"

"Somewhere safe where we can think about this."

* * *

ONCE SAFELY WITHIN the walls of his Park Lane mansion, Drago ushered Meg into the library. Having registered that it was approaching lunchtime, he'd given orders for the meal to be served as soon as it was ready. Now, he shut the door on the rest of the household and followed Meg to the armchairs grouped before the fireplace.

The day was gray and cool, and a cheery fire was burning in the grate.

Meg sat, drew off her gloves, and held her hands to the blaze.

Drago sat in the armchair opposite.

"I've been thinking." Meg looked at him. "These attacks—you haven't had anything like this happen to you before, have you?"

He shook his head. "No one's ever come at me with a knife before."

"Exactly. And the first attack occurred after the notice of our engagement appeared in the *Gazette,* and the second occurred the morning after our engagement ball." She fixed him with a solemn and serious look. "The timing has to be significant."

Slowly, he nodded, not sure where she was heading but willing to follow.

Meg felt the talons of an emotion rather like fear close around her heart. "The motive has to be something to do with the succession, don't you think?" When Drago blinked at her, she rushed on, "That's the first issue that leaps to anyone's mind when a nobleman announces he's about to marry. Everyone assumes that once we wed, we'll set about filling your nursery, and the corollary of that is that your current heir will soon be displaced."

He frowned, but held her gaze. "Are you suggesting that Denton is behind these attacks?"

She flung up her hands. "I don't know, but surely he's the first person one has to suspect."

Drago's rejection of the idea was plain in his face.

Throwing caution to the winds, she reached across and gripped his hand tightly. "We might not yet have made our final decision to marry, but I don't want to lose you before we get a chance to say our vows!"

He blinked, then studied her face, searching her eyes more intently. After several seconds, he said, "I will admit that, in the general way of such things, Denton would have a motive—if he was so inclined."

Drago spoke carefully, feeling as if he was skating on very thin ice. From the roiling emotions clouding Meg's eyes, it was clear that she was truly agitated over the prospect of someone attempting to murder him.

On the one hand, he felt distinctly gratified; she plainly cared for him in the same way that he cared for her, which made him feel rather better about—less exposed by—his own possessively protective instincts, all of which were currently insisting that it was she who had been the villains' target, not he.

While he had no evidence that would prove that point, certainly not to her, inside, he was convinced that the men—all three of them—had been after her, not him.

Meg had been studying his eyes. "Are you sure he isn't? Are you certain that Denton doesn't secretly harbor a wish to step into your shoes?"

He was, but how to convince her? "Perhaps we should see how he reacts on finding us both alive and unharmed."

She nodded decisively. "Yes. That's an obvious first step." When he didn't say more, she prompted, "So where can we find him?"

A tap on the door heralded Prentiss.

Drago held up a silencing hand to Meg as the butler entered and announced, "Luncheon is served, Your Grace. Miss Cynster."

Drago nodded. "Thank you, Prentiss." He rose and held out a hand to Meg. As she laid her fingers across his palm and allowed him to raise her, he continued, "Is my brother in?"

"Lord Denton went out earlier, Your Grace, but he expected to be back in time for luncheon."

"Excellent. When he returns, please ask him to join us."

"Indeed, Your Grace."

Drago offered Meg his arm, and together, they walked out of the room. As they crossed the front hall, he closed his hand over hers on his sleeve. "Denton's at that age when one rarely intentionally misses a meal. If he said he'd be back for luncheon, he'll be here soon."

She accepted that with a dip of her head.

Drago sat her in the chair to the right of his place at the head of the table.

She glanced at the only other place set, opposite her. As Drago took his seat, she arched her brows at him. "Your mother and Mrs. Weekes?"

Drago glanced down the expanse of empty table. "Apparently not in. I daresay they'll be out at some luncheon or other."

Meg nodded, then looked up to thank Prentiss as he served the soup.

She and Drago were quietly supping the excellent celery soup when confident footsteps crossed the hall.

The next instant, Denton appeared in the doorway.

Drago watched as his brother's face lit with obviously genuine pleasure.

"Meg!" Smiling with his own brand of charm, Denton came down the table to take the hand Meg offered and bow over it. "It's a delight to see you here, enlivening our otherwise dour brotherly meal."

With a genial nod to Drago, Denton rounded the carver and dropped into the chair on Drago's left. "Have you been out braving the dowagers in the park?"

"No, as a matter of fact." Meg waited until Denton had been served and Prentiss left the room to ferry the soup tureen back to the kitchen. "We went to visit my old governess in Manchester Street." She caught Denton's gaze and arched her brows. "But you knew that, didn't you?"

The look of complete and utter puzzlement that descended on Denton's face—whose features were far easier to read than his brother's —could not have been faked.

Denton stared at her. "I...had no idea that your old governess lived in Manchester Street." Patently at sea, he glanced at Drago. "Should I have known? Was she Mel's governess before Meg's or...something like that?"

Obviously struggling to keep his lips straight, Drago said, "What Meg has omitted to mention is that on leaving her governess's building, we were set upon by two thugs."

"With knives," Meg supplied.

"Luckily," Drago smoothly continued, "I had Papa's swordstick, and they got the worst of the encounter."

"Good Lord!" Stunned, Denton looked from Drago to Meg and back again. "A knife attack in broad daylight, virtually in Mayfair?"

Drago studied Denton's face, then looked at Meg and arched a laconic brow.

She sighed and pushed her empty soup plate away. "You're right. It isn't him."

Denton was still confused. "What isn't?"

Drago's brow lifted again, and Meg inwardly sighed and explained her reasoning that the motive behind the attacks might have something to do with the dukedom's succession. "But obviously, it's not you behind the attacks."

Instead of being incensed over being suspected, Denton had fixed on a different point. "*Two* attacks?" He stared at Drago, then, his jaw setting, looked across the table at Meg. "It isn't me—which I'm glad you realize— but that doesn't mean you're wrong." He, too, looked at Drago with concern. "I'm your immediate heir, but if you were to die in some fashion that implicated me in your death..."

Meg looked at Drago. "Who would inherit then?"

Drago looked from one to the other, then reluctantly conceded, "Warley. He's next in line."

"Exactly. And as you very well know, our dear uncle is perennially short of the ready." Denton tossed up his hands. "Who knows what he might have got himself into? Creditors snapping at his heels or worse."

Drago warned the other two to silence as Prentiss returned, followed by two footmen, all carrying platters of various delicacies, cold meats, and fruit. Once the dishes were laid before them and their soup plates removed, Drago signaled to Prentiss to leave them and close the door.

The instant the latch clicked, Denton added, "And don't forget what Warley said when he first heard of your engagement."

Meg looked at Denton. "What did he say?"

"That he was relieved that Drago had taken the plunge and finally decided to marry, but that even with you being a Cynster, he wouldn't be surprised if the marriage never actually occurred."

Drago swallowed a sigh and met Meg's pointed gaze. "Yes, he said that, but first, that was before he met you, and second, Warley is a confirmed misogamist."

She frowned. "He hates marriage?"

"He's been known to label the institution the devil's own invention."

She huffed. "Even so"—she glanced at Denton—"I think we should at least speak with Warley."

Denton was nodding. "Even if only to rule him out, just as you did with me."

Faced with two belligerently determined faces, Drago held up his hands. "All right. But"—he reached for the nearest platter—"after we've lunched."

* * *

WARLEY LIVED IN BAKER STREET, in an apartment in a house apparently given over to bachelor gentlemen's residences.

Meg, Drago, and Denton arrived a little before four o'clock. Warley's man admitted them. Plainly recognizing Drago and Denton and no doubt guessing who Meg was, the man immediately showed them into a rather luxurious sitting room, all leather-upholstered furniture and highly polished dark wood.

After Meg denied any wish for tea—she was far too tense for such pleasantries—Drago dismissed Warley's man and, with Denton, joined Meg in the large, well-padded armchairs angled before a neat fire.

"He'll be here soon." Denton relaxed into the dark-green leather. To

Meg, he explained, "Warley always returns home at four o'clock to get ready before heading out for the evening. He's rarely in otherwise. He tends to live at his clubs."

Meg nodded. She was starting to have second thoughts about Warley being the one behind the attacks. As Denton had pointed out, to step into the duke's shoes, Warley would have to make the attacks look to be the work of Denton, and she couldn't see how anyone would connect Denton —relatively innocuous sprig of a noble family that he was, one who, as far as she had ever heard, led a blameless existence compared to his notorious older brother—to the men who had carried out the attacks thus far. The three simply hadn't been the sort of men one could imagine Denton consorting with, not even to hire to commit murder.

The same caveat applied even more definitely to Warley.

She drummed her fingers on the chair's arm and frowned at the fire.

The *click* of a latch was followed by the sound of heavy footsteps in the front hall.

"Jeffries! Where the devil are you, man?" After shrugging off his heavy coat, Warley walked into the sitting room and, seeing them, came to an abrupt halt. "Ah!" His eyes lit, and a smile wreathed his face. "I have visitors! Excellent!"

Drago and Denton had risen, and Warley shook hands and thumped their shoulders. "What-ho, nephews!"

Meg rose, too, and when Warley turned to her, somewhat weakly offered her hand.

He took it and bowed with extravagant gallantry. "My dear Miss Cynster. Welcome to my humble abode." He released Meg and glanced at Drago and Denton, then at her. "Drinks, anyone?"

When they all shook their heads, still smiling genially, Warley looked from one to the other. "Well, then. What's this all about, heh?"

Drago waved them all to take seats, and Meg was cravenly grateful when, as soon as they'd all settled, Denton seized the baton and told Warley about the attacks on Drago and Meg.

The utter horror that overtook Warley's countenance was impossible to question. He was sincerely, indeed quite alarmingly, shocked. His expression beyond serious and edging into panic, he looked at Drago. "What precautions are you putting in place, m'boy? You'll at least take a guard with you from now on, I hope?"

Drago studied his uncle's face, then looked at Meg and arched a brow.

She sighed and, defeated, shook her head. "It's not him, either."

Warley goggled at her. "What?"

It took a little time and considerable verbal ingenuity to explain Meg and Denton's thinking, but when Warley finally understood what, exactly, they'd wondered, he stared at them as if they'd run mad. *"What? Me* wanting to be the duke? No, no!" He waved his hands. "You have that entirely wrong. Why, it was me who ensured that Ryland put that clause in his will to make sure Drago married. Why would I do that if I wanted the title?" Before they could answer, as if struck, Warley added, "If I'd wanted to be the duke, I would have bumped you both off when you were little. Always running headfirst into danger, the pair of you. Easy enough to engineer an accident or two."

"Uncle!" Denton exclaimed.

"Well, I didn't, did I?" Warley waved at him and Drago. "You're both still here, which is my point."

Drago waved both hands, urging Warley and Denton to calm down. "I hope"—he looked at Warley—"that you understand that, in the circumstances, we needed to check, as Denton put it earlier, to at least eliminate you from the list of suspects."

Warley huffed, but allowed, "I suppose that's true enough."

Drago leaned back. "Now, what's this about you being behind that clause in the pater's will?"

Warley looked at Drago warily.

When Drago stared implacably back, Warley sighed and said, "You have to remember that when he—your father—made his will, you were what? Early twenties? And sowing your oats left and right. You were a typical reckless Helmsford hellion." Warley lifted a shoulder. "We all are to some degree, at least at that age, but the family tendency always seems to manifest most strongly in the eldest son and heir. Your father himself was exactly the same."

Drago merely nodded. "And?"

"And…we, your father and I, could both see that you had all the necessary credentials and required talents to, eventually, in time, become an exceptional head of the family, a worthy successor in every way. That you would step into the shoes of the Duke of Wylde and do us all proud. But we wanted—me especially—to ensure that you would marry, so I badgered your father into putting in that clause."

Warley glanced at Denton, then met Drago's eyes. "Despite there being the two of you, accidents do happen, and I never, ever, wanted to be placed in the position of shouldering the responsibility for the family, let alone the dukedom. I knew that I didn't have it in me. I simply don't. You could even say, with justification, that I'm allergic to responsibility. And if the title ever did come to me, well, likely it would die with me, what? So your father agreed and, knowing you as well as he did, knowing that if it came to a question of having to knuckle down and marry suitably in order to protect Wylde Court and all those there, as well as Wylde House and the staff there, well!" Warley spread his arms. "No one doubted you would step up and do the right thing. That you would give up your hedonistic lifestyle and find some suitable lady"—Warley beamed approvingly at Meg—"just as you did."

Warley returned his gaze to Drago, and his genuine approbation was easy to see. "We all recognized that you are a true Helmsford. You will not fail to act to protect those you see as in your care."

Drago's eyes had narrowed. He continued to study Warley. "So that clause had more to do with you than with me."

"Well, yes and no. We all wanted to make certain that you lived up to your potential, and I have to say"—Warley's gaze again shifted to Meg—"from all I'm hearing, Meg is the perfect bride to assist you in that endeavor." Warley returned his gaze to Drago. "To help you pick up and manage all the ducal reins that you've largely been able to ignore until now but that, once you're wed, you'll no longer be able to let slide."

Determinedly, Warley nodded. "And those aspects are yet more reasons why I should never, ever, inherit." He appealed to all three of them. "Can you imagine me addressing the Lords?"

Meg struggled to keep her lips straight. Warley had a point; he was simply not the sort people tended to take all that seriously.

But as she absorbed the insights Warley's revelations had offered, Warley sobered.

He looked at Drago. "Now we're all clear that it's not me or Denton behind these dastardly attacks, who is? Surely that's the most urgent question." Abruptly, he paled. "You haven't informed the police, have you?"

"No." Drago's tone was decisive. "Nor do I intend to."

"Thank God for that," Warley returned. "Last thing the family needs— a scandal of that sort. The ton's already salivatingly focused on the Helmsfords as it is."

"But who the devil could it be?" Frowning, Denton looked at Drago. "Who is trying to kill you, and what do they hope to gain?"

Drago nodded. "Those are, indeed, the pertinent questions." He caught Meg's gaze. "But we've been assuming it's me the attackers are targeting, yet in both instances, Meg was there, too." He arched a brow at her. "Could someone be intent on harming you? The attacks started after our engagement was announced. What about disgruntled former suitors?"

Meg made a scoffing sound. "I'm Miss Prim, remember? I've never allowed any gentleman to even imagine I might entertain an offer, so no, it won't be—can't be—that." She frowned at Drago. "But could the attacks be in revenge from someone who had expected you to marry someone else? We know of Alison, but were there others who might, conceivably, have had expectations, expectations the announcement of our engagement dashed?"

Although his expression remained as inscrutable as ever, Drago nevertheless clearly considered the point but, ultimately, shook his head. "There's no one." He grimaced and conceded, "Other than Alison and her family."

"Could it be Hubert?" Denton asked.

Drago snorted. "Hubert is such a stuffy prig. Can you see him going to some sleazy tavern on the docks to hire the men who accosted us in Manchester Street?"

Both Denton and Warley looked as if they were trying to imagine such a scene, but neither could quite manage it. The subsequent suggestions were half-hearted at best.

When appealed to by Drago, Meg had nothing sensible to advance. She looked at the three Helmsford men and felt distinctly stymied.

Drago also looked around the circle, then concluded, "At present, there's nothing we can do in terms of identifying whoever is behind these attacks, not until we learn more." He locked eyes with Meg. "Until then, I suggest we—you and I—should take all reasonable precautions."

Denton and Warley adamantly agreed and were quick to make suggestions.

Meg held Drago's gaze and wondered what precautions he, her ducal betrothed, would consider "reasonable."

CHAPTER 11

"*I*'ve been thinking."

Meg looked at Drago. He'd unexpectedly called that morning to take her for a drive in the park and had just steered his grays through the gates and turned the horses' heads south—toward the Serpentine and away from the more fashionable stretch. As he hadn't brought Milton, his tiger, she asked, "What about?"

He looked ahead, then said, "Let me pull up, and we can stroll."

After drawing in to the verge and handing over the reins to the same stable lad who had held his horses before, Drago handed her down from the elegant carriage, then wound his arm in hers and set course for the banks of the Serpentine.

At that hour, that area of the park was mostly inhabited by nursemaids and their charges; while there were other couples strolling, they were not so plentiful that she and Drago would be forced to acknowledge others every few yards, nor were those others close enough to inhibit a private conversation.

She glanced at him curiously. "So what have you been thinking about?"

He looked at the well-clipped grass before their feet. "Correct me if I'm wrong, but given these attacks started after we announced our engagement, regardless of whether they're aimed at you or me or both of us, their purpose, one has to suppose, is to prevent us marrying."

She considered that, then nodded. "That's logical."

He flung her a wry grin. "So...while we agreed to wait until June to make our final decision"—he looked ahead—"from where I stand, I definitely want to marry you, and I'm willing to count my decision made." He brought his dark gaze to her face. "In light of that, I wondered where you currently stand on that question—to marry me or not—and whether, if we're both of a mind to finalize our union, we shouldn't declare our hand and marry as soon as possible."

Meg blinked, but before she could reply, he, again looking ahead—scanning their surroundings for threats, she realized—smoothly continued, "As I see it, bringing our wedding forward will achieve two desirable additional aims. It will end the social circus and, more importantly, remove all incentive for any further attacks."

To Meg's mind, the latter was by far the more persuasive argument. The emotional upheaval of yesterday and the resulting tension—which had remained unresolved and continued through their evening's events, as she'd found herself constantly on edge, glancing all around—had underscored just how much her inner self already had invested in Drago.

In Drago alive and being his usual, not-so-easily-managed self.

On him being the challenge she needed and, now, wanted above all else.

"Yes," she said.

The single word had him glancing sharply at her. "Yes? As in...?"

She firmed her chin. The longer she thought about it, the better his idea seemed. "Yes, I agree that we should proceed to a wedding with all speed."

He halted and faced her. He took her hands and searched her eyes. "You're certain you want to marry me?"

And there it was—that hint of vulnerability that made her so very sure.

She smiled and nodded decisively. "Like you, I've made up my mind. Bringing our wedding forward won't change anything other than those things we want to change."

"Thank you." Honest relief and gratitude infused the words. He smiled, and for once, his social mask fell away entirely, and his face reflected every bit of joy and delight she might have hoped to see. "I'm glad—no, I'm thrilled." He raised her hands and, holding her gaze, dropped a kiss on each set of knuckles. "I swear to you on all I hold holy that you will never regret agreeing to be mine."

Despite his reputation, she'd now heard enough and learned enough of him to feel certain that she wouldn't.

They were attracting attention. Both realized and, twining their arms, started strolling again.

Given their determination to be protective of each other, attested to by how far both were prepared to go to secure the right to be openly so, even to initiating a rushed wedding with all that would entail, was merely a symptom of what had already grown between them—the link, the emotional connection—she had little doubt they would both feel much happier, more emotionally secure, once they were wed.

"No one else needs to know the reason behind our rush to the altar." Drago's quiet comment mirrored her thoughts.

"I agree." She slanted a ruefully teasing glance his way. "Doubtless, those inclined to question what's driven our decision will think the predictable."

His lips twisted, and he met her gaze. "Indeed."

Drago studied her eyes, then looked forward and squeezed her fingers where they rested on his sleeve. "So what's next? In this, you're at the helm."

She pondered for an instant, then replied, "We tell my parents, then your mother." She looked up and met his gaze. "And then we'll merely have to stand back and let them run the show. I'll wager they're going to be very, very happy to do so."

He gave an amenable nod. "In that case..." He turned her around, and they retraced their steps to the curricle. "Let's head for Half Moon Street without delay."

He was quietly thrilled by her ready acquiescence to his plan. He'd spent all of the previous evening and most of the night evaluating and debating the best way forward, searching for the surest way to get himself into position to protect her as his inner self demanded.

Marrying immediately—as soon as the knot could be appropriately tied—was unquestionably his best option. Once she was formally his, he would have a much freer hand to ensure nothing befell her, even if he had to hedge her around with guards.

They reclaimed the curricle and started for Half Moon Street. Along the way, they perfected their argument for a wedding as soon as possible.

"A week from now." Meg looked at Drago. "Do you foresee any difficulty in obtaining a special license?"

"None whatsoever." He grinned and turned out of the park in style. "The archbishop is a distant cousin of sorts and will be only too happy to see me leg-shackled."

"In that case, I can't see any hurdle that might trip us up."

Of course, breaking the news of their latest decision to Meg's parents took a certain degree of tact. As Meg had foreseen, the predictable reason—namely that she was already expecting his child—immediately leapt to her parents' minds, but without actually addressing that point, they managed to allay such suspicions. Or so Drago hoped.

"In truth," he confessed, "I've already endured more than I can take of the ton's avid interest. Every ball is becoming a trial—draining my reserves of politeness, let alone my temper—and this way, we can marry without any unfortunate incident erupting."

"I can certainly understand that." Demon Cynster snorted. "I still remember the weeks before our wedding—I always thought my brother did the right thing in eloping. And being a duke with Meg your prospective duchess, it'll only be worse for you both." His shrewd blue gaze rested on his daughter's face. "And as you're both of one mind on the matter, I can't see any reason not to roll forward to the wedding without further ado." He arched his bushy brows at his wife. "What say you, my dear?"

Felicity—Flick, as she'd instructed Drago to call her now that he was set to join the family—had narrowed her eyes, but not, thankfully, on either him or Meg. Rather, she seemed to be considering some distant vista. Then her gaze refocused on Drago and Meg where they sat side by side on the drawing room sofa. "As far as I recall, no mention has yet been made of the wedding. No date alluded to, even within the families."

Drago nodded. "To my knowledge, that's correct."

Flick smiled in delighted anticipation. "In that case, my dears, I see no reason at all that you shouldn't marry as you've suggested, next Saturday. Indeed"—she nodded sagely—"the degree of excitement the announcement will engender will prove your point. It will be a frenzy, but at least this way, it'll all be over within a week. And trust me, it would have been a frenzy regardless of when the wedding took place. This way, the nonsense will be done with and the unavoidable disruption to everyone minimized."

Drago was so relieved to have that agreed to so readily that he smiled equally delightedly and accepted Flick's invitation to remain for a celebratory lunch.

* * *

AFTER LUNCH, Drago descended the steps of the Cynster house and walked to where one of Demon's grooms had just drawn Drago's grays to a halt, having driven his curricle around from the mews.

Smiling appreciatively, the groom climbed down and handed over the ribbons.

"Thank you." Drago accepted the reins and stepped into the curricle.

The groom nodded at the horses. "They're a bang-up pair, Your Grace." The groom grinned. "Has the master seen them yet?"

Drago thought, then shook his head. "I don't believe so—not unless he's given to peering out of the windows at the street."

"Trust me." The groom saluted. "If he hasn't said anything, he hasn't seen them."

Drago grinned back, tipped his whip to the groom, and set the grays trotting.

He'd intended to head home and speak with his mother and brother about the now-settled date for the wedding, but the pealing of the city's bells signaling that it was two o'clock reminded him that, assuming that his mother had stayed in for luncheon, she would almost certainly be enjoying her postprandial nap.

That meant he had an hour to kill before he would be admitted to her presence.

"And there are others I need to warn about my impending nuptials."

On reaching the junction with Piccadilly, Drago turned his horses to the left and proceeded toward Lincoln's Inn.

Twenty minutes later, having navigated the traffic through Trafalgar Square and along the Strand, he left his horses with a lad in the Fields— no longer fields but a square surrounded by tall narrow residences—and walked beneath the archway and into the courtyard of the ancient inn, now home to the chambers of England's finest solicitors.

Much like Oxford colleges, each building around the central court-yard boasted staircases with rooms—known as chambers—giving off to either side of several landings. The Helmsford solicitors, Crawthorne and Quartermaine, occupied one of the prize chambers on the first floor.

After climbing the stairs, Drago walked into the outer office. Before he'd closed the door behind him, the senior clerk had leapt to his feet.

"Your Grace." The clerk bowed low. "I'll inquire if Mr. Crawthorne can see you."

"Thank you, Fitts." Drago waved his permission, and the clerk whirled and hurried down a narrow corridor to the door at the end.

Drago paused before the wooden railing that separated the small waiting area with its well-padded armchairs from the raised desks behind which the clerks toiled.

In less than a minute, Fitts returned. "Mr. Crawthorne is available to see you, Your Grace." Fitts opened the gate in the railing and bowed Drago through.

With a nod for the man, Drago walked down the corridor and entered Crawthorne's inner sanctum, a pleasant room sporting a bow window that overlooked the courtyard with its leafy trees, clipped lawns, and ferociously tidy paths.

"Your Grace!" Crawthorne stood behind his desk, smiling in welcome.

Drago nodded and met Thomas Hayden's gaze as Thomas dutifully closed the door.

As Crawthorne's junior partner, Thomas had a desk tucked in one corner of the room.

Drago shifted his gaze to the dukedom's principal legal eagle and inclined his head. "Crawthorne."

"No need to ask if you're well." Crawthorne waved to one of the armchairs angled before his massive mahogany desk, a good half of which was covered by files. "Please, take a seat and tell me how Crawthorne and Quartermaine might be of assistance."

Drago obliged, sitting and elegantly crossing his long legs while Thomas drew up a straight-backed chair and sat a little beyond one end of the desk.

Feeling very much in charity with the world, Drago glanced at Thomas, then shifted his gaze to Crawthorne, who now sat with his hands clasped on his blotter, an attentive expression on his lined face. Drago hid a fond smile; over the years, old Crawthorne had extricated him from more than one scrape. While the solicitor transparently disapproved of Drago's recklessness, he'd never preached. Smoothly, Drago said, "I informed you some weeks ago of my intention to oblige my late father by satisfying the clause in his will requiring me to marry before my thirty-fifth birthday."

Crawthorne nodded. "I was, consequently, unsurprised to read the notice of your engagement to Miss Cynster in the *Gazette*. Although"—Crawthorne's gaze flicked briefly to Thomas—"Mr. Hayden informed me that he believed you and Miss Cynster intended to wait until June or so to marry, I have, of course, commenced preparing the information necessary for determining the marriage settlements."

"Excellent." Drago smiled approvingly; this was why Crawthorne was the dukedom's solicitor. "I've come to inform you that Miss Cynster and I have concluded that there's no reason to wait, and we've elected to confound society by making next Saturday our wedding day."

"Next Saturday!" Thomas exclaimed.

When Drago and Crawthorne looked at him, Thomas blushed and cleared his throat. "Sorry." He offered Drago a bashful smile. "I was just… surprised. Well, stunned."

Drago smiled back. "To be expected—Meg and I hadn't really discussed our wedding date as such." To Crawthorne, he explained, "Earlier today, Miss Cynster and I made up our minds as to when we should wed. I've come straight from the Cynster house in Half Moon Street."

"I see." Crawthorne had seized a legal pad and pencil and was already making notes. "Half Moon Street. Yes, I believe I know the house." All business, he looked up and skewered Drago with a glance. "Do you know which firm the family employs?"

"No. I didn't think to ask."

"No matter." Crawthorne scribbled. "I know Montague and Sons manages the family's business affairs and has for decades. Montague will know who handles the legal side." Crawthorne sat back and, gaze shrewd, regarded Drago. "Now, as to what I would recommend." He went on to list various sums, properties, and caveats.

Drago listened attentively and made a few remarks, but when Crawthorne waded deeper into the legal issues, Drago held up a staying hand. "Crawthorne, considering how much the dukedom relies on your wisdom, I have full confidence in your advice. Whatever is required to reach an agreement, do it." He smiled, deliberately charming. "I place the dukedom's future unreservedly in your hands."

Despite his age and revered position in his profession, Crawthorne all but preened. "Indeed, Your Grace. You may rely on Crawthorne and Quartermaine to ensure that a generous settlement is agreed while, of course, preserving all that is the dukedom's due."

With that assurance ringing in his ears, Drago rose, bringing Crawthorne and Thomas to their feet. His expression easy, Drago said, "In that respect, I know I can safely place my trust in Crawthorne and Quartermaine. I'll leave you to it."

With a nod to Crawthorne and a smile for Thomas as his friend moved to open the door, Drago murmured as he passed Thomas, "I'll see you later." Then he left and, in short order, quit the chambers and strode for his curricle.

* * *

DRAGO AND MEG spent Saturday evening attending a dinner at the home of one of the ton's foremost hostesses followed by a select soirée. At neither event did they have even a whisper of a chance to speak privately, and of necessity, they had to keep their decision regarding their wedding a secret. Both had been warned exceedingly strictly by their mothers that on no account was the news to leak out just yet.

Indeed, under threat of all manner of retribution, all lips were to remain sealed until Monday, when a notice would run in the *Gazette*.

Until then, their mothers were busy notifying family members, in some cases by courier.

"If we don't give everyone a chance to get here in time for the wedding, we'll never hear the end of it!" his mother had exclaimed, a sentiment emphatically shared by Flick.

Apparently, formal invitations would be sent out on Tuesday; his mother, his aunt, and even his sisters had been drafted to help Flick and her familial peers inscribe and address each of the hundreds of invitations that would have to be dispatched.

Drago would have preferred to lie low until next Saturday, but doubted he would be allowed to hide. By midmorning on Sunday, he'd grown restless enough and curious enough to seek clarification as to what he might expect in the coming week. Consequently, he had the grays put to and drove to Half Moon Street.

On being admitted to the front hall, he immediately heard the chatter of female voices—many more than one—and froze on the threshold. Having no wish to find himself dragged like some prize exhibit into a morning gathering of Cynster females, he rolled a questioning eye at the butler. "Miss Cynster?"

The butler understood perfectly. Keeping his voice low, he replied, "Miss Cynster accompanied the Countess of Glengarah and the countess's son, Master Dougal, to the Zoological Gardens, Your Grace. They departed about a half hour ago. I daresay they will still be there."

Drago smiled. "Thank you."

Still holding the door, the butler bowed low, and Drago swung around, went down the steps, and leapt into his curricle. He accepted the reins from Milton, glad that today, he'd allowed the young tiger to come along.

As Drago set the grays pacing, Milton asked, "Where we headed to then, Y'r Grace?"

"Miss Cynster has gone to the Zoological Gardens, and we're off to hunt her down."

* * *

MEG HELD one of her nephew Dougal's small hands, and Pru held on to the other as they progressed from enclosure to enclosure, viewing the animals pacing within, much to Dougal's delight.

Meg and Pru had quickly learned not to let Dougal free. The now-three-year-old lordling was fast on his feet, which was why, as well as Dougal's nursemaid, Deaglan had insisted they were accompanied by

Diccon, a tall, lanky, long-legged footman who was accustomed to running down and recapturing his young master.

Both nursemaid and footman were trailing two paces behind, both keeping a watchful eye on their charge.

Meg wasn't sure whether she was amused or appalled that it took four adults to corral and oversee one small boy. Of course, with his round, still-chubby face framed by black curls and the wide cerulean-blue eyes he'd inherited from Pru, Dougal was already a charmer and a cheeky one at that.

"Next one!" he shouted and threw himself into towing Meg and Pru to the next set of railings.

Over his head, the sisters shared a smilingly resigned look and allowed him to drag them along.

The three zebras in the next enclosure fascinated Dougal. Being Pru's son and a true grandson of Demon Cynster, he was familiar with and could already name most of the points of a horse, and after frowningly studying the zebras, he looked up at Pru and said, "Mama, these look like horses with stripey skin, but they're not, are they?"

Pru smiled proudly. "No, darling, they're not. They are distantly related to horses—to equines, you remember that word—but they are a different group to our horses. No one rides them or puts them in harness or anything like that."

Dougal looked at the zebras. "So they just run around and crop grass all day?"

Pru arched her brows. "In the land from where they come, that's probably what they do."

Dougal stared at the zebras some more, bending and squinting at their hooves, then commenting on their manes and tails.

Meg listened to the exchanges between Pru and her son and had to smile.

When Dougal finally lost interest and consented to move on, Meg cast a laughing glance at Pru. "I must remember to ask Mama and Papa if you were as horse-obsessed when you were Dougal's age."

Pru blinked her blue eyes wide, then smiled and glanced at her son. "I rather suspect I was."

They walked slowly on along the garden's winding walk toward the last cage, the one housing the gorillas. Meg knew of it from when she was young, and she and Toby had been brought to the gardens. Toby had insisted on spending ages before that cage, staring in; the large apes had always fascinated him.

They halted before the gorillas' cage.

Dougal studied the two large apes inside. After a moment, he wrinkled his nose. "They smell bad."

Meg refrained from pointing out that the zebras had been smelly, too.

Dougal took a large step back. "I don't think I like g'rillas." But he continued to watch the pair closely, while Meg and Pru simply waited.

After a moment, Meg's attention drifted. She glanced around and saw Drago striding along the path toward them. Hands in his greatcoat pockets, he was scanning the groups about the cages.

Pru had followed Meg's gaze and cynically murmured, "I seriously doubt His Grace of Wylde is here to see the animals."

From the way Drago's expression lit when he spotted them, Meg doubted that, too.

Drago walked up and swept them both an elegant bow. "Good morning, ladies." His gaze fell to Dougal, and Drago grinned. "And Lord Dougal as well."

Dougal clung to Pru and Meg's hands and looked up at Drago. "Are you a lord, too? Like my papa?"

Drago crouched, bringing his face closer to Dougal's level. "I am, indeed."

Pru bent down to say, "Drago is a duke, which means he's a higher-ranking lord to you, my sweet, so you should practice your bow."

"Oh." Dougal looked at Drago with renewed interest. "All right." He drew his hand from Meg's and bobbed in a clumsy half bow, then looked up at his mother. "Is that right?"

Drago answered, "Perfectly acceptable." He held out his hand. "It's also acceptable for lords like us to shake hands."

Dougal grinned hugely, grasped Drago's elegant fingers in his chubby fist, and pumped enthusiastically.

"Excellent! You now have greeting a duke down pat." Drago retrieved his hand and rose. His gaze lifted to the gorilla enclosure. "What do you think of the gorillas?"

Dougal pulled a face. "I suppose they're all right for animals, but I don't really like them." Eagerly, he looked up at Drago. "I like the zebras best."

Drago nodded. "I always preferred the zebras, myself. Gorillas are...a trifle rough and crude, don't you think? Nowhere near as graceful as a zebra."

"The giraffes were good, too. They have such long necks."

"Indeed." Drago took a step back. "And they walk like this." Using his arms and stiffening his long legs, he demonstrated, to the amusement of all in sight.

"Yes!" Dougal pulled his hands free and tried to copy Drago and laughed delightedly when he managed a passable imitation.

Bemused, Meg watched as, with Dougal by his side, Drago did a "giraffe walk" in a small circle.

Both she and Pru were smiling irrepressibly. Pru leaned close and whispered, "I've noticed that all men have an inner little boy."

Meg nodded. "And it comes out at the most unexpected times."

"And in the most unexpected ways." Pru smiled and, when Drago halted and straightened, held out her hand to Dougal. "On that note, it's time we headed home for luncheon. You must be hungry by now."

The mention of food fixed Dougal's attention, and he nodded. Then he glanced up—all the way up—to Drago's face. "Thank you for playing with me, Lord…"

Looking down, Drago smiled. "Just Drago, Dougal." He ruffled Dougal's curls. "As I'll soon be your uncle, you can call me Drago."

Dougal looked thrilled at the prospect of another uncle to play with. "Uncle Drago." He skipped to his mother and took Pru's hand. "Are we going, then?"

Pru laughed. "We are, indeed."

Drago fell in on Meg's other side as they left the zoo and crossed Broad Walk to continue beneath the trees along the path that would take them to the Gloucester Gate. They'd left the Glengarah carriage waiting in Gloucester Terrace.

Meg glanced at Drago. "Will you join us for luncheon?"

His gaze drifted down to Dougal's dark head. "Actually, I was wondering if I might steal you away." He waved ahead. "My curricle is waiting behind Glengarah's carriage." He met her gaze. "I'm sure we could find somewhere quieter to eat."

She chuckled. "I believe your mother and aunt, and your sisters, too, are at Half Moon Street, and they were expecting to be there all day."

"Ah. Well, in that case, Wylde House sounds like our perfect bolt hole."

Dougal had been earnestly impressing on Pru how much he wanted a zebra. As they emerged through the Gloucester Gate, Dougal's expression set in mulish lines, and he halted on the pavement and looked challengingly at Pru. "I'm sure Papa would say I could have a zebra."

Drago shared an amused glance with Meg, then stepped around to face Dougal. "Actually, Dougal, zebras come from Africa, which is very warm, not to say decidedly hot."

"Exactly." Pru bent down to assure her son. "So you see, a zebra wouldn't thrive at Glengarah. They're not used to our winters at all, and they would sicken and die."

"Oh." Dougal's face fell—but only for an instant. Blue eyes lighting, he looked at Pru. "But I can ask Gran'papa to get one and keep it for me, can't I?"

The thought of Demon Cynster training a zebra brought a smile to all their faces.

Hard hands closed around Meg's shoulders and roughly hauled her away.

"No!" She struggled, but the man holding her was strong.

Then Drago was there, one hand closing on her forearm while his other fist flew past her face.

A howl rent the air, and the meaty hands fell from her shoulders.

Drago pulled her to him, then thrust her behind him, shoving her toward Pru.

One look at her sister's shocked face and the way she was clutching Dougal to her skirts was enough to assure Meg that this was entirely real.

She caught her balance and whirled and saw Drago duck a punch thrown by a beefy man, apparently the partner of the man who had grabbed her.

That man was groggily picking himself up from the pavement where he'd landed.

Drago set his jaw and took great delight in slinging a roundhouse punch that connected with a satisfying *thud* with the head of the second man, who had tried to grab Meg.

That man reeled back, and Drago swung around, expecting the first man to come at him again.

Instead, in a shambling run, that man barreled straight past Drago, seized his partner by the arm, and dragged him away. The pair fell into a stumbling run along the pavement.

The instinct to give chase had Drago on his toes, but...

Meg.

He glanced back to see that she was standing, shocked, only a few paces away, and except for him, she was more or less unprotected.

Looking back at the escaping thugs, he watched the pair veer between two stationary carriages and stumble onto the road, where a nondescript black carriage waited, the driver holding his horses on a tight rein.

The pair tumbled into the coach. "Go! Go!" one of them yelled, and the driver lowered his hands, and the horses bolted. The carriage rocketed past, careening on around the curve of the carriageway.

His hands on his hips, Drago exhaled, then he shook out his coat, resettled his sleeves, and walked back to Meg. She'd swung around, following the carriage with her gaze. He ducked to look into her face. "Are you all right?"

She focused on him, then nodded. "Yes." Her gaze raced over his features. "Thanks to you." She blinked. "Again."

A chill gripped his spine as the implications of what had just occurred rolled through his mind, but he kept all hint of reaction from his face. Calmly, he took her arm and wound it—safely—with his. "We do seem to be making a habit of this." It wasn't a habit he liked.

At the time of the attack, the only others on the pavement had been nursemaids or ladies with their children. Everyone was shocked, but now, several footmen and a few gentlemen who had been within the park and had seen what had occurred came up to inquire after their state.

Drago and Meg reassured all who asked and did their best to douse all interest.

When they were finally free to stroll back to Pru, Meg murmured, "I didn't see anyone from our circle, did you?"

Drago shook his head. "Let's hope the news doesn't make the rounds."

Pru was still wide-eyed, but for Dougal's sake, she found a smile. Looking down at her son, she said, "See? They're both unharmed."

Halting before Pru, Drago smiled and nodded to Dougal. "We are, indeed, perfectly all right." With a glance, he took in the serious faces of the nursemaid and footman, both of whom had come running to protect their mistress and young master. In accepted fashion, the pair had been trailing behind their charges—too far, in this instance, to have been of any help, but then who expected an abduction attempt at the gates of Regent's Park?

"It might be best," Drago suggested with what he thought was quite remarkable calm, "if Meg and I return to Wylde House." He focused on Pru. "You might let your husband and father know what occurred and that we'll be there."

Pru blinked, then her chin firmed, and she nodded. "An excellent idea. I'll tell the others."

She looked along the pavement toward the waiting carriages and waved, and the Glengarah carriage drew out of the line and came rolling up, closely followed by Milton, carefully managing the grays.

Drago and Meg waited until Pru and Dougal climbed inside their carriage, along with the nursemaid, then leaving the footman to shut the carriage door, Drago led Meg to his curricle. He helped her to the seat, then rounded the horses, accepted the reins from Milton, stepped up, and sat.

Keeping his mind ruthlessly focused on what he was doing—on

driving his horses and negotiating the traffic through town to Park Lane —gave him time to come to grips with the possessive protectiveness that was coursing so powerfully through his veins.

He knew what it was he felt; he even knew why. He just hadn't expected to feel it so intensely, to the point where he found it all but impossible to take a step back and view the incident from a wider perspective.

To the point where the only thing that mattered was protecting Meg.

She'd been silent as he drove through the streets, but as they turned onto Park Lane, she blew out a breath. "That was an attempted abduction, wasn't it?"

His jaw clenched so hard, he was amazed it didn't crack. After a moment, he managed a nod. "Yes."

Meg frowned. "But you were right there. Obviously, you would defend me. Making a bid to seize me there makes little sense."

Drago checked his horses to a slow walk. "I wasn't supposed to be there, and if you think of how we were standing just before those thugs tried to seize you, they might well have thought I was Pru's husband and that I would act to protect her and Dougal rather than immediately move to free you."

She was aware of tension rolling off him in waves. She studied his face. "What is it?"

After a second, he met her gaze. Usually dark and warm, his eyes seemed almost black, and his gaze was as hard as obsidian. "If," he bit out, "I hadn't been there, hadn't, purely on the off chance, come to find you, and they had succeeded… Think about it." His face as hard as granite, he shifted his gaze forward and flicked the reins. "If they'd stolen you away even for an hour, I wouldn't have been able to marry you."

She sat back, stunned, as that realization washed over her.

Followed by the conviction that he was absolutely right.

Her mind reeled, conjuring all the possibilities, none of which were good. Even if she'd been returned, unharmed, to her home within the hour…

Society would think the worst. Guaranteed.

She would be deemed soiled goods, and Drago's entire family would have risen up and refused to accept her as his duchess.

And all of the ton—including every last one of the hostesses who had encouraged her to become his bride—would have agreed.

In one simple step, in a single hour, all prospect of her marrying Drago would have been wiped off the cards.

But it hadn't happened. Whatever Fate was watching over her—over them—had sent him to Regent's Park that morning.

Her characteristic stubbornness rose inside her, this time with such power it was virtually a living force. She would be damned if she was going to allow some cowardly villain to stop her seizing what she now wanted, namely Drago and his duchess's coronet.

In her heart—in fact, to her soul—she now accepted that she was the right lady to fill those shoes.

She managed to find her breath again as he drew the curricle up before the steps of Wylde House. "So whoever is behind this is intent on preventing you from marrying."

He stepped down, tossed the reins to Milton, and held out his hand for hers. As she placed her fingers in his and felt his close tight about them, he caught and held her gaze. "Or on stopping me from marrying you."

* * *

Fifteen minutes later, Drago was still trying to wrestle his unruly emotions under some semblance of control. The fact that Meg was sitting safely in an armchair by his library fire helped, but he was still a long way from his usual calm and collected self, that self who was accustomed to controlling everything in his world.

He told himself that feeling this way about a threat to the lady he'd chosen to be his duchess was only to be expected.

The rationalization didn't help; he knew that the impulses battering him owed their power to something else.

Something more.

He was still pacing before the fireplace—under Meg's watchful and faintly wondering gaze—when Prentiss opened the door and announced, "The Countess of Glengarah, the Earl of Glengarah, Mr. Cynster, Mrs. Cynster, and Mr. Toby Cynster."

Drago blinked. He'd expected Deaglan and Demon, and he supposed he shouldn't be surprised to see Pru, but Flick and Toby as well?

Meg rose and was immediately enveloped in a motherly, then a fatherly hug. She patted her father's shoulder. "I'm quite all right." She glanced at Drago. "Thanks to Drago."

Demon pried his arms from around his youngest daughter and held out a hand to Drago. "I'm in your debt, Wylde. Pru told us what happened. It didn't sound in any way like a chance attempt."

"No. I'm sure it wasn't." Drago shook hands with Deaglan, then Flick tugged him down to place a motherly kiss on his cheek.

She gripped his hand and whispered, "Thank you."

His lips actually lifted slightly. "Hitting those thugs was truly a pleasure."

Their eyes met for a second; what Flick saw in his, he had no idea, but whatever it was seemed to satisfy her. With a nod, she released him and moved to claim one of the multitude of armchairs.

Before Drago had a chance to realign his wits, Prentiss was back to announce more visitors.

Meg wasn't surprised to find herself welcoming Drake and Louisa. Toby would have sent word to Wolverstone House, which doubtless accounted for the presence of their Cynster cousins, Aiden and Evan, both of whom arrived in Louisa and Drake's train; Meg had heard that Lucifer Cynster's eldest sons were members of the group that Drake often called on in his investigations.

The newcomers were still sorting out seats when George Bisley and Harry Ferndale arrived. As Drago had sent summonses to the pair, their appearance was no surprise.

As, after greeting Meg and Drago, the pair moved to find chairs, Meg glanced at Drago. "Not Thomas?" She kept her voice low, beneath the hum of the others talking.

"He'll be in chambers," Drago replied, speaking just for her. "I don't think I mentioned it, but he's a junior partner at Crawthorne and Quartermaine, the Helmsford solicitors."

Meg blinked. "I see."

"Aside from that meaning he won't be free for guard duty during the day, I don't want to interrupt his work." He met her gaze. "He's working on the marriage settlements, and I don't want them delayed."

"No, indeed." She wasn't going to protest that she didn't need guards. If she had guards, then he would, too, for she had every intention of sticking as closely to him as possible.

The thugs might have attempted to kidnap her, but ultimately, Drago marrying was what they were seeking to disrupt, and while the reason behind that wasn't yet clear, it had to have something to do with Drago and his future. And as far as she was concerned, Drago and his future were now all hers.

Hers to share. Hers to defend.

The library door opened again, and Drago's mother, Warley, and Denton came in.

The gentlemen rose, and greetings were exchanged.

The duchess squeezed Meg's hand and touched her lips to her cheek. Drawing back, she searched Meg's face. "Thank God, you're safe, my dear." She looked at her son. "And Drago, too." She smiled softly. "But he's always had the luck of the devil. As long as you're safe…" The duchess squeezed Meg's fingers again, then released her and moved into the room.

Finally, everyone found chairs and settled.

Meg sank into hers and joined all the others in training her gaze on Drago as he stood before the fire.

CHAPTER 12

"Thank you all for coming at such short notice." Drago looked around the faces. "Some of you will have heard what occurred this afternoon outside the Gloucester Gate of Regent's Park, but for those who are as yet in the dark…" With as little extraneous detail as possible, with additions from Meg and also Pru, he described what had happened. He concluded, "The men had an unmarked black carriage waiting, with the driver ready to whip up his horses. When they realized kidnapping Meg was not going to be as easy as they'd thought, they rushed back to the carriage and drove off."

Some were shocked, others less so.

"Anything notable about the carriage or horses?" Drake asked.

Drago shook his head. "You would see a hundred such carriages passing through Trafalgar Square in an hour at midday."

"Someone had to have been watching the house." Toby glanced at his father. "The Half Moon Street house." He looked at Drago. "They saw Meg leave with Pru. They must have spotted Dougal and followed, hoping for just such a chance as, in fact, presented itself, albeit by then, you'd joined the ladies."

Drago nodded and explained how their company was disposed on the pavement outside the park. "I suspect they thought I was connected to Pru and Dougal, not to Meg. When we exited the park, we were all looking at Dougal and interacting with him. Meg and I had been walking next to each other, but she wasn't on my arm."

Everyone took that in, then Drake leaned back in his chair and steepled his fingers. "Have there been any other odd happenings of late? Any other attacks?"

Drago glanced at Meg, who shot him a rueful look and nodded resignedly. He looked at Drake. "There were two previous incidents." Most there hadn't heard of those; he quickly outlined what had occurred.

Drake frowned, his dark gaze shifting to Meg. "So there have actually been three attacks, all apparently targeting Meg."

Drago nodded. "Precisely. And in all three instances, there was no reason anyone would have supposed I would be there." That was why the compulsion to lock Meg in a tower was riding him so hard.

"But what is the point of all this?" Studying Meg, Deaglan shook his head. "Why would anyone want to kill Meg, of all people?"

The question elicited opinions from all sides, most of which boiled down to no one having any idea other than to stop her marrying Drago, and with that conclusion, he agreed. He waited until the last exclamation had faded, then with his gaze, swept the gathering. "After today's attempted abduction, I feel it's safe to conclude that for whatever reason, the villain's intention is to prevent Meg from marrying me." Before anyone could comment, he went on, laying out in straightforward fashion how even an hour's abduction would have ended all hope of him and Meg marrying.

His thesis caused consternation, with Meg's family and his own exchanging horrified glances as the reality of what had almost transpired sank in.

Finally, as grimly aghast as the others, Drake nodded to Drago. "Sadly, I suspect you have it right. The purpose of the abduction was not to *kill* Meg but to void all chance of you and she marrying."

"But *why*?" Meg looked more exasperated than frightened.

She looked around the faces and waited—everyone waited—but no one had any idea.

Drago dipped his head to her. "That, indeed, is the critical question."

"And if we can find the answer," Drake added, "we'll likely be able to identify whoever is behind this." Then he frowned. A second later, he looked intently at Drago. "Is there any person who might imagine they would benefit were you not to marry Meg?"

Drago's mother huffed. "I do hope, Winchelsea, that you're not suggesting that some overzealous mama with a debutante to settle is trying to do away with Meg in the hope Drago—of all men—will then turn to her daughter instead?"

Drago was grateful that, other than to Meg, George, and Harry, he hadn't mentioned having considered Alison Melwin as his duchess to anyone present. Although all three looked at him, they didn't speak, and he was grateful for that, too. Alison didn't need to be dragged into this.

Drake grimaced. "When you put it like that, it does sound far-fetched."

Denton caught Drago's gaze. "But there is another reason. Someone might think that by removing Meg, Drago will be unable to marry before his thirty-fifth birthday, thus plunging the dukedom into a financial hole."

"What?" The loudest exclamation came—understandably—from Demon Cynster. He skewered Drago with a sharp blue gaze. "What's this?"

Drago swallowed a sigh and explained about the clause in his father's will. "But my birthday's in mid-August. Removing Meg now would still leave ample time—"

"No, it wouldn't." Louisa made the statement with absolute authority. She met Drago's eye. "If Meg died now, you would be deemed to be in mourning. Yes, you might wish to marry before mid-August, but your chances of finding another ton family willing to make that alliance and risk social censure, led by the Cynsters and connections no less… Well, at the very least, it would limit your choices quite dramatically, dukedom or not."

Both Drago's mother and Flick were nodding.

"And," his mother added, "the truth of why you would need to marry with such unseemly haste would come out, and that would create all sorts of questions."

Pru looked at Meg. "Did you know about this? Before you accepted him?"

Meg met Pru's gaze. "I knew before our engagement ball."

Pru nodded and grinned at Drago. "Just checking."

He muted a snort.

"So," Drake said, "there's a chance that whoever is behind the efforts to scupper your wedding is seeking to prevent you from accessing the funds required to keep the ducal estates running." He focused on Drago. "I take it that would harm the wider family and damage the estate?"

Tight-lipped, Drago nodded.

"That means," Drake continued, "that we might be searching for someone with a grudge against the Helmsfords." He glanced at Drago's mother and Warley. "Any ideas?"

Both clearly thought, then both shook their heads.

"I can't think of anyone who would fit that bill," Warley said.

Drake nodded. "That leaves us with two other possibilities." He looked at Aidan.

Apparently following Drake's thoughts, Aidan nodded. "Leave it with me. I'll check and make sure that the funds in question are still where they're supposed to be."

Deaglan cocked an eyebrow at Drake. "Embezzlement?"

"That's one possibility." Drake transferred his gaze to Evan. "The other is whoever stands to benefit from those funds if Drago doesn't marry in time."

Drago frowned and looked at Warley. "It's a list of charities, isn't it?"

Warley nodded. "A short list. Three, I believe. I can't remember which off the top of my head."

"No matter," Evan said. "I'll check the will and then delve into the current financial state of each of the potential beneficiaries." He looked at Drago. "It's possible someone is desperate, and your father's potential bequest... Well, I imagine it's sizeable and, consequently, would be highly attractive were someone needing to cover a shortfall in their accounts."

Drago considered that, then shook his head. "I find it difficult to believe that either of those possibilities will prove to be correct. As far as Warley and I know, the money is still safely in the Funds, and knowing my father, the charities, whichever ones they are, will be established and sound." He shook his head again. "There has to be something else behind this."

Deaglan raised his brows. "If not that, then what?"

Drake nodded. "There has to be some reason, but it's possible that this villain, whoever he proves to be, has a motive none of us can yet see."

Drago didn't find that reassuring, and from the expressions on the faces around the circle, neither did anyone else.

There followed several half-hearted attempts to speculate as to what such a motive might be, none of which were taken seriously, until Constance said, "Could it be Hubert?" When others looked her way, she elaborated, "Hubert Melwin, a neighbor at Wylde Court." She looked at Drago. "Edith mentioned that at one point—before you met Meg—you had flirted with the notion of Alison, Hubert's sister, as a possible candidate for the role of your duchess."

Thank you, Edith. Drago shook his head. "I made no mention of my thoughts regarding Alison to Hubert or any of the Melwins. I'd merely sounded out Edith—or rather, she made the suggestion to me. It never went beyond that." *Because, thank God and all the saints, whisky and Fate intervened.*

From beside Constance, Warley snorted. "Can't see it, myself. Hubert's a decent-enough sort, but not given to action, y'know? Bit of a high-stickler and definitely stiff-rumped with it. I can't see him unbending enough to deal with any uncouth types like these knife-wielding attackers, what?"

"Hmm." Regarding Warley, Constance frowned. "While in the main, I agree with your assessment, I would nevertheless allow that Hubert is probably *capable* of organizing these attacks, and as we don't know what pressures might have caused him to do so, or indeed, how he learned of Drago's however-fleeting interest in Alison—"

"Or," Denton put in, "if Hubert has simply got it into his head that Alison should be Drago's duchess and has grown fixated on achieving that." He met his mother's and uncle's eyes. "Can any of us say that Hubert couldn't be behind this?"

The answer was silence—a clear negative.

Drake looked around the circle. "It seems that, at this point, we lack sufficient information to point the finger at anyone."

Reluctant agreement came from all sides.

Far from growing calmer as the discussion had progressed, Meg now felt significantly more shaken than she had on entering the library. Courtesy of Drago's more detailed explanation and the others' extrapolations, comments, and exclamations, the reality of just how close she'd come to not being able to marry Drago or, indeed, any eligible gentleman at all had not just registered but sunk deep. She truly had come within a whisker of having her life ruined.

Yet even as that realization resonated in her brain, as had happened earlier, in reaction to the potential horror, indomitable and unquenchably stubborn determination surged high and yet higher.

We're getting married in a week.

Her lips set. They were, and they would. She'd never felt more fiercely determined on achieving a particular outcome.

Chin firming, she looked at Drago, and as if hearing her thoughts, he reached for her hand, closed his around it, and said, "Thank God we're getting married in a week."

Her smile held a sharp edge as she nodded. "Indeed."

The announcement caused mild consternation, as some there hadn't yet caught up with their latest news.

Meg left it to her mother and Drago's to elaborate.

Once they had and various questions had been asked and reassurances had been forthcoming, Meg wasn't surprised to hear Toby suggest and Drago and Drake agree that she would need to be guarded whenever she was outside either the Half Moon Street house or Wylde House.

She listened in critical silence as they made plans that involved all the unmarried gentlemen in the room in keeping a close-yet-not-obvious protective eye on her at all times. She found it interesting that everyone deferred to Toby regarding the organization of guards and was taken aback when Pru volunteered to act, as Pru put it, "as the keeper of Meg's diary."

Pru met Toby's gaze, then Drago's. "I'll also liaise with the other ladies of the family, the older as well as the younger."

Everyone else was quick to agree that Pru doing so would be most helpful.

"And I'll help," Louisa put in. "So will Therese."

Meg inwardly sighed and accepted that she would simply have to grin and bear with the attention, with being watched and hemmed in by her nearest and dearest for the next week.

At least it will be for only one week.

And from the wordless yet meaningful looks shared between Denton, George, and Harry, she felt confident that Drago, too, would rarely find himself alone.

She could live with that.

Along with Louisa, Pru had had her head close to their mother's, listening intently while her mother conferred with Constance. As the gentlemen's planning drew to a close, Pru looked up and announced, "Meg has to visit the modiste tomorrow morning. Toby and I will call at Half Moon Street for breakfast and work out her day from there."

Drago nodded. "I think it best if Meg remains for dinner at Wylde House. There are several matters we need to discuss. Denton and I"—he glanced at his brother, who promptly nodded—"will see her safely home to Half Moon Street later in the evening."

Then Drago looked at Flick. "Also, I wouldn't mind joining you over breakfast tomorrow."

Flick smiled back. "Please do."

Demon rumbled in assent.

Constance caught Flick's eye. "We should discuss which events Meg and Drago most need to attend over the coming week."

Flick nodded. "And of course, there are the family events that will need to be scheduled, too."

With Pru and Louisa listening intently and interjecting comments and suggestions, the two older ladies grew absorbed with discussing the rival merits of this soirée over that ball, and which evenings of the week should be assigned to the family gatherings that were expected in the lead-up to a wedding of such stature.

Meg considered their mothers' heads, both blond, one sleek, the other a cloud of curls, tipped close as their owners patently bent their minds to crafting the most socially effective route along which to steer their children to the altar.

After a long moment, she glanced around the room, noting the groups that had formed among the gentlemen, all discussing the situation, too. Each group was a mix of Cynsters and Helmsfords or Drago's friends. Looking at Drago, she met his gaze and smiled. Leaning closer, she whispered, "I'm starting to see a sliver of a silver lining."

Drago looked about them, then brought his gaze back to her face and returned her smile. "There's nothing like a threat to make everyone band together."

She nodded. "Everyone's starting to behave as one big family with a common goal." She paused, then added, "Given our marriage will effectively link our families, both old and large and long established, such a development is nothing to sneeze at."

Drago reached out and twined his fingers with hers. "No, indeed." He glanced around again. "And yes, while not quite a merger, there will be a living, breathing, potentially ever-evolving link that will be brought into being with our wedding and extend into the future." He brought his gaze back to hers. "There'll doubtless be challenges in managing that."

Meg found herself returning his easy smile with something akin to eagerness backed by rising confidence.

Drago studied her expression, then his smile deepened, and he raised her fingers to his lips and kissed them. "You seem to be looking forward to the fray."

She grinned. "As Stirs—Miss Stirling—confirmed, I require challenges to thrive."

He laughed softly. "Between your family and mine, I predict you'll have more than enough challenges to keep you thoroughly absorbed."

A soft tap on the door heralded Prentiss. He made his way to Drago's side and quietly said, "Your Grace, Mr. Hayden has called to see you."

Drago blinked, exchanged a surprised look with Meg, and straightened. He nodded to Prentiss. "Please ask him to join us."

As Prentiss left to do so, Drago glanced at Meg. "I wasn't expecting Thomas, but perhaps there's some question about the settlements."

They both looked toward the door, and others turned to do the same as it opened and Thomas Hayden walked in.

Abruptly, he halted, and his gaze flitted over the grouped chairs, taking in the small crowd.

"Thomas." Drago waved him nearer. "Come in."

Transparently uncertain, Thomas approached, nodding to the others, all of whom he'd previously met. He held several rolled sheets in his hand; on reaching Drago, Thomas held them out. "The draft marriage settlements. Given the urgency, Crawthorne and I thought you'd want to go over them as soon as possible."

"Yes, indeed." Drago eagerly took the document. "The sooner we get the details decided, the better."

Thomas looked around and, his expression hardening, asked, "What's going on?"

Already unrolling the sheets, Drago explained in broad terms, then looked up and gratefully acknowledged the assistance of those assembled in providing protection for Meg henceforth. "So until the wedding, she'll be under constant guard."

Thomas looked shocked and rather stunned. "Good Lord!"

George nodded soberly. "Quite a turn-up, what?"

Drago had swiftly scanned the draft. "I'll need to go over this later." Re-rolling the document, he looked at Demon. "Perhaps, sir, if I bring this"—he held up the roll—"with me tomorrow morning, while the ladies are visiting the modiste, you and I could go over the details together."

Demon nodded decisively. "The sooner we agree on the specifics and get our respective solicitors to finalize the thing, the better." He glanced sidelong at his wife and Drago's mother. "We don't want any unexpected impediments arising between now and Saturday."

Drago agreed. He looked at Thomas, who had settled beside Harry and George and was listening to them and Aidan and Evan relate the highlights of the earlier discussion. "Thomas?" When Thomas looked his way, Drago saw he was as grimly unhappy with the situation as the rest of them. Drago raised the rolled papers. "I anticipate sending back the draft with any corrections to your office around noon."

Thomas nodded. "I'll get working on it as soon as it arrives." He glanced at the others, then reluctantly got to his feet. "I should get back to chambers." He looked at Drago and Meg and nodded gravely. "I'll see you...most likely tomorrow evening." Thomas glanced around, meeting the others' gazes. "I'll happily assist whoever's been assigned to keep Meg safe."

Toby raised an acknowledging hand. "I'll send you"—he looked around the faces—"and everyone else a list of which events Meg and Drago are slated to attend each evening, sometime around noon each day."

Everyone murmured in determined agreement, and as Thomas made his way to the door, others rose to follow.

* * *

THE RUSH to the wedding started within the hour, with Meg and Drago, assisted by Constance, Denton, and Warley, going over the arrangements for Drago and Meg's honeymoon at Wylde Court.

As Meg had never visited the estate and was unfamiliar with the sprawling mansion, she had to rely on the others for advice, but with four Helmsfords, three of whom had grown up in the house and the fourth who had gone there as a young bride exactly as Meg would, offering insights and correcting each other frequently, she felt confident she'd been informed of all the relevant particulars.

In the end, she and Drago decided on a set of orders he undertook to convey to the Wylde Court staff as to what would be expected when he and Meg arrived there late in the afternoon on Saturday.

As promised, Drago and Denton escorted Meg home. After leaving Denton in the town carriage, Drago accompanied Meg to her door, then stole a kiss—a far-too-short kiss—before surrendering her into Fletcher's care.

The following morning, as arranged, Drago joined her family around the breakfast table.

With somewhat cynical amusement, Meg noted how seamlessly Drago connected with Toby and Demon in the matter of protecting her. When it came to protecting their ladies, Cynsters and Helmsfords were clearly cut from the same cloth.

With her and Drago's events for that day and evening decided, Toby left to notify those who would act as guards at each event. Rising from the table as well, Meg's mother collected Meg and Pru with a glance and, leaving Drago and Demon to settle in the library and go over the marriage settlements line by line, led her daughters across the front hall toward the drawing room.

"We thought it best," her mother explained to Meg, "not to risk traveling to Bruton Street, so we organized for Madame LeClaire to attend us here."

They entered the drawing room, which had been transformed by stacks of materials and lace and three long cheval glasses, to find not only the elegant French modiste and her two assistants but also a bevy of Meg's female relatives who had obviously decided they needed to be there to tender their opinions.

When Meg paused just inside the room and, bemused, surveyed the already-chattering horde, her grandmother, Horatia, flanked on one sofa by Meg's great-aunt Helena, correctly interpreted Meg's expression and grinned. "You didn't think we'd miss this, did you? Even in our family, it's not that often that we have a rush-to-the-altar wedding and a ducal one to boot."

Helena smiled, her pale-green eyes twinkling. "You have made excellent choices thus far, my dear." She waved at the stacks of fabrics. "We are all agog to see what choices you will make here."

One of Meg's closest cousins, also one of her bridesmaids-to-be, Lydia —betrothed herself, but not yet wed—turned her dark-blue gaze on Meg and incredulously widened her eyes. "Surely you didn't think the rest of them"—with a wave, she indicated the assembled ladies—"would allow you, me, and Anthi to keep the fun of choosing our fabrics and styles all to ourselves?"

Meg laughed. She went forward and hugged Lydia, then was grabbed and hugged hard by Anthi—Lydia's younger sister, Amarantha—who would also be one of Meg's attendants. "This is all so exciting!" Anthi enthused. "I can't wait to walk down the aisle with you."

"Yes, well, in that case"—Meg exchanged a smile with Madame LeClaire, who with her assistants was waiting patiently beside her wares —"we'd better get started on creating our gowns."

With that, everyone agreed, and encouragement rained thick and fast.

Madame LeClaire clapped her hands, and fabrics were unrolled and displayed.

Pru, slated to be Meg's matron of honor, left the room and returned minutes later with two footmen carrying a large round ottoman. Once the footmen had departed and the door was closed, the others encouraged Meg to shed her plum-colored day dress and stand on the ottoman, now surrounded by the cheval glasses, so that the sumptuous materials could be draped around her and judged against her hair and complexion.

She'd half expected her choices to be questioned, or at least for the older ladies to voice opinions before she had a chance to form her own, but no. Everyone held back, offering no more than mild comments, until she'd declared her preference for a delicately shimmering pink-hued silk that, somewhat to her surprise, met with the approval of everyone there.

Then the discussion turned to styles, first for her gown, then for those of her three attendants, and finally, there was the material for the matron of honor's and bridesmaids' gowns to be chosen.

Meg hadn't foreseen the giddy rush of excitement and happiness that had enveloped her, more or less from the first. Everyone there was genuinely delighted and supportive and happy to be there, to be a part of her wonderful morning.

The hours sped past, punctuated by tea, cakes, and cucumber sandwiches. And for all those minutes, Meg forgot entirely about the hovering threat to her and Drago's happiness. More, the last remnants of awareness that she had never set out to be Drago's duchess or he to marry her slid away. This moment in time was so very right it was impossible to question.

Impossible to doubt that this was exactly where she was supposed to be.

This was exactly how she'd imagined the days before her wedding would unfold.

Surrounded by family, buoyed and made giddy by a collective feeling of mutual joy.

* * *

THAT EVENING, following the schedule his mother and Flick had deemed most appropriate, Drago presented himself at the Half Moon Street house in good time for dinner with Meg's family.

She met him in the front hall, and he allowed himself an extended moment to stare and drink in the sight of her—his duchess-to-be—in her eau-de-nil gown, the color of which made her hair look even more like spun gold than usual.

Quirking a brow at him, she caught his gaze and came forward, offering her hands. "Your Grace."

He took her hands in his and smiled into her eyes as he raised her hands, first one, then the other, to his lips for a kiss. "You are exquisite." He wasn't only commenting on the gown, a fact he was more than equal to conveying with his eyes.

She primmed her lips and retrieved her hands. "Thank you." As she turned toward the drawing room, she threw him a look that clearly said, "Behave."

He offered his arm, and she wound hers with it. As they walked toward the drawing room, she dipped her head closer to say, "I noticed that you couldn't resist organizing for men to watch this house."

He arched his brows at her. "What did you expect?" *My most precious treasure is currently residing here.*

A second later, he frowned. "Although I'm less than impressed that you've already spotted them. I had instructed them to not be obvious."

She chuckled. "Not obvious, but we don't usually have that many street sweepers on this street."

"Ah. I see."

Smiling, he strolled with her into the drawing room, into the warmth and relaxed ambiance of a—relatively speaking—simple family dinner.

Immediately the dessert course was dispensed with, they all rose and, with Demon, Drago escorted Meg and Flick to the Grosjean house in Albemarle Street. Toby waved them off, saying he'd meet them at Hamilton House later.

Lady Grosjean's soirée—a highly select affair—and the Hamilton House ball were the events Drago's and Meg's mothers had decreed to be the must-attend events for Drago and Meg that evening.

While no one imagined any attack would occur within the refined confines of the haut ton's drawing rooms and ballrooms, Drago was grateful that several Cynster males were circulating among the crowd in Lady Grosjean's drawing room. Although they all disguised the focus of their attention, their gazes constantly touched on Meg.

Just checking.

Of course, with the announcement of their wedding, which had appeared in the *Gazette* that morning, there were many, even among that select crowd, who wished to remind Drago and Meg and their parents—Drago's mother and Warley had arrived ten minutes after Drago and Meg—of their existence.

Everyone who was anyone wanted an invitation to what was shaping to be the wedding of the Season, and that wasn't solely due to the prominence of their families. Their unexpected union coupled with their equally unforeseen rush to the altar had captured imaginations in ton circles, presently devoid of any other scandal over which to whisper.

After parting from a pair of older matrons who had been insistently probing as to the reason for Meg and Drago's "tying the knot in such a rush" and having witnessed Drago perform the remarkable feat of, successfully yet without giving offence, explaining to said matrons that inquiries such as theirs were, in fact, the principal reason, Meg murmured to her husband-to-be, "I stand in awe. That was nothing short of amazing."

His easy smile curving his lips, Drago inclined his head. "I'm delighted that my well-known dislike of the drawing rooms and their customary inhabitants can be put to such good use in our very worthy cause."

"Color me amazed that you pulled it off." She sighed. "I almost wish we could tell people the truth so they would stop speculating."

"Sadly, informing them of the truth won't stop their imaginations. Indeed, I suspect that learning the truth would only inflame them."

She huffed. "You're probably right."

"No probably about it," he murmured and steered her to the next couple waiting to waylay them.

Meg smiled and played the role assigned to her. In truth, it required little effort; engaging with the ton was all but second nature.

But while she smiled and chatted and, with Drago, batted aside any too-intrusive questions, she was constantly aware of just how close to her he now remained and of the aura of protectiveness that emanated from him, a defensive cloud that enveloped her.

She was aware of the others, too—Denton and several of her cousins, male and female—circulating like satellites about them, yet as, in Drago's library, the combined families had agreed that it would serve no one should the ton at large learn of the situation, all their guards were self-effacingly discreet.

She would have predicted that she would find such protectiveness cloying and irritating, but curiously, when she examined her feelings, she discovered she found the attentiveness and protectiveness reassuring. Indeed, at least in Drago's case, she found his absolute focus on her rather revealing. Encouragement and more bloomed in her breast when she dwelled on what, beneath all else, was driving his reaction.

Finally, with her parents, and with his mother and uncle and others following, she and Drago left the soirée and traveled on to Hamilton House.

The ball was in full swing when they arrived. Despite that, their appearance in the ballroom's doorway caused a fractional pause in conversations, and a ripple of interest flowed through the crowd.

What followed was much the same as what they'd weathered at the soirée.

"Only," Drago murmured, resetting her arm in his, "in a much more tightly packed arena."

As the ball would qualify as a "crush," that was certainly true. They had to weave their way through the crowd and managed to advance by only a few feet at a time. She glimpsed several "guards" drifting through the crowd around them.

At one point, Drago lowered his head and murmured, "George, Harry, and Thomas are here as well." Drago's eyes danced. "We should be especially grateful that they've braved even a ball such as this to lend their aid."

Meg grinned and nodded. "Will we ever live it down if one of them is unexpectedly snared while assisting us?"

Drago chuckled and raised his head. "It has to happen sometime."

They forged on, making little headway through the crowd, many of whom could barely wait to approach them. Nevertheless, by dint of constant practice, their ability to deflect over-inquisitive queries and dance around the subject of the guest list for the wedding only grew, and by the time the musicians finally returned to play a waltz and they could escape to the dance floor, they were both smiling in quiet triumph.

The waltz and the two that followed gave them some respite, then it was back to the jungle of overwhelming ton attention.

Denton caught up with them in the crowd. "Thought you'd like to know that Alison and her beau are here." Denton pulled a face. "Along with Hubert, who apparently thinks he has to play gooseberry."

"Where?" Meg asked.

Denton pointed toward one of the side walls, and Drago looked over the heads, then nodded. "I see them." He arched a brow at Meg. "Shall we?"

"Yes, please. I'm keen to learn how they're faring."

When they came up with the other couple, who had thankfully managed to separate from Hubert, they discovered that the answer to Meg's question was not as any of them had hoped.

Joshua grimaced. "We've still not managed to convince Hubert to drop his opposition to our match. I suppose I can understand why Alison's parents wish us to have Hubert's blessing as well as their own, but I have to wonder for how long he's going to make us wait."

"It doesn't matter," Alison declared, her expression showing more determination than Drago had previously seen in her. "We're going to marry, and given it is the Season, there's no reason we can't be patient for a few more months. And as we are *immovable* in our decision to wed, Hubert will eventually have to give way."

Meg murmured encouragingly, and Drago smiled. "You'll get there eventually. Hubert might be stubborn and set in his ways, but I've never heard him described as stupid."

That got a grin from Joshua and a smile from Alison.

As they parted from the pair, a little farther along the side wall, Meg saw the archway to the corridor leading to the ladies' withdrawing room. Sliding her arm from Drago's, she tipped her head that way. "I won't be long."

He looked, then scanned the crowd ahead and pointed to an older couple. "Friends of my parents. I'll wait for you with them."

She nodded and slipped through the crowd and into the corridor.

The withdrawing room was large and well appointed. There was no queue, and mere minutes later, Meg stepped back into the passageway.

A shadow moved farther along the corridor, away from the archway through which the noise of the ball spilled. Meg squinted, then smiled as she recognized Denton. With a dip of her head, she turned and headed for the ballroom.

She stepped over the threshold and paused. Since she'd left, the crowd had shifted, and she could no longer see Drago or the couple he had gone to join.

"Meg."

She looked in the other direction and saw Thomas sidle through the crowd. If anything, the crush had intensified.

He reached her and smiled. "You seem to have lost your fiancé."

She smiled back and waved in the direction in which Drago should be. "He's not far." She tipped her head, studying Thomas. "Earlier, Drago and I were talking of the risk you, and George and Harry, too, are courting in coming here to help with our current situation." She brightened her smile. "We truly are grateful."

Still smiling easily, Thomas shrugged. "Just part of being friends." He glanced around, then looked back at Meg. "I probably shouldn't comment, but you're looking a trifle flushed." He tipped his head toward the end of the room, which wasn't all that far away. "If you'd like to take a quick stroll on the terrace, I'd be happy to accompany you."

Meg was, indeed, feeling flushed; in the overcrowded room, it was warm to the point of being one step removed from suffocating. But she knew Denton was lurking somewhere in the corridor at her back, and even if she couldn't spot them in the crowd, others would very likely have their eyes on her. Smiling with genuine regret, she put her hand on Thomas's arm. "While I would love to take you up on that offer, I fear that doing so will only result in mild apoplexies occurring elsewhere in the room before we're hauled back inside and have a peal rung over our heads."

Thomas blinked, then understanding dawned on his face. "Ah. I see."

His gaze slid over her head to the archway, and he grimaced lightly, then looked down at her and smiled again. "Perhaps we'd better not risk it, then."

The musicians started up, and gallantly, he offered his arm. "We could dance."

She laughed and shook her head, but reached for his arm. "You can escort me to where Drago must be waiting." She turned him in the right direction. "He should be somewhere over there."

Thomas nodded and obligingly set himself to cleave a path through the crowd.

CHAPTER 13

The following evening, Drago and Meg dined with their immediate families at Wylde House.

Thereafter, they piled into various carriages and set off for Harcourt House for the first of two events, attendance at which their mothers had decreed to be their necessary fate.

The front of Harcourt House in Audley Street was a blaze of lights. The simply termed "party" was a select affair, the guest list limited to those of the oldest and foremost families who comprised the most rarefied circle of the haut ton. A small crowd of onlookers—maids, foot-men, and the avidly curious—had gathered on the pavement to either side of the front steps to watch and exclaim at the gowns and jewels and feathered headdresses as the upper echelon of society rolled up to Lady Harcourt's door.

As he handed Meg down from the Wylde town carriage, Drago had to fight a compulsion to look searchingly in every direction. Thus far, they'd managed to smother all ton awareness of the attacks they'd weathered, and the last thing he wished to do was raise questions in ever-inquisitive minds.

Nevertheless, as he escorted Meg—eye-catching in teal silk with matching feathers in her hair—up the steps to the front door, he swiftly scanned the watching crowd and spotted two reassuring faces—Wylde House staff he'd set on guard duty.

He hadn't really had to order anyone to it; merely through her few visits to the house, by her confident, relaxed, and appreciative manner when dealing with the staff, Meg had won them to her side. Drago had been given to understand that, one and all, they very much approved of her as his duchess.

While within the walls of ton events, the various gentlemen of their families could effectively guard her, outside on the streets of London, he had greater faith in his staff's abilities to blend in and watch for anyone taking too close an interest in their future mistress.

Old Lady Harcourt welcomed him and Meg to her ballroom with overt delight. Indeed, with such rapture that Drago realized that, within her ladyship's august circle of ageing matrons, Meg, or rather seeing Meg wed, was something of a cause célèbre.

As they parted from her ladyship and moved into the crowd, Meg cast him an amused smile. "She's one who is thoroughly thrilled to see me marrying you."

Arrogantly confident, he smiled back. "I never thought to say it, but in that, she and I agree."

Meg laughed, which seemed a good omen, and so it proved. Together, they moved effortlessly around the room, exchanging greetings with some, chatting at greater length with others; in large part, he left it to Meg to decide with whom they spent more time.

Her assurance in these circles went bone deep, and he was increasingly aware of how lucky he was to be able to rely on her extensive knowledge of virtually all those present.

At one point, as they progressed between groups, he lowered his head and murmured in her ear, "Have I mentioned how very thankful I am that you never accepted any other offer for your hand and so remained moving through these circles, gathering information and understanding for... Is it nine years?"

She glanced sidelong and met his eyes. "This will be my tenth Season."

"Would have been." He looked ahead and smiled at the pair of matrons waiting to engage them. "We're cutting it short, remember?"

Donning her social smile, she retorted, "I'm unlikely to forget."

They continued to circulate through the crowd, strengthening connections and becoming more widely known themselves.

"I have to admit," he whispered at one point, "that I never imagined myself becoming one with this crowd quite so easily."

Meg met his eyes. "But this was always destined to be the sphere in which, ultimately, you would move."

"I know. But even after I succeeded to the title, I put it off." He paused, then stated what, at least to him, was the obvious. "No matter how appropriate, I wouldn't be here if I wasn't marrying you."

A simple truth. Yes, moving in this sphere was a part of his destiny, yet if she—specifically she—hadn't come into his life, would he ever have claimed his rightful place?

He honestly couldn't say. Possibly once he'd got much older and had grown bored with everything else.

Strangely, with Meg by his side, he didn't find interacting in this sphere boring at all.

Eventually, they'd circumnavigated the room, and as they paused, considering their next move, their mothers approached, approval writ large on both their faces.

His mother patted his arm and smiled at Meg. "You are both doing excellently well. Your stepping into this circle has been noted by everyone."

Flick nodded decisively. "As it ought to be."

His mother went on, "Everyone is pleased that you've signaled your intention to shoulder the social mantle of the dukedom."

Flick glanced around. "And as you've covered the room, it's time to move on to your next port of call."

"Indeed," his mother agreed. "Appearing at the Cambridge House soirée is even more important. As the Duke and Duchess of Wylde, you will be expected to grace such events without fail."

Flick smiled encouragingly at them. "Just like Therese and Alverton, and indeed, Sebastian and Antonia and Drake and Louisa, even though the latter four have yet to succeed to their respective titles."

"All of you," his mother went on, "are expected to make your mark in some appropriate fashion, and attendance at events such as these tonight is the necessary avenue to establishing and securing your position in our world."

"I couldn't have put it better," Flick said. "And now, it's time you left. Our hostess is over there"—she pointed to a chaise along one wall—"and I can see Therese and Devlin moving in the same direction. As neither Constance nor I will be at Cambridge House, if you need any assistance there, Therese is the one to ask."

"Thank you, Mama." Meg flashed a smile at Flick, then also extended it to his mother, who, Drago noticed, looked quietly pleased.

With a bow to their mothers, without further ado, he steered Meg toward their hostess so they could take their leave.

* * *

THERESE AND DEVLIN were waiting in the foyer of Cambridge House when Meg and Drago arrived, and together, the four went up the stairs, bound for the elegant drawing room.

Ascending beside Meg, Therese looked ahead, then glanced at Meg. "Given you're both still finding your feet, I would recommend remaining together. Between you, your combined understanding should allow you to avoid the pitfalls, and I warn you there will be several snares waiting for anyone unwary enough to step into them."

When Meg looked faintly surprised, Therese cynically said, "This is the political sphere after all, which translates to 'here be dragons.'"

Meg laughed and nodded in agreement.

Once they'd been welcomed—enthusiastically and encouragingly—by Emily, Lady Palmerston, the four moved together in the direction her ladyship indicated; no one gainsaid the wife of the Prime Minister. But soon after, Meg and Drago parted from Therese and Devlin and forged a path of their own around the room, approaching others with whom they'd engaged during her ladyship's previous soirée.

At the end of the room, they paused to take stock.

Surveying the groups, all busily discussing this issue or that, for Meg's ears alone, Drago murmured, "Previously, I would have found this daunting. I daresay I would have coped, but"—he captured her gaze—"having you by my side has made taking my first steps into this arena so much more straightforward." He grinned. "So relatively painless."

She laughed and tipped her head his way. "I know very little about the political issues of the day, but you seem able to hold your own on that front, and when it comes to social matters, to connections and standing, my ten years swanning about the ton have taught me all we need to know." She met his eyes. "It seems we make an accomplished team."

He smiled and raised her fingers to his lips and kissed. "Precisely my point."

Even though his gaze returned to their surroundings, she still felt a sizzle spreading along her nerves, evoked not just by the pressure of his lips on her knuckles but even more by the unshielded warmth lurking in the depths of his dark eyes that he now allowed her to see.

Bedroom eyes. She now understood the saying.

Unnerved by the prospect that, being so experienced, he might see how sensually affected by him she was, she thrust the thought deep; this really wasn't the venue at which to explore such sensibilities. Casting about for distraction, she said, "I realize that, on this stage, we're still feeling our way, but do you have any thoughts as to what"—he looked back at her, and she met his gaze—"for want of a better term, political direction you might take?"

He thought for a moment, then said, "Despite assumptions and any appearances to the contrary, since I succeeded to the title and thus to managing the dukedom, I've had to grapple with many of the outcomes of government policies. There are quite a few that really need adjusting, while other issues have yet to be addressed." He started them strolling again; if they stood for too long, they would assuredly be approached by someone wanting to sound him out about something. "I'm speaking of issues that, when taken over the entire country, significantly impact the country's prosperity and the people's well-being." He paused, then went on, "One point my father went to great lengths to pound into my head was that we—the aristocracy of England, by which he largely meant the Lords—should never forget what happened to our French counterparts when they failed to take care of their people. He maintained that the original concept of 'lordship' was not to accumulate lordly wealth but to defend and protect a group of people." After a moment, he added, "Those lessons are ones I'll never forget."

Feeling a novel sense of enthusiasm well, Meg nodded eagerly. "So that's your framework. Your guide." She met his eyes. "So is there any particular tack you think we should therefore take?"

He smiled. "I've been talking with Alverton, and he tells me there's a group in the Lords—a loose alliance, if you will—who share similar views. Each has their own perspective, their own particular interests."

"Like Alverton with the railways?"

"And Chillingworth—Antonia's father—with agriculture, and Devil more with financial management and investments." Drago looked at Meg. "I've been told that Chillingworth is the convener of the group, as far as anyone is, but I haven't seen him about town this year."

She nodded. "He and Francesca rarely come to town other than for a specific reason, but"—she grinned at him—"I believe they'll be down for our wedding, so you'll be able to chat with him then."

Drago nodded. "You'll have to introduce us. I haven't met him in years."

"I will."

"Now"—he looked over the shifting crowd—"is there any particular area represented here in which you have an interest?"

Pleased, indeed impressed that he'd asked, she beamed at him. "As a matter of fact..." She proceeded to tell him of the association of many of her female connections with the Foundling House. "I've considered other causes, but the need fulfilled by the Foundling House is the most compelling to me."

He nodded. "Well, then." He scanned the heads. "Why don't we see if there's anyone here who might be of use in furthering the interests of the Foundling House?"

"And we should see what more we can learn about the issues espoused by Chillingworth's group."

With their enthusiasm renewed and specifically directed, they moved once more into the clusters of guests, but this time with purpose, and to their mutual surprise, the hours flew.

* * *

MEG AND DRAGO dutifully attended three events on Wednesday—one luncheon and two balls. Being so very much the cynosure of attention was growing increasingly wearying, but Thursday—finally—brought relief.

The Countess of Glencrae's party, held at Glencrae House in Bury Street, was strictly a family-and-close-friends-only affair.

More, the older generation had opted to reserve their energies for the formal family pre-wedding dinner on Friday, leaving the middle-aged and younger cohorts free to chat and share news of their lives in more relaxed fashion.

Meg was thrilled to be able to catch up with so many of her cousins. "Although," she informed Drago, "strictly speaking, many are second or even third cousins."

Taking in her eager expression, Drago smiled. "Our older families do tend to spawn many twigs on multiple branches of our family trees." He glanced around. "That said, I doubt many families can rival the Cynsters in sheer fecundity."

They were surrounded by a gay, rambunctious horde, all chattering at once. The noise level far exceeded anything one would encounter in a ton drawing room, but as they'd been instructed on their arrival by their hostess, Angelica, tonight was "All family, no holds barred, and no one needs to concern themselves over how they appear to anyone else."

With all customary ton restraints removed, the Cynsters were in their element.

Drago found Meg and himself passed from group to group, as if waltzing through a kaleidoscope of the family from the senior members present—Devil and Honoria, Vane and Patience, Demon and Flick, Lucifer and Phyllida, Gabriel and Alathea, Simon and Portia, Henrietta and James, Mary and Ryder, Amanda and Martin, Amelia and Luc, Angelica and Dominic, Eliza and Jeremy, Heather and Timothy—to their numerous offspring, many of whom were now married and had their spouses in train. It wasn't long before Drago's head was spinning, trying to keep track of all the names.

At one point, Meg looked at his face and laughed. "Don't worry. You'll eventually learn who everyone is."

He wasn't so sure about that. "They are legion," he replied in awe. When she laughed again, he smiled, smugly satisfied.

Angelica's husband, Dominic, Earl of Glencrae, was their host for the evening, and on his way across the room, he stopped beside them, handed Drago a glass, and poured a finger of amber liquid into it. "Try that."

Nothing loath, Drago complied. As ambrosia burst upon his tongue, he felt his eyes go wide. He swallowed, raised the glass, and stared at the golden liquor. "That's...exquisite."

Dominic grinned. "Welcome to the family. We'll send a keg as a wedding gift." With a salute to Meg, he wandered off, bottle in hand.

Enlightenment dawned. "Glencrae—of course!" Drago looked at the glass he still held, then sipped again, closing his eyes to better savor the smooth, smoky flavor. "This stuff is rarer than hen's teeth."

"Dominic's always very good about supplying the family." Meg linked her arm in his and towed him on. "Come and meet his wards. They can tell you all about the distillery."

That was a subject he truly was fascinated by, although he had to concentrate to decipher the soft burr of the Guisachans' Highland accent.

When they left the pair, Meg informed him, "Angelica said the rest of the Scottish contingent will be arriving tomorrow. They rarely come to town, so have to rush to get here in time."

"Which ones are they?"

She reeled off another string of names; he really had no hope of remembering them all. "Oh, but Carter and Calvin—they're Richard and Catriona's youngest two—must already be here." On her toes, she peered over the heads. "They spend most of their time in London these days. There they are!" And she towed him on.

Sipping the excellent whisky, Drago went with a smile on his face.

As the evening wore on, he grew more aware of a realization unfurling in his brain, occasioned by a common thread he perceived in all the Cynster unions. Pru had spoken nothing but the truth: Cynsters married for love.

It was there, constant and unwavering, in the swift, shared, private looks, in the effortless interaction between each married couple. In an underlying, unstated joy, and in the confidence each demonstrated in the other.

Every couple present was a team, partners in life. An active partnership much as his parents' marriage had been.

It wasn't exactly an epiphany, yet it hit him with the force of one. The Cynster ideal was precisely the sort of marriage he wanted.

The sort of marriage he needed.

He'd known for some time that Meg was the right lady for him, had seen and had demonstrated just how well they could work together in forging a shared life.

All that, he already knew.

But it isn't only that I need and want.

No, indeed, and that evening's revelations underscored just what lay within his grasp.

Everything I've ever wanted and secretly hoped to have.

The couples about them were living, breathing testaments that his instincts weren't wrong. The power in that room, the potential of the unions, was simply breathtaking.

He drained the glass, then Meg was there, removing it from his grasp. He'd been talking to Aidan and Evan while she'd been chatting to several of her female peers, including her two bridesmaids.

With a nod to Aidan and Evan, she took Drago's hand. "Come along."

He threw a laughing exculpatory look at Aidan and Evan, who both grinned, then Meg towed him toward the wall, set the empty glass on a sideboard, and continued to a paneled door that she opened, then she drew him on, into the corridor beyond.

He shut the door behind them. "Where are we going?"

"You'll see."

He'd started wondering—speculating—even before they reached the small parlor at the rear of the large house.

She drew him over the threshold, then whirled around him and closed the door.

No lamps were lit, but moonlight poured through the uncurtained bay window.

He turned to her—just in time to catch her as she flung herself at him, anchored his face between her palms, and kissed him with a degree of innocent enthusiasm that caused his lungs to seize and wiped every last thought from his brain.

They could count the number of times they'd kissed on the fingers of one hand. And up to now, it had been he who had initiated every exchange, stealing kisses when the situation allowed. The places and company in which they'd found themselves, day after day, evening after evening, hadn't offered many opportunities, even for a kiss.

He wanted—lusted for—more, much more, and apparently, she did, too.

Typically, she'd seized the reins and was intent on steering them…he wasn't sure to where.

Regardless of what she had in mind, he wasn't about to complain.

Swamped by the unexpected heat of the engagement and aware of her escalating demands, he nevertheless took a few seconds to savor the moment, to register and appreciate the supple curvaceous body impressing itself against his harder frame…

She made a frustrated sound, one he understood, and obedient to her prompting, he caught her face between his palms and took control of the kiss.

He increased the subtle pressure on her lips, and on a sigh, she let him in. He sent his tongue questing, then tangling with hers, luring her, teaching her, and delighting in her eager responses.

Her mouth was a cornucopia of delight, then her hands fell from his face to rest on the upper planes of his chest, and the simple accepting touch spurred him on.

He angled his head, deepening the kiss, then let his hands drift from her face. With his palms, he traced the alluring curves of her nearly bare shoulders, then paused the delicate caress, even while he continued to engage her in the kiss, waiting, wondering…

She stepped into him, a deliberate incitement that left no room for doubt.

Slanting his lips over hers, he slid one arm around her waist, cinched her to him, then turned her in to the darkened parlor.

A large armchair with a high back was positioned facing the windows. Without breaking from the kiss, he steered her around to the front of the chair, then sat and drew her down with him, and still holding to the kiss, she settled on his lap.

Meg approved of his sense in sitting; she hadn't been sure how much longer her legs would hold her. With just a kiss, he seemed able to sap her strength and turn her muscles to jelly.

He truly was a master, and she'd been itching—simply *itching*—to have him take her just a little further, to explore at least the threshold of what waited for her on their wedding night.

This evening, with so many of her familial peers—so many married and therefore far more knowing than she—all around her, she'd lost patience and decided she simply had to know…more.

At least as much as he could and would show her in this parlor.

Seated on his hard thighs, she wriggled so she was facing him more fully, so she could prosecute her demands more effectively through their kiss.

More. Now.

The words resonated in her head, beat in her blood, and—thank God—he seemed to hear.

His lips moved on hers, almost teasingly languid now, tempting her to fall even further under his spell.

She went willingly, wanting to know, then with one hand cradling her jaw, holding her face at just the right angle so he could plunder her mouth, from where it had been gripping her waist, his other hand rose, skating over the taut silk of her bodice to skim over the curve of her breast.

Her breath, what she had left of it, hitched. Then her heart beat faster, and she murmured and shifted, leaning in to press her breast—firm mound and aching tip—into his waiting palm.

And suddenly, his kiss grew hotter, more heated, his lips more demanding.

His fingers drifted, oh-so-delicately tracing the swollen curves of her breast, the upper, then the lower.

Then he cupped her breast, and she ceased breathing.

He closed his hand, and her senses reeled. His clever fingers found the tight bud of her nipple and gently squeezed, then tweaked. Then he kneaded the mound, and every last iota of her mind locked on the sensations evoked—provoked—by his lazy knowing exploration, by his artful, expert pandering to her senses and, even more, her desire. Feeding it. Stoking it.

Sending it soaring to new heights.

Lost in whirling pleasure, her wits tantalized by the promise of what might come, she only distantly registered the *click* of the door latch.

"Ahem!"

With a start, she opened her eyes. Over the top of the raised back of the chair, in the doorway, she saw Angelica outlined against the faint light in the corridor.

"I daresay you're absorbed at the moment, but the pair of you need to reappear in the ballroom without delay. Your elders are growing restive."

Meg couldn't marshal sufficient wit to make any reply.

She looked down at Drago, only to see that his shoulders were shaking with silent laughter.

Angelica tsked. "You both must know that Drago's reputation is such that there's no way Honoria and Patience, let alone Flick—let alone Demon—will countenance you both disappearing for long. However, because I remember how being in your situation feels, might I suggest that you take the roundabout route via the terrace to return to the ballroom? If you continue along this corridor, you'll find a door at the end. If you go through it, you'll be on the far end of the terrace. I've already left the ballroom's terrace doors open, so you'll be able to stroll in and claim that you've merely been taking the air."

She paused, then amended, "Not that that is any guarantee of avoiding suspicion, but it's better than saying you've been sampling forbidden delights in the back parlor."

With that, Angelica turned to leave. "Just hurry up before someone else comes looking for you."

Drago roused himself to call, "Thank you, Angelica!"

She huffed and departed.

Rather bemused, Meg looked into Drago's dark eyes, then grinned. "She's always had a soft spot for handsome rakes."

Drago helped her up off his lap. "Just as well I qualify, then."

"Don't grow conceited."

"With Cynsters all around, I doubt that will happen."

He waited while Meg shook out her skirts and straightened her bodice, then he offered his arm. "Angelica's right. We should take the terrace route back."

They set out at a brisk pace.

He had far too much experience with illicit encounters not to have kept a tight rein over his own desires. The chances of actually sating his hunger had been distant at best, so he wasn't perturbed by the slow burn of desire and unslaked passion; both would keep, and indeed, the end to such necessary restraint was in sight.

As they slipped onto the terrace and into the cool night air—which would help cool both their ardors—he was conscious of a feeling of light-headedness. It was, indeed, heartening to learn that his chosen bride wanted him as much as he wanted her.

That much, she'd made abundantly plain through her kisses, her insistent lips, and her inviting actions.

Despite the interruption—in the circumstances, very likely necessary—in his estimation, the evening had gone exceedingly well.

* * *

FRIDAY EVENING BROUGHT the final formal event that Drago and Meg were expected to attend prior to their wedding. As that event was a dinner for their combined families hosted by Meg's grandmother, Lady Horatia Cynster, and as all the family members had already met, in some cases multiple times, although technically still a formal affair, the evening wasn't as tension-inducing as it might otherwise have been.

Nevertheless, Drago remained alert and focused as, before dinner, with Meg on his arm, he circulated among the guests in the drawing room. There were several far-flung Cynsters he hadn't met before—such as the branch from the Scottish Lowlands and others from Devon—and by now he'd learned that each and every Cynster was potentially an ally. Some in estate business, some with investments, and others in a host of endeavors including horse breeding, wolfhound breeding, jewelry, antiques, and artworks.

He didn't have to feign interest. When, after chatting with Gerrard Debbington, the renowned painter, and Meg's cousin Carter Cynster, as Drago and Meg moved on and she cocked a questioning brow his way, he could assure her with absolute sincerity, "Your family's accumulation of talents truly is amazing." Faintly, he frowned. "I can't understand why the Helmsfords haven't diversified to the same extent."

That was a potential weakness he should attend to at some point.

Possibly by having a quiverful of children and sending them questing in every direction of modern life.

As if reading his mind, she replied, "There's always time."

He grinned to himself and allowed her to steer them on.

The overwhelmingly encouraging, happy, and positive atmosphere was universally supported. The ancient ones smiled benevolently, and the middle-aged generation were plainly delighted with the alliance. Many were already busy forging connections and making plans.

As for his and Meg's generation... Drago had thought he, his siblings, and his cousins were close, but they had nothing on the huge tribe of Cynsters. They, it seemed, didn't just keep abreast of the major milestones in each other's lives but actively engaged with each other, dabbling and assisting in each other's business, and their spouses were also active members in what seemed akin to a teeming cauldron of practical support to which all members freely contributed and drew from at need.

The idea that through marrying Meg, he and the dukedom of Wylde would gain open access—indeed, be expected to call on—such an immense range of knowledge and skills left Drago a trifle giddy.

Suddenly, the future looked filled with an immense potential he hadn't known might be there.

All through marrying Meg.

He raised her hand from his sleeve and, gripped by a sense of gratitude to both her and Fate, pressed a kiss to her knuckles and, ignoring her questioning glance, allowed her to lead him on.

Soon after, they were summoned to dinner. As the guests of honor, he and Meg were seated in the center of the long banquet table, surrounded by their siblings and cousins. The meal was predictably sumptuous, the many courses nothing short of superb. Wine flowed freely, and toasts were duly offered and drunk, while otherwise, a steady hum of conversation enveloped the entire table.

While the desserts were being set out, Drago stole a moment to look up and down the long board, surveying the faces he could see. Every single one was aglow; everyone there was engaged and absorbed. Indeed, if the bright expressions were any indication, everyone was enjoying themselves immensely.

This, he reflected, was unquestionably the most pleasant of the many such evenings he'd participated in over the years.

After dinner, with the gentlemen forgoing the chance to sit apart and instead joining the ladies, the company repaired to the large drawing room and continued to chat in the more relaxed vein facilitated by excellent food and wine.

Standing beside Drago before the ornate fireplace and surrounded by a constantly shifting crowd of her siblings, cousins, and their assorted spouses, Meg was aware of a rising tide of excitement, of eagerness for the wedding tomorrow, that swirled about them, buoying her spirits and those of everyone there.

As Anthi gushingly observed, "Thank goodness the wedding is tomorrow! Being this giddy is exhausting!"

Everyone around them laughed, although fellow-feeling gleamed in many an eye.

This wouldn't be the last Cynster wedding of this generation—there were several members younger than Meg who had yet to find their match —yet for some reason, possibly due to Drago's rank and the potential importance of the alliance, significantly more attention than usual had been focused on their union.

Then Drake, with Louisa on his arm and accompanied by Aidan and Evan, strolled up, and under cover of the wider conversation, with a nod to her and Drago, Drake said, "We thought you should hear this."

Louisa smiled. "So you can trip up the aisle with rather fewer cares."

Aidan huffed. "I don't know about walking up the aisle—you'll be doing that regardless—but I can confirm that the funds your late father left in trust are exactly where they should be and, as one would hope, have grown substantially over the years."

Drago nodded. "Thank you. So there's nothing amiss there."

They all looked at Evan, who duly reported, "I checked into the potential beneficiaries named in your father's will. All three are well-known charities, and all are well-governed and entirely solvent and operating within their means. I looked, but could find no hint of a reason any of the three would be desperate for more cash. Well," he temporized, "other than for their usual purposes. Charities always want more funds, but there's no unusual or suspect activity at any of those three."

Drake nodded. "And I can add that Toby, Carter, Justin, and several others I thought might have useful contacts have quietly and discreetly asked around, but no one's found anything to indicate that anyone we don't know about might benefit in any way from you two"—he dipped his head toward Meg and Drago—"failing to tie the knot."

"Or alternatively," Louisa put in, "be disadvantaged in some strange way because of you marrying." She shook her head. "Aside from pointless jealousy, I couldn't turn up a whisper of a possibility from even the most ancient of the grandes dames."

Of all their number, Louisa was acknowledged as having the ear of the older generation of ton matriarchs.

Reassured, Meg smiled gratefully.

But then she noticed that Drago, Drake, and indeed all the others weren't smiling. If anything, they'd grown more serious. Toby came up and joined the circle, and he looked equally somber.

"That means," Drago said, his expression unreadable, "that we still have no idea what the motive behind the attacks is."

Drake pulled a face, and the other men all looked equally unhappy.

Louisa, too, was studying their expressions. "Well," she declared in bolstering tones, "at least we're almost to the moment when your marriage becomes a fait accompli."

"And hopefully," Evan added, "once it does, these peculiar attacks will cease."

Drake shrugged noncommittally.

Drago, too, wasn't so sure putting an end to the attacks would be that simple.

Not that getting married is exactly simple.

Pru appeared and looped her arm with Meg's. "Mama and the others want to go over the arrangements for tomorrow morning." She rolled her eyes. "Yet again." Pru collected Louisa with her gaze. "Your presence wouldn't hurt. See if you can calm them. I swear they're more nervous than Meg."

Drago found a commiserating smile for Meg, but as he watched her, Pru, and Louisa, all arm in arm, stroll toward the gathering of ladies clustered around Meg's mother and his, the charmingly nonchalant expression fell from his face.

After a moment, he glanced at the gentlemen standing with him. They, too, were watching Meg and looking quietly concerned.

He returned his gaze to Meg, now standing before her mother, who was seated on a chaise, and murmured, "Given we've yet to divine the villain's motive, I believe I'll feel much happier if, even after we wed, I keep a very close eye on my soon-to-be bride."

Drake made a sound of agreement.

Toby shifted. "If you need any help, don't hesitate to call on us. Any and all of us."

Drago met his soon-to-be brother-in-law's eyes and nodded. "If it comes to that, I will."

Tomorrow, with family all about them from morning until the end of the wedding breakfast...

He realized that with the wealth, depth, and breadth of family he now possessed, the chance of anything adverse happening before they were married was vanishingly slight.

CHAPTER 14

"No, no! Not like that!" Warley batted away Maurice's hands and, frowning critically, adjusted the folds of Drago's silk stock. "There! Where's that pin?"

At a glance from Drago, Maurice rather grudgingly handed over the large gold-and-diamond pin, part of the Helmsford family jewels. The pin had been worn by successive dukes at their weddings since at least the fourteenth century.

Warley took the pin and, squinting ferociously, slid it carefully into the silk folds at Drago's throat.

After tipping his head from side to side, finally satisfied, Warley lowered his hands, stepped back, and nodded. "That's how it should go."

Drago noticed his uncle's eyes growing damp, and to distract the others present—Denton and Maurice—Drago swung around to survey his reflection in the long looking glass on his dressing room wall. No doubt Warley was remembering Drago's father on his wedding day. Warley would have attended the duke on that occasion as well.

Examining his reflection, Drago could understand why the sight would affect his uncle. His mother, his aunt, and many others who had known his father well had often commented that Drago was his spitting image, a state that seemed to have grown only more pronounced with the years.

Surveying the end result of the combined efforts of tailor, shirt maker, and boot maker, he took his time checking the lines and creases and allowed Maurice to tweak the skirt of his coat to lie just so. Finally, he let his lips curve approvingly. "I believe I'll do."

A species of excited anticipation, laced with subtle apprehension over the unforeseeable combined with the uncertainty inherent in doing something he'd never done before, had been fermenting inside him since he'd woken with the dawn. He couldn't recall feeling anything similar, not since he'd been a small child.

The ducal signet ring never left his right hand, but from Maurice, he accepted the ornate gold ring he habitually wore on his left middle finger, slid it into place, then took his gold fob watch, tucked the watch into his waistcoat pocket, and slipped the fob into position and looped the chain across the black-and-gold brocade of his waistcoat.

One final glance at the looking glass, and he nodded. "Right, then." He turned to Denton; quietly amused, his brother had been watching the proceedings from the safe distance of the window seat. "Do you have the ring?"

Denton patted his right pocket. "Yes." He grinned. "Can you imagine what would happen if I didn't have it to hand over? Given Meg's family as well as our own, I would never live it down."

"No, you wouldn't," Warley said sternly. "You wouldn't be able to show your face for years."

Battling a grin as wide as his brother's, Drago met Denton's eyes. Their uncle was taking Drago's wedding more seriously than anyone. Indeed, Drago marrying had in large part come about because of Warley's drive to ensure that the responsibility for the dukedom never fell on his shoulders. His uncle was, therefore, hell-bent on making sure the wedding went off without a hitch.

Warley had earlier joined Drago and Denton for breakfast, so there was nothing more they needed to do. Drago glanced at the clock, then arched a brow at Maurice. "Has the duchess gone down yet?"

It wasn't quite time to leave for the church.

"No, Your Grace. I understand Her Grace is still at her toilette."

"In that case"—Drago gathered Denton and Warley with a glance—"I suggest we wait in the library." Smiling, he turned toward the door. "Glencrae sent a bottle of his whisky around. This might be an opportune moment to sample it."

He wasn't surprised that Denton and Warley happily followed him downstairs.

* * *

In Half Moon Street, excitement had been building since before dawn, and welling wedding frenzy now pervaded the house. The staff had never seen a bride walk down the stairs on her way to a new life and were determined to make the most of the occasion. Pru had married at Glengarah Castle in Ireland, so today's event was the only chance the Half Moon Street staff would have to be a part of such proceedings.

In Meg's bedchamber, amid a froth of lace, silks, and endless chatter, she and her bridesmaids, Lydia and Anthi, sorted out their gowns, then Meg sat on her dressing stool while Rosie brushed her hair and Lydia and Anthi were helped into their gowns by their maids.

Then Meg's mother and Pru arrived, along with their maids— everyone wanted to be a part of the day and, preferably, to play a role, however small—and Meg found herself swept up in the moment, enveloped in warmth and family affection, in the blessings of good wishes and the delights of shared joy.

The oohs and aahs when she finally stood clad in her wedding gown— as she stared, wide-eyed, at the vision her cheval glass revealed—would forever live in her memory.

A pearl-encrusted band had been set amidst her burnished curls and secured a gossamer-fine veil edged with tiny seed pearls. Although presently set back, when down, the veil hung to her waist in the front, but swept lower at her sides and still lower at her back to drape in a short train that Lydia and Anthi would carry as Meg walked down the aisle.

The gown beneath the veil was of the shimmering pink-tinged silk she'd chosen, with seed pearls edging the neckline, the cuffs of the fitted sleeves, her waistline, the silk peplum, and finally, the hem of the skirt.

Teary-eyed but beaming, her mother stepped up behind her and clasped a three-strand pearl choker about her throat. The necklace matched the pearl bobs that already hung from her earlobes.

"A wedding gift from your father and me." Her mother rested her hands on Meg's shoulders and, in the mirror, met her gaze, then with a final pat, her mother stepped back, allowing Pru, smiling fit to burst, to step forward.

Pru raised Meg's right arm and deftly secured a matching three-strand pearl bracelet about her wrist. She, too, met Meg's eyes in the mirror. "From Deaglan and me. Just for you."

Meg smiled mistily back. She blinked several times, willing the tears not to pool and fall.

"Now, now—none of that!"

They all whirled to find Meg's grandmother, Horatia, stumping through the now-open doorway.

At the universal looks of surprise, Horatia humphed. "You didn't seriously imagine I would miss this, did you?"

There was no correct answer to that.

Horatia waved her cane at Meg. "Turn around, my dear, and let me see."

In a rustle of silk skirts and petticoats, with Lydia and Anthi rushing to help with her train, Meg complied.

Horatia, who ranked as one of the senior grandes dames in the ton, raked Meg with her gaze, then Horatia beamed and met Meg's eyes. "You look divine, my child." With blatant satisfaction, she added, "Wylde is going to swallow his tongue."

With a satisfied cackle, Horatia nodded to the others. "You all look well and will do the family proud." Then with a last glance at Meg, she waved and turned to the door. "George is waiting downstairs, no doubt having a bolstering drink with your father and Glengarah, but it's time we were making for the church." Horatia directed a final nod at Meg. "We'll see you there."

Horatia pulled the door closed behind her, and the room erupted with exclamations.

"Good heavens!" Meg's mother looked faintly horrified. "Is that the time?"

"When did you ask for the carriage to be brought around?" Lydia asked.

"The flowers are downstairs," Anthi said. "We mustn't forget them."

"The fan!" Rosie pounced on the delicate pearl-decorated fan with a design picked out in bright-blue silk embroidery, which Horatia had sent as a personal wedding gift. Swiftly, Rosie looped the fan's ribbon about Meg's right wrist.

"Your father will be waiting to propose a toast to the bride." Along with everyone else—especially the five maids—Meg's mother scanned the room, trying to spot anything else they'd missed.

"In that case," Pru said, running a critical eye once more over Meg, "we'd better hurry, or there won't be any champagne left!"

Two minutes later, arm in arm with her mother and Pru, with Lydia and Anthi practicing their veil-holding skills and bringing up the rear, the bridal party, missing only Demon, slowly descended the stairs.

In the front hall, Fletcher, the butler, was returning through the front door, no doubt having assisted Horatia and George into their waiting carriage. Fletcher saw the group as they reached the landing. He beamed, then darted into the drawing room to alert Demon and Glengarah.

Managing her skirts down the stairs took concentration. Meg and her party were only halfway down the last flight when her father and brother-in-law strolled out of the drawing room. Each carried glasses, and Glengarah held a magnum of champagne.

Meg smiled down at the pair, noting both wore expressions of approbation and appreciation.

Her older brother Nicholas, his wife, Adriana, and Toby had volunteered to oversee matters at the church, so the group currently in the front hall included all the rest of her immediate family.

When she stepped down to the second-last stair, her father waved. "No—stop there. That's perfect." He beamed at her, and his blue eyes, courtesy of the two steps level with hers, were alight with paternal love and pride.

He beckoned to the others. "Come down and get your glasses."

Meg's mother and Pru slipped their arms from Meg's and complied, while Lydia and Anthi carefully laid down her train, then scampered down to join the others.

Deaglan and Demon handed around glasses of champagne, then with a delighted smile, Deaglan presented one to Meg.

Her smile a trifle wobbly, she accepted it.

The instant she had, Demon raised his glass. "A toast!" He lowered his arm, and his gaze captured Meg's. "To my darling girl. Today, you do us and the entire family proud! May you and that devil Wylde enjoy a long and happy marriage." He looked at Meg's mother, then caught her hand, raised it to his lips, and kissed her fingers. Lowering their now-linked hands, he looked back at Meg and raised his glass. "As we have."

"To Meg and Drago," Deaglan called, and everyone else, including all the staff who had gathered to see her leave the house, echoed the words.

Minutes later, wrapped in the warmth of good wishes, Meg was helped into the carriage that would take her to her wedding.

* * *

DRAGO AND DENTON took refuge in the vestry of St. George's Church in Hanover Square. Warley had elected to escort Drago's mother into the church, and two minutes after arriving in the vestry, the brothers were joined by George and Harry, whom Drago had asked to stand with him on this most momentous occasion.

"Saw Warley and your mother come in and guessed you must have arrived." Harry closed the vestry door on the babel of voices filling the body of the church.

"It's already shoulder to shoulder out there." George grinned. "That's one good thing about standing alongside you—we won't have anyone breathing down our necks."

Drago scoffed, but he was already starting to feel a trifle nervous. Not a common occurrence for him.

He'd also asked Thomas to stand up with him, but after some thought, Thomas had begged to be excused. Aware that, although as well-born as the rest of them, Thomas sometimes felt the weight of his relatively penniless state when exposed to the haughtily arrogant and judgmental upper echelons of the haut ton, Drago hadn't pressed.

"Lots of Cynsters and also your cousins looking alert out there," Harry told him. "Don't think you need fear anything will get past them."

George nodded. "Very much on watch and looking every which way at once."

Toby had seen Drago and Denton on their way in and assured them there were eyes and ears everywhere, including in the church's long colonnaded porch, and knowing that Meg would be accompanied to the church by her father and brother-in-law, plus their various coachmen and grooms, Drago felt somewhat relieved on that score. Nevertheless, he hadn't called off his trusted men—grooms, stable hands, and footmen from the Wylde House staff—who were circulating among the considerable crowd that had gathered outside to watch the procession of haut-ton carriages and exclaim over the ladies' gowns. "Hopefully," Drago said, "once today is over and our marriage is set in stone, whoever our villain is will accept defeat and retreat and leave us alone."

George, Harry, and Denton murmured agreement.

"I can't see what he could possibly hope to gain by continuing his campaign," Harry said.

George stirred. "And besides, it's not as if you and Meg will be easy to get at down at Wylde Court, surrounded by your exceedingly loyal and devoted staff."

Drago was counting on that.

The minister joined them. A connection of the Helmsfords, he was decked out in full regalia in honor of the occasion. He smiled at Drago, then extended the gesture to include the other three. "Gentlemen, I've just received word that the bride has arrived outside the church. It's therefore time we took our places." He met Drago's eyes. "If you will follow me, Your Grace?"

Drago inclined his head in acquiescence.

Immediately the minister exited the vestry, the noise in the church started to fade, replaced by the rustle of clothing as people shifted, searching for a better view.

As Drago walked out in the minister's wake, he reflected that if, two months ago, anyone had asked him how he expected to feel at this particular moment in his life—about to vow to cleave to a single female for the rest of his days—his answer would have been some combination of resignation and the acceptance of his doom.

Instead, on his way to marry Meg, he was prey to steadily building impatience. An impatience to have this day over and done so that, hand in hand, he and she could embark on the adventure of creating their joint life, the one they would live side by side, sharing and supporting each other through whatever the years might bring.

The eagerness to seize and secure that shining future that was coursing through him was so intense it stole his breath and left him humbled.

As he took up his position on the step before the altar, he looked up at the large window beyond the choir and literally prayed that all would run smoothly through the day, and that at the end of it, Meg would be his.

* * *

MEG PAUSED in the foyer of the church while her attendants fluttered and fussed about her. Her mother waited by the presently closed doors leading into the nave and watched in a way that reminded Meg that she was the baby of the family and about to leave her home. Her father stood to the side, waiting to escort her down the aisle, while Toby, standing guard by the door, watched over their mother's head, an understanding, indulgent smile on his lips.

Pru was among the flutterers. After primping the fern leaves in Meg's bouquet of white roses and lilies, Pru stepped back, and as Lydia and Anthi took up their places behind Meg, the edge of her train in their hands, Pru ran her gaze critically over them all. Frowning, she imperiously waved Demon to his position beside Meg, then after one last comprehensive glance, Pru nodded decisively. "We're ready."

She scurried around and took up her position behind Lydia and Anthi, and everyone looked at Toby.

He cracked open the door and signaled through it. A moment later, Carter and Calvin, their cousins, slipped into the foyer and took up stations at either side of the heavy double doors sealing off the nave.

Toby offered his arm to his mother. "Mama?"

She smiled, bustled the few steps to Meg, raised her veil, and bussed Meg's cheek. "I'm so proud of you, my love," she whispered. She resettled the veil, then turned to Toby and took his arm, and Calvin held open one of the double doors for them to slide through into the aisle.

Carter grinned at the assembled party. "The organist is on his toes. He'll start the wedding march as soon as Toby and Aunt Flick are seated."

During that final minute as she waited to start her walk down the aisle, to take Drago's hand and forge a new life by his side, Meg felt none of the apprehension she'd expected would consume her. Instead, despite the unresolved threats, despite the rush, despite everything, a heady sense of joyful eagerness welled inside and buoyed her.

The first strains of the wedding march rang out in a summoning peal.

Demon patted her hand. "Here we go, my darling girl. Are you ready?"

She looked up at him and knew happiness filled her eyes. "Yes."

Moving in ceremonial concert, Carter and Calvin, both beaming, swung the doors wide.

Meg hauled in an excited, expectant breath and held it, then Demon stepped out, and she paced with him.

They passed under the archway and into the nave, and her gaze flashed down the long aisle to the altar steps and landed on Drago.

Tall, dark-haired, superbly elegant in formal wedding attire, he waited, watching her, his dark gaze, even at this distance, compelling.

Mesmerizing.

She couldn't look away. Screened by her veil, her smile was all for him as on her father's arm, she traveled down the aisle, Demon's presence by her side the only thing restraining her from rushing.

Regardless of how they had got to this place, to this point in time, this moment was so right. So very right for both of them.

With that certainty in her heart, she halted and waited while her father ceremonially placed her hand in Drago's.

As his long fingers curled about hers, Drago's gaze was fixed on her veiled face; in that moment, he was every bit as consumed by her as she was by him.

Their gazes locked, then both drew in a breath and, as one, turned to face the minister.

For Drago, the ceremony passed in a blur of familiar phrases and words spoken by rote.

They exchanged their vows in clear, sure tones, yet instead of focusing on such physical manifestations, his awareness was overwhelmed by a deep, intense, and shatteringly complete understanding of what taking this step and marrying Meg truly meant for him.

The possessive protectiveness that had been steadily building from the moment he'd first met her was there to stay and would only grow more powerful with the years. The vulnerability that underlay that, that gave it birth and drove it, was now ineradicable and, likewise, destined to grow even more acute once she was formally his duchess.

In marrying Meg today, he was acknowledging that and accepting it. Willingly.

For a man like him, until now blithely hedonistic, today signaled a profound, bedrock-reshaping change.

The wonder of the moment was the emotion that had him so joyously embracing that reorienting of his life.

He was smiling with genuine happiness when the minister prompted him, and after receiving the wedding band from Denton, he slid the simple gold ring onto Meg's slender finger.

He looked into her face, into her eyes. Expectant excitement lit the sky-blue orbs, and her lips were as curved as his. Her entire expression was simply radiant.

The minister droned on through the various prayers, and Drago and Meg, their fingers now entwined, continued to play their prescribed roles. Then finally, he heard the minister declare that they were man and wife.

Closing the tome he had held throughout, the minister beamed on them both and, to Drago, said, "You may now kiss your bride."

His smile broke free, and he swept Meg into his arms. Laughing, she came readily, and they kissed—given the circumstances, not too passionately, yet the promise was there, rich and warm and alluring—to the sound of applause, laughter, and cheers.

They broke apart and turned to the congregation, only to be enveloped by a crowd of family and friends, all eager to press their congratulations and good wishes for a long and happy life.

Working in tandem, in the polished, free-flowing partnership they'd perfected over the past weeks, he and Meg didn't miss a beat in responding appropriately to each and every felicitation.

Eventually, courtesy of their mothers and various family members, they managed to beat a path to the church door and across the porch to the steps, at the bottom of which a barouche bedecked with white roses, lilies, and ribbons waited to carry them to St. Ives House. As the invited guests would join them at the wedding breakfast, all were happy to see them set off, and rice and flower petals rained upon them as hand in hand, smiling and laughing, they dashed down the steps to the carriage.

Drago helped Meg in, then followed. The footman—one of Drago's in full Wylde livery—shut the door and scrambled up to stand behind the seat. The footman, the coachman, and everyone Drago saw in the crowd was smiling delightedly.

The carriage moved off to cheers and waves.

As the barouche rolled into quieter surrounds, Drago sat back with a satisfied sigh. He was still smiling.

He glanced at Meg and found her regarding him, her expression relaxed and serene. She studied his face as he studied hers. Wondering what she was thinking, he arched a brow.

The curve of her lips deepened, then she said, "I feel as if I've stepped through some door and into a new life." She tipped her head. "I'd expected to feel something of the sort, but nothing so definite, so sharp and clear."

He thought, then replied, "I suppose, for you, the change is dramatic. Your identity has altered. You've just become the Duchess of Wylde. You've left your childhood home and will go to a new one, of which you'll be the mistress." He paused, then went on, "For you, the change is far more physically manifest than it is for me."

She searched his eyes, then head still tipped, prompted, "But…"

He flashed her a private smile, acknowledging that she'd read his thoughts correctly. "But despite the lack of physical change, for me, the sense of embarking on a new, fresh, and as yet entirely unwritten chapter of my life is equally real."

Holding her gaze, he reached for her hand, raised it to his lips, and pressed a kiss to her white-gloved knuckles. "We did it. We bowed to Fate, and now we're here. And we'll go forward together."

She looked into his eyes and, her expression still radiantly serene yet serious, nodded. "And together, we'll shape our joint future as we wish it to be."

He smiled, leaned closer, and kissed her lightly. "Amen." There was no doubt in his mind that they would do just that.

They arrived at St. Ives House to find members of their families already there, waiting to welcome them and direct them and all the guests that were following to the ballroom.

The next hours vanished in a giddy celebration, one full of laughter, happiness, and sincere good wishes.

With Drago, Meg circled the room, receiving the accolades and the congratulations heaped upon them with outward serenity; all of that, she'd been prepared for.

What set excitement and anticipation bubbling inside her was the realization that, in marrying Drago, she'd secured all she'd ever hoped to achieve—all she'd ever dreamed of achieving—through her marriage.

She'd married the right man for her; so many told her so, and in her heart, she knew that to be the unvarnished truth.

And as they'd agreed on the drive from the church, it was now up to them to make of their life what they would.

She couldn't wait to get started.

The wedding waltz she and Drago shared was, to her, a reflection of that. She laughed and let him whirl her down the room, keeping pace as he effortlessly swept her along.

To her mind, with the wedding now behind them, there was no cloud —no threat, no danger—any longer on their horizon.

The future beckoned, unfettered and full of promise.

Drago couldn't decide which of the many emotions surging through him was most dominant. Satisfaction, relief, joy, and eagerness for what lay ahead all had their moments. With Meg on his arm, he moved through the crowd, all intent on celebrating their union, and knew that, for him, today would always rank as a highlight of his life.

As he and Meg had alluded to earlier, today was the day when so much changed. Today marked the beginning of the rest of his life and hers.

With that certainty solidifying within him, he unreservedly gave himself up to enjoying the hours with their extensive families, connections, and friends.

In the melee, he and Meg caught up with George, Harry, and Thomas. All three were quick to offer their congratulations and wishes for a happy future.

George glanced at the celebratory crowd. "Excellent outcome all around!"

Harry nodded earnestly. "Haven't seen so much consensus in a crowd such as this…well, in my lifetime. Amazing, really."

Grinning, Thomas arched a brow at Drago and Meg. "So are you off to Wylde Court, then?"

Smiling, Drago met Meg's eyes and gently squeezed her hand. "Later today." He looked at his friends and pointedly added, "For at least several weeks."

"It's going to take me that long to find my way around the place." Meg's expression assured everyone that she was looking forward to the challenge.

Harry and George promptly fell to recalling all the highlights of the estate that, as visitors over many years, they had found of note.

"Don't forget the tower, either," Harry said. "The views from there are amazing!"

They chatted for several minutes, all in the vein of encouraging Meg in enjoying her time at Wylde Court, picking up the reins there as Drago's duchess. Then Drago and Meg moved on through the guests, stopping and chatting and being delighted.

Twenty minutes later, Meg directed Drago's attention to a couple ahead of them. "There's Alison and Joshua." The Melwins had received an invitation as a matter of course, and Meg and Drago had made sure that Joshua had been invited as well. Buoyed on happiness, Meg glanced at Drago. "Surely the Melwins have agreed to countenance their betrothal by now."

Looking at the couple standing at the edge of the crowd with their backs to Meg and Drago, Drago murmured, "So one would hope. Perhaps we can congratulate them. Let's find out."

On hearing Drago call their names, Alison and Joshua turned. On seeing who was approaching, the pair were quick to smile and offer their felicitations.

But Meg had seen the glumness both had leapt to hide, and she was sure Drago had, too. While the four of them exchanged the usual compliments, Meg glanced around. She and Drago had been circulating for long enough that others were no longer lying in wait, wanting to speak with them. No one was close enough to overhear. When the first rush of congratulations faded, she fixed Alison and Joshua with a direct look. "Have the Melwins agreed to your betrothal being announced?"

There was really no way to avoid answering that question.

Alison sighed, and her face fell. "No." She shared a grimly determined look with Joshua. "But we're not giving up. Hubert will have to climb off his high horse sometime."

"So he's still being difficult?" Drago asked.

Joshua nodded. "I—" He glanced at Alison and amended, "We are at our wits' end. If Hubert would give us some idea of what he sees as an issue—why he's advising his father not to agree to our betrothal being announced—I'm sure we would be able to address any perceived problem, but..." Joshua raised a hand in a gesture of helplessness. "We can't counter an argument that's not advanced."

Drago frowned. "I take your point." After a moment, he said, "If you think it would help"—he glanced at Meg—"we would be happy to speak with the Melwins on your behalf."

Meg nodded. "Absolutely. You can count on our support."

Alison smiled weakly. "Thank you." She looped her arm in Joshua's and glanced up at him. "But I'm determined to wear Hubert down. We will prevail, even if it takes a few more months." She smiled more confidently. "He can't resist forever. Not even Papa will allow that."

Others came up to hover, clearly waiting to speak with Meg and Drago.

Meg smiled at the newcomers, then said to Alison and Joshua, "If we can help, let us know."

With nods, the four parted, and with Drago, Meg moved on to the two matrons with daughters eager to engage with them.

Then the musicians returned, and the next hour flew.

Drago found Meg pried from his side to dance with her brothers, Nicholas and Toby, and subsequently, several of her cousins. He, in turn, was captured by his sisters, then by several cousins, all older than he, and all of whom took great delight in teasing him over him choosing to marry a Cynster.

They, it seemed, had heard about the "Cynsters only marry for love" mantra, and all were openly curious as to what he thought of it.

Assuming the cool haughtiness of the head of their house, he refused to give them even a hint.

His sense of self-preservation shuddered at the thought.

Finally—*finally!*—it was time for the newlyweds to depart.

Of course, Meg had to throw her bouquet, which she did from halfway up the mansion's main stairs. Although she closed her eyes before flinging the flowers high over the jostling group of unmarried young ladies, the bouquet nevertheless fell on Lydia's head. As Lydia was already engaged, that surprised no one, but put big smiles on the faces of Lydia and her bridegroom-to-be.

Her hand in Drago's, Meg hurried up the stairs, and he cooled his heels in the corridor while, with Pru, Lydia, and Amarantha in attendance, Meg hurried out of her wedding gown and into a carriage dress and bonnet suitable for the drive to Wylde Court.

When the door opened and she stepped into the corridor, Drago rose. As always, she looked enchanting to him—to all his senses—and if anything, being finally married had heightened the possessiveness he'd always felt toward her.

Mine. All mine.

He managed to find a smile that was merely charming and didn't reflect the more primitive emotions coursing through him. He held out his hand to her. "Shall we?"

Her glorious smile bloomed, and she walked forward and set her hand in his. "Let's go."

Let's start on our journey together.

Her eyes filled in the words she didn't say, but he needed no further encouragement to close his hand about hers and turn with her to the stairs.

They descended to applause and cheers and something akin to acclaim. Their nearest and dearest lined their path to the front door, waiting to press their hands, kiss their cheeks, and wish them well. It was one of those rare times in life when Drago felt that emotion referred to as "family feeling" wrapping about and weaving through the gathering like some tangible entity.

Finally, after shaking hands with a beaming George and Harry and a smiling yet serious Thomas, with Meg by his side, Drago stepped through the heavy doors of St. Ives House and onto the porch.

Immediately before the steps, in the short gravel forecourt, his curricle stood waiting, the grays champing at their bits. Of course, some wags had decided to decorate the curricle with white ribbons and ribbon-rosettes, and several cans dangled from the rear.

A nervous Milton held the horses' heads and was looking anywhere but at his master.

Denton leaned close and whispered, "Don't blame Milton. The Cynster and Helmsford younger crew weren't about to listen to anything he said."

"I don't suppose," Drago murmured back, "that you thought to intervene?"

"Good God no!" Denton slapped Drago on the shoulder. "I've lived to see you set off on your honeymoon in appropriate style."

Others around them chuckled.

Meg, too, had been studying the curricle. "I have to say, that isn't as bad as I'd expected."

Drago decided to say no more.

Instead, he glanced at Meg, tightened his grip on her hand, and caught her gaze. "Are you ready, my dear duchess?"

She smiled the smile she reserved just for him. "Never more so, Your Grace."

He chuckled and led her down the steps. Others followed them.

After helping Meg up to her seat, Drago rounded the horses, accepted the reins from Milton, and paused to set the lad's mind at rest and to release him to return to Wylde House.

In their earlier planning, their various supporters had agreed that Drago and Meg should head directly for the Court rather than pause for no real reason in Park Lane.

Not that anyone expected any further attack, not now they were wed.

The reins in his hand, Drago leapt into the curricle. Their well-wishers crowded around, but all were wary of the heavy-hoofed grays and didn't get too close, allowing Drago to salute everyone with his whip and call out their thanks one last time, with Meg echoing his sentiments, then he eased the reins, and the curricle rolled smoothly forward to cheers and several more-raucous suggestions.

As they turned out of the St. Ives House gates and the yells from behind them faded, replaced by the clattering of the cans banging on the cobbles, facing forward, Meg sighed, a happy sound.

When Drago glanced her way, she caught his eye and smiled. "That was entirely predictable in every way."

He smiled back, then concentrated on tooling the curricle around Grosvenor Square. As soon as they were out of sight of St. Ives House, he drew the curricle to the curb, handed the reins to Meg with a "Hold them," and stepped down to remove the cans.

While he did, Meg pulled off every ribbon she could reach. When, having stowed the cans in the boot, Drago returned, she handed him the reins. "Wait while I finish deribboning us. I don't fancy driving all the way into Kent advertising our newlywed state."

"No, indeed."

Drago waited patiently while the ribbons, too, were thrust into the boot. When Meg clambered back up and took her seat beside him, he met her gaze and smiled. "Ready?"

She beamed and faced forward. "Let's go." A few minutes later, she leaned her shoulder against his and added, "And if I might suggest, once we're free of the traffic and on the open road, it would be fitting for you to give your horses their heads."

Drago's smile deepened. As was so often the case, he and she were in absolute agreement.

CHAPTER 15

*T*he sun's last rays were slanting across the lawns and the front façade of Wylde Court when Drago steered the now-docile grays up the long, curving drive to the graveled forecourt.

A sense of relief spread through him, along with welling anticipation.

He drew the horses to a halt and glanced at Meg. "Here we are."

She met his eyes, expectation and awareness in her gaze. "Indeed."

His staff had been on watch. Grooms came running to take charge of the horses. Drago descended, passed on the reins, then rounded the curricle and handed Meg down.

As she stepped onto the gravel, the grooms, both older men, bowed ceremonially. "Your Graces."

Drago felt Meg's fingers flutter in his and tightened his grip. When she looked at him, he smiled reassuringly. "The rest of the staff will be waiting inside to welcome you."

Her answering smile was a little less certain.

They'd brought no baggage with them; all their luggage would already be there, sent down earlier in a heavy carriage with Maurice, Tisdale, and Rosie. Consequently, no footmen came running, but the front doors had been propped wide, and Fothergill, the Court's butler, stood waiting.

Drago drew Meg's arm through his and led her toward the shallow steps leading up to the porch. "Chin up," he murmured. "Believe me, they'll welcome you with open arms."

She glanced at him questioningly. "Because I'm your duchess?"

They started climbing, and he confided, "Despite my wider reputation, I'm something of a favorite here."

Meg found that easy to believe. She'd already realized that her husband was a complex man with multiple façades he showed to different groups. At base, at heart, he was, however, always the same—a kind and caring nobleman who accepted his responsibilities and took them seriously.

She didn't doubt that his staff there, on his principal estate, loved him for that.

Just as I've come to do.

The understanding that she shared that trait with the very formal butler, Fothergill, who maintained a neutral expression but whose eyes twinkled warmly, with his wife, the bobbing housekeeper who eyed her with open hope, and with all the staff members in the long line snaking up the grand staircase made the ceremonial introductions and induction into the ways of Wylde Court easier than she'd imagined.

When they reached the youngest scullery maid and the bootboy, both of whom looked at Meg with awe and something close to reverence, she couldn't hold back and acknowledged Fothergill's introduction and the little maid's awkward curtsy and the boy's overexuberant bow with a bright, appreciative smile.

Before she could turn away, Drago stepped to her side. He, too, smiled at the young pair, and Meg saw both smile back.

They're not nervous of him at all. Fancy that.

"Thank you, Fothergill." Drago nodded in dismissal to the butler and caught Meg's eyes. "We can find our way from here."

Fothergill bowed. "Of course, Your Grace." Straightening, his expression softened, and he inclined his head deferentially to Meg. "Your Grace. Once again, welcome to Wylde Court."

The assembled staff, who had turned to watch her progress up the stairs, cheered and clapped.

Meg felt herself blushing. Spontaneously, she raised her hand and waved. "Thank you!" she called, then Drago closed his hand about hers and tugged her on.

She went, allowing him to draw her with him along the gallery.

He turned through an archway, and his fingers tightened about hers. With his other hand, he gestured down the corridor along which they were now walking quite rapidly. "The ducal apartments are at the end."

She'd expected to feel nervous, tentative at least. Instead, excitement and eagerness and searing impatience bubbled up inside her.

They reached the double doors at the corridor's end. Drago released her hand to set them swinging wide, then waved her through, and without the slightest hesitation, she walked in.

She paused in a foyer of sorts with three doors—one ahead, one to the left, and another to the right. The one ahead stood open, and she continued through. She heard a *click* behind her as Drago closed the main doors before following.

She'd walked into an airy, comfortable apartment that stretched across the width of the wing. Large mullioned windows overlooked an expanse of formal gardens delimited by the tall trees with which the estate seemed liberally endowed. To her left was a sitting area, with two well-padded armchairs upholstered in gold velvet arranged before a fireplace, on either side of which two large windows admitted the last of the evening's golden light. The room's walls were paneled to waist height in the same dark wood of the heavy, ornate mantelpiece; she thought it was black walnut. The floors, too, were of the same wood, polished to an obsidian sheen, but the darkness was alleviated by richly patterned, jewel-toned carpets that even her undereducated eye could see were little short of masterpieces.

After shutting the door, Drago had paused just inside, watching her drink in the room. "The rugs are from the Near East, courtesy of one of my roving great-uncles."

"Hmm." Above the paneling, the walls were plastered and painted a soft ivory and hosted several paintings of landscapes she suspected were scenes from the estate—wooded hills rolling away, a forest glade, the still waters of a large lake.

Drawing in a breath tense with rising anticipation, she turned to survey the massive four-poster bed that dominated the right half of the room. Like the mantelpiece, the bed was flanked by two windows and carved from the same black walnut, its posts, headboard, and footboard all richly patterned with acorns, roses, oak leaves, and vines. The heavy brocade curtains, presently looped back, were in the black, gold, and silver of the Helmsford livery. The silk counterpane was gold, edged with black and silver, and the mounded pillows looked to be covered in silver-hued silk.

There was furniture placed throughout the room—a writing desk and chair set before the main window, a sideboard, two chests of drawers, and a credenza, plus small tables on either side of the bed—but she barely noticed them; her gaze had fixed on the sumptuous luxury of the huge, tempting bed.

She moistened her lips and glanced at Drago. "Who sleeps here?"

His dark gaze met hers. "I have been. I was hoping we would."

Oh, good. She forced herself to glance around. "Your parents didn't have separate rooms?" Not that she cared.

"I was informed that they never saw the need."

When she looked at him, she saw he was smiling. "My parents never did, either."

"Ah. Well, in lieu of an extended tour"—he pointed to a door in the inner wall to the right of the bed—"through there you will find your dressing room and a bathing chamber beyond." He swiveled to point to a matching door in the inner wall to the left of the fireplace. "And my dressing room and bathing chamber are through there."

She nodded. "In that case..." She drew in a deeper breath. He'd drawn closer as they'd spoken. She swung toward him and flung herself at him with absolute confidence that he would catch her.

On a chuff of surprised laughter, he did, his hands fastening tight about her waist, capturing and anchoring her against him, and as she raised her head, his swooped, and he covered her lips with his.

They'd previously shared precisely four kisses. None had been like this one.

The heat, the erupting passion, the surge of greedy, compulsive desire simply hadn't been there before.

Then again, before, they hadn't been married, and now they were.

Now, they were not just free to indulge, but this—this rabid hunger, feeding it, assuaging it—was expected, even encouraged.

She raised both hands and speared her fingers into his black locks, holding his face as she pressed what was nothing less than an urgent entreaty upon him. Since he'd first kissed her on the cottage stairs, she'd longed to do just this, but hadn't dared. She hadn't known what might ensue and had been wary about stepping into a situation that might have veered out of control.

Now, with their wedding behind them, she was free to expand her horizons in this sphere. To cast off all restraint and learn what would come when she lay in this man's arms.

With boundless eagerness and enthusiasm, she threw herself into the task.

His palms eased from her waist and slid lower. He cupped his hands about the globes of her derriere and gathered her even closer, explicitly molding her hips to his even as he angled his head, with his tongue found hers, and with blatant mastery, took control of the incendiary kiss.

And taught her how physically engaging a kiss could be. With a deliberation—a determination and intent—that captured her utterly, he opened her eyes to unexpected pleasures. She lost touch with the world as he languidly stroked and evocatively plundered, teasing her senses and artfully drawing her wits into a game of thrust and caress that quickly devolved into a duel of tongues that second by second grew even more heated.

The rampant ridge of his erection pressed against the curve of her belly. Registering the fact and its implications—its promise—her greedy heart leapt, and she murmured incoherent encouragement into the kiss.

Then she caught her mental breath, seized the moment figuratively with both hands, and using her lips, her mouth, her tongue, her hands, her fingers, and the pressure of her slim frame sued for more.

More. Everything. Every last element of passionate lovemaking that he could teach her.

Given his reputation, she felt certain she was in good hands and flung her considerable will into encouraging him to show her every last aspect he could.

In flagrant pursuit of that, she pressed even closer, and his arms locked about her, and he lifted her off her toes and waltzed them toward that gigantic bed.

Again, she expected to feel at least a twinge of trepidation; she was a virgin, after all. Yet once again, caught up in the driving heat of the moment, in the building urgency, with her senses consumed and desire lashing her with a fiery whip, all she was conscious of was an utterly compelling, giddy-making impatience to rid themselves of the layers between them so she could feel his body against hers.

That was what she wanted; that was what she was determined to have.

Drago had expected this engagement—the first of many, or so he hoped—to proceed by slow and cautious steps. He'd steeled himself to pander to and delicately overcome some degree of maidenly modesty and shyness.

Clearly, his bride—his new duchess—was made of sterner stuff and had other ideas.

Or more precisely, she had only one.

One that had captured his own raging desire and whipped it into a frenzy.

He'd thought he'd been waiting with sophisticated patience. In reality, his inner self had merely been craftily holding back, biding its time and seeking the right moment to rise to the fore, slip every leash, and seize her.

With her greedy hands and urgent, hungry kisses, she'd given his primal, primitive inner self permission to do just that.

As if to emphasize her direction, the instant he halted beside the bed, without breaking from the conflagrationary kiss, she snatched her hands from his hair and fell on his cravat. She freed the large pin, anchored it in the lapel of his coat, and set her quick fingers to the silk folds.

What was he supposed to do?

With his more primitive side in the ascendancy, he sought out the buttons closing the bodice of her carriage dress and expertly slid them free.

This wasn't at all how he had envisaged the engagement progressing, but he saw no reason—had no wish much less any will—to cavil as, in a flurry of hands and grasping fingers, they peeled layer after layer from each other.

Fine fabrics went flying, discarded with abandon. Shoes and socks were dispensed with in short order.

At one point, gripped by a guilty sense that he should make some effort to be more attentive, he tried his damnedest to slow down, but she gave vent to a frustrated sound and all but ripped his shirt away.

He gave up, gave in, and helped her free his hands from the cuffs— before she realized the advantage his hands and arms being tangled afforded her.

In between scorching, searing kisses marked by increasingly flagrant and provocative caresses, they proceeded with frenzied alacrity to strip each other of every last stitch.

Exuberantly, she flung the shirt aside, and his inner self chuckled, amused and delighted. He couldn't recall ever having such a blatantly enthusiastic partner.

They swayed together while their lips and mouths continued their ravenous plundering, and her fingers wrestled with the buttons anchoring his trousers while he unpicked the laces of her full petticoats that some unkind person had knotted at the back of her waist.

Finally, the laces came free, and with a well-judged push, he sent the fine frothing cotton sliding down her long, long legs.

Still engrossed in kissing him, she raised one foot, stepped free, then used her other foot to kick the petticoats away. Angling his gaze down, he saw she was wearing silk stockings anchored above her knees with ruched blue-silk garters.

On impulse, as his waistband loosened, he broke from the kiss and her grasping hands and slid to his knees before her. "Allow me."

The words emerged in a gravelly growl.

Her body was still teasingly sheathed in a fine translucent silk chemise. Sliding his hands beneath the chemise's edge, he set his palms to the bare skin of one thigh, just above the garter, and her breath hitched and her fingertips sank into the muscles of his shoulders.

Smiling inside, he glided his palms down, smoothing garter and gossamer-silk stocking over the sleek muscles of her calf to her foot, then when she raised that foot, he drew stocking and garter free and dropped them to one side.

He leaned into her, his head against the soft swell of her belly, and repeated the exercise with her other leg.

Her fingers slid into his hair and gripped, clutching his head to her as she fought to find her balance in what, to her senses, was no doubt a careening world.

The scent of her arousal reached his nostrils and wove into his brain, an aphrodisiac like no other.

Driven by a surge of primitive need, he rose—and discovered that she'd succeeded in loosening both his trousers and the silk smallclothes he'd worn beneath. Both garments slid from his lean hips and puddled about his feet.

She pushed into him, and her lips found his again. He stepped forward, into her, lifting his feet free.

He was naked, she was almost so, and as his hands instinctively found their way beneath the hem of her chemise and his palms glided over the luscious globes of her bottom and the shock of skin-to-skin contact seared through them both, the expertise of years raised its head.

He hadn't thought this through. He had no plan for how matters would proceed. He hadn't allowed for the heightened urgency that had gripped them both and derailed all hope of him controlling the play, yet with her lips and greedy urging hands, she continued to make her demands crystal clear, and he needed to decide on the right next move immediately if not sooner.

He'd been an acknowledged rake of the highest order for over a decade. There was a reason for that.

This was nothing more than his latest challenge.

With blinding rapidity, he reviewed and discarded a slew of possibilities; there was really only one that met the needs of an enthusiastic lady-virgin.

As if to confirm that, her hands were streaking over him, exploring the contours of his body and eagerly reaching for areas he would prefer she didn't yet touch. Decision made, he didn't bother to relieve her of her chemise, but hauled her hard against him, trapping her hands, then he bent slightly, looped an arm beneath her bottom, and hoisted her up against him.

She broke from the kiss on a gasp. Her hands fell to his bare shoulders. Her breasts, screened only by the finest gossamer silk, rose and fell dramatically right in front of his face. His mouth watered, but he held to his course, the one he knew would be best for her. Prompted by the slide of his hands along the backs of her thighs, all but instinctively, she clamped her knees to his hips. From beneath heavy lids, through her long lashes, she looked down at him, and her blue eyes smoldered.

Before she could think enough to attempt to direct him, he turned and sat on the bed, then fell back onto the silk coverlet.

She uttered a small shriek as she followed him down, then discovering herself straddling his waist, settled and slowly pushed up. Once she was sitting across his hips, her knees to either side, predictably, she tried to frown, although the effect was nothing like her best efforts. "What...?"

His gaze drinking in the sight of her, he let his lips slowly curve. "We'll get to what's next in a moment, but first..." Firming one hand at her back, he half sat, propping on one braced arm. "You're still wearing too many clothes."

He breathed the last word against the peak of one breast, then licked the silk over the jutting tip, wetting the fabric until it stuck to her heated flesh, then he opened his mouth and drew the luscious bud in. She made a shocked, choked sound, and her fingers slid into his hair and gripped. Tight. They tightened even more as he licked, laved, and curled his tongue about her distended nipple. He played, and she fought to catch her breath, which only grew more ragged with every passing second.

Eventually judging her too far gone to attempt redirecting him, he slid his hand from her back and closed it about her other breast, kneading in time to his devouring. Then he drew back—to a wordless, breathless protest from her—but only to transfer his attention to her thus-far-neglected breast.

The relief that slid through her as she realized his intention set his lips curving again.

He would have taken more time to savor the delights of the luscious mounds, but part of his so-experienced brain kept track of her responses, following each movement, logging every sigh, waiting for the right moment...

When for the third time, she squirmed against him, grinding her hips across his, he drew back and, grasping her chemise with both hands, drew the filmy garment up, over her head. Without hesitation, she lifted her arms and freed them, leaving him to fling that last barrier away.

Before the material even left his fingers, she fell on him, clasping his face between her hands and pressing a kiss that was all fire and demand upon him.

Then she drew back just enough to focus on his eyes. "Show me. Now."

His reaction—instinctive in the face of such blatant challenge—was to spear the fingers of his hands into her hair and hold her steady as he plundered her mouth anew. He gradually sat up, easing her hips back.

"How?" she whispered through the shockingly ardent exchange.

"Like this." He showed her how to position herself, then from close range, met her gaze. Their heated breaths mingled as he whispered, "The reins are in your hands."

She blinked, and he watched—delighted anew—as understanding dawned, infusing her delicate features.

Then her eyes locked with his and, holding his gaze, she eased down.

Taking him in, inch by excruciatingly slow inch.

His hands rode her hips. His palms itched with the impulse to push firmly down. He set his jaw and resisted. Endured. This might be torture, but it was the best way for her, for her first time…

The head of his erection butted against the barrier he'd expected to find, and she frowned.

Before he could gather his wits enough to issue direction or encouragement, she tightened around him, shattering his ability to think, then apparently realizing the inadvisability of that action, she relaxed her inner muscles and, with typical determination, pushed forcefully down.

"Oh—" She bit off the pained sound.

"Shh." He kissed her gently, drawing her into the kiss, distracting her even while his senses reeled. She was tight, so tight; he felt as if, behind his lids, his eyes had crossed with sheer pleasure…

Easing back from the kiss, he whispered against her lips, "Just wait a moment." Then he kissed her again, more deeply, snaring her skittering senses and drawing them into the exchange.

She followed his lead, at first. But seconds later, she pulled back from the kiss and, eyes closed, experimentally shifted.

It was his turn to bite his lip and cling to sanity. Then he hauled in a breath, expanding his lungs, and gripping her hips, said, "Like this."

He showed her how to ride him, initially helping her set the pace, but she soon caught the rhythm, and he could lean back, let his eyes feast, and try to hold his own demons at bay enough to wallow in the view.

Her curly golden tresses had slid free of the French knot and bounced about her alabaster shoulders. Her breasts were full and swollen and, here and there, flaunted the marks of his earlier attentions.

The sight tightened something in his gut, something primal and powerful.

As, now confident and sure, she rode him, her lips curved with pure delight, and her features all but glowed with an open sensuality that literally stole his breath.

He'd never—ever—been with such a captivating lover. Somehow or other, she—his wife, his duchess—drew on some hitherto unsuspected part of him and held that entity in her hands, a willing prisoner.

Meg had to keep her eyes closed in order to catalog everything her overloaded senses were relaying to her brain. The feel of him inside her was simply indescribable. So large, hard, and rigidly ungiving, yet as she rode him and he filled her slick channel, the friction was exquisite, the sensations sublime.

She finally understood why her sister and all her married cousins and cousins-in-law smiled so fondly upon their husbands. She hadn't realized that passion and desire could move one to such sensual heights. To the point where the physical act became merely a way of connecting with emotions that ran much deeper.

She'd felt that tumbled jumble of raw and powerful emotions in his kiss, could feel it even now in his touch as his hands sculpted her body with a reverence that was impossible to miss.

She focused on that, on the feelings and emotions, and followed where they led. Rising and falling upon him, helped by the strength in his hands and arms, in increasing desperation, she forged on, knowing there had to be a destination to this journey, although she wasn't entirely sure what it was.

The molten heat within her constricted, tightened, a heated spring winding tauter with every solid impaling thrust of his body into hers.

With every thudding beat of her heart.

Involuntarily, her body tightened about his, and still she pressed on.

Then suddenly, between one gasping breath and the next, she was flying.

Flying apart.

She screamed as her senses shattered, and she saw stars. Bright, brilliant explosions, a kaleidoscope of sensations fired and fled down every nerve.

Heat followed, a wash of glorious sensual warmth unlike any sensation she'd felt before.

The joy of it flooded her, washed through her, then slowly, very slowly, receded, and she slumped forward, catching herself on hands splayed across Drago's damp chest.

Slumping fully down on his back, he drew her close, into his arms, then he rolled, taking her with him, placing her beneath him. Then he rose above her and moved inside her, and to her considerable surprise, her body, already humming with delight, responded anew.

Drago felt her rise to his next thrust and swallowed a groan. This engagement had—entirely unexpectedly—taken him into an arena unknown.

The unforgiving desperation to claim her, to make her his, was an order of magnitude greater than any compulsion he'd felt before. The experience of being wholly at the mercy of such ungovernable urges was both novel and beyond unsettling. Almost scarifying.

But Meg was his—his in a way no other lady had ever been.

His to hold, to protect. To cleave to in life's storms.

Where did that thought come from?

Yet he knew it was true. She was destined to be his everything. She was slated to be the kernel of his life henceforth.

Even as he acknowledged that, he let the reins slide from his grasp and let his body take over. Knowing that the exigencies of the age-old dance could and would subsume all thought, he bowed his head, let go, and let Fate and whatever this was that had risen so powerfully between them have him.

Losing himself in her did, indeed, consume him.

She shattered anew, a sensation, a sight, he would never tire of, then as all tension drained from her, in a series of powerful thrusts that left him utterly undone, his body claimed its own release.

All strength drained from him, and on a muted groan, he slumped on his forearms, careful not to squash her into the mattress, soft though it was.

In the darkness that had fallen, in the country silence that now cocooned them, their breaths were labored, hers a warm puff against his cheek, their hearts still thudding as one in his ears.

It took several long minutes before he could summon sufficient strength to raise his head and look into her face. When he focused on her features, his ego preened. Even though she seemed asleep, a smugly satisfied smile curved her lips.

With his gaze, he traced the full curve of those luscious lips and realized that he was smiling inanely.

Gazing at her, he felt the warmth in his chest that she and only she evoked swell until it filled him. He stared at her for long moments as full realization sank in.

I've fallen ineradicably in love.

He studied her, waiting for something—anything—inside him to rise up in mocking rejection.

Nothing did.

After several seconds of surprise over that unqualified acceptance, he lifted from her, then rearranged them in the bed. He slumped on his back, one arm cradling her as she huffed and snuggled against him, then she settled her head on his chest, and all tension fled her limbs.

He tried to think, to imagine what this not-entirely-unexpected turn of events would mean. Yet the only coherent thought his brain produced, just as he slid over the edge of sleep, was that as a Cynster, she'd run true to her family's form.

CHAPTER 16

Over the following days, Meg happily settled into her role as Drago's duchess. While being constantly addressed as "Your Grace" took a little getting used to, the contentment she felt in going about the huge house, in interacting with Fothergill and Mrs. Fothergill and the other staff, was both relief and encouragement.

Indeed, the atmosphere pervading the massive mansion was universally one of positivity and optimism, of looking forward with hope and eagerness. Meg was reassured to discover that the large staff apparently got along very well; most were children of the estate, and their fathers and grandfathers—or mothers and grandmothers—had worked in the same roles in decades past.

Over those decades, the day-to-day procedures had been refined and perfected, until now, the entire household rolled smoothly along under the steady hand of the Fothergills with nary a hitch along the way.

Rosie, who had come with Meg from Half Moon Street, had reported that she'd been made very welcome and had found the household remarkably calm and well ordered. "It's a happy place, miss—Your Grace, I mean. I haven't come across anyone even given to moodiness yet."

For his part, Drago endeared himself to her—even more than he had to that point—by understanding that she would need a few days to find her feet.

In that regard, by the Wednesday after the wedding, Meg felt she was making solid progress; to her and, apparently, to all others at Wylde Court, it was increasingly clear that being Drago's duchess was exactly the right occupation for her.

All in all, she felt relieved, reassured, and was actively enjoying settling into her new home.

As for the private hours she and Drago spent in the ducal apartments, that was another source of delight, not to say pleasure. Not to say revelation. She hadn't really thought about how having a husband and being intimate with him—often several times a day—might alter, more specifically strengthen, their relationship. She was starting to grasp that reality and develop a deeper appreciation of her family's long-held belief that Cynsters should only marry for love.

Love, she'd realized, was one of those emotions impossible to comprehend until one experienced it oneself. That she was in love with Drago was impossible to deny, and while neither had yet admitted their state, she firmly believed he loved her. He certainly acted like it, not just in their bedroom but in every facet of their life.

Their love-based marriage was currently a work in progress, and with that, too, she was content.

Unexpectedly, at least to her, Ridley, the puppy, had arrived with their luggage from London. Still decidedly half grown and gangly and awkward with it, the pup had taken to following her everywhere and, when she sat, if he could, curling up on her feet.

Drago was the only other human Ridley showed such signs of loyalty toward; the pup seemed to consider everyone else as to be tolerated or cultivated where necessary, but not worthy of his allegiance.

As on that Wednesday morning, with Ridley at her heels, she made her way to her private sitting room, a spacious parlor abutting her end of the ducal suite, she turned her mind to what challenge she should next address in donning the mantle of Drago's duchess.

She was almost to the door when it opened, and Fothergill came out.

Seeing her, the butler smiled and bowed. "Good morning, Your Grace. The mail arrived early, bringing several letters for you. I placed them on your desk." He held the door for her and the pup.

Passing him with a smile, Meg replied, "Thank you, Fothergill. I'll attend to them now."

Eager to see who had written, she crossed to the escritoire set before a large window overlooking the gardens. Three letters lay on the leather-edged blotter. She picked them up. The first was from her mother, the second from Pru, while the third... "Interesting." She hadn't expected Drago's mother, who had remained in London, to communicate with her at this point.

Fothergill had shut the door. Meg picked up a letter knife and broke the seal on all three letters, then leaving the knife on the desk, she carried the letters to the comfortable chair angled before the hearth, in which a small fire cheerily popped and crackled.

She settled in the armchair, and after Ridley had made himself comfortable, she opened her mother's missive. As she'd anticipated, it contained a report of how the wedding had been received by the wider ton. Apparently, everyone was genuinely pleased, and high hopes were being entertained regarding their future in both political and social spheres. While Meg had expected that, it was nevertheless gratifying to have it confirmed. Once she and Drago returned to London, they would have plenty to keep them occupied on multiple fronts.

Pru's letter was a mixture of cousinly gossip and sisterly advice, much of which made Meg laugh. As the oldest and youngest of the four in their family and six years apart in age, she and Pru had not been that close through their childhoods. But as adults, they'd grown progressively closer, and ever since her engagement to Drago, Meg had felt a greater and stronger bond with Pru, and from the revelations and frank if often hilarious advice Pru imparted, she felt the same.

Feeling a glow of familial contentment, Meg folded Pru's letter, set it aside with their mother's, and with curiosity welling, unfolded the three sheets of the dowager's communication. Meg scanned past the usual salutations and transparently fond wishes for success in their marriage, then slowed as she reached the meat of the missive. The dowager had very helpfully written a short list, with descriptions appended, of the local ladies Meg could expect to have bowl up to the front door once the first week of their marriage had passed and the locals commenced paying bride visits.

As everyone knew, the touted purpose of such visits was to welcome the new bride to local society. Equally, it was an opportunity for those who visited to take stock of her and make judgments over how she might fit into their circles.

Twice, Meg read through the information Constance had thought fit to impart. It was extremely pertinent and useful intelligence, and Meg was grateful to have it. While many new brides were left to find their way unassisted, Constance had taken the time and thought to reach out and support Meg in taking up what had been, previously, Constance's role.

Feeling heartened, relieved, and undeniably more confident over embarking on an aspect of her new life that she'd yet to spend much time contemplating, Meg laid the letter with the others, then sat and stared at the flames in the hearth while she considered her initial approach to local society. Should she wait for them to come to her? Or should she, perhaps, steal a march and take more definite control of the situation?

She knew which path she felt more inclined to follow, but despite the weeks she'd spent with Christopher and Ellen at Walkhurst Manor over the years, she didn't know enough about the local area, of potential events much less the likely attendance of local gentry, to be able to craft any campaign.

Deciding that she did, indeed, favor taking control of how she engaged with local society and, therefore, needed more information, she rose and, with Ridley trotting behind, set off for the library. At that hour, Drago would almost certainly be there, dealing with his correspondence and estate business.

She tapped on the door, then opened it and looked in.

Seated at his desk, Drago glanced up and saw her. Straightening in his chair, he smiled in welcome and waved her in. "What is it?"

He watched as his ever-engaging wife closed the door after Ridley and, a slight frown on her face—one he now knew signified thinking and planning—came to sink into the armchair to the side of his desk, the one he'd placed there just for her.

"I've been thinking," she began, meeting his eyes, "that from Sunday onward, we're likely to see the local ladies, possibly with husbands in tow, rolling up to the front door to pay their respects."

"To get a good look at you and take the temperature of our marriage?"

She reached down and scratched Ridley behind his ears. "Just so."

He rapidly reviewed what he knew of the surrounding gentry. "While I'm acquainted with the local gentlemen, I have to admit that, to date, I've avoided their wives like the plague, so I fear I won't be much help with them."

She waved dismissively. "Never fear. Your mother has come to our rescue. She wrote with details of the ladies we can expect to call and what I should anticipate with each."

He smiled. "Remind me to be suitably grateful when next I see Mama."

She nodded in mock-seriousness. "Indeed, you should be." Then her expression eased, and she studied him. "I was wondering…"

When he arched a brow, she continued, "While I'm not at all keen for our week of peace to end, it will all too soon. What do you think of us making a preemptive foray into local circles?"

He blinked. "Instead of waiting here like sitting ducks?"

"Precisely."

He swiveled to fully face her. "What do you have in mind?"

They discussed the possibilities. While he might not know the local ladies, he knew every local event held within twenty miles. After they'd defined what they wanted to achieve—an appearance at some local event at which other members of the surrounding gentry would be present—he suggested, "We could attend the market in Sissinghurst. It's held on Saturday and is the largest local market. I would expect to see most of the local gentlemen, usually with their wives, there."

She smiled, eager and approving. "That sounds perfect!"

He loved the way her expressions reflected her emotions. That made his life much easier; he rarely couldn't immediately identify what she was feeling. What she was thinking wasn't always so easy to guess, but her feelings were usually clear.

She continued, "That's exactly the right sort of event. Informal, and our appearance there this Saturday will be seen as you showing me around the local entertainments."

"As a fond husband should." He smiled indulgently, aware of sinking just a little more deeply, a little more comfortably into married life. Not in a million years would he have imagined such a life would suit him so well, but there was no denying the sense of having finally found his right path nor the reassurance evoked by knowing he would have Meg's hand in his as they went forward in life.

She, too, had relaxed into this new state of being. She glanced at his desk, then caught his eye and arched a brow. "Is there anything note-worthy going on in town?"

He glanced at the letter he'd been perusing when she'd arrived. "I haven't heard of anything in general, but"—he looked back at her—"I received a note from Chillingworth seeking confirmation that, now I'm finally a married man, I'm serious about becoming more active in Parliament."

Her brows rose. "This is following on from our exchange at the wedding breakfast?"

Drago nodded. "I told you that various members of that group had approached me, and in the main, our ideas and opinions run largely parallel."

She tipped her head. "So what does Chillingworth actually mean?"

He grinned; trust her to focus on the crux of the issue.

They spent the next twenty minutes discussing possibilities and options, including what interests he might personally pursue and how best to respond to the group's overture, leaving Drago reassured and relieved by the evidence freely offered that Meg considered herself his partner in the political arena, too.

* * *

AS THEIR FIRST step in controlling their entrance into local society, on Saturday morning, Meg strolled on Drago's arm into the busy market-place located next to the Milk House Inn in the village now known as Sissinghurst.

She'd seen the new signs as they'd driven in along the lane. "I remember this village being called Milkhouse. That was its name, wasn't it?"

Drago nodded. "They officially changed the name only recently."

"I knew they'd started to call it Sissinghurst instead, but why?"

"The old name has a strong association with the Hawkhurst Gang and evokes too many bad memories for people around here."

"Ah. I see." She surveyed the three rows of stalls ahead of them. "Where should we start?"

"Given we're here to see and be seen rather than buy anything, I doubt it matters."

She opted for a methodical approach, moving down the row on the left first.

They weren't even halfway down the row before they were bailed up by the local squire. A bluff, genial man clearly well acquainted with Drago, the squire was all delight when Drago introduced him to Meg.

Meg smiled and chatted easily, then after directing a questioning look at Drago and receiving an infinitesimal nod in response, she invited the squire and his lady to call on them the following afternoon.

The squire professed himself beyond delighted. "And the dear wife will be *aux anges*, have no doubt!"

"Lovely. Shall we say at about three o'clock? I hope to have several others join us, and if the weather holds fine, we'll have tea on the lawn."

The squire assured them he and his wife would be there.

They parted from the beaming man and proceeded down the row of stalls, but from that moment on, Meg barely had a chance to examine any of the goods for sale as, for all the local gentry attending, she and Drago became the primary feature of the market. A succession of locals sought them out to greet Drago and be introduced to his new bride.

Meg bore the avid attention with ease; county people were never as pushy as those in town. Indeed, she found herself enjoying several infor-mative exchanges with various ladies, some of her age, others much older.

At one point, when she and Drago walked on, she murmured, "There are several real characters among the local circles."

"Indeed. So how many have we invited for tomorrow thus far?"

"Six couples. A few more won't hurt if we meet any others you think we should invite."

They continued along the rows of stalls, meeting, chatting, sometimes inviting, then moving on.

"Although in some ways similar, this is nowhere near as demanding as a ton soirée." Smiling, Meg glanced at Drago. "Incidentally, I meant to ask. Where does the family normally attend church?"

"If I'm at the Court, I usually appear at the estate chapel. We've so many workers, there's always a small congregation there, and the local minister and the curate take the service turn and turn about."

"Hmm. That should be where we go tomorrow morning, but I suspect we should consider attending elsewhere on other Sundays so that we become better known through the district."

"Where do you suggest?"

Meg questioned him as to the other local churches, and they discussed the pros and cons, finally deciding to venture to St. George's Church at Benenden on the following Sunday. "Many of the congregation there know me, and I would like to reconnect with the Bigfield House people as well as Christopher and Ellen and others from the manor."

Drago nodded. "Given you already have those links, you should keep them alive."

Meg looked ahead, then grasped Drago's sleeve. "Look! There's Alison and Joshua."

Drago caught her hand and wound her arm with his, and they went forward to meet the other couple.

Everyone was all smiles and happy greetings, yet Meg sensed that all was still not well with Alison and Joshua. She fixed them both with a direct look. "Don't tell me Hubert is still being difficult."

Alison's face fell, and her expression grew mulish. "Worse! He's convinced Papa that we should put off announcing our engagement until at least the end of summer!"

Glumly, Joshua confirmed, "To at least the end of August."

"But it's not even May." Meg was incredulous. "That's four whole months away."

"I know!" Alison said. "It's utterly unreasonable."

Drago frowned. "Has Hubert given any reason at all for his peculiar stance?" He glanced at Joshua. "Does the end of August have any significance that you know of?"

Joshua shook his head. "I've thought and thought, but there's nothing I can see that would account for Hubert's insistence."

"And he is *very* insistent," Alison confirmed. "So much so that Papa won't listen to any arguments Joshua and I make."

Drago caught Joshua's eye. "I confess, Joshua, that in light of Hubert's resistance, I had my man look into your situation, and he's assured me that all is definitely aboveboard with you. Consequently, I'm entirely willing to stand behind you, and if and when you think it might help, I'm happy to have a word with Melwin—Alison's father, that is."

Relief spread across Joshua's face. "Thank you." He looked at Alison, smiled, and squeezed her hand. "We hope it won't come to that, but if it does, it's comforting to know that we have your"—his gaze flicked to Meg, and he smiled—"and your duchess's support."

"Indeed. And our approval, too," Meg staunchly declared.

"Thank you." Alison, too, looked happier. "Your support means a lot to us." She shook her head. "I really don't want to be an autumn bride."

Soon after, the four parted, and Meg and Drago continued down the last row of stalls.

"That must be so frustrating." Meg glanced at Drago's face. "Being kept apart for no reason—apparently just for a whim of her brother's."

Drago nodded. "One can't help feeling for them." He met Meg's eyes. "Especially now that we're enjoying the benefits of marriage that they're being denied."

He watched as she searched his eyes and gentle color rose in her cheeks. Then she nodded and faced forward. "Indeed."

After meeting with one last lady and inviting her to join the party at the Court the next day, they returned to the curricle, left nearby in Milton's care, and set off for home.

As with Meg beside him, Drago tooled the grays homeward, he was alive to how relaxed she was and aware, at some deeper level, of her contentment with her lot.

To him, now, that meant...a great deal.

And that, he thought, was simply one indication of what love had done to him.

He was still grappling with all the changes.

"Well," Meg mused, "as we'd hoped, it seems the attacks have ceased."

"Thus far, yes. Let's hope that holds." He remained concerned that no amount of investigating had as yet turned up even a hint of what the motive behind the attacks had been. Had that motive, whatever it was, truly been rendered null and void by their wedding? Or was it simply in abeyance, possibly due to them being at Wylde Court and therefore not easily reached?

"Well, we've gone a whole week, and nothing's happened." She threw him a smile. "I have to admit it's so peaceful down here, it's difficult to imagine anything intruding on the serenity."

He wasn't so convinced, but dipped his head. "It's always very peaceful down here."

* * *

IN THE WAKE of their successful tea party on the south lawn on Sunday, on Monday afternoon, Meg set out on one of the regular visits Constance had mentioned she usually undertook when she was in residence, namely ferrying a basket of provisions to two older widows who lived together in a small cottage on a corner of the estate.

As, in a way, it was due to Meg and Drago marrying that the dowager was presently fixed in London, Meg had spoken with Mrs. Fothergill and arranged to go in the dowager's stead.

"The old dears will be that thrilled to meet you," Mrs. Fothergill predicted.

With Ridley dogging her heels, Meg stopped in the kitchen and picked up the hamper Cook had ready and waiting, then left the house via the rear door to walk to the stable. Fothergill had ordered the gig to be made ready for her, and the simple carriage was standing in the stable yard— along with her husband.

Drago saw her and smiled. "There you are."

"Hello." She held up the hamper. "I'm on my way to visit the widows."

"So I gathered." He arched a black brow at her. "Do you know the way?"

Vaguely. She waved in the general direction. "I know I should follow the lane to the northeast."

He considered her for a moment, then glanced at the black mare harnessed to the gig. "Can you drive?"

She made a rude sound. "I'm a Cynster. Of course I can drive. I drove your grays, remember?"

"You're the Cynster who isn't fond of horses, and if you recall, I wasn't exactly awake to watch you handle my grays." He met her gaze. "Perhaps I should come with you"—he smiled charmingly—"just so you can set my mind at ease."

It was a lovely late-spring day, and she wasn't about to turn him away. "Why not?" She noted the relief that was there and gone in his dark eyes. Pretending she hadn't noticed, she advanced on the gig. "But I'm driving."

He followed, took the hamper from her, and helped her climb to the seat. "If you're to convince me of your prowess, I suppose that's unavoidable."

She settled on the seat, took up the reins, and waited while he stowed the hamper, then joined her on the bench. The stable lad caught Ridley and assured them he would tie the pup up to await their return. Smiling her thanks, Meg flicked the reins and guided the docile mare out of the stable yard. "I thought you were going to spend the afternoon in the library."

"I was, but the sunshine called, and I came out to check on Morgan, the horse I rode this morning. I thought he was favoring a leg, but he seems fine now."

She nodded. Drago often rode before a late breakfast, which suited her; after he'd left her in a boneless heap, she could lie in and recover before joining him at the table.

The mare obediently trotted along the track that crossed to the north of the Court's gardens and entered the woods to the northeast. These were old woods—more correctly, forest—with tall, mature, thick-canopied trees and dense undergrowth lining both sides of the winding track. It was peaceful driving through the dappled sunshine, with the only sounds the rattle of the gig's wheels, the occasional jingle of harness, and intermittent birdcalls.

Meg's mind was lazily meandering when Drago nodded ahead.

"Just after that corner, the track dips. The corner's so sharp, you can't see the dip until you're all but in it."

"Thank you." She slowed the mare a trifle, and they rounded the blind curve.

Immediately, the mare snorted and danced.

A second later, the wheels hit a branch, one small enough for the horse to step over but large enough to badly jolt the occupants of the gig as one wheel rose, tipping them wildly one way, before slamming back to the flat.

Meg shrieked, and Drago seized her, anchoring them both via his hold on the seat's back as the second wheel went over the branch and they were violently flung the other way with the gig angling down into the dip.

The second wheel thumped back to earth, and the seat leveled, then the mare screamed and reared.

Shocked, Meg fought to hold her.

Drago swore, let Meg and the seat go, and seized the reins—just as the mare tried to bolt.

On three legs.

Only Drago's strength allowed him to rein in the panicked horse.

The mare responded to the absolute authority she sensed through the reins and stopped trying to break free. Gradually, she quieted, then stood, head down, muscles quivering, with one hoof held suspended and her hide flickering.

Drago stared at the horse and tried to sort out what had happened. He hauled in a huge breath, refilling lungs cinched tight, then glanced at Meg.

Her face paper-white, her blue eyes huge, she stared at the horse and breathed in deeply.

Crack!

The sound of a branch snapping had them jerking their heads to stare to the left.

Dense undergrowth was all they could see.

A second later, they heard a definite rustle, a disturbance much larger than that caused by a fox or a badger, then several moments later and more distantly came the distinctive sound of fleeing footsteps.

Drago was growing accustomed to being torn between the instinct to give chase and the compulsion to remain and protect Meg. The latter always won.

When they could no longer hear the fleeing man, he looked at Meg.

She met his eyes, her own deadly serious. "The attacks haven't stopped."

He eased his clenched jaw enough to say, "No. They haven't." He looked at the horse. "But whoever set this up has fled. We should be safe enough. Here. Hold these."

He handed her the reins, then stepped carefully from the gig. Making soothing sounds, he approached the nervy horse. After stroking her long nose and shoulder, he reached for her injured hoof. "Let me see."

He looked and bit back a curse. He released the hoof, injured but not, he thought, irreparably, and cast around on the ground.

"What are you looking for?"

"Some sort of caltrop—nails set to pierce horses' hooves."

"Good Lord!"

He saw one, bent, and scooped it up. He examined it, then grunted. "It's a primitive, homemade affair. Just three big nails twisted together." He showed her, then looked around. "Can you see any others?"

Meg tied off the reins, pulled on the brake, climbed down, and helped him search.

They found two more of the diabolical devices.

Drago scanned the lane one last time. "I think that's it."

He rejoined Meg by the gig. She glanced at the caltrops, then looked into his face. "Whoever planned this thought I would be alone. I would most likely have been thrown when the gig tipped or when the horse reared and kicked. Then whoever was waiting, watching, would…"

He felt his face harden and forced himself to nod.

Blue eyes filled with confusion, she asked, "But *why?*"

Holding her gaze, he shook his head. "I've no idea, but we need to make an end to this."

* * *

AFTER SOME DEBATE, they decided to free the horse from the gig, leave the carriage in the lane, and leading the mare, walk back to the stable.

By the time they reached the stable yard, they'd been spotted by several stablemen and gardeners, and a small group of concerned staff had gathered. Once the men heard their tale, shock and disbelief abounded, but were soon replaced by anger and determination.

While Meg reunited with a frantic Ridley—how did dogs so unerringly know when their people were in danger?—Drago assured the men of their intention to bring the matter to a head and expose and appropriately deal with whoever was behind the accident. Meg waited while he handed over the caltrops, explained the mare's injury, consigned the poor beast into the head stableman's care, and directed two grooms to retrieve the abandoned gig. Then he, she, and Ridley set off for the house.

They'd reached the stable arch when Drago paused, looked back, caught the head stableman's eye, and called, "Have three riders get ready to courier messages to London."

The head stableman saluted. "Aye, Your Grace."

Drago turned, and they continued toward the house.

Meg guessed, "You're calling in reinforcements?"

Lips thin, he nodded. "If we're to catch this bastard, we'll need to set a trap."

Her expression tight, she smiled intently. "What an excellent idea."

CHAPTER 17

On the following day in the late afternoon, while in the drawing room watching Meg sip her tea, in an effort to distract her and himself from the threat hovering over them, Drago suggested they take the boat out on the lake.

It was a glorious, lazy early-summer day. A week before, on the second day they'd been at the Court, at Meg's eager suggestion, he'd rowed them out, and they'd spent a quiet hour lying back in the mild sunshine and talking. Golden moments that they'd both enjoyed and that he hoped to replicate today.

He wasn't surprised when she set down her teacup and, her face alight with eager agreement, asked, "Now?"

He smiled, rose, and waved her to the door.

She hurried past him. "Let me get my bonnet."

He stood back to let Ridley follow her out. "I'll wait for you on the front porch." From there, he could signal the men—grooms, stablemen, and gardeners—who were going about their business while surreptitiously watching for any sign of strangers creeping near.

When Meg came out, tying her bonnet ribbons under her chin, he smiled, reached out and took her hand, and together, they walked briskly down the steps and crossed the forecourt to stroll over the south lawn toward the lake.

"Ridley?" he asked.

"I left him in the kitchens."

On reaching the shore, they followed it around to the left, to the small boathouse tucked into the trees that clustered about the far end of the long, teardrop-shaped lake.

It was the work of a moment to lower the rowboat, stored on a canvas sling above the water, into the lake. Drago handed Meg in, then followed. She sat on the wide stern bench and settled her skirts. He doffed his jacket, dropped it beside her, then rolled up his sleeves and sat on the middle bench, facing her. He slid the oars into their locks, then dipped the blades and pulled, and the small boat glided out of the cover of the boathouse and onto the still waters of the lake.

Holding on to the boat's sides, Meg tipped her face up to the sky, closed her eyes, and sighed. Then she opened her eyes and looked around. After a moment, she observed, "This isn't an ornamental lake, is it?"

"No. It's a natural feature. We assume it's fed by a spring. As far as I know, it's never run dry." He bent to the oars, and the boat slid over the water's surface. "That's why we have a rowboat and not a punt."

"It's deep?"

"Too deep for poling, especially in the center of the widest part. It's very deep there."

She studied him, then smiled. "I'd wager that, as children, you and Denton dove for the bottom."

He hesitated, then tipped his head. "When we were young, we did. We never found it."

There were gardeners pruning a line of bushes to one side of the lake and a pair on the other side, clipping the edges of the drive. Safe enough, Drago reasoned, to row to the lake's center and lounge in the sun and chat.

They were more or less in the middle of the lake when Meg's until-then-serene expression clouded, and she frowned and looked down. "Drago..." She raised one foot, shod in a garden slipper, which was dripping.

Startled, he looked down and saw his own boots were an inch deep in slowly rising water. "I don't believe it. The boat's sprung a leak." He met Meg's gaze and felt his features set. Then he gripped the oars and started to row as fast as he could for the nearest shore.

Within yards, he realized that the stern, where Meg was sitting, was sinking faster than the rest of the boat. He paused in his rowing to reach out a hand to her. "Get behind me, into the prow. The hole must be under the stern bench."

She took his hand and sloshed and scrambled forward, but even as he bent to the oars again, he knew they had no chance of reaching the shore before the boat sank.

Nevertheless, he rowed with rapid, powerful strokes as the boat wallowed ever deeper.

He glanced over his shoulder, past Meg to the shore. He hadn't wasted breath yelling for help; it was likely the gardeners, in common with most Englishmen, couldn't swim.

Luckily, he could.

The water level was now mere inches from flooding the boat. Within minutes, it would sink beneath them.

He freed the oars from the locks and laid one flat in the water, where it floated. He swiveled and handed the second oar to Meg. "Can you swim?" Most males of their class had some ability, but ladies rarely did.

She wrinkled her nose. "A little. My father made sure we all could. But I'm not by any means a strong swimmer."

He nodded reassuringly. "That's all right—I am."

They were still more than fifty yards from the shore, and while the gardeners had noticed their plight and rushed up, as he'd foreseen, none were able to do more than wade out a few yards and wait to assist them when they got closer.

"If we stand up, the boat will sink and create suction when it does. Better for us to roll over the side." He looked at Meg. "You go first. If you can, keep hold of the oar." He tipped his head to where the first oar still floated a yard or so from the boat. "I'll be right behind you, and I'll tow you to the shore."

Staring at the floating oar, she swallowed and nodded. "All right."

She shifted to the side of the boat, then curled over the side.

Drago scooped up her legs and skirts and tipped her over.

She went in with a splash. Gasping, she turned onto her back, still clutching the oar with one hand.

"That's it." He grabbed his jacket and shrugged it on. He glanced at the stern, then bent and reached under the seat and blindly ran his hand across the planks.

His fingers snagged in fabric, and he gripped and tugged.

A clump of soaked white cotton came free. He held it up, then realized the boat was sinking even faster. He thrust the sodden lump into his jacket pocket, then went over the same side of the boat as Meg.

He came up and slicked his hair out of his eyes just in time to see the rowboat sink silently into the lake.

Meg was floundering. She'd turned on her side and was attempting to kick and push the oar toward the shore, but with her skirts and petticoats hampering her efforts, she hadn't managed more than a few yards.

The boat vanished into the depths, and Drago swam to her. "Ease up." He closed one hand about the oar's shaft. "Don't try to swim as such. Just hold onto the oar and float, and I'll tow you to shore."

She met his eyes, and he could see she was holding back rising panic, but her lips firmed, and she nodded.

He reorganized the oar so that it lay before her and she was gripping the shaft with both hands, then he grasped the wooden rod between her hands and set off, slowly but steadily swimming for the shore while towing her beside him.

On the shore, the men had been doing what they could. One had run back to the house, and from the corner of his eye, Drago saw Fothergill and Mrs. Fothergill hurrying across the porch with towels and blankets in their arms.

"Nearly there." He kept his gaze on Meg, on her eyes, letting her see his unshakeable confidence that all would be well.

Her chin was set, and she was still trying ineffectually to kick, but although her white-knuckled grip on the oar didn't loosen, he sensed she was tiring.

Then two of the gardeners who had waded in until the water was chest high stretched forward and snagged the tip of the oar. The pair gripped and pulled, and Drago and Meg were drawn smoothly on.

The instant Drago got his feet under him, he released the oar and stood. Once sure of his footing, he reached for Meg and scooped her— sodden bonnet, skirts, and all—into his arms. He hoisted her against his chest and ducked his head to plant a kiss on her wet forehead. "It's all right. We're safe."

Her fingers curled into his lapel, and she nodded slightly.

Supported by the gardeners, one on either side, he slogged out of the lake and stepped onto the grassy bank. With her drenched skirts, Meg was amazingly heavy. Slowly, he bent and set her on her feet, but he didn't move away, instead encouraging her to lean against him.

He could feel her trembling uncontrollably, and he didn't think it was due to any chill. In truth, the water hadn't been that cold, a minor blessing.

The clop of hooves and the faint jingle of harness reached them.

Everyone looked across the lake to see a group of horsemen trotting up the drive.

Then the horsemen saw them.

Even across that distance, Drago heard the shocked curses, then the riders pushed their mounts on to the forecourt, where they tumbled from their saddles and rushed toward him and Meg.

"Naturally," he murmured for Meg's ears alone, "they had to arrive at the most exercising moment."

She snorted softly. "You did invite them, but yes. There'll be no holding them back now."

"They must have dropped everything and come running. I didn't expect them until later today at the earliest."

"That might have been the case had it been left to Denton, George, and Harry, but with Toby and my cousins? With excitement on offer, of course they came running."

At that moment, the Fothergills reached them and wrapped towels around them, and once the towels were saturated, Mrs. Fothergill, clucking all the while, draped a blanket around Meg and relieved her of her dripping bonnet.

Drago thanked the pair, with Meg echoing his words, then ordered that a bath be prepared for Meg, and for Maurice and Rosie to attend their respective dressing rooms, only to have Fothergill assure him all was already in hand.

At Drago's nod, the Fothergills turned and, taking stock of the newcomers, Fothergill murmured, "By your leave, Your Grace, we'll return to the house and ensure the gentlemen's rooms are prepared."

"Thank you. Please do." Drago watched the butler and housekeeper hurry back to the house, then he refocused on the seven gentlemen striding purposefully toward him and Meg. He grasped Meg's elbow and gestured at the group. "We'd better go and allay their fears."

She nodded, and he stepped out, but when she went to move with him, her legs seemed to fail, and she all but sank to the grass.

Muttering a curse of his own, Drago wasted no breath complaining that she should have said she felt too weak to walk. He swung her into his arms again, settling her there before thanking the outdoor staff who had helped them, and Meg added her gratitude as well. Drago recommended that the pair who were drenched return to the house to dry off, then he started walking—slowly and carefully—to meet the bevy of concerned males descending in a hyperalert and ready-to-be-vengeful platoon.

Predictably, Toby was in the lead, with Aidan, Evan, and Carter close behind. Denton, George, and Harry brought up the rear, their expressions as close to wordlessly horrified as Drago had ever seen them.

The instant he was close enough, Toby demanded, "What the—"

"Yes," Drago calmly stated, "this was another attack. The second of two since we've been here. The first was yesterday afternoon. Obviously, our villain's motive wasn't nullified by our wedding." He paused as Toby halted in front of them.

When Meg's brother stared frowningly at her, she smiled faintly, reached out, and patted his cheek. "Truly, I'm all right. Just a trifle weak from trying to swim in all these skirts. For the record, I don't recommend ladies go for a dip fully clothed."

Aidan snorted. "You sound like your usual argumentative self, so you can't be all that damaged."

"She'll be rather less damaged," Drago stated in a tone that brooked no argument, "if we go inside and she gets warm and dry."

"Yes, of course." Denton stepped back, getting out of Drago's way.

The others took the hint and did the same.

They all looked grave as they flanked Drago as he carried Meg to the house. Regardless, he thought, none of them were anywhere near as gravely concerned as he.

As they crossed the forecourt, Meg stirred in his arms. "I can walk from here."

"No need." He imbued his clipped tones with enough ducal authority to have not just her but the seven gentlemen surrounding them cast swift glances his way.

While the gentlemen were reassured and some of their tension left them, Meg eyed his features, then softly snorted and faced forward.

He carried her up the steps, across the porch, but paused in the front hall to glance at Denton.

His brother nodded. "You go up. We'll wait in the library."

Drago nodded his thanks, turned toward the stairs, and carried Meg up and on to their suite.

* * *

FIFTEEN MINUTES LATER, dry and dressed in fresh clothes, but still rubbing his damp hair with a towel, Drago walked through their bedroom and Meg's dressing room and into her bathing chamber.

With her eyes closed, Meg was reclining in the full-length tub, the water of which was gently steaming. Her hair looked to have been washed, partly dried, and was now piled atop her head.

Rosie was putting bottles of salts and oils away in a small cupboard. At Drago's signal, the maid quickly set two thick towels on the bench beside the bath, then bobbed a curtsy and left via the corridor door.

At the *click* of the latch, Meg cracked open her eyes. She looked at the door, then her gaze swiveled and landed on Drago. "Ah. You're here."

"I am." He leaned against the doorframe and continued to dry his hair. "How do you feel?"

"Truly?" She closed her eyes again. "I feel so thoroughly languid and relaxed, I could lie here for at least another hour, but if I do, the others will start to fret, and with Toby, one never knows what that might lead to."

Drago decided he didn't need to defend Toby even if, on this subject, he agreed with her brother. "Out there, beside the lake, you were in shock. You were shivering even though it wasn't that cold."

"Shock? I suppose, but it really felt more like horror." Before he could probe, she went on, "I told you I'm not a strong swimmer. Because of that, I always feared being in deep water and drowning, and of course, with the weight of my skirts, the fear was even worse."

Unalloyed fury welled, strong and undeniable, inside him.

Then she opened her eyes, found his, and smiled. "But you were there, right beside me, so all was well." She gripped the sides of the bath and sat up, sending water sluicing over the swells of her breasts. "Regardless, the horror has faded. Now, I'm feeling decidedly angry."

Drago could understand that.

Meg studied Drago's face and saw enough in his stony features to suggest that distraction might be wise. "I can't believe the others are already here. They couldn't have got your notes until late last night or even this morning."

Drago grunted and lowered his towel. "I suspect, like me, they had a lingering concern over whether our wedding would put an end to the attacks."

She grimaced. "Their concern makes it difficult to take umbrage over them maintaining such a focused interest in our doings." She picked up a towel and rose. Shaking out the length, she fixed Drago with an assessing look as he crossed toward her. "You didn't ask them to hold themselves ready to come down, did you? Before sending for them yesterday, I mean."

His gaze on her body, he shook his head. "Clearly, they felt sufficiently unsettled to hold themselves ready to come down at a moment's notice, which only underscores the need to act and put an end to our villain's game. He's kept all of us dancing on his hook for long enough." He offered her a hand to help her from the bath.

She gripped his fingers and stepped down to the tiles, but when he would have helped her dry off, she waved him back. "We have to get downstairs in short order, remember?"

His lips quirked, but he obligingly retreated to lean in the doorway again.

While she dried herself, they talked about household arrangements now the others were there, then he helped her don the day dress Rosie had laid out in the dressing room.

After she'd brushed her hair, wound it up, and anchored it, and put on delicate gold earrings and a matching necklace Drago had given her, she sighed, then turned and reached for his arm. "I'm as ready as I can be to face the inquisition waiting for us downstairs."

* * *

AFTER PAUSING to confer with Fothergill in the front hall, they entered the library to find their supporters lounging in the armchairs before the hearth.

Denton and George leapt up to offer Meg and Drago their places, then fetched other chairs from farther down the room.

Once everyone was settled, Drago began, "First, thank you all for responding to my summons so promptly."

George waved dismissively. "Of course we came!"

"This," Toby stated, "whatever this is, has been going on for too long."

Drago dipped his head in agreement.

Frowning, Aidan glanced at George and Harry. "I thought there were three of you. Where's"—he looked at Drago and Meg—"Thomas, is it?"

Drago nodded. "I sent Thomas word of what had happened, but recommended that he didn't hie down here." Drago glanced at Meg, then at the others. "Thomas is dependent on his position at Crawthorne and Quartermaine, my solicitors, and I would rather he didn't risk his place in chambers to assist us in this."

"Aside from all else," Harry put in, "you never can tell when having a friend reviewing your legal documents will come in handy."

"Just so," Drago concurred.

Toby stirred and fixed his hazel gaze on Meg and Drago. "So what happened out there?" He tipped his head toward the lake.

Drago explained that they'd taken out the rowboat the previous week. "And after yesterday's excitement—I'll get to that in a moment—I thought Meg and I could do with a quiet sojourn on the lake, so we took the boat out again. While not in use, the boat is kept in the boathouse, held out of the water in a canvas sling. We lowered it into the lake and set off. We'd reached the widest section of the lake before we realized the hull was taking in water." Drago suddenly remembered and held up a hand. "Wait."

He rose and tugged the bellpull and, when Fothergill appeared, asked for Maurice. While they waited for the valet, Drago returned to his chair. "Apparently, since Monday last week, a hole had appeared in the hull, hidden under the stern bench."

Toby arched his brows. "Just appeared?"

Drago looked toward the door as a rap on the panels heralded Maurice.

"Your Grace?"

"Maurice, there should be a handkerchief in the right outer pocket of my jacket—the one that was soaked."

"Indeed, Your Grace. I found it, but it's not one of yours."

"No, it isn't. Could you fetch it, please?"

Maurice bowed and departed.

Drago looked at the others. "I found the handkerchief—a plain white handkerchief as far as I saw—stuffed in the hole. When I pulled it out, the boat sank more rapidly."

Toby said, "So whoever put the hole in the hull wanted you to row well out before the boat sank."

Meg nodded. "We were in the middle of the lake before we noticed water was leaking in."

Studying Drago and Meg, Toby frowned and focused on Drago. "But you can swim. I know Meg doesn't swim well and might have been in trouble if she'd been alone, but you were there and, clearly, were able to haul her as well as yourself out. While this is obviously another attack, it seems something of a long shot, especially as within weeks of your wedding, it was odds on that you'd be with Meg—" Toby noticed that Denton, George, and Harry were all shaking their heads and looking exceedingly grave. "Ah," Toby said, "what have I missed?"

Denton looked at Drago. "I, for one, would never have imagined you would row out on the lake." He glanced at Meg, who was clearly as mystified as her brother and cousins. "Not even to please Meg." Denton looked at George and Harry, both of whom nodded solemnly, then continued, "If anyone had asked any of us"—he arched his brows at George and Harry, and both quickly shook their heads—"not that anyone did, but if they had, we each would have sworn that while Meg might have taken out the boat, under no circumstances would you have been with her."

Meg turned her blue gaze on Drago. "What don't we know?"

Drago met her eyes. After a few tense seconds, he said, "Denton and I had a younger brother—our youngest sibling, Edward. One spring, when both Denton and I were away at school, Edward drowned in the lake. We"—he gestured at Denton—"came home for the funeral. After that day…neither of us, nor our sisters or our parents, ever went out on the lake again. The rowboat was kept ready and in good order for guests, but the family never again indulged."

Meg reached across and closed her hand about one of his. "You should have told me when I asked to go out last week."

He smiled faintly, turned his hand, and gently squeezed hers. "Our marriage and us coming here has signaled the start of a new era for the Helmsfords. It seemed time to let that particular piece of the past fade."

For several seconds, no one spoke, then Toby said, "That actually tells us something about our villain."

Before anyone could ask what, Maurice returned, bearing the still-damp handkerchief.

Drago took it and, spreading it over one hand, checked the corners. "As I thought, it doesn't have a monogram."

"Let me see." Meg lifted the linen square from Drago's fingers and examined it more closely.

"Your Grace." Maurice bowed, preparing to depart.

"Maurice, wait." Meg looked up and held out the square to the valet. "You know your handkerchiefs. What does this one say of its owner?"

Maurice glanced at Drago, and at his nod, came forward and took the handkerchief. He, too, examined it, even more closely than Meg had. Then he looked at her. "In my opinion, Your Grace, this is the handker-chief of a gentleman, a reasonably well-to-do one. The quality of the linen is excellent, and although there's no monogram, the hems are expertly sewn." He bounced the handkerchief on his palm. "Conduit Street quality, I would say."

"Thank you." Meg took back the handkerchief, and Maurice bowed and withdrew.

The instant the door closed behind the valet, Toby nodded. "That fits with what I was about to say." He met Drago's eyes. "The expectation that you wouldn't have gone out on the lake—that it would be Meg alone or at best with a footman who most likely wouldn't have been able to swim at all—isn't widely known." He glanced at Meg and his cousins. "For instance, we didn't know. If one of us had planned this latest attack… well, we wouldn't have bothered because we would have assumed you would be with Meg and most likely can swim better than she can and you would get both of you out."

Aidan was nodding. "We would have anticipated the attempt playing out exactly as it did—meaning that it wouldn't have worked."

"Precisely. Instead," Toby continued, "our villain took a risk and came here, onto the estate, sometime between last Monday and today, put a hole in the rowboat's hull, stuffed it with his handkerchief to slow the leak sufficiently, then left the boat exactly as it should have been." He arched a brow at Drago. "Did you notice anything out of the ordinary before you put the boat in the water?"

Drago consulted his memory, then shook his head. "Everything was as I expected to find it. And with the way the boat's always left—in a sling just above the water—the hole beneath the seat wasn't visible."

"That suggests," Carter put in, "that whoever's behind the attacks knows this place quite well."

"More," Toby said, his expression intent, "he knows your family. He knew of your reason for not going on the lake. He knew about your reaction to your brother's death."

Drago felt his expression harden as that reality sank in. Slowly, he nodded, then met Toby's eyes. "That reduces the list of suspects quite a lot."

"I thought it might." Toby looked at Denton, George, and Harry. "You three knew. Who else?"

"Well," Harry said, "Thomas, of course. All of us spent part of our summers here, so of course we all know."

"Who else?" Meg looked at Drago.

"Our sisters, our mother, Edith, and Warley, plus all of the staff here, at the Court itself. Grooms, stable hands, gardeners—all likely know. Many were here even then and attended Edward's funeral." He hauled in a breath, then exhaled and said, "However, I believe we can absolve all of the above of any villainous intent. It's all but impossible to imagine a motive."

"Besides," Meg said, "none of the staff here have been up to London. Unless we postulate some conspiracy of sorts, our villain must be someone who can move freely between London and Kent."

"And we mustn't forget that our villain is a gentleman," Evan said.

Silence fell as they all digested the latest revelations.

Then Evan looked at Drago. "You called us down here because of some accident that happened yesterday. What was that?"

Between them, Drago and Meg described their ill-fated excursion of the previous day.

The others asked questions, clarifying details.

Finally, Toby huffed. "Again, the placement of the branch at just that spot—leading into a steep dip—suggests someone who knows this place well."

"Also," Denton said, "that's a regular visit paid by Mama in her role as duchess. For decades, she's been going there—in the gig, along that track

—on every fourth Monday of the month like clockwork, but as Meg is here and Mama isn't, it was a good bet that Meg would have the gig out to take the hamper to the old dears."

"Is it possible for someone to watch the stable yard to see if Meg was on her way?" Aidan asked.

Drago frowned. "Not the stable yard itself. If they'd been keeping watch on the yard, they would have seen I was with Meg. But they could easily have seen her walking alone from the house toward the stable yard, carrying the hamper." He met Aidan's eyes. "I'd gone to the stable earlier for another reason altogether. It was sheer luck I was there and saw the gig being prepared for Meg and decided to go with her."

Toby fixed Drago with a level look. "One day, your luck will run out."

Drago returned the look. "That's why you're here."

Toby's swift grin flashed, and he inclined his head.

Frowning, Denton summarized, "So we're looking for a gentleman who knows the ins and outs and routines of this place very well, and he's targeting Meg." Denton looked at Drago. "Specifically Meg."

Grimly, Drago nodded. "That, I think, is now beyond question. Whoever he was, he was lying in wait by the lane where he'd set his trap for the gig. When he realized I was with Meg, he took off."

"Running." Meg looked at Drago. "Now I think of it, he ran off very quickly."

Drago thought back to the sound of fleeing footsteps and nodded. "Yes, he did. Which suggests—"

"That he's someone you know," Toby concluded. "Someone you would recognize. He didn't want you to catch even a glimpse of him."

Having envisioned the scene, Harry and George looked quietly horrified.

"If you hadn't been there…" Harry said.

George shook himself. "That doesn't bear thinking about."

"Indeed." Speaking more forcefully, Drago looked around the circle. "That's why we need to bring this game—whatever it is—to an end."

Toby nodded. "Casting your mind over all who would think that you wouldn't go out on the lake, is there anyone among that apparently small number who are acting strangely?"

Drago considered the question, then glanced at Meg. "Hubert."

Aidan frowned. "Who is Hubert?"

Between them, Meg, Drago, and Denton explained.

"And he's been acting strangely how?" Toby asked.

That took a little longer to make clear, but eventually, everyone was nodding in understanding.

"So Hubert's interference is all to do with stopping his sister, Alison, from marrying her chosen beau, who by anyone's standards is perfectly acceptable," Aidan said, "and Alison is the young lady Drago almost offered for before meeting Meg."

Having successfully glossed over the facts of that meeting, Meg and Drago both nodded.

"Ah." Evan leaned forward, resting his forearms on his thighs. "It seems pertinent to mention that I've spent a little time going over the wording of Drago's father's will more carefully, and if I'm reading the clause in question correctly—and I believe I am—then if Drago isn't actually married on his thirty-fifth birthday, there might be an issue satisfying that clause and getting the funds released."

When the others looked at him in confusion, Evan explained, "Even if Drago is married now, if he isn't then, on his thirty-fifth birthday, then the way the clause is worded, it won't be satisfied. In other words, there's no mention of or allowance made for him being a widower."

The information made them all sit back.

Eventually, Meg put their thoughts into words. "What you're saying is that, even though Drago has married me, if I die now or at any time before his birthday in August, he'll need to find another bride in a very short space of time."

Evan nodded. "That's how it appears to me." He looked at Drago. "I suspect it was an oversight in the legal drafting that no allowance was made for you being a widower, but that's the way it's written, and there's no arguing with it now."

Drago tipped his head in acceptance, then looked at Meg. "August," he said and watched her eyes widen.

She turned to stare at him. "You think that's why Hubert is insisting that Alison and Joshua wait until the end of August before announcing their engagement?"

Toby looked from one to the other. "Well, well. That does rather point the finger at Hubert." He focused on Drago. "Would Hubert know about your previous aversion to going out on the lake?"

Drago's features hardened. "Yes, he would. The family are close neighbors, and over the years, he's been around here often enough to have seen and heard of the family's refusal to venture onto the lake, and he definitely knows why. He was here for Edward's funeral. I'm sure of that."

"He was," Denton confirmed. "He might even have been standing close enough to hear us all swearing that we would never go out on the lake again." He looked at Drago. "We did that at the graveside, remember?"

Harry raised a hand and waved it. "I remember that, and I was standing about a yard behind your family."

George was nodding. "I remember that, too. Most of those around you would have heard, and I'm fairly certain Hubert was there, in that group."

Aidan shifted. "Would Hubert know about the stipulations in your father's will?"

"I can't imagine how he learned of them," Drago said, "but I suspect the answer is yes. It was the reason I was thinking of offering for Alison's hand, and my aunt Edith was the intermediary in…exploring the possibilities there. She might have let something slip."

Toby looked at Evan. "Would Hubert have been able to learn about the lack of mention of Drago being a widower?"

Evan nodded. "In the same way I did." He looked around the circle. "After a will is granted probate, it can be viewed by anyone who knows to ask for it. Once Hubert realized there was such a clause in the late duke's will, learning its details would have been easy."

"Right, then." Toby spoke decisively. "Hubert is the one gentleman we know of who had access to all the relevant information and who is also behaving in a manner that could be interpreted as keeping himself, via his sister, in a position to capitalize on the difficult situation that will arise if Meg dies."

Toby looked around the circle of faces, inviting comment. When no one spoke, he focused on Drago. "It appears that Hubert is the principal candidate for the role of our villain."

Drago grimaced feelingly. "There's just one stumbling block. Hubert is not a man of action. He's never struck me as having any great degree of gumption. That said, I haven't had much to do with him over the years. He's a few years my senior, and he was always one of the pompously correct brigade."

Toby and the others considered that, then Toby inclined his head. "Your caveat is duly noted. However, given that we have no better suspect —indeed, no other suspect at all—I suggest we set our minds to the task of how to prove our villain's identity. If it's not Hubert, then it's someone else. Either way, we need to flush him out."

Grim-faced, Drago looked at Meg. "Indeed. That's the challenge before us. How do we bring this situation to a head and, thus, to an end?"

* * *

DESPITE DRAGO'S CAVEAT, the discussion over the dinner table was entirely focused on how to prove Hubert was behind the attacks on Meg.

Seated opposite Drago at a table that had been reduced in size to more comfortably accommodate their company of nine, Meg listened carefully to all the arguments advanced.

The more ideas that were floated, the more they talked, discussed, and argued, it became increasingly plain that there was really only one viable path to achieve what they wanted.

"We can't just confront Hubert," Toby maintained. "We have no real evidence to say it's him, only that it might be him. All he'll need to do is deny it, and we'll have tipped our hand to him—and if it's not him but someone connected with him, then to the real villain as well—for no gain."

"And there's no saying," Drago added, "that tipping our hand to the villain, whoever he is, won't just make him try all the harder." His gaze rested on Meg. "Precipitating a more violent and possibly more unpredictable reaction isn't what we want."

"No, indeed." Toby narrowed his eyes. "What we need to do is control his reaction and confine it in such a way that it exposes his identity without risking any harm to Meg."

Meg bit back a comment to the effect that there was really only one path to achieving that laudable aim.

Eventually, with the dessert plates empty and the gentlemen agreeing that whisky before the library fire sounded just the thing, the company retreated to the armchairs there.

As, after handing around crystal glasses of amber liquor, Drago resumed his seat, Meg stated, "We need to come up with a feasible plan that will lure the villain into the open in an unequivocal way."

There. I've stated the obvious. Now let's see how long they can drag their feet before acknowledging the inevitable solution.

She sat and listened as Drago, supported by Toby, insisted that, while they might feel reasonably convinced that the villain was Hubert, any plan they came up with had to allow for the villain being someone else. "We're not going to get two chances at this," Drago stated. "We need to flush out our villain at our first attempt."

Meg saw no reason to disagree; she wanted this over with, the villain exposed and dealt with, and normalcy restored as soon as possible.

Finally, with a swift glance at her, Toby stated, "The only way forward that I can see is for Meg to act as a lure of sorts—as very well-protected bait."

Drago's lips tightened. "I would prefer any other way. There must be one."

Gamely, Aidan shook his head. "If so, I can't see it, and none of us have despite the past hours of racking our brains."

"None of us," Denton told his brother, "are happy about the prospect of Meg being in any sort of danger, however slight, but the alternative— letting this situation go on—is potentially worse."

"Indeed." Meg decided it was time she spoke up and reminded them all that she had a mind of her own. She fixed her gaze on Drago. "As one who has a large stake in this matter, on multiple fronts, I, too, can see no other way to achieve our necessary goal, and I believe we need to accept what must be and direct our energies into crafting a plan that will draw the villain into the open while simultaneously ensuring my absolute safety."

Drago held her gaze for a very long moment, and everyone else held their breath. Then almost imperceptibly, his stony features eased a fraction, and he inclined his head to her before shifting his dark gaze to the others. "Very well. Given those parameters, what can we devise?"

Subtle relief spread through the company, and once again, the ideas started flying, although now the suggestions were a great deal more focused and practical.

Step by step, they constructed a sequence of events that, they hoped, would cast Meg as an obvious target, apparently unprotected and alone, although in reality, she would never be out of sight of several—always more than one—of her dedicated champions.

Naturally, Drago didn't like the plan, but he reluctantly agreed.

"This way," Toby assured him, "should Hubert prove to be the villain, we'll be able to watch him all the way to the point where he incriminates himself and then step in, yet at the same time, should the villain prove to be someone else and close enough to see our lure and think to take advantage—as we would hope—then our guards will ensure that he won't be able to reach Meg, either."

Denton nodded eagerly. "Whoever he is, we'll have him." He looked at Drago. "Tomorrow."

His expression utterly impassive, Drago looked at them all, then raised the hand of Meg's that he'd appropriated during the discussion, pressed a kiss to her knuckles, and met her gaze. "We'd better."

CHAPTER 18

*S*oon after, the gathering broke up, and anticipating a day full of activity on the morrow, the company made their way up the stairs. Denton volunteered to show the others to their rooms, leaving Drago and Meg to continue down the family wing to the ducal suite.

Drago followed Meg into their bedroom and shut the door on the world. He stood watching her as, lit by the warm glow of the lamps set on various side tables, she reached up to unpin her hair.

She turned and saw him watching. She met his gaze, her own direct yet mysterious, embodying the age-old allure of a confident lady, a siren's call to which he'd always been susceptible.

She studied his expression, then softly smiled. "I know you don't like the plan, but it is the only one we have, and at base, you're as determined as I am to bring this nonsense to an end."

He prowled toward her. "You're right. I'll never approve of, much less like, any venture that places you at any risk whatsoever. And yes, I've had more than enough of our joker's games. They end tomorrow. One way or another." He slid an arm around her waist and drew her to him. "There's just one thing."

She settled against him and, with gentle playfulness, arched her brows. "Just one?"

"Yes, you confounding woman—just one." He looked into her upturned face and felt all levity drain from him. "Regardless of what happens, you have to remain safe. When I get back here, you have to promise you'll be here, unharmed, untouched, waiting for me."

She smiled reassuringly. "With all my guards about me, there's no chance Hubert or anyone else will reach me."

Drago knew the plan, yet something in him still paced, uncertain, unconvinced. "Remember, before our engagement ball, we spoke of what we felt for each other and what we hoped to find in our marriage?"

She thought back, then refocused on his eyes. "We wanted a love match. Both of us did, even if we didn't know if it would come."

"But it did come, didn't it?" He raised a hand and wound his fingers in one curling tress, then he shifted, raised both hands, and sank his fingers into the rich bounty of her golden hair. Holding her face between his palms, he searched her eyes. "Love came and caught us, and the very thought that the next attempt on your life might succeed is enough to bring me to my knees." He tipped his head forward and rested his forehead on hers. "I find that now, I cannot conceive of a life without you." He raised his head and looked into her eyes. "How did that happen in just a few weeks?"

Her smile turned rueful. "I really don't know." Raising her hands, she curled her fingers about his wrists. "But rest assured that what you feel for me, I feel for you. I cannot conceive of a life without you, either."

"Good."

The fierceness in the response didn't shock Meg. She'd long realized that the glibly sophisticated, charming veneer Drago displayed to the world overlay a much more serious man. Practical, sensible, compassionate; he was all those things and more. And people like Emily Temple and the more senior in political and social circles had seen through the façade to the real man, and it was he they wanted in their ranks.

She understood that he was torn over allowing her to play her part in their plan. She understood exactly what he was feeling because over his involvement, she felt much the same. Perhaps not with the same intensity and force, but the quality of the emotion was identical.

In his dark eyes, she could see the turmoil that racked him. Knowing of no other way, certainly no more appropriate way, to distract him and herself, using her hold on his wrists, she stretched up and pressed a kiss—an open-mouthed invitation—to his lips.

His response, immediate and heated and so very much in tune with their needs, was everything and more than she'd hoped for.

In seconds, the flames of their always-ready passion had flared, and desire swirled about them, heightening their senses, goading and tempting and driving them on.

Even so, they didn't rush but savored each second as they divested each other of their clothes, layer by layer, garment by garment. Reverence and worship had become their watchwords, underpinned by commitment to the other, to their pleasure, with the achievement of that being their greatest reward.

They came together in an achingly slow dance, one that stretched and expanded their awareness of all that was physical and all that was emotional in the simple intimacy.

In the communication that flowed between them in the moment that, hand clutching hand, bodies clamped tight, they reached the peak in a rush of togetherness, and their senses soared, then shattered.

They clung as they spiraled slowly back to earth.

As one, together, determined never to be parted.

Finally, Drago stirred, lifted from her, and slumped onto his back.

She curled toward him, and he gathered her in, and she pillowed her head on his chest.

A moment later, staring up at the canopy, he sighed. "I didn't expect this."

She pressed a soft kiss to his chest. "This what?"

"In all honesty, hopes and dreams aside, I never expected to fall in love." He paused, then went on, "I know my parents' marriage was a love match. I just didn't expect to have one myself." He shifted his head to glance down at her face. "I never expected to be so blessed."

She smiled softly and smoothed a hand over the crisp black hair before her face. "If it's any consolation, I didn't expect to fall in love, either. Especially not with you." She glanced up, and when he waited, went on, "I'd been looking for the right gentleman for me, the one man above all others I would love, but by the time I met you, I'd lost hope of ever encountering him. Yet the instant I set eyes on you, inebriated though you were, I suspected you might be the one. Against all the accepted precepts, against all odds, that proved to be the case."

He smiled down at her and tightened his arms in a gentle hug. "So here we are."

She nodded. "Indeed."

He raised his head and pressed a kiss to her forehead. "Sleep."

As if he'd cast some spell, she felt the lethargy arising from their recent activities well and swell, then flow in an ocean of oblivion over her. On a sigh, she slipped under, into peaceful dreams.

Drago watched her slide into slumber. He waited until he was sure she was fathoms deep, then he carefully eased from her lax embrace and ultimately from the bed. He found his silk robe, shrugged it on, and belted it.

Then he quietly crossed the room to the door, opened it and left, then closed the door silently behind him.

He padded along the familiar corridors to the other end of the wing and took the servants' stairs to the attic.

On reaching the head of the stairs, he stepped into the narrow attic corridor and tapped quietly on the first two doors.

When Maurice and Tisdale appeared, he beckoned them down the stairs to the landing and proceeded to make his own arrangements.

* * *

As AGREED, they set their plan in motion the very next day.

After confirming the details over breakfast, at eleven o'clock, Drago mounted his black hunter, Vulcan, and rode across the estate toward Melwin Place.

Having steeled himself to play his part, he'd remained in the stable yard and chatted amiably with his stable hands while they'd saddled the big horse, then he'd ridden off with not the slightest sign that his entire awareness remained centered on Wylde Court.

Specifically on the family parlor at the rear of the mansion, where Meg was waiting with the others.

Their plan called for Meg to wave off George and Harry as if the pair were returning to London. Then Denton was to leave with Toby, Aidan, Evan, and Carter, ostensibly to show them the way to Walkhurst Manor.

They'd reasoned that if their villain was watching the house—or had men doing so—they would deduce that Meg was, however temporarily, without protectors.

So when she went out to the rose garden...

With tension locked like a vise about his head and heart, Drago cantered up the gravel drive of Melwin Place. As he dismounted before the steps, a groom came running. Drago handed over the reins. "I'll be about an hour."

"Yes, Your Grace."

The groom led Vulcan away, and Drago climbed the steps to the front door.

The butler recognized him and bowed low. "Your Grace!"

"Good morning." Ducal arrogance on show, Drago strolled inside. "Is Miss Melwin at home?"

The butler looked flustered. "Ah..." Then he pulled himself together. "Miss Melwin is presently in the morning room, Your Grace. With her brother and...another gentleman."

Drago arched his brows. "Mr. Bragg, by any chance?" That would be a stroke of luck.

The butler's face cleared. "Indeed, Your Grace."

"Excellent." Drago smiled charmingly and waved the man ahead of him. "Please take me to them."

After closing the front door, the butler hurried to do so. He led Drago to a room toward the rear of the manor house, tapped, opened the door, and proudly announced, "His Grace, the Duke of Wylde."

Drago entered to see surprise overtake the faces of the trio seated in the parlor—Alison and Joshua on the sofa and Hubert in an armchair facing them. Hubert's expression was one of stunned astonishment, while Alison and Joshua looked unexpectedly and pleasantly relieved.

"Wylde." Hubert shot to his feet. Previously, Hubert had thoroughly disapproved of Drago, as much as a gentleman of Hubert's rank could disapprove of a neighboring duke. Today, however, Hubert manufactured what he no doubt believed was a welcoming smile and advanced with his hand outstretched. "We're delighted to see you at Melwin Place, Your Grace."

Drago hid all suspicion behind his usual charming smile. "Hubert." He grasped Hubert's hand and resisted the urge to crush it, reminding himself that they needed Hubert to incriminate himself.

Apparently oblivious to any undercurrents, Hubert gestured to Alison, who, with Joshua, had risen. "You're acquainted with my sister, of course."

Drago smiled sincerely at Alison and half bowed as she hurriedly curtsied, then Drago transferred his smile to Joshua. "And with Mr. Bragg. I hoped I might find you here." Drago strolled forward to offer Joshua his hand.

Joshua shook it and bowed. "Your Grace."

Both Drago and Joshua looked at Alison.

She leapt to wave Drago to an armchair. "Do please have a seat, Your Grace."

With a deepening smile, he elegantly sat, and Alison and Joshua resumed their places on the sofa, leaving Hubert, somewhat uncertainly, to reclaim the other armchair.

Studying Drago's face—trying to gauge what he wanted of them—Alison tentatively ventured, "I expect the duchess is still settling into life at Wylde Court."

"Indeed." Drago smiled encouragingly at Alison. "Meg would have accompanied me, but she's still finding her way with the various demands on her time, so I am here representing us both. We wished to invite you"

—he transferred his smile to Joshua—"and Mr. Bragg to an alfresco luncheon next Sunday." Avoiding glancing at Hubert, Drago waved languidly. "An entirely informal affair."

Alison looked at Joshua, then returned her gaze to Drago. "I would be delighted to attend, Your Grace."

"As would I." Joshua half bowed.

"Excellent!" Drago beamed. "Now I've done my duty in that regard, I wonder, Bragg, if I might seek your opinion on a matter of estate business." Drago fleetingly glanced at Hubert, then looked at Alison. "Perhaps, Miss Melwin, you would be agreeable to accompanying Mr. Bragg and myself on a stroll about the gardens." He waved toward the French doors that stood open to the terrace. "It's such a lovely day, it seems a shame to waste it, even while discussing business."

"Yes, of course." Now intrigued, Alison obligingly rose.

The gentlemen got to their feet, and Drago waved Alison and Joshua ahead of him. Hubert, of course, followed them out.

Once on the terrace, over Alison's head, Drago spoke to Joshua. "When we met in London, you mentioned that your firm was thinking of opening an office in Tunbridge Wells. I'd like to pick your brains as to those plans." He smiled at Alison, standing between them, and gallantly offered her his arm. "Let's stroll on the lawn. I'm sure Alison won't mind indulging us."

Alison readily smiled and took his arm, then glanced questioningly at Joshua.

Her intended nodded encouragingly and waved her and Drago to the steps. Joshua walked down with them, and in relaxed fashion, the three of them set out across the lawn.

After several yards, Drago changed direction so that they were walking parallel to the terrace. A quick glance revealed Hubert quitting the terrace and heading in the direction of the stable.

"Has he gone?" Alison whispered.

"Yes." Drago watched Hubert round the corner of the house and disappear from view. "I think he's gone to the stable."

"Good." Alison slowed and, gripping Drago's arm, turned concerned eyes his way. "So what's going on?"

Briefly, he told them.

"So Meg's alone, and you don't know who will turn up and try to lure her away?" Joshua asked.

Drago grimaced. "That's the nub of it, yes."

"But her brother and cousins and your brother and your friends are all keeping watch." Alison pressed his arm. "I'm sure they'll keep her safe."

He hoped so. He didn't add that Hubert was their prime suspect. "Meanwhile," he went on, "I have to be seen to be elsewhere and believably occupied." He managed a smile for Alison and Joshua. "We hoped you two might help me with that."

They assured him that they would be honored to assist in whatever way they could.

He explained that he was supposed to remain in sight of anyone watching for at least an hour, and to their credit, the pair did their best to engage and entertain him as they strolled the lawn in full view of whoever might be interested.

Drago gritted his teeth and did his best to be grateful for their chatter, all the while wondering what his wife was up to and whether the villain had swallowed their bait.

* * *

ACCORDING TO THE PLAN, Meg was supposed to remain inside until an hour after Drago had left. They'd judged that to be time enough for all those delegated to be on watch—watching her, watching Hubert, and generally watching the approaches to the estate—to surreptitiously get into position and for the villain to realize that a window of opportunity had opened for him and for him to act to seize it.

After Drago had left, standing on the front porch where she was readily visible, Meg had duly waved off George and Harry. She had laughed and called down to them while they'd mounted, waved, and ridden away.

Shortly after, Denton had led Toby and her three cousins out of the house via the side door. In a noisy group, they'd headed for the stable yard. There, with much noisy chatter, they'd mounted up and headed south and onto the road to Walkhurst Manor.

All of that had taken place as arranged. The opening act in their scripted play was complete. Now they simply had to wait to see what happened next. Or more specifically, who appeared in or around the Court, either intent on harming her or, as they'd all thought more likely, trying to lure her to some place where the villain could do away with her in secret.

While she'd been all for the plan—she wanted this ridiculous state of siege to end—now the moment was upon her, she was no longer feeling quite so enthusiastic about being on her own through the next stage, no matter how essential that was.

Once Denton and her brother and cousins had left, she found the silence in the house oppressive.

She'd been instructed to keep away from the windows while she waited and had been warned not to be seen pacing anxiously in any of the downstairs rooms.

"There's no way that I can read a book or sit embroidering." She pulled a face, then went upstairs to the room she shared with Drago, sat in one of the armchairs by the hearth, and tried not to think.

After several minutes, she realized that there was one sure distraction she hadn't set eyes on since they'd left the breakfast parlor. Frowning, she rose and went to look for Ridley.

In London, it had soon been established that, despite his uncertain origins, the pup was house-trained, and subsequently, he'd been allowed the run of the house, and that freedom had been extended at the Court. Alongside his devotion to Meg, he was developing into a gregarious animal, ready to be friendly with any human he came across. To Ridley, fawning over men's boots was a special delight.

In contrast, Drago's wolfhounds were standoffish with strangers and, indeed, had yet to fully accept Meg. Currently, they preferred to sleep in a kennel off the stable and otherwise roam the gardens; while they would attach themselves to Drago and follow him to the library or his study, at present, they were not being encouraged to venture elsewhere in the house and especially not upstairs. Consequently, Ridley's range overlapped that of the hounds only when he followed Meg into the library or when he gamboled about her in the gardens. The wolfhounds, older and more established in their territory, had merely sniffed the puppy, then disdainfully left him to wander as he would.

Ridley usually dogged Meg around the house, flopping on her feet to nap whenever and wherever she sat. It was odd that he hadn't been haunting her steps that morning.

She glanced into all of the rooms in the ducal suite in case he'd got trapped when someone had closed a door, but he wasn't anywhere there. She walked up the family wing and into the gallery, calling his name, but he didn't bound up from any of the corridors, and when she paused to listen, she heard no whining, scratching, or yipping.

Increasingly concerned, she started down the stairs and paused on the half landing to call more loudly.

Fothergill emerged from the rear of the front hall and looked up. "Your Grace? Is something wrong?"

"I can't find Ridley. Have you seen him?"

Clearly consulting his memory, Fothergill frowned. "Now that you mention it, ma'am, I can't say I have. Not since after breakfast." He met her gaze. "I'll ask the staff. I'm sure someone will know where he is."

Meg summoned a grateful smile. "I'll be in the family parlor."

Fothergill bowed and departed, and Meg continued down the stairs.

But when fifteen minutes later, Fothergill tapped on the parlor door, he didn't have a golden bundle of fur in tow. A slight frown on his usually impassive face, the butler bowed. "I regret, ma'am, that we've yet to lay hands on the pup, but about half an hour ago, Flora, the kitchen maid, heard the beast scratching madly at the back door and let him out, assuming he needed to do his business. When he goes out like that, he normally returns and whines at the door to be let back in, but as of yet, he hasn't come back. If you wish, ma'am, I could send some of the footmen and gardeners out to search for him."

Meg frowned. On the one hand, she was anxious about Ridley, but on the other, if footmen and gardeners were seen quartering the grounds, that might well discourage their villain.

They'd gone to such lengths to set their trap; she didn't want to jeopardize their plan over an errant pup who would no doubt turn up for his next meal, utterly unrepentant over any fuss he might have caused.

Then she remembered that Drago had expressly ordered the wolfhounds kept in their run for the day.

Inwardly, she sighed. "No, Fothergill. Let's wait until after luncheon. If he hasn't turned up by then"—by which time the villain either would have made an appearance or wouldn't be going to—"we'll set up a search."

"Very good, Your Grace." Fothergill bowed and departed.

When the door closed, Meg glanced at the clock on the mantelpiece. It was almost time for her to go out and promenade through the rose garden. When the assembled gentlemen had suggested the rose garden as the best site for her to show herself and tempt the villain to approach, they'd wanted her to be cutting blooms, but as she'd pointed out, anyone who actually knew anything about roses would know one didn't cut flowers in the middle of the day, not unless there was some other reason to be doing that at that time.

Grudgingly, they'd agreed that it would work just as well for her simply to stroll about enjoying the perfumed blooms. While she hadn't specifically thought about it at the time, Meg had mentally seen herself as having her until-now-faithful dog with her, snuffling about under the roses as he usually did.

It was, she was fast discovering, one thing to agree to play bait, but she hadn't thought she would be entirely alone while waiting for the villain to bite.

Arms folded, she stared at the clock as the hands ticked inexorably on. Then she huffed and swung toward the French doors. If she didn't go now…

Drago would be riding home soon, and if she didn't flaunt herself sufficiently in front of the villain before Drago arrived, all their efforts would be for naught.

She drew in a bolstering breath, opened the French doors, and stepped out onto the rear terrace.

After closing the doors, she strolled at an easy, lackadaisical pace along the terrace, paused at the end to survey the gardens, then went down the steps and walked unhurriedly along the gravel path that led to the rose garden.

The rose garden at Wylde Court was a series of long curving paths, bordered on either side by deep beds planted with roses. The bushes were old and large and currently heavily weighted with blooms. The profuse shows of color and the heady medley of scents rising in the midday sunshine made the notion of the lady of the house choosing to stroll there before luncheon entirely believable.

They'd chosen the rose garden for her promenade because there were no walls and, overall, the area was flat, making it easy for her protectors, hidden in the trees that ringed the gardens, to watch over her.

Doing her best to convey a real interest in the roses, she stopped here and there to admire specific flowers and to sniff appreciatively. She hoped and expected that the villain or his henchmen would come out of hiding fairly soon. She was, after all, presenting the blackguards with the easiest of kidnapping scenarios. By arrangement with the staff, that morning, there were no gardeners working on that side of the house, and the rose garden was out of direct sight of the stable yard, and the open lawns stretched, invitingly empty, to either side.

Only the forest that lay twenty yards beyond the end of the garden offered any close cover, and indeed, it was from that direction that she expected the villain to appear.

Slowly, she followed the path as it wound left, then right. She slowed even further along the last winding arm, the section closest to the edge of the forest.

On reaching the end of the path, she paused and muttered, "Has he even noticed I'm out here?"

On a sigh, she turned on her heel and—still keeping to a crawling pace, but with her hopes sinking with every yard—retraced her steps along the rose-lined path toward the house.

By the time she walked out of the rose garden and onto the path crossing the lawn, she'd dismissed their plan as an abject failure and turned her mind to the worrying problem of Ridley and what orders she should give regarding a search for the golden-pelted pup.

She raised her gaze and looked toward the house and saw Thomas striding rapidly toward her from the direction of the forecourt.

Clearly, he'd ignored Drago's directive not to risk his position by excusing himself from chambers and had come down to help.

Thomas's purposeful approach across the lawn would have scared off any villain, but that no longer mattered as, regardless, said villain hadn't swallowed their bait.

Meg halted and summoned a smile; it was kind of Thomas to have come. But as he neared and she made out his features, she realized he was tense and worried.

She started toward him. "Thomas. What is it?"

He glanced around as if searching for anyone else approaching, then grimaced and, as they met, halted and transferred his gaze, serious and sober, to her face.

She gripped his sleeve and fought to restrain herself from shaking his arm. "Has something happened to Drago?"

"Not as far as I'm aware."

"What, then?" From his careful tone, he was aware of something that he knew would upset her.

"That dog of yours."

"Ridley?" She couldn't keep the eagerness from her voice. "Have you seen him?" She gripped his arm more tightly. "Do you know where he is?"

Grim-faced, Thomas met her eyes. "I arrived in time to meet Drago as he left for Melwin Place. He told me about the others watching over you and suggested how I could best help. Long story short, I was scouting through the forest to the south of the house when I heard whimpering. I found your pup in the cellar of an old ruined cottage. He must have gone investigating and fallen in. I would have got him out, but he's injured, and he won't let me anywhere near him. He's bleeding and, from what I could see, might have broken a leg."

"Oh Lord!" Meg put her fingers to her lips.

Thomas glanced searchingly around the lawns again. "As the plan doesn't seem to have worked, I thought I should come and tell you." He met Meg's eyes. "Do you want to stay here longer? I could walk on to the stable—"

"No!" Using her grip on his sleeve, she towed him around. "To hell with the villain, whoever he is. If he arrives now, the others will see him, and Drago should be back soon anyway. We'll have to come up with some other plan, but there's only one Ridley. Please show me where he is immediately."

"All right." Thomas started walking quickly and pointed ahead. "We need to go into the forest and head southeast a little way."

Releasing his arm, Meg nodded. She raised her skirts and hurried to keep up with his longer strides.

They rounded the front corner of the house and rapidly crossed the south lawn.

As they neared the trees, she said, "I know Drago told you not to come, but I'm glad you did."

Somewhat stiffly, Thomas inclined his head. "I received his note, but..." His lips tightened. "I couldn't not come." He waved into the trees. "It's this way."

Meg nodded and hurried on beside him.

* * *

MEG FOLLOWED Thomas through the heavily shadowed woods. It was taking much longer than she'd thought to reach their destination.

Thomas glanced at her and, as if divining her thoughts, admitted, "It's farther than I'd realized."

She nodded, and they continued on their winding, twisting path through the thickening trees. Much of the estate surrounding Wylde Court was given over to forest, most of it quite old.

At last, Thomas pointed ahead, and between the tall trunks, she spotted a crumbling ruin that had once been a small cottage.

Originally, the cottage had stood in a clearing, but over the years, the forest had encroached, and now, only a few yards separated the encircling trees from the cottage's lichen-covered walls.

Meg hurried forward. "Ridley?"

A volley of barking drew her around the side of the long-abandoned cottage to the mouth of its cellar. The door was flung back, revealing a set of stone steps covered in dust and debris stretching downward into the gloom.

Meg crouched and peered into the darkness shrouding the cellar. "Ridley?"

Bark! Yip! Bark!

He was definitely in there and, by the sounds of it, quite agitated.

"Wait," she called. "I'm coming."

She rose and carefully started down the steps. She had to work to keep her balance, testing each stone to make sure it was stable before trusting her weight to it.

Ridley continued to yip and bark, if anything growing more hysterical.

As Meg descended and her eyes adjusted to the prevailing gloom, she saw that, except for the roof formed by the well-aged, solid oak planks of the cottage's floor, the entire cellar was faced with stone. This would once have been an excellent place for storing grains, fruits, vegetables, and herbs. Indeed, if the door was fixed and the detritus of the years cleared away, the cellar appeared sufficiently sound that it would be useable now.

Finally, she stepped onto the cellar's stone floor.

"Careful," Thomas warned, descending the steps just behind her. "There's all sorts of rubbish strewn about."

The only illumination came from the open doorway, and given they were deep in the forest, the light falling through was diffuse and did little to penetrate the dimness deeper in the cellar.

Meg blinked several times, then looked toward where the barks, now interspersed with growls, were emanating from. As her eyes adjusted further, Ridley's golden body gleamed through the shadows.

Relief hit her, and she dashed forward. "Ridley!"

She reached him and, crouching, set her palm on his head to calm him, but he continued to struggle, trying to leap and lick her face, all the while alternating between barks and growls. "Quiet." She tried to keep him down as, gently, she ran her hands over his quivering body and limbs. "Don't jump! You'll hurt yourself more…"

Instead of any evidence of injury, her searching fingers found a rope tied to his collar.

She blinked, and her improving vision verified what touch was telling her. Ridley wasn't hurt. He was tied to an anchoring ring set in the wall.

Relief was short-lived as realization poured over her in an icy wave.

She shot upright and spun to face Thomas, only to discover that he was standing squarely between her and the cellar door with a length of rope in his hands.

Fear joined the roiling emotions coursing through her, but anger—for Drago and for everyone else this man had taken in—was far stronger. "You must be mad!"

"Not at all." His voice exuded an almost unnatural calmness. "My plan is so brilliant no one will ever guess until all the pieces have fallen into place, and by then, even those who might suspect won't be able to do anything about it." Smug certainty colored his tone. "You'll see..." Then his features hardened, and he shrugged. "Actually, you won't."

Her only hope was to delay whatever he had planned and pray that others had seen her leave with him. "Was it you behind all the accidents?"

"Of course it was."

His gloating spurred her on; men always liked to boast, didn't they? "So it was you who hired the man who came at me with a knife in Bond Street and those thugs who attacked Drago and me in Manchester Street."

He gave vent to a disgusted snort. "I suppose one gets what one pays for. They said they were professionals, but clearly, they were the sort of amateurs who didn't think it mattered if, as I'd instructed, you were alone when they attacked or if you were accompanied. They escaped Drago, but you'll be pleased to know that they didn't escape me. I couldn't leave any loose ends flapping. Once my life is on the track I've planned, I don't want to be constantly looking over my shoulder, so I removed those three and the earlier man as well, then moved on to a higher class of villain-for-hire."

"Wait." She frowned. "Earlier man? Wasn't the Bond Street attack the first?"

The gloating was back. "No. My first attempt was really quite inspired and so very nearly worked." His gaze lowered from her to Ridley, who was now plastered against her leg and growling low in his throat.

Meg knew just how the pup felt.

"You said you liked dogs. I was watching from a nearby carriage, and the man who released the mutt timed it perfectly. You should have died under Carmichael-Craik's horses' hooves. Instead, Drago saved you." Thomas shook his head. "I should have known then that I'd have to do the deed myself, but I hoped never to directly show my hand." He sighed. "However..." He raised his hands and uncoiled the rope. "In a way, it's rather poetic, don't you think, that the mutt you rescued in escaping that first attack should be the bait that lures you to your death? And his, too, of course."

Hurriedly, she said, "The least you can do is tell me the rest." *Delay, delay, delay.* "Was it you who put the branch on the track and hid in the bushes, waiting for me to be flung from the gig?"

"Yes. And dammit! Drago shouldn't have been with you. Why he decided to accompany you to visit two old women..." He shook his head. "That was plain bad luck."

"And it was you who put a hole in the rowboat?"

"Of course—and again, that should have spelled your doom! What possessed Drago to overcome his sensibilities over his dead brother? After that, I started to think your existence was charmed." He paused, staring at her, then he drew the rope taut between his hands. "But this time, I've got you away from him, and this time, I'll succeed."

He took a step toward her.

Meg clamped down on the urge to cower and stood her ground. "I cannot conceive," she said, deploying her grandmother's haughtiest tones, "how you imagine you're going to get away with this." She waved at the rope. "Whatever this is."

He took another step toward her, and she could hear the smile in his voice as, entirely unperturbed, he replied, "Trust me, I will." Then he paused, head tipping, and more pensively went on, "Indeed, you might say my entire plan is based on trust. On the fact that the others trust me implicitly, without question, and so they believe everything I tell them. Whatever I say, they take as truth." He was close enough now for her to make out his smile. "As they will in this case."

Meg's heart was thudding, but the warmth of Ridley's body pressing against her leg reminded her she had him to fight for as well. She summoned every ounce of bravado, crossed her arms, and tipped up her chin. "As I'm going to be the one affected, what is it that you plan to do?"

She'd meant with the rope, but he took the question to refer to his entire plan and, proving her earlier observation, showed he was definitely a man. He all but preened as he told her, "My plan is so unlike anything that anyone's done before, I have no qualms at all that Drago or anyone else will guess my intention, not even after everything is done and the coffers of the dukedom fall into my hands."

She frowned. "How on earth...?"

His answering smile was unnervingly close to ecstatic. "It all hinges on Drago's father's will. And on Drago, of course, but it was entirely predictable that he'd wait until the last minute—well, the last Season before his thirty-fifth birthday—to find a bride. That, after all, was the impetus behind that clause—making sure he actually married. But you see, that gave me a chance to find him the perfect bride. Meaning the perfect bride for my purposes, and Alison Melwin satisfied my every last requirement."

One penny dropped in Meg's brain. Eyeing Thomas, she asked, "Are you acquainted with Hubert Melwin?"

Thomas's smile deepened. "I see you're following my strategy. And yes, indeed, Hubert and I have become close friends. Confidantes, you might say, at least on his side."

She still couldn't see his point. "So you...what? Kill me, making Drago a widower, then…" She could guess the immediate next steps, but not what came after.

Sure enough, Thomas confirmed, "Then I explain to him—or better yet, get Crawthorne to—that in order to satisfy the terms of his father's will, Drago has to actually be married on his thirty-fifth birthday."

She nodded. "So he'll have to find a suitable bride very quickly, and most families would find that difficult to accept, given he'll be in mourning."

"But the Melwins—via Hubert—will understand and encourage Alison to do the right thing and put aside her beau to become a duchess. And then," he rolled on, warming to his exposition, "I'll wait until Alison bears Drago's heir and the child proves to be healthy, then I'll arrange for Drago to have a fatal accident. How tragic." His tone dripped with fake sympathy. "By then, of course, Crawthorne will have retired, and I'll have taken over the legal affairs of the Helmsfords. Although Denton might be named executor and guardian, I'll be able to deal with him, especially as I will be in a position to ensure that, as Alison's older brother, Hubert will be named co-guardian for the Helmsford heir."

Thomas's features assumed an expression of intense, almost-beatific anticipation. Meg stared as he went on, "After that, of course, it'll be a simple matter to slowly drain the coffers dry. I'll be wealthy beyond anyone's wildest dreams."

Then he refocused on Meg, and his expression sobered, growing unnervingly intense. "You can see, now, why I couldn't let you—a Cynster —be Drago's duchess. If you bore his heir and he then died, I wouldn't have a hope of getting anywhere near the dukedom's riches. You and your meddlingly protective family would see to that."

He tipped his head, took one last step, and brandished the rope. "So be a good girl and let me tie you up."

Meg blinked. "Tie me up?" She'd assumed he was going to hang her or strangle her or, in some dramatic way involving a rope, murder her.

"It's that or"—he reached into his pocket, and she heard a *click*, then saw he was aiming a small revolver at Ridley—"watch as I blow the mutt's brains out. And then yours, of course. Messy, but it'll achieve the same end, meaning the one I want."

She swallowed. "And if you tie me up?"

He smiled. "I'll leave you here—you and your dog—to die. If and when anyone finds you, who knows what they might think? Regardless, there'll be nothing to connect me to your sad demise."

They were far too far from the house for anyone to hear her shouting. And while she didn't doubt that when she didn't return, a search would be mounted, how many people knew of this cottage, let alone the cellar beneath it?

His gaze locked with hers, Thomas weighed the rope in one hand and the revolver in the other. "Lady's choice as to which way you both meet your end."

Earlier, he'd spoken more accurately than he knew; both plans—his and theirs—hinged on trust. She had to trust that regardless of whatever tale Thomas had spun, someone had still been watching her and had followed them from the house. She knew Drago had slipped from their bed last night; she strongly suspected he'd gone to arrange for more protection for her, but she'd fallen asleep again before he'd returned.

She hadn't heard anything—not the crack of a twig or the rustle of leaves. She had no idea if anyone was out there, but she'd wanted to play bait to draw out the villain, and she'd succeeded. Now she had to trust her co-conspirators to keep her alive.

"All right." She held out her hands.

But Thomas shook his head. "No. Turn around and cross your wrists behind your back."

Meg hesitated, but then complied. Ridley whined when she moved her leg, but when she took up her new stance, he quieted and leaned against her other leg. He growled softly at Thomas as he stepped forward and lashed her wrists together. Tightly. Painfully so.

She gritted her teeth. At this point, protest would be useless. Then she thought of another question. "What are you going to—"

Fabric circled her face and cinched tight over her lips. A muffled "Mm-hmm!" was all the sound she could make.

The fiend behind her chuckled. "You didn't think I'd leave you able to scream for help, did you?"

She clenched her jaw, then sensed that he'd backed away.

She swung around and saw Thomas swiftly climbing the cellar steps.

He reached the doorway and stepped outside, then turned and bent and raised the old door. Before he set it in place, he looked down at her. "Pity. You were simply in the wrong place at the wrong time and chose to save a man you should have left to reap his just rewards."

With that, he lowered the door into place.

Meg stood in the dark, testing the bonds holding her wrists, but he'd known what he was doing, and the knots didn't ease by even a smidgen.

Then she heard a scraping noise and realized that Thomas was pushing a heavy rock across the cellar door.

Even if she freed her hands, given how much difficulty he was having shoving the rock into place, she doubted that, pushing from the inside, she would be able to escape.

Reaction hit her, and she decided to sit down before she fell.

Immediately, Ridley crowded close, trying to comfort her as he sought comfort.

Meg pressed her face, gag and all, into the pup's soft coat.

Now, we just have to wait and put our trust in everyone else.

Just as Drago had had to do when he'd ridden out that morning.

CHAPTER 19

$\mathcal{U}$ nbelievably tense and alert, Drago rode up the Wylde Court drive.

Has anything happened?

Is Meg all right?

Who is our villain?

It was an effort to preserve a nonchalant, unperturbed façade as he slowed Vulcan in the forecourt.

Masham, one of the older grooms, was waiting to take Vulcan's reins. Drago's first intimation that something had, indeed, occurred was the pointed look Masham sent him. "Your friends, the viscount and his lordship, just raced in and are waiting in the front hall."

Drago's pulse spiked. "Her Grace?"

"I understand Her Grace is safe, but not here at the moment."

Drago gave his customary nod of dismissal and had to fight not to take the porch steps two at a time and, instead, proceed at a normal, unruffled pace up and across the porch and in through the front door, which, as usual at that time of year, was propped wide.

As soon as he passed into the hall proper, George and Harry all but leapt on him. Both were breathing hard, and they literally seized his arms and all but shook him.

"It's Thomas!" George gasped.

"Truly, it is." Eyes wide, Harry nodded like a bobbing doll.

Both looked shocked to their back teeth, but...

Drago frowned. "Thomas?" What the devil were they trying to tell him? "Thomas is what?"

"The villain!" his friends all but howled.

George grasped Drago's shoulders and looked him in the eye. "We couldn't believe it any more than you, but we saw and heard him with our own eyes and ears."

"It's him," Harry confirmed, still struggling to catch his breath. "It was him all along. He confessed it all to Meg."

Drago's head was spinning, but at that, fear reared and gripped tight. "Where is she?"

Harry and George released him to hold up calming hands. "She's all right," Harry assured him. "Maurice and Tisdale are getting her out of the cellar of that ruined cottage in the forest."

"They'll escort her back here," George said. "She's definitely all right, but everyone agreed we should hightail it back here to tell you about Thomas before he turns up."

Drago frowned. He glanced at the open doorway, unsurprised to see Fothergill and two footmen lurking in the shadows. He looked at Fothergill. "I take it the staff are watching for Mr. Hayden's approach?"

Fothergill half bowed. "Indeed, Your Grace."

Drago looked at his friends and waved them into the shadows of a corridor leading away from the hall. "Start at the beginning." He halted inside the corridor, out of sight of anyone in the hall, and focused on George and Harry. "Thomas met me as I rode out. I told him I was going to Melwin Place and you were on watch. I told him where you would be and sent him to join you."

Harry snorted. "He joined us all right, but he told us you'd asked him to tell us to drop back along the drive and keep watch for anyone approaching the house. Meanwhile, he would take over watching Meg himself."

"We weren't sure that was wise, but if you'd said to do that..." George grimaced. "We started to head down the drive, but it didn't feel right, you know?"

"The simple fact was that we couldn't imagine you *reducing* the guards around Meg." Harry shook his head. "That wasn't you."

George nodded. "So we turned back, and as we were approaching the house—"

"Still keeping to the cover of the trees," Harry put in.

"We saw Meg and Thomas coming around the house," George continued. "They'd left the rose garden and were hurrying across the front lawn."

"We didn't know what that was about, so we followed."

"We were suspicious by then," George said, "so we didn't join them, and luckily, it's easy enough to track people through your type of forest."

"Mind you, we nearly gave the game away by squealing like girls when Maurice and Tisdale crept up on us." Harry shook his head. "Those two are very good stalkers. No wonder you always take them when you go hunting."

George was nodding.

Drago clenched his jaw, then prompted, "What happened then?"

"Ah," George said. "The four of us followed Thomas and Meg—he was leading her through the forest, but she was right on his heels—to the ruins of the old cottage."

"We heard a dog barking, and Meg rushed ahead," Harry said. "She went down into the cellar, and Thomas followed."

"You may be sure all four of us rushed to see, and luckily, the dog was barking and they were talking, so they didn't hear us, and…" George blew out a breath. "Well, Meg got it all out of him."

Harry nodded. "She kept asking questions, and Thomas was so pumped up in his own conceit, he told her all about his scheme. He couldn't resist telling her—and the four of us listening as well—how he'd arranged for all the accidents."

"Including the incident when Meg rescued the puppy." George met Drago's eyes. "That was Thomas, too, right from the get-go. And he used the puppy again to lure her away and get her to rush down into the old cellar."

"But…" Stunned, Drago spread his hands. *"Why?"*

"Oh, she got him to explain that, too, and it all made horrible sense, but" —George darted a glance toward the front hall—"he'll be here any minute." He looked at Drago. "As soon as we'd heard enough and knew Thomas was planning to tie Meg up and leave her and the dog trapped in the cellar to die, your men said we should get back here and tell you what had happened the instant you returned. They stayed to free Meg once Thomas left."

"We were still close enough to see that Thomas did as he'd said," Harry reported. "He climbed out of the cellar and shut the door. He was pushing a rock over it when we raced off to get here and warn you."

Drago was starting to piece together the sequence of events. "How long were you waiting for me in the hall?"

"Only about a minute," Harry said.

Drago nodded curtly. "You're right. Thomas will arrive soon." While one part of his mind was reeling over Thomas's betrayal—wanting to know the how, when, where, and most importantly, why—another part, a more pragmatic and incisive part, was swiftly analyzing and adjusting. "He'll want to be with me when I learn that Meg is missing. He'll want to be here to manage things—to help organize the search to ensure no one other than him goes near the cottage."

George and Harry stared at him, mutely waiting for orders.

Grimly, Drago thought through the prospects. "We need to keep Thomas here, preferably unsuspecting, until we're sure Meg is safe and as many others as possible are present to bear witness to the revelations." He focused on George and Harry. "If Thomas lays eyes on either of you as you are, still breathless and disheveled, he'll guess we know, and who knows what he might do then?"

Drago paused, imagining possible scenarios, then waved down the corridor and led the way. "He'll expect me to hold court in the library." He walked faster and glanced at George and Harry. "You two can take refuge in the study next door. With the connecting door ajar, you'll be able to hear everything said in the library."

George and Harry nodded, and Drago went on, "Once the others start returning, that's the time you two should come in as well—make sure you go out of the study into the corridor and come into the library from there."

Harry said, "As if we've arrived with the others."

"Exactly." Drago paused at the door to the library and pointed at the next door along. "That's the study. I'll open the connecting door."

He waited to see the pair disappear into the study and close the door, then went into the library and quickly crossed to the connecting door. He opened it and nodded to George and Harry as they positioned themselves just out of sight around the now-open panel. Satisfied, Drago turned, swiftly crossed the large library, and sat in the chair behind his desk.

He'd only just leaned back—only just allowed his mind to shift to Meg —when a rap on the door heralded Fothergill. The butler walked in and impassively announced, "Mr. Hayden, Your Grace."

Thomas walked in, a frown on his face. "Drago. Have you seen Meg?"

Rather than answer, Drago nodded a dismissal to Fothergill. "Thank you, Fothergill. Lord Denton and Her Grace's cousins will, no doubt, turn up shortly. Please show them in when they arrive."

"Yes, Your Grace." Fothergill bowed and retreated.

Drago waved Thomas to a chair before the desk. Maintaining any semblance of equanimity in the light of what Drago now knew was difficult. Contrarily, when he looked at Thomas, he saw the same man he'd known since Eton, who had remained close—a friend, supposedly— through all the years.

Still frowning, Thomas dropped into the chair.

Drago noted Thomas remained alert. Drago found a slight smile, but he couldn't make it reach his eyes. "You know I didn't expect you to come down."

Thomas waved dismissively. "As I said earlier, I couldn't stay away." He grimaced lightly. "Although I'm not sure what good my presence did. I didn't see anyone who shouldn't be around while I was patrolling outside —well, other than George and Harry. They were so obvious, I suggested they fall back a trifle. But then"—Thomas frowned as if puzzled—"I couldn't see Meg anymore. She was in the rose garden. Did she come inside?" He sobered. "Or has something happened?"

Drago throttled the urge to fling himself at his so-called friend and beat the truth out of him. Adopting a faintly surprised expression, he replied, "Not that I'm aware of." He manufactured a sigh. "It seems our villain was too canny to be taken in by our trap." He heard the tramp of boots approaching. "Here come the others." Drago looked toward the door. "Perhaps they have news."

The door opened, and Toby, Aidan, Evan, Carter, and Denton trooped in.

Toby grinned good-naturedly and nodded at Thomas, then looked at Drago. "We just saw George and Harry. They're on their way in."

Drago inclined his head, taking that to mean that George and Harry had alerted the others as to who their villain was.

Glancing at Thomas, Drago noticed that he was gripping the arms of the chair rather tightly. He was holding himself still, ready to act; Drago's failure to comment about Meg's whereabouts was confusing him, and having all the other males about was making him nervous.

The others claimed chairs, all except Toby, who prowled toward the French doors that gave onto the terrace, and pretended to be looking out.

When Denton, in one of the armchairs facing the desk, looked at Thomas as if about to ask how he came to be there, Thomas forced a smile and preempted the question. "I had to come and help." He gestured with one hand. "I couldn't let you lot have all the fun."

The door opened again to admit George and Harry. Both came in as if expecting…something.

Thomas glanced swiftly around, but there was nothing in anyone's faces to give him any clue. Finally, Thomas looked back at Drago and manufactured a concerned frown. "So…where's Meg?"

"Right here." The ringing declaration swung everyone's attention to the connecting door as Meg walked in, with Ridley held on a rope leash and Tisdale and Maurice a step behind.

Meg's gaze—hard, crystal-blue—landed on Thomas.

Ridley saw Thomas as well. Teeth baring, the golden-pelted puppy snarled and snapped.

Everyone looked at Thomas.

He stared at Meg, at the dog, then wet his lips and raised his gaze... and realized everyone was watching him.

He started to rise, and Meg cried out, "He has a gun!"

His features contorting, Thomas drew the revolver from his pocket and aimed it at her. "Why won't you just die?"

Ridley's snarl filled the room, and the dog lunged, yanking the rope from Meg's hand. In a golden blur, Ridley bounded, leapt, and locked his jaws around Thomas's arm.

Thomas yelled and dropped the gun. Trying to shake Ridley off, Thomas stumbled back and fell over the side of the armchair.

Meg rushed up to catch the trailing rope and pull Ridley away.

Drago flung himself over the desk to reach Meg and put her behind him.

Denton and Evan both dove for the gun.

Toby closed in on Thomas from behind—only to be flung aside as Thomas sprang to his feet, looked wildly around, then lunged for the French doors.

In a flash, he was through them and outside.

With curses flying, the others—so many they were bumping into each other in their haste to reach the French doors—rushed to give chase.

Drago was more concerned with, more focused on, Meg. Slumping against the front of the desk, he hauled her to him and clutched her tight. That she clung to him equally fervently went a long way to calming his galloping heart. When he could control his voice, he murmured into her curls, "Are you all right?"

She nodded, then she raised her head, looked into his eyes, and reached up, framed his face, and kissed him. Hard. Forcefully. Confidently. Then she pulled away, stepped back, and caught his hand. "Come on! We need to be there when they catch him. We can't fall too far behind."

Drago wrestled his mind back to the action at hand and nodded. "I want to hear his reasons for what he's done directly from him."

Meg studied his grim expression. "He told me what he planned to do, but he didn't tell me why. You—and George and Harry, too—need to know that. You deserve to know that."

She turned to hand Ridley's lead to Maurice, but Drago intervened.

"Bring him. He's a scent hound, and he's definitely got Thomas's scent. He might be useful."

"And we're not about to stay here," Maurice added. "We want to see the end of this, too."

Drago nodded, and the four of them followed Ridley, already straining at his makeshift leash, through the French doors.

Thomas had made it into the trees. Drago and Meg stepped onto the terrace just in time to see the last of the pursuers vanish into the forest to the east of the house.

"Come on!" Closing his hand around Meg's, Drago jogged with her in that direction. Maurice and Tisdale kept close behind, while Ridley, nose to the wind, bounded ahead.

They reached the trees and plunged into the forest.

Drago knew the entire estate like the back of his hand. He listened to the shouts as, some way ahead of them, the others called out, directing each other as they followed Thomas's erratic trail. He was tacking side to side, trying to lose them.

Ridley now had his nose to the ground and, with the leash taut, kept Drago and company unerringly on track.

Drago plotted their route in his mind. Thanks to Ridley, who never paused to take stock, they were steadily gaining ground.

Then Drago realized what lay ahead. "He's going to run onto the cliffs of the old quarry." He glanced at Meg. "It's where they dug up the stone for the house, but it's been unused for centuries." He looked ahead, gauging the distance. "It's overgrown, but the cliffs are still there. I don't think I ever took Thomas that way. He won't know the quarry's there." He thought, then added, "Other than Denton, none of the others will know, either." In his head, Drago extrapolated the route Thomas was now following. Abruptly, Drago stopped jogging and pulled Meg and Ridley to a halt beside him. "We need to get ahead of him, so to speak, or he might run straight over the edge without realizing."

Meg looked at the puppy, still straining on his leash.

"Yes, he went that way," Drago said, "but we need to go a different way." Increasingly sure of that, he gripped Meg's hand tighter. "Come on!"

He set off at an angle to the route Thomas had taken. Meg tried to follow, but Ridley stood his ground and whined.

Tisdale scooped up the dog and nodded to Drago. "Go. We'll follow."

Drago went, wending his way through the trees, intent on getting to the quarry's edge before Thomas. His hand still locked about Meg's, without looking at her, he explained, "We'll reach the edge of the quarry some way around from where Thomas will, but we should be within hailing distance. We should be able to warn him of the danger before he runs over the edge."

He was aware of Meg looking at him curiously, presumably wondering why he was so concerned over saving Thomas—the villain of the piece—from plunging to his death. The truth was that some part of Drago's mind was still grappling with the reality that it had been Thomas —*Thomas!*—all along. While he accepted that Thomas was, indeed, their villain, the betrayal cut deep. He needed to hear the reason that had driven Thomas to such acts, and for that, he—and George and Harry, too —needed Thomas alive.

The sky glimmered blue through the trees ahead. A minute later, they burst out onto a narrow shelf of clear land that ringed the gaping scar of the quarry. Drago halted, looping an arm about Meg's waist to prevent her from venturing closer. "The edge is unstable and can crumble away at any time."

They'd arrived close to the head of the quarry, a little way around the northern rim. The opening to the quarry lay some way to the east, and directly across on the opposite side lay the spot where Drago thought Thomas would fetch up.

He scanned the forest, listening to the crashes and curses and calls as the pursuit neared. Then he glimpsed a body twisting, almost staggering, through the trees.

Drago released Meg and cupped his hands about his mouth. "Thomas! Watch out for the cliff!"

Thomas burst through the last of the undergrowth and rushed on, only to pull up at the last second, literally teetering with the toes of his boots on the cliff's edge. Wild-eyed, he stared briefly at Drago and Meg, then spun around and frantically looked to either side, searching for some way to escape.

But the others were closing in, more or less in an arc about him.

Drago heard a clatter and saw several small rocks break off from the cliff below Thomas to fall, bouncing and pinging, all the way down to the quarry floor far below.

"Thomas!" Drago yelled. "Step away from the edge." He waved Thomas back. "The cliff's unstable."

His expression utterly blank, Thomas looked at Drago, but instead of moving away from the edge, he swung to face the others as, one by one, they appeared, keeping within the trees but surrounding Thomas's position.

Thomas stood poised, arms spread for balance, his weight on his toes as if he intended to make a dash one way or the other and break through the cordon.

What he would have done, they were destined never to know.

A sullen rumble was all the warning anyone had. In the next instant, the earth roared, and the cliff beneath Thomas's feet fell away.

One second, he was there, and then he was gone.

Meg gasped. She clutched Drago's jacket and pressed her face to his chest.

Drago watched Thomas's body twist and turn, flung like a rag doll, multiple times before landing on the rubble far below. Then dust rose and obscured the sight, and Drago closed his eyes and buried his face in Meg's hair.

On the opposite cliff, held silent by shock, the other men stared at where Thomas had been.

Still held in Tisdale's arms, Ridley whimpered.

The sound of rocks smashing and dirt raining down continued for a full minute, then the dust cloud, denser now, rose even higher, and an eerie silence descended.

Slowly, the other men stepped out of the trees, but wisely didn't go any farther. They peered, but couldn't see down as Drago and those with him could.

As the dust settled and the cloud thinned, they could see Thomas's body sprawled, facedown, on the quarry floor.

Drago stared at the sight, then sighed, gently squeezed Meg, then released her and took her hand. "We need to go down."

He led their group back into the trees and around and down to the mouth of the quarry.

On the quarry's other side, Denton did the same, leading the other pursuers to the quarry's entrance. When Drago and Meg reached the quarry mouth, the others were waiting, silent and still.

Impassively, Drago nodded to them all, then led the way into the quarry.

He glanced at Meg questioningly, and she met his eyes and tightened her grip on his hand. She wasn't about to leave him to endure this on his own.

George and Harry fell in behind them, and the others brought up the rear.

When they reached Thomas, Drago crouched by his head and lightly touched his shoulder, and to everyone's surprise, Thomas softly groaned.

A single glance at his broken and twisted limbs, at the angle of his spine, assured them all that he wasn't long for this world.

Drago leaned close. "Why, Thomas? Why did you do this?"

Standing beside Drago, Meg waited, wondering.

George and Harry crouched on Thomas's other side, straining to hear anything he managed to say.

Thomas made a hacking sound—a hoarse laugh. "Because"—his voice was thready, but in the prevailing silence, they all heard it—"you were so rich. So unthinkingly wealthy. All three of you. While I… Courtesy of my father, I had nothing. You got to enjoy the lives you'd always been destined to have, while I…I had to scrimp and save and work. Work!" Disgust etched his tone. "Work with that doddery fool Crawthorne just to be able to dress well enough to move in the same circles as you."

The outburst had drained him, but there was nothing any of them could say to that that wouldn't sound trite.

Thomas breathed in, clearly a painful act. His head was angled toward Drago. Thomas hadn't opened his eyes, and Meg saw that his lips were now white. After a second, he murmured, so low the others shifted closer to hear, "I couldn't stand it. I couldn't see any way forward, and I was almost at the point of simply vanishing into London's hordes—maybe taking ship somewhere and starting a new life far from England—when Crawthorne asked me to review your father's will. I read that clause—the one stipulating that you had to be married on your thirty-fifth birthday—and the entire plan simply came to me. Point by point, it just spooled out in my mind. The perfect plan, one no one would ever suspect given how long it would take to come to fruition. But in order to get my hands on the coffers of the dukedom, I was more than willing to play a long game."

He seemed to relax, and his voice took on a dreamy note. "I started years ago. I became acquainted with the Melwins and became their solicitor. I cultivated Hubert. He was so easy to manipulate that was no challenge at all. And when the time was ripe, I casually dropped a hint in Edith's ear, steering her to Alison as a suitable duchess. My plan was progressing perfectly. Everything was on track. Until you got drunk and fell into the arms of a Cynster and proposed to her instead."

Thomas seemed to be failing. When, frowning, Drago said, "I still don't understand," Meg was about to step in and explain the rest of Thomas's plan, but apparently spurred by Drago's confusion, Thomas rallied.

His graying lips curved. "It was so ridiculously simple. You were to marry Alison, and once you'd fathered an heir and the boy proved healthy—I was willing to wait years to make sure of that—then you, old son, would have met with a fatal accident, leaving the boy to succeed you as duke, but he would be a minor. Denton would have been one guardian, and I was in a position to ensure that Hubert would be named as guardian, too."

Thomas made another hacking sound—a dying man's cackle. "Just think. By then, I would have been solicitor to both sides. I would have ensured I was the one holding the financial reins, and then, finally, I would have systematically drained the dukedom dry."

Drago stared at the man he'd thought a lifelong friend. "So your friendship was all about money?"

His eyes still closed, Thomas smiled. "From the first day at Eton. I picked you three. Don't you remember? It was me who brought us together. You were all wealthy and destined to become even more so once you came into your inheritances. I reasoned that, at some point in the future, one of you would provide me with an opportunity to better my financial standing. And you, Drago—or rather, your father—did."

Thomas's face clouded, pain etching his features. He coughed, then his voice barely there, breathed, "But then you met Meg, and no matter what I tried, she simply wouldn't die. But my plan couldn't work with her as your duchess. Can you imagine it? If she bore your heir, even if you died, her family as well as yours would have closed ranks, and there was no way I would have been allowed to get my hands on the Helmsford coffers. There would have been Cynsters watching. That would never have worked."

He tried to shake his head, but that was one movement too far. His body spasmed once, twice, then his features fell slack, his shoulders slumped, and all tension drained from his limbs.

Drago hung his head for a second, then he raised it and stared at the dead man. After a moment, he lifted his gaze to George and Harry, crouched, equally stunned and disbelieving, on Thomas's other side. Drago shook his head. "We never knew him, did we?"

"No." George moistened his lips. "That was awful."

Harry pushed upright, his horrified gaze still locked on Thomas's body. "He was...not who we thought he was."

Drago rose, and George slowly got to his feet.

Meg held tightly to Drago's hand as he turned to Tisdale and, with an utterly impassive countenance, gave orders for a gate to be fetched and the body brought up to the house.

Tisdale dipped his head. "At once, Your Grace." He put Ridley down and handed the rope to Maurice.

Maurice took the rope, and Tisdale left, but then Maurice glanced at Drago. "If I might suggest, Your Grace, I'll wait with the body to deter any scavengers."

Drago felt numb inside. The only sensation anchoring him to the here and now was Meg's hold on his hand. He looked at her, and she met his eyes, then turned to Maurice and held out her hand for Ridley's leash. "Thank you, Maurice. Ridley can come with us."

After winding the rope about her other hand, she looked at Drago, then squeezed his hand and simply said, "It's over. Let's go home."

He nodded and, with her, turned away. The others parted, then fell in behind them as they walked with heavy tread out of the old quarry, leaving the crumpled body of Thomas Hayden lying in the dust of the quarry floor.

CHAPTER 20

"*E*vil." George shook his head. "There's just no accounting for it any other way."

They'd returned to the house, passing the group of stablemen and grooms who, led by Tisdale, were on their way to retrieve the body.

Now the company sat sprawled in the library, trying to come to terms with what had happened and, even more, with what they had learned.

Meg looked at the glum faces around her. Despite Denton, Toby, and her cousins not having been directly involved, they were all wealthy enough, privileged enough, to understand being greatly envied and resented for it.

But the company had been sunk in gloom for long enough; it was time to talk and move on. She stirred, drawing the men's eyes. "I still can't believe it's over. Or if it comes to believing, that it was Thomas behind everything, even the incident with Ridley."

Drago huffed. "I can't quite wrap my mind about that—any of that —either."

After a moment, Harry gruffly said, "I honestly don't think there was anything any of us could have done. He started laying the groundwork for this when he was what? Thirteen?"

George slowly nodded. "He was rotten at the core, but his outer skin was glossy and perfect. There was no way any of us could have seen the blackness inside."

"We couldn't have known," Drago agreed. "Looking back, I can't recall that he ever gave us any indication of how he felt regarding our wealth."

Harry and George murmured agreement.

Toby was looking from face to face, from George and Harry to Drago. "Ultimately," Toby said, "there is no way to see what truly lies in a man's heart."

Meg bit her tongue. She glanced at Drago, then at the others, all of whom had put themselves out to help friends or family members weather a battle of sorts.

To her way of thinking, how a man behaved usually shone a light on what was in his heart. Perhaps Thomas had proved the exception to that rule, using his behavior to pull the wool over everyone's eyes, even those who were usually more observant and perceptive, but the men around her? They rang true. Their behavior was genuine, a reflection of their natures. Their attitudes spoke to what lived at their core.

Drago shook his head and, into the silence that had fallen, said, "All I can think about is what a waste Thomas made of his life. He might not have been wealthy, but he had prospects."

George huffed. "But rather than work to make the most of those, he chose a shortcut via murder."

"Multiple murders," Harry pointed out.

After a moment, in a different tone, Harry said, "Do you remember..."

Meg listened as the three men who had thought they'd known Thomas Hayden reminisced about long-ago larks and adventures.

It was a eulogy of sorts for a man who hadn't really existed.

Then the gong sounded for dinner, and Meg silently blessed Fothergill and the staff. They didn't normally dine this early, but today, the company needed the distraction.

They rose, and the others waved Drago and Meg into the lead, then followed them to the dining room.

Drago sat in the carver at the head of the table, and with Meg directly in his line of sight at the table's other end, let the normality of the meal wash over him, drawing him back to the reality of his life.

Gradually, so gradually he was almost unaware of it, the vise about his chest eased, and he found himself smiling at a joke offered by Carter. Indeed, he felt increasingly grateful to Meg's brother and cousins and even Denton, all of whom helped carry the conversation into lighter spheres, drawing him, George, and Harry along, submersing them in the familiar habits of their normal lives, until it became plain that while Thomas's death had signaled the end of a life, it had also drawn a line under a stage of their lives as well.

Thomas and his evil intentions had been vanquished, and they remained to carry on.

As they should. As so many people needed them to do.

When the meal ended, they rose and, in deference to the day and the company's composition, repaired not to the drawing room but to the library to relax in greater comfort in the well-padded armchairs. Denton helped Drago pass around tumblers of whisky.

As Drago and Denton claimed their seats, Fothergill came in.

When Drago looked his question, Fothergill bowed, straightened, and inquired, "I was wondering, Your Grace, whether the gentlemen will be staying."

"Oh, goodness!" Meg looked at George, Harry, her brother, and her cousins. "You will stay, won't you? After what we all went through, surely you won't want to hie back to London tonight."

Drago smiled and gestured with his glass, feeling almost back to his usual expansive self. "You all contributed a great deal to the House of Wylde today and are very welcome to stay."

Harry and George exchanged looks, then George raised his glass to Drago. "Happy to stay, as always."

Toby looked at the other three Cynsters, who nodded. "We'll stay," Aidan, Evan, and Carter chorused.

Toby held up his glass and studied the amber liquid. "As it appears that Glencrae has honored you with the good stuff, it's only fair we remain to help you savor it."

The others laughed, and the men all sipped.

Almost smiling, Fothergill bowed and retreated.

Meg looked around the faces, studying their features, relieved to see them all relaxing.

Then the door, which Fothergill must have left unlatched, was thrust wide, and the scampering of paws on polished boards was followed by Ridley barreling across the rug to joyously leap at Meg's knees. Then he bounded off to sniff around the circle of boots before returning to her and curling up, literally on the toes of her half boots.

She looked down at the furry golden lump anchoring her feet to the floor. "I hope that someone knows how to explain to this beast that I no longer need to be watched over through every minute of my day."

Mock-sorrowfully, Toby shook his head. "I don't like your chances."

"If you think about it from his point of view," Denton said, his gaze on the pup, "then today is the second time you've rescued him. I seriously doubt he's going to consent to be separated from you anytime soon."

With his glass, Drago pointed at Ridley. "Just as long as he doesn't think he's won entry to the ducal suite."

Unsurprisingly, that occasioned several comments about who was top dog there, with her brother and her cousins maintaining that it wasn't likely to be anyone whose name started with a *D*.

Meg played up to the suggestions, and Drago and Denton got into the mood of defending the honor of Helmsford males.

With ridiculous quips flying thick and fast, Meg sat back in her chair and smiled.

Everything was—finally—on the way to being all right.

* * *

BY THE TIME the company ambled from the library and headed up the stairs, Meg felt certain that her brother, her cousins, and Denton had largely recovered from the shocks of the day. Indeed, in her relatives' cases, she knew they thrived on excitement, and all had been involved with Drake and his missions for long enough to take encounters with evil in their stride.

For Drago, George, and Harry, the healing would take longer. Thomas had been a part of their lives for more than twenty years, and his betrayal had cut to the bone. Although it had been Drago whom Thomas had eventually targeted, his words had made it clear that he'd been prepared to exploit any avenue to wealth his manufactured friendship with the three had afforded. He'd deliberately chosen Drago, George, and Harry to befriend because...

Hand in hand with Drago, Meg walked down the family wing, and the voices of the others faded as they made for their rooms elsewhere in the large house. She tipped her head against Drago's shoulder. "When Thomas trapped me in the cellar and I asked him about his plan, he said that it was based on trust." She glanced up and met Drago's eyes. "He intentionally presented himself to you, George, and Harry in the guise of a person all three of you would instinctively trust."

His eyes full of memories, Drago nodded. "He was one of us. That was something we never questioned." He paused to open the door of the ducal suite, then followed her inside and shut the door on the world. "Our failure, if one can call it that, lay in not seeing, not understanding, and indeed, remaining blissfully oblivious to the chip on his shoulder and the resentment he bore"—Drago tipped his head—"not just toward us personally but against all those of our class who come by our wealth through being born to it."

He halted in the middle of their bedroom, and Meg went into his arms.

She raised her hands, framed his face, and held it so she could meet his gaze. "The failure wasn't yours. It wasn't George's or Harry's, either. Not one of you are naive or foolish or prone to befriending those of poor character." She held his gaze and fiercely stated, "Deliberately, with full knowledge of his purpose, Thomas preyed on you from an early age. From when you were just emerging from childhood." She shook her head. "You didn't have the necessary awareness to counter such an attack. Nor should you have had. People learn to distrust others as they grow older. Distrusting your peers from childhood isn't a recipe for a happy life."

With his hands about her waist, the supple warmth of her body a tactile reassurance he'd been craving all day, Drago looked into her eyes and let her words slide like balm through him. After a moment, with a wry lift of his lips, he admitted, "One of the true weaknesses of being born to power is that a part of that mantle makes one feel that one should be able to—and indeed, should—put anything and everything right."

She tipped her head, her expression faintly rueful. "I suppose I can see that. That having the power—as you say, being born to it—anyone with a conscience would feel compelled to use it to right wrongs."

He arched his brows as insight hit him. "Like you and your cousins and connections with your work at the Foundling House. And like me and my peers in engaging with the issues before Parliament."

She nodded. "Thomas chose his own road, one that would have benefited only him at the expense of others. He reaped the rewards of that choice, and while it might take time, you, George, and Harry have to accept that the Thomas you thought you knew was a fabrication and the real Thomas was a villain who is now gone from this world."

He drew her closer until her body rested against his and bent his head to touch his forehead to hers. "I'm hoping you'll help me absorb those facts."

Her response was instantaneous. "I will."

"I can't tell you—can't find the words to explain—what it was I felt when George and Harry told me that the villain was Thomas and that he'd succeeded in getting his hands on you." His lips twisted wryly. "I'd ridden back from Melwin Place already anxious over you, and to hear he'd seized you…"

The memory of the moment lived vividly in his mind. He drew in a long, still-tortured breath. "For one interminable instant, I feared I had finally run out of luck and lost you."

He raised his head and met her gaze. "I've come to see you—crossing paths with you and being able to marry you—as the greatest stroke of luck I'm ever likely to have. To lose you when we'd found our way into a marriage that's well-nigh perfect... Luckily for my sanity, in virtually the same breath, George and Harry blurted out that you weren't hurt and were being rescued by Maurice and Tisdale."

She nodded with ready comprehension. "When I realized the villain was Thomas and that he'd lured me into that cellar, I should have been afraid. Indeed, I would have been terrified except that, when he spoke of how he'd exploited your trust, he reminded me that I could trust you. That with complete assurance, I could place my trust in you and in all our helpers. And in my heart, I knew I could—I didn't doubt it. That made waiting for rescue—which in reality, came only a few minutes after Thomas left—much easier." She smiled. "They didn't leave me in the cellar alone long enough for me to start doubting and grow frantic. But then we had to rush back to the house. I feared what Thomas would do once he realized that I was free and you and all the others knew the villain was him. Maurice and Tisdale assured me you would handle it, and their confidence was so absolute, it rubbed off on me."

He smiled. "They'll be getting a bonus, both of them."

"Good." Her eyes on his, Meg tipped her head. "So, finally, here we are."

"Indeed." He searched her eyes, his features softening. "Able, at last, to get on with our lives—with being the Duke and Duchess of Wylde— without either of us fearing we'll lose the other."

She nodded. "To freely go forward, crafting our lives into the best future we can."

"With no more unexpected interruptions." He bent his head, and his lips covered hers.

She parted her lips and welcomed him in, then kissed him back with spiraling ardor.

She'd expected that they would take things slowly, that they would savor each moment, knowing now that they had forever. Instead, beneath all their talk, beneath their logical reasoning, had lurked a need neither had fully appreciated. A desperate yearning for confirmation at the most elemental, fundamental level that they still had each other, that their love still lived, whole and potent and so very powerful.

Through the eruption of mutual hunger and passion, throughout the torrid engagement that followed, love—simple, powerful, and undeniable —ruled.

Between them, there was no gainsaying that, no closing their eyes and pretending that most compelling of emotions didn't govern, command, and direct them. Didn't invest and drive each touch, each caress, each grasping clutching, each greedy kiss.

Love—their love—infused the heated moments with a bright, brilliant truth that seared them to their souls.

In the moment that they joined and through their racing, scorching ride to the peak, they acknowledged that truth, over and over, both holding to it with renewed commitment and deepening joy.

Inevitably, the peak reared before them, and culmination seized them, shattered them, and re-formed them.

Pleasure rose up and broke over them, washing in a giddying tide through them and on, leaving them wrung out and gloriously sated, wrapped in each other's arms.

After long moments of lying on his back and struggling to regain his breath, Drago lifted Meg from where she lay slumped over him and settled them both in the depths of the ducal bed.

Their bed. Now and forever.

As his mind realigned, Drago realized he'd never felt so alive, so content, so perfectly aligned with his world. So perfectly poised, with all the right supports, to make his mark upon it.

Ducking his head, he pressed a kiss to Meg's curls. "Having finally fully realized what fate I escaped in marrying you, I freely admit that I am and always will remain immensely grateful to whatever gods, whatever Fate, arranged for you to stumble across me in my inebriated state that morning."

Locked in his arms, still lying half atop him, Meg huffed out a breath, tickling the hairs on his chest, then in a sultry tone, murmured, "I believe I know just how you can thank me—and Fate and the gods—over the next several decades."

Drago smiled into the darkness. "I'll be more than happy to pay my dues."

As he lay there, content and happy, reality intruded, but already, Thomas's demise was growing more distant. "I would never have imagined I could be labeled innocent, not on any count—or George or Harry, either—yet when it came to Thomas, in a sense, we were. We—none of us —ever had the slightest inkling he was as he was."

"As I've already pointed out, that is in no way a reflection on you, George, or Harry. Because of the men you are—loyal and caring—your minds couldn't encompass such a betrayal." After a moment, she added, "Such darkness."

He had to agree. "You're right. Betrayal isn't in our lexicon, and none of us have what one might term a dark side."

"No, you don't." Meg tightened her arms about him and confidently stated, "You might be the Duke of Wylde, but your wildness is grounded in joy and love more than any other emotions. Joy and love and loyalty and caring." She tipped her head up to look into his face. "Those are the emotions that define you."

Joy and love. Loyalty and caring. Drago met her eyes and smiled. "I believe I can live with that."

* * *

LATER, once they'd settled again and were waiting for sleep to come creeping in, with Meg warm and snuggled against his side, Drago murmured, "I've always seen marrying as a step toward becoming a better man, specifically becoming the best duke I can be." He glanced at Meg as she lifted her face to look into his. "I don't want to reach the end of my life and look back with regret for what I might have accomplished. I might have inherited the title, but what I make of the position, what I achieve in this life as the Duke of Wylde, lies in my hands." He smiled into her eyes, raised his head, and brushed a kiss to her forehead. "With you by my side, my perfect and fated duchess, the possibilities are endless."

He was looking forward to the inevitable challenges.

Even as sleep drew nearer, they spent the next minutes exchanging ideas, visions of what might be possible that grew bolder and more inno-vative the longer they spoke and the more it sank in that their future was no longer hostage to inexplicable threats.

Meg grinned as she snuggled even closer. "There's so much to look forward to."

"Indeed." The tone of Drago's voice signaled his content.

Meg felt that content settle about them, enveloping and embracing them. She smiled and admitted, "In all my years of imagining the man I would marry and what my married life would be like, I never dreamed that I would find myself eager to race into the future with the notorious Duke of Wylde."

Drago smiled and kissed her, and she held him to her as the kiss spun on, a simple statement that she was his and he was hers, now and through all that would come.

EPILOGUE

ELEVEN MONTHS LATER...

*D*rago lounged against the post at the end of their bed and watched his son and heir suckle at his mother's breast. Despite quite overweening paternal pride, his gaze lingered more on the woman than the child.

Meg. She'd been radiant as a bride, radiant as a mother-to-be, and she was even more gloriously radiant now. The changes in her body had been fascinating, and the flush on her cheeks was utterly captivating.

She continued to hold his interest and his heart effortlessly. As if by right.

And perhaps that was, indeed, the truth. Even more so than before, he was convinced she was his perfect match, his perfect mate. His perfect duchess.

The past months had been spent finding their feet, socially and politically, and they'd met every challenge head-on and triumphed. They'd taken their first and definite steps toward crafting their roles, by mutual agreement and equally mutual determination positioning themselves to make a difference in steering the country to becoming one in which all children could thrive and prosper.

Meg's inclination to assist foundlings had dovetailed with a need he'd found within himself to better the situation of children born to those less fortunate. Whether Thomas's death had influenced him in that, he couldn't say, yet he was now actively involved in finding ways to merge master and servants' interests so that families at all levels of society could grow and build and better themselves.

To his mind, their quest could be stated simply as building a better future by setting the feet of the next generation on the right, most equitable path.

That had become their joint direction.

And now they had the beginning of their own personal endeavor in that regard.

His gaze shifted to the dark head of his son. The first installment in what he and Meg hoped would be a large family—one aspect of their future to which they were determined to devote themselves. In all its many iterations, family was important to both of them, and they were as one in their fierceness over protecting their own.

Even if he was not even a fortnight old.

"Woof!" Ridley, now fully grown, reared up to place his front paws on the coverlet beside Meg.

Meg frowned. "No, Ridley. You can't play with him yet. He's too small."

She looked at Drago and grinned. During her confinement, Ridley had managed to worm his way into the ducal suite. The fact that it was usually Drago, or if not him, Maurice, who let the pushy dog in never failed to make her smile. She studied her handsome husband's face as he sharply instructed the dog to get down, and Ridley grudgingly complied.

Her son released her breast on a contented sigh, and she reswaddled him, settled her nightgown, and lifted him to her shoulder. Gently patting his back, she looked at Drago, who had watched every move like a hawk. She wasn't sure he was aware of just how intently focused on the baby's well-being he was. "Your mother is asking, as is your aunt. And as you might imagine, an unending parade of my female relatives, young and old, as well. So"—she fixed Drago with a pointed, almost-belligerent look—"what is his name to be?"

To her surprise, on that point, Drago had ummed and aahed. Now, he looked uncertain, not an expression she was accustomed to seeing on his arrogantly aristocratic face.

"I wondered if," he ventured, "in light of what brought us together, we might call him after my father—Ryland."

She'd expected as much and nodded. "How about Ryland Harold, honoring both our fathers? Ryland Harold Helmsford, future Duke of Wylde."

Drago smiled. "Done." He blinked, then admitted, "I didn't think it would be that easy."

She met his gaze. "I think you know there's only one name I would have vetoed."

Sobering, he nodded. "And that was one I would never suggest."

For a second, the specter of Thomas Hayden hovered between them, but it was a fading shade, almost insubstantial now, and no longer held any power over them.

"Now we've settled that so amicably"—Drago pushed away from the bedpost and, ignoring Ridley's outraged stare, sat on the bed beside Meg —"before I forget, I met with Joshua earlier. As soon as I saw him, I knew something momentous—something good—had occurred, and he couldn't wait to blurt it out. Alison is expecting their first child, and wonder of wonders, Hubert is finally engaged to be married."

"No!" Meg's eyes went wide. "Well, I was expecting to hear about Alison one of these days—they've been married for months, after all—but Hubert? Who has he chosen?"

"If I understood correctly, the shoe was on the other foot. The lady chose him. She's a Miss Sinclair from the Lowlands. According to Joshua, Hubert was smitten from the first, and while Miss Sinclair tends to play her cards close to her chest, the general view is that she is also taken with Hubert, rather than simply with the notion of being the eventual mistress of Melwin Place."

"That's splendid." Meg lowered her contented son to her lap and leaned back against the piled pillows. "That will give Hubert something to do instead of hovering over Alison and Joshua."

Absentmindedly, Drago nodded, distracted by his heir's large dark eyes, which were studying him with blatant curiosity.

On learning of Thomas's demise and his plot to beggar the Wylde estate by, through Hubert, controlling Alison's putative son, Hubert had been horrified and mortified, and his confidence had suffered a considerable blow. Thomas had built Hubert up in his own esteem to the point that Hubert had believed he was a very knowing gentleman working to secure the best outcome for his family. That in reality he'd been the puppet of a would-be ducal murderer had come as an ego-shattering shock, and ever since, Hubert had been much less sure of himself and much less inclined to disapprove of anyone else.

"I'm glad Hubert's found someone who will stand beside him." Meg looked at Drago. "I assume this Miss Sinclair can be counted on to support him?"

"Apparently she's of a managing disposition, so I hope that means yes."

"Regardless, Hubert marrying will mean a lot less attention focused on Joshua and Alison, which given their situation, I'm sure they'll appreciate."

Drago looked up, and Meg smiled understandingly at him. He smiled back, then leaned forward and, over the head of their offspring, pressed his lips to hers.

A *thump* on the bed jerked them from the kiss.

"Ridley!" Meg stared at the dog, who ignored her and circled beside her legs.

Drago muttered a curse and shifted, intending to catch the dog, but Ridley dropped, nose to tail, his back tucked against Meg's legs.

Meg laughed and caught Drago's arm. "No, leave him. If you put him off, he'll just give us that mournful look as if we're being the world's worst owners."

Drago huffed, but left the dog lying. "At least," he said, looking back at his son, "he doesn't seem overly interested in the baby—in Ryland."

"No." On hearing Drago use the baby's name, Meg felt her heart swell. "I suspect Ridley sees Ryland as an unwanted interloper for my affections. However, I predict that will change the instant Ryland starts to crawl. After that, it will be them against the world."

"Heaven help us!" Drago met her eyes, read her happiness, and smiled. He caught her hand, raised it, and holding her gaze, pressed a kiss to her knuckles. "Regardless, dear wife, I suspect we'll survive."

With love in her eyes, Meg nodded. "You and me, partners in life— come what may, we'll triumph."

* * *

Seven years later...

In Wolverstone House, Toby walked into the study that Drake had made his own and wasn't all that surprised to find his cousin Louisa waiting to pounce.

She didn't even give Toby time to claim the chair Drake, seated behind his desk, waved Toby to before fixing her pale-green gaze on his face and demanding, "How are Nicholas and Addie getting on with their latest?"

Toby blinked and sank into the chair. "I assume in the same manner they coped with the previous four, although possibly with greater confidence, don't you think?"

Louisa threw him an unimpressed look. "Does she have a name yet?"

"No. I gather there's been considerable discussion about that, what with Meg and Drago's two girls plus Pru's three already in the family. Not to mention the other female sprigs sprouting on the other branches of the family tree. The choices are getting more limited."

"Hmm. Yes, I suppose that's true."

"Don't," Toby warned, thinking to head Louisa off, "ask me about Meg and Drago, or Pru and Deaglan for that matter. You two probably see more of them than I do."

"Indeed. Now that we've persuaded all those with seats in the Lords to become active, I do see their wives more frequently." Louisa smiled and opened her eyes wide. "But what, dear Toby, of you?"

His lips thinned. "About me, there's next to nothing to report." He looked pointedly at Drake. "I gather you have some issue you'd like me to attend to?"

Drake had been leaning back in his chair, observing the interplay between his wife and Toby. Now, he looked at Louisa and arched his brows.

She sighed. "All right. I'll leave you to it." She rose and added, "But don't forget what I said," before sweeping regally from the room.

To Toby's mind, Louisa might be merely a marchioness, but she could give any queen lessons in how to use deportment to make one's point.

Regardless, he wasn't about to ask Drake what she'd meant. Hearing the door click shut behind her, Toby relaxed, stretched out his long legs, crossed his booted ankles, and looked inquiringly at Drake. "So what is it?"

Drake wasn't one to waste time. "We have a situation in Austria. One of our contacts there, an English doctor of medicine who has attended several of the families at court for decades, all the while quietly passing any useful information he hears to us, has unexpectedly come into possession of a packet of dispatches destined for the German embassy. The courier who was carrying the packet got caught up in an unrelated incidental brawl at a local inn and was knifed. The good doctor was summoned to attend him, but although the doctor did his best, the courier died. But before he breathed his last, the courier entrusted the packet to the doctor. As the doctor has lived in Austria for decades, he speaks perfect Austrian and also perfect German. It's likely the courier assumed he was entrusting his mission to a fellow countryman."

Toby nodded. "So I'm to go to Austria—Vienna, I assume—and pick up the packet and bring it home?"

"Would it were that simple." Drake caught and held Toby's gaze. "The doctor sent one of the reports the packet contained plus a list of the packet's contents, but no further details of what those contents reveal." Drake sighed. "The single report plus the list is enough to assure us that the packet contains intelligence of the highest order regarding German interests and intentions in southwest and central Africa."

Toby frowned. "So you need the packet and all it contains." He still didn't see the problem.

Drake nodded. "However, the reason the good doctor sent just enough to ensure he whetted our appetite was that he has a daughter who lives with him and he's grown fearful that, however unwittingly, him intercepting the packet will expose her as well as him to unwanted scrutiny and potentially hostile reactions from the Germans and the Austrian authorities." Drake held Toby's gaze. "The doctor wants me to arrange and guarantee his and his daughter's safe passage to England with appropriate escort."

Toby looked disgusted. "You want me to play nursemaid." It wasn't a question.

Drake's lips twitched. "I knew you would say that. Regardless, yes. I don't have many agents as fluent in German and Austrian as you, and…a certain amount of persuasion might be needed."

Toby frowned. "I thought the good doctor wanted to come home?"

"He does. According to other sources in Vienna, the daughter doesn't and is likely to prove difficult."

Toby blinked. "And how, exactly, am I to persuade the lady to up stakes if she's set against it?"

Drake smiled. "I'm counting on you to do whatever it takes to ensure she happily troops all the way back to England."

Toby looked even more disgusted. "Really?"

Drake nodded decisively. "This is too important—too vital to the country's future—to quibble over means. Get the doctor and his daughter and bring them home, along with the packet of dispatches."

Toby grimaced, but nodded. "So when do I leave?"

Drake gave him the details of the ship on which passage to the Continent had been arranged. "From there, I'm leaving it to you to choose your path. In some circles, you're sufficiently well known as one of ours to necessitate playing safe."

Toby nodded. "So I slip into Vienna and out again, with the doctor, his daughter, and dispatches in tow, preferably without anyone knowing I was within a hundred miles of the place."

Drake nodded. "Exactly." He signed and handed over a sizeable bank draft drawn on Crown funds.

Toby took the draft, examined it, then nodded and rose. "This should see me through."

He pocketed the draft, then saluted Drake, but before he could turn away, Drake said, "One last thing…"

Something in Drake's voice made Toby freeze and set his instincts on high alert. When Drake didn't continue, Toby asked, "What?"

"Much against my will, this will be your last mission for me and the Crown."

Toby frowned. "Why?"

Drake sighed. "Because it's been borne in on me from multiple quarters—your family, my family, the grandes dames, half of whom are related to either you or me, as well as umpteen hostesses—that I need to stop giving you an excuse to flee the capital whenever you choose."

Toby scowled. "That's ridiculous."

Drake met his gaze. "Sad to say, it's not. That, old son, is life in the haut ton, and you as well as I were born into it. And as you very well know, in such matters, there is no escape."

* * *

* * *

Dear Reader,

The conundrum Meg Cynster confronts at the start of this story is one faced by many young women, even today. Do I settle for something less than love or wait, possibly in vain, for true love to come my way? Luckily for Meg, Fate decides to send her the answer in the unexpected guise of Drago, Duke of Wylde.

Although aware of the other's existence and despite the other's obvious suitability, these are two people who, in the normal course of events, would never bother looking at the other in terms of a potential spouse, purely due to inaccurate visions of the other's character and a lack of appreciation of what are, for each of them, the most important traits in a life-partner.

Consequently, having to spend a Season supposedly betrothed to the other becomes a journey of discovery—both about the other's true nature and also their own desires, wants, and needs.

Of course, how much anyone wants anything can be measured by how fiercely they will seize, hold on to, and defend that thing, and Drago and Meg's growing desire for a life together is severely tested, and I have to admit that unraveling the villain's plot proved a feat for me as well as my characters!

I hope you enjoyed following Meg and Drago's embracing of their fates and their fight to protect and defend a love and a marriage that they come to view as immeasurably precious.

As usual, the Epilogue ends with an indication of which Cynster's romance will be next to be published, and in this case, we're jumping seven years ahead to the scene that sees Toby, Meg's brother, dispatched on his last mission for Drake, Marquess of Winchelsea—last mission because, in late 1863, Toby is the very last Cynster of his generation yet to wed and the ladies of his family have put their feet down regarding him flitting away out of society.

Naturally, Fate intervenes!

Toby's tale, *A Family of His Own*, will be released in March, 2024.

With my very best wishes for lots more happy reading!

STEPHANIE.

For alerts as new books are released, plus information on upcoming books, exclusive sweepstakes and sneak peeks into upcoming novels, sign up for Stephanie's Private Email Newsletter https://stephanielaurens. com/newsletter-signup.php

Or if you don't have time to chat and want a quick email alert, sign up and follow me at BookBub https://www.bookbub.com/authors/ stephanie-laurens

The ultimate source for detailed information on all Stephanie's published books, including covers, descriptions, and excerpts, is Stephanie's Website www.stephanielaurens.com

You can also follow Stephanie via her Amazon Author Page at http:// tinyurl.com/zc3e9mp

Goodreads members can follow Stephanie via her author page https:// www.goodreads.com/author/show/9241.Stephanie_Laurens

You can email Stephanie at stephanie@stephanielaurens.com

Or find her on Facebook
https://www.facebook.com/AuthorStephanieLaurens/

COMING NEXT:

A FAMILY OF HIS OWN

Cynster Next Generation Novel #15
To be released in March, 2024.

Toby Cynster is not amused to have been informed that his present mission is to be his last in the shadowy service of Drake, Marquess of Winchelsea. Courtesy of Toby's status as the last unmarried Cynster of his generation and the consequent insistence of his female relatives, he will be given no more excuses to avoid society and hopefully, instead, will devote himself to finding a suitable bride. But Toby sees no point in marrying—thanks to his siblings and cousins, he has plenty of nephews, nieces, and connections with whom to play favorite uncle, and he cannot see any point in establishing a family of his own. But then the mission takes an unexpected turn, with Toby having to escort the irritatingly fascinating Diana Locke plus the three young children of a dying Englishman from Vienna to England. Because of Toby's mission, their journey becomes a flight from deadly pursuit, and their most effective disguise is to pass themselves off as a family—the sort of family Toby had been certain he would never want.

Available for pre-order by December, 2023.

RECENTLY RELEASED:

MISS FLIBBERTIGIBBET AND THE BARBARIAN
Cynster Next Generation Novel #13

#1 New York Times bestselling author Stephanie Laurens returns with a story of two people thrown together on a journey of discovery that defines what each most want of life, love, and family.

A gentleman wishing to buy a fabulous horse and a lady set on protecting her family find common ground while pursuing a thief who upends both of their plans.

Nicholas Cynster rides up to Aisby Grange determined to secure the stallion known as The Barbarian for his family's Thoroughbred breeding stable, only to be turned away by the owner's daughter. Nicholas retreats, but is not about to be denied by any lady, no matter how startlingly beautiful and distracting.

Lady Adriana Sommerville knows Nicholas will be back and resigns herself to having to manage his interaction with her aging father. She successfully negotiates that potential quagmire only, at the very last moment, to discover the horse is missing.

Stunned, Addie insists on setting out in pursuit and is not so silly as to refuse Nicholas's support.

But as they follow on the heels of The Barbarian, their adventures and encounters open both their eyes to the prospect of a more enduring partnership. Yet before they can follow that trail farther and before they can lay hands on the horse, through shock after shock, their pursuit uncovers a complicated plot that strips away masks and rescripts everything Addie and her siblings thought they knew about the Sommerville family.

A classic historical romance of adventure, discovery, and reconciliation set in the English countryside. A Cynster Next Generation novel. A full-length historical romance of 103,000 words.

RECENTLY RELEASED:

THE TIME FOR LOVE
Cynster Next Generation Novel #12

#1 New York Times *bestselling author Stephanie Laurens explores what happens when a gentleman intent on acquiring a business meets the unconventional lady-owner, only to discover that she is not the biggest or the most lethal hurdle they and the business face.*

Martin Cynster arrives at Carmichael Steelworks set on acquiring the business as the jewel in his industrialist's crown, only to discover that the lady owner is not at all what he expected.

Miss Sophia Carmichael learned about steelmaking at her father's knee and, having inherited the major shareholding, sees no reason not to continue exactly as she is—running the steelworks and steadily becoming an expert in steel alloys. When Martin Cynster tracks her down, she has no option but to listen to his offer—until impending disaster on the steelworks floor interrupts.

Consequently, she tries to dismiss Martin, but he's persistent, and as he has now saved her life, gratitude compels her to hear him out. And day by day, as his understanding of her and the works grows, what he offers grows increasingly tempting, until a merger, both business-wise and personal, is very much on their cards.

But a series of ever-escalating incidents makes it clear someone else has an eye on the steelworks. The quest to learn who and why leads Martin and Sophy into ever greater danger as, layer by layer, they uncover a diabolical scheme that, ultimately, will drain the lifeblood not just from the steelworks but from the city of Sheffield as well.

A classic historical romance, incorporating adventure and intrigue, set in Sheffield. A Cynster Next Generation novel. A full-length historical romance of 100,000 words.

FOES, FRIENDS, AND LOVERS
Cynster Next Generation Novel #11

#1 New York Times *bestselling author Stephanie Laurens returns with a tale of a gentleman seeking the road to fulfillment and a lady with a richly satisfying life but no certain future.*

A gentleman searching for a purpose in life sets out to claim his legacy, only to discover that instead of the country residence he'd expected, he's inherited an eccentric community whose enterprises are overseen by a decidedly determined young lady who is disinclined to hand over the reins.

Gregory Cynster arrives at the property willed to him by his great-aunt with the intention of converting Bellamy Hall into a quiet, comfortable, gentleman's country residence, only to discover the Hall overrun by an eclectic collection of residents engaged in a host of business endeavors under the stewardship of a lady far too young to be managing such reins.

With the other residents of the estate, Caitlin Fergusson has been planning just how to deal with the new owner, but coming face to face with Gregory Cynster throws her and everyone else off their stride. They'd anticipated a bored and disinterested gentleman who, once they'd revealed the income generated by the Hall's community, would be content to leave them undisturbed.

Instead, while Gregory appears the epitome of the London rake they'd expected him to be, they quickly learn he's determined to embrace Bellamy Hall and all its works and claim ownership of the estate.

While the other residents adjust their thinking, the burden of dealing daily with Gregory falls primarily on Caitlin's slender shoulders, yet as he doggedly carves out a place for himself, Caitlin's position as chatelaine-cum-steward seems set to grow redundant. But Caitlin has her own reasons for clinging to the refuge her position at Bellamy Hall represents.

What follows is a dance of revelations, both of others and also of themselves, for Gregory, Caitlin, and the residents of Bellamy Hall. Yet even as they work out what their collective future might hold, a shadowy villain threatens to steal away everything they've created.

A classic historical romance set in an artisanal community on a country estate. A Cynster Next Generation novel. A full-length historical romance of 118,000 words.

RECENTLY RELEASED:

THE MEANING OF LOVE
A spin-off from Lady Osbaldestone's Christmas Chronicles

#1 New York Times *bestselling author Stephanie Laurens explores the strength of a fated love, one that was left in abeyance when the protagonists were too young, but that roars back to life when, as adults, they meet again.*

A lady ready and waiting to be deemed on the shelf has her transition into spinsterhood disrupted when the nobleman she'd once thought she loved returns to London and fate and circumstance conspire to force them to discover what love truly is and what it means to them.

What happens when a love left behind doesn't die?

Melissa North had assumed that after eight years of not setting eyes on each other, her youthful attraction to—or was it infatuation with?—Julian Delamere, once Viscount Dagenham and now Earl of Carsely, would have faded to nothing and gasped its last. Unfortunately, during the intervening years, she's failed to find any suitable suitor who measures up to her mark and is resigned to ending her days an old maid.

Then she sees Julian across a crowded ballroom, and he sees her, and the intensity of their connection shocks her. She seizes the first chance that offers to flee, only to discover she's jumped from the frying pan into the fire.

Within twenty-four hours, she and Julian are the newly engaged toast of the ton.

Julian has never forgotten Melissa. Now, having inherited the earl-dom, he must marry and is determined to choose his own bride. He'd assumed that by now, Melissa would be married to someone else, but apparently not. Consequently, he's not averse to the path Fate seems to be steering them down.

And, indeed, as they discover, enforced separation has made their hearts grow fonder, and the attraction between them flares even more intensely.

However, it's soon apparent that someone is intent on ensuring their married life is cut short in deadly fashion. Through a whirlwind courtship, a massive ton wedding, and finally, blissful country peace, they fend off increasingly dangerous, potentially lethal threats, until, together, they unravel the conspiracy that's dogged their heels and expose the villain behind it all.

A classic historical romance laced with murderous intrigue. A novel arising from the Lady Osbaldestone's Christmas Chronicles. A full-length historical romance of 127,000 words.

THE SECRETS OF LORD GRAYSON CHILD
Cynster Next Generation-Connected Novel
(following on from The Games Lovers Play)

#1 New York Times bestselling author Stephanie Laurens returns to the world of the Cynsters' next generation with the tale of an unconventional nobleman and an equally unconventional noblewoman learning to love and trust again.

A jilted noblewoman forced into a dual existence half in and half out of the ton is unexpectedly confronted by the nobleman who left her behind ten years ago, but before either can catch their breaths, they trip over a murder and into a race to capture a killer.

Lord Grayson Child is horrified to discover that *The London Crier*, a popular gossip rag, is proposing to expose his extraordinary wealth to the ton's matchmakers, not to mention London's shysters and Captain Sharps. He hies to London and corners *The Crier's* proprietor—only to discover the paper's owner is the last person he'd expected to see.

Izzy—Lady Isadora Descartes—is flabbergasted when Gray appears in her printing works' office. He's the very last person she wants to meet while in her role as owner of *The Crier*, but there he is, as large as life, and she has to deal with him without giving herself away! She manages—just—and seizes on the late hour to put him off so she can work out what to do.

But before leaving the printing works, she and he stumble across a murder, and all hell breaks loose.

Izzy can only be grateful for Gray's support as, to free them both of suspicion, they embark on a joint campaign to find the killer.

Yet working side by side opens their eyes to who they each are now—both quite different to the youthful would-be lovers of ten years before. Mutual respect, affection, and appreciation grow, and amid the chaos of hunting a ruthless killer, they find themselves facing the question of whether what they'd deemed wrecked ten years before can be resurrected.

Then the killer's motive proves to be a treasonous plot, and with others, Gray and Izzy race to prevent a catastrophe, a task that ultimately falls to them alone in a situation in which the only way out is through selfless togetherness—only by relying on each other will they survive.

A classic historical romance laced with crime and intrigue. A Cynster Next Generation-connected novel—a full-length historical romance of 115,000 words.

THE GAMES LOVERS PLAY
Cynster Next Generation Novel #9

#1 New York Times *bestselling author Stephanie Laurens returns to the Cynsters' next generation with an evocative tale of two people striving to overcome unusual hurdles in order to claim true love.*

A nobleman wedded to the lady he loves strives to overwrite five years of masterful pretence and open his wife's eyes to the fact that he loves her as much as she loves him.

Lord Devlin Cader, Earl of Alverton, married Therese Cynster five years ago. What he didn't tell her then and has assiduously hidden ever since—for what seemed excellent reasons at the time—is that he loves her every bit as much as she loves him.

For her own misguided reasons, Therese had decided that the adage that Cynsters always marry for love did not necessarily mean said Cynsters were loved in return. She accepted that was usually so, but being universally viewed by gentlemen as too managing, bossy, and opinionated, she believed she would never be loved for herself. Consequently, after falling irrevocably in love with Devlin, when he made it plain he didn't love her yet wanted her to wife, she accepted the half love-match he offered, and once they were wed, set about organizing to make their marriage the very best it could be.

Now, five years later, they are an established couple within the haut ton, have three young children, and Devlin is making a name for himself in business and political circles. There's only one problem. Having attended numerous Cynster weddings and family gatherings and spent time with Therese's increasingly married cousins, who with their spouses all embrace the Cynster ideal of marriage based on mutually acknowledged love, Devlin is no longer content with the half love-match he himself engineered. No fool, he sees and comprehends what the craven act of denying his love is costing both him and Therese and feels compelled to rectify his fault. He wants for them what all Therese's married cousins enjoy—the rich and myriad benefits of marriages based on acknowledged mutual love.

Love, he's discovered, is too powerful a force to deny, leaving him wrestling with the conundrum of finding a way to convincingly reveal to Therese that he loves her without wrecking everything—especially the mutual trust—they've built over the past five years.

A classic historical romance set amid the glittering world of the London haut ton. A Cynster Next Generation novel—a full-length historical romance of 110,000 words.

PREVIOUS CYNSTER NEXT GENERATION RELEASES:

THE INEVITABLE FALL OF CHRISTOPHER CYNSTER
Cynster Next Generation Novel #8

#1 New York Times bestselling author Stephanie Laurens returns to the Cynsters' next generation with a rollicking tale of smugglers, counterfeit banknotes, and two people falling in love.

A gentleman hoping to avoid falling in love and a lady who believes love has passed her by are flung together in a race to unravel a plot that threatens to undermine the realm.

Christopher Cynster has finally accepted that to have the life he wants, he needs a wife, but before he can even think of searching for the right lady, he's drawn into an investigation into the distribution of counterfeit banknotes.

London born and bred, Ellen Martingale is battling to preserve the fiction that her much-loved uncle, Christopher's neighbor, still has his wits about him, but Christopher's questions regarding nearby Goffard Hall trigger her suspicions. As her younger brother attends card parties at the Hall, she feels compelled to investigate.

While Ellen appears to be the sort of frippery female Christopher abhors, he quickly learns that, in her case, appearances are deceiving. And through the twists and turns in an investigation that grows ever more serious and urgent, he discovers how easy it is to fall in love, while Ellen learns that love hasn't, after all, passed her by.

But then the villain steps from the shadows, and love's strengths and vulnerabilities are put to the test—just as Christopher has always feared. Will he pass muster? Can they triumph? Or will they lose all they've so recently found?

A historical romance with a dash of intrigue, set in rural Kent. A Cynster Next Generation novel—a full-length historical romance of 124,000 words.

A CONQUEST IMPOSSIBLE TO RESIST
Cynster Next Generation Novel #7

#1 New York Times *bestselling author Stephanie Laurens returns to the Cynsters' next generation to bring you a thrilling tale of love, intrigue, and fabulous horses.*

A notorious rakehell with a stable of rare Thoroughbreds and a lady on a quest to locate such horses must negotiate personal minefields to forge a greatly desired alliance—one someone is prepared to murder to prevent.

Prudence Cynster has turned her back on husband hunting in favor of horse hunting. As the head of the breeding program underpinning the success of the Cynster racing stables, she's on a quest to acquire the necessary horses to refresh the stable's breeding stock.

On his estranged father's death, Deaglan Fitzgerald, now Earl of Glengarah, left London and the hedonistic life of a wealthy, wellborn rake and returned to Glengarah Castle determined to rectify the harm caused by his father's neglect. Driven by guilt that he hadn't been there to protect his people during the Great Famine, Deaglan holds firm against the lure of his father's extensive collection of horses and, leaving the stable to the care of his brother, Felix, devotes himself to returning the estate to prosperity.

Deaglan had fallen out with his father and been exiled from Glengarah over his drive to have the horses pay their way. Knowing Deaglan's wishes and that restoration of the estate is almost complete, Felix writes to the premier Thoroughbred breeding program in the British Isles to test their interest in the Glengarah horses.

On receiving a letter describing exactly the type of horses she's seeking, Pru overrides her family's reluctance and sets out for Ireland's west coast to visit the now-reclusive wicked Earl of Glengarah. Yet her only interest is in his horses, which she cannot wait to see.

When Felix tells Deaglan that a P. H. Cynster is about to arrive to assess the horses with a view to a breeding arrangement, Deaglan can only be grateful. But then P. H. Cynster turns out to be a lady, one utterly unlike any other he's ever met.

Yet they are who they are, and both understand their world. They battle their instincts and attempt to keep their interactions businesslike, but the sparks are incandescent and inevitably ignite a sexual blaze that consumes them both—and opens their eyes.

But before they can find their way to their now-desired goal, first one accident, then another distracts them. Someone, it seems, doesn't want them to strike a deal. Who? Why?

They need to find out before whoever it is resorts to the ultimate sanction.

A historical romance with neo-Gothic overtones, set in the west of Ireland. A Cynster Next Generation novel—a full-length historical romance of 125,000 words.

The first volume of the Devil's Brood Trilogy
THE LADY BY HIS SIDE
Cynster Next Generation Novel #4

A marquess in need of the right bride. An earl's daughter in search of a purpose. A betrayal that ends in murder and balloons into a threat to the realm.

Sebastian Cynster knows time is running out. If he doesn't choose a wife soon, his female relatives will line up to assist him. Yet the current debutantes do not appeal. Where is he to find the right lady to be his marchioness? Then Drake Varisey, eldest son of the Duke of Wolverstone, asks for Sebastian's aid.

Having assumed his father's mantle in protecting queen and country, Drake must go to Ireland in pursuit of a dangerous plot. But he's received an urgent missive from Lord Ennis, an Irish peer—Ennis has heard something Drake needs to know. Ennis insists Drake attends an upcoming house party at Ennis's Kent estate so Ennis can reveal his information face-to-face.

Sebastian has assisted Drake before and, long ago, had a liaison with Lady Ennis. Drake insists Sebastian is just the man to be Drake's surrogate at the house party—the guests will imagine all manner of possibilities and be blind to Sebastian's true purpose.

Unsurprisingly, Sebastian is reluctant, but Drake's need is real. With only more debutantes on his horizon, Sebastian allows himself to be persuaded.

His first task is to inveigle Antonia Rawlings, a lady he has known all her life, to include him as her escort to the house party. Although he's seen little of Antonia in recent years, Sebastian is confident of gaining her support.

Eldest daughter of the Earl of Chillingworth, Antonia has abandoned the search for a husband and plans to use the week of the house party to decide what to do with her life. There has to be some purpose, some role, she can claim for her own.

Consequently, on hearing Sebastian's request and an explanation of what lies behind it, she seizes on the call to action. Suppressing her senses' idiotic reaction to Sebastian's nearness, she agrees to be his partner-in-intrigue.

But while joining the house party proves easy, the gathering is thrown into chaos when Lord Ennis is murdered—just before he was to speak with Sebastian. Worse, Ennis's last words, gasped to Sebastian, are: *Gunpowder. Here.*

Gunpowder? And here, where?

With a killer continuing to stalk the halls, side by side, Sebastian and Antonia search for answers and, all the while, the childhood connection that had always existed between them strengthens and blooms...into something so much more.

First volume in a trilogy. A Cynster Next Generation Novel – a classic historical romance with gothic overtones layered over a continuing intrigue. A full-length novel of 99,000 words.

The second volume of the Devil's Brood Trilogy
AN IRRESISTIBLE ALLIANCE
Cynster Next Generation Novel #5

A duke's second son with no responsibilities and a lady starved of the excitement her soul craves join forces to unravel a deadly, potentially catastrophic threat to the realm - that only continues to grow.

With his older brother's betrothal announced, Lord Michael Cynster is freed from the pressure of familial expectations. However, the allure of his previous hedonistic pursuits has paled. Then he learns of the mission his brother, Sebastian, and Lady Antonia Rawlings have been assisting with and volunteers to assist by hunting down the hoard of gunpowder now secreted somewhere in London.

Michael sets out to trace the carters who transported the gunpowder from Kent to London. His quest leads him to the Hendon Shipping Company, where he discovers his sole source of information is the only daughter of Jack and Kit Hendon, Miss Cleome Hendon, who although a fetchingly attractive lady, firmly holds the reins of the office in her small hands.

Cleo has fought to achieve her position in the company. Initially, managing the office was a challenge, but she now conquers all in just a few hours a week. With her three brothers all adventuring in America, she's been driven to the realization that she craves adventure, too.

When Michael Cynster walks in and asks about carters, Cleo's instincts leap. She wrings from him the full tale of his mission—and offers him a bargain. She will lead him to the carters he seeks if he agrees to include her as an equal partner in the mission.

Horrified, Michael attempts to resist, but ultimately finds himself agreeing—a sequence of events he quickly learns is common around Cleo. Then she delivers on her part of the bargain, and he finds there are benefits to allowing her to continue to investigate beside him—not least being that if she's there, then he knows she's safe.

But the further they go in tracing the gunpowder, the more deaths they uncover. And when they finally locate the barrels, they find themselves tangled in a fight to the death—one that forces them to face what has grown between them, to seize and defend what they both see as their path to the greatest adventure of all. A shared life. A shared future. A shared love.

Second volume in a trilogy. A Cynster Next Generation Novel – a classic historical romance with gothic overtones layered over a continuing intrigue. A full-length novel of 101,000 words.

The third and final volume in the Devil's Brood Trilogy
THE GREATEST CHALLENGE OF THEM ALL
Cynster Next Generation Novel #6

A nobleman devoted to defending queen and country and a noblewoman wild enough to match his every step race to disrupt the plans of a malignant intelligence intent on shaking England to its very foundations.

Lord Drake Varisey, Marquess of Winchelsea, eldest son and heir of the Duke of Wolverstone, must foil a plot that threatens to shake the foundations of the realm, but the very last lady—nay, noblewoman—he needs assisting him is Lady Louisa Cynster, known throughout the ton as Lady Wild.

For the past nine years, Louisa has suspected that Drake might well be the ideal husband for her, even though he's assiduous in avoiding her. But she's now twenty-seven and enough is enough. She believes propinquity will elucidate exactly what it is that lies between them, and what better opportunity to work closely with Drake than his latest mission, with which he patently needs her help?

Unable to deny Louisa's abilities or the value of her assistance and powerless to curb her willfulness, Drake is forced to grit his teeth and acquiesce to her sticking by his side, if only to ensure her safety. But all too soon, his true feelings for her show enough for her, perspicacious as she is, to see through his denials, which she then interprets as a challenge.

Even while they gather information, tease out clues, increasingly desperately search for the missing gunpowder, and doggedly pursue the killer responsible for an ever-escalating tally of dead men, thrown together through the hours, he and she learn to trust and appreciate each other. And fed by constant exposure—and blatantly encouraged by her— their desires and hungers swell and grow...

As the barriers between them crumble, the attraction he has for so long restrained burgeons and balloons, until goaded by her near-death, it erupts, and he seizes her—only to be seized in return.

Linked irrevocably and with their wills melded and merged by passion's fire, with time running out and the evil mastermind's deadline looming, together, they focus their considerable talents and make one last push to learn the critical truths—to find the gunpowder and unmask the villain behind this far-reaching plot.

Only to discover that they have significantly less time than they'd thought, that the villain's target is even more crucially fundamental to the realm than they'd imagined, and it's going to take all that Drake is—as well as all that Louisa as Lady Wild can bring to bear—to defuse the threat, capture the villain, and make all safe and right again.

As they race to the ultimate confrontation, the future of all England rests on their shoulders.

Third volume in a trilogy. A Cynster Next Generation Novel – a classic historical romance with gothic overtones layered over an intrigue. A full-length novel of 129,000 words.

If you haven't yet caught up with the first books in the Cynster Next Generation Novels, then BY WINTER'S LIGHT is a Christmas story that highlights the Cynster children as they stand poised on the cusp of adulthood – essentially an introductory novel to the upcoming generation. That novel is followed by the first pair of Cynster Next Generation romances, those of Lucilla and Marcus Cynster, twins and the eldest children of Lord Richard aka Scandal Cynster and Catriona, Lady of the Vale. Both the twins' stories are set in Scotland. See below for further details.

BY WINTER'S LIGHT
Cynster Next Generation Novel #1

#1 New York Times *bestselling author Stephanie Laurens returns to romantic Scotland to usher in a new generation of Cynsters in an enchanting tale of mistletoe, magic, and love.*

It's December 1837 and the young adults of the Cynster clan have succeeded in having the family Christmas celebration held at snow-bound Casphairn Manor, Richard and Catriona Cynster's home. Led by Sebastian, Marquess of Earith, and by Lucilla, future Lady of the Vale, and her twin brother, Marcus, the upcoming generation has their own plans for the holiday season.

Yet where Cynsters gather, love is never far behind—the festive occasion brings together Daniel Crosbie, tutor to Lucifer Cynster's sons, and Claire Meadows, widow and governess to Gabriel Cynster's daughter. Daniel and Claire have met before and the embers of an unexpected passion smolder between them, but once bitten, twice shy, Claire believes a second marriage is not in her stars. Daniel, however, is determined to press his suit. He's seen the love the Cynsters share, and Claire is the lady with whom he dreams of sharing *his* life. Assisted by a bevy of Cynsters— innate matchmakers every one—Daniel strives to persuade Claire that trusting him with her hand and her heart is her right path to happiness.

Meanwhile, out riding on Christmas Eve, the young adults of the Cynster clan respond to a plea for help. Summoned to a humble dwelling in ruggedly forested mountains, Lucilla is called on to help with the difficult birth of a child, while the others rise to the challenge of helping her. With a violent storm closing in and severely limited options, the next generation of Cynsters face their first collective test—can they save this mother and child? And themselves, too?

Back at the manor, Claire is increasingly drawn to Daniel and despite her misgivings, against the backdrop of the ongoing festivities their relationship deepens. Yet she remains torn—until catastrophe strikes, and by winter's light, she learns that love—true love—is worth any risk, any price.

A tale brimming with all the magical delights of a Scottish festive season. A Cynster Next Generation novel – a classic historical romance of 71,000 words.

THE TEMPTING OF THOMAS CARRICK
Cynster Next Generation Novel #2

Do you believe in fate? Do you believe in passion? What happens when fate and passion collide?
Do you believe in love? What happens when fate, passion, and love combine? This. This...

#1 New York Times bestselling author Stephanie Laurens returns to Scotland with a tale of two lovers irrevocably linked by destiny and passion.

Thomas Carrick is a gentleman driven to control all aspects of his life. As the wealthy owner of Carrick Enterprises, located in bustling Glasgow, he is one of that city's most eligible bachelors and fully intends to select an appropriate wife from the many young ladies paraded before him. He wants to take that necessary next step along his self-determined path, yet no young lady captures his eye, much less his attention...not in the way Lucilla Cynster had, and still did, even though she lives miles away.

For over two years, Thomas has avoided his clan's estate because it borders Lucilla's home, but disturbing reports from his clansmen force him to return to the countryside—only to discover that his uncle, the laird, is ailing, a clan family is desperately ill, and the clan-healer is unconscious and dying. Duty to the clan leaves Thomas no choice but to seek help from the last woman he wants to face.

Strong-willed and passionate, Lucilla has been waiting—increasingly impatiently—for Thomas to return and claim his rightful place by her side. She knows he is hers—her fated lover, husband, protector, and mate. He is the only man for her, just as she is his one true love. And, at last, he's back. Even though his returning wasn't on her account, Lucilla is willing to seize whatever chance Fate hands her.

Thomas can never forget Lucilla, much less the connection that seethes between them, but to marry her would mean embracing a life he's adamant he does not want.

Lucilla sees that Thomas has yet to accept the inevitability of their union and, despite all, he can refuse her and walk away. But how *can* he ignore a bond such as theirs—one so much stronger than reason? Despite several unnerving attacks mounted against them, despite the uncertainty racking his clan, Lucilla remains as determined as only a Cynster can be to fight for the future she knows can be theirs—and while she cannot command him, she has powerful enticements she's willing to wield in the cause of tempting Thomas Carrick.

A neo-Gothic tale of passionate romance laced with mystery, set in the uplands of southwestern Scotland. A Cynster Next Generation Novel – a classic historical romance of 122,000 words.

A MATCH FOR MARCUS CYNSTER
Cynster Next Generation Novel #3

Duty compels her to turn her back on marriage. Fate drives him to protect her come what may. Then love takes a hand in this battle of yearning hearts, stubborn wills, and a match too powerful to deny.

#1 New York Times bestselling author Stephanie Laurens returns to rugged Scotland with a dramatic tale of passionate desire and unwavering devotion.

Restless and impatient, Marcus Cynster waits for Fate to come calling. He knows his destiny lies in the lands surrounding his family home, but what will his future be? Equally importantly, with whom will he share it?

Of one fact he feels certain: his fated bride will not be Niniver Carrick. His elusive neighbor attracts him mightily, yet he feels compelled to protect her—even from himself. Fickle Fate, he's sure, would never be so kind as to decree that Niniver should be his. The best he can do for them both is to avoid her.

Niniver has vowed to return her clan to prosperity. The epitome of fragile femininity, her delicate and ethereal exterior cloaks a stubborn will and an unflinching devotion to the people in her care. She accepts that in order to achieve her goal, she cannot risk marrying and losing her grip on the clan's reins to an inevitably controlling husband. Unfortunately, many local men see her as their opportunity.

Soon, she's forced to seek help to get rid of her unwelcome suitors.

Powerful and dangerous, Marcus Cynster is perfect for the task. Suppressing her wariness over tangling with a gentleman who so excites her passions, she appeals to him for assistance with her peculiar problem.

Although at first he resists, Marcus discovers that, contrary to his expectations, his fated role *is* to stand by Niniver's side and, ultimately, to claim her hand. Yet in order to convince her to be his bride, they must plunge headlong into a journey full of challenges, unforeseen dangers, passion, and yearning, until Niniver grasps the essential truth—that she is indeed a match for Marcus Cynster.

A neo-Gothic tale of passionate romance set in the uplands of southwestern Scotland. A Cynster Next Generation Novel – a classic historical romance of 114,000 words.

And if you want to discover where the Cynsters began, return to the iconic
DEVIL'S BRIDE

the book that introduced millions of historical romance readers around the globe to the powerful men of the unforgettable Cynster family – aristocrats to the bone, conquerors at heart – and the willful feisty ladies strong enough to be their brides.

ABOUT THE AUTHOR

#1 *New York Times* bestselling author Stephanie Laurens began writing romances as an escape from the dry world of professional science. Her hobby quickly became a career when her first novel was accepted for publication, and with entirely becoming alacrity, she gave up writing about facts in favor of writing fiction.

All Laurens's works to date are historical romances, ranging from medieval times to the mid-1800s, and her settings range from Scotland to India. The majority of her works are set in the period of the British Regency. Laurens has published more than 80 works of historical romance, including 40 *New York Times* bestsellers. Laurens has sold more than 20 million print, audio, and e-books globally. All her works are continuously available in print and e-book formats in English worldwide, and have been translated into many other languages. An international bestseller, among other accolades, Laurens has received the Romance Writers of America® prestigious RITA® Award for Best Romance Novella 2008 for *The Fall of Rogue Gerrard*.

Laurens's continuing novels featuring the Cynster family are widely regarded as classics of the historical romance genre. Other series include the *Bastion Club Novels*, the *Black Cobra Quartet*, the *Adventurers Quartet*, and the *Casebook of Barnaby Adair Novels*.

For information on all published novels and on upcoming releases and updates on novels yet to come, visit Stephanie's website: www.stephanielaurens.com

To sign up for Stephanie's Email Newsletter (a private list) for heads-up alerts as new books are released, exclusive sneak peeks into upcoming books, and exclusive sweepstakes contests, follow the prompts at http://www.stephanielaurens.com/newsletter-signup/

To follow Stephanie on BookBub, head to her BookBub Author Page: https://www.bookbub.com/authors/stephanie-laurens

Stephanie lives with her husband and a goofy black labradoodle in the hills outside Melbourne, Australia. When she isn't writing, she's reading, and if she isn't reading, she'll be tending her garden.

www.stephanielaurens.com
stephanie@stephanielaurens.com